PENGUIN BOOKS

A Kingdom This Cursed and Empty

Stacia Stark is a fantasy romance author who loves writing about found families, self-reliant heroines and brooding, grumpy heroes. Originally from New Zealand, Stacia spent over a decade traveling and living in various countries around the world as a freelance copywriter, and attributes both her wanderlust and creativity to those adventures. When not traveling or writing, Stacia is usually lost in the pages of a good book.

Come say hi on Facebook: facebook.com/groups/starksociety
Or learn more at Staciastark.com

T0322064

A KINGDOM

This

CURSED

and

EMPTY

STACIA STARK

PENGUIN BOOKS

PENGUIN BOOKS

UK | USA | Canada | Ireland | Australia
India | New Zealand | South Africa

Penguin Books is part of the Penguin Random House group of companies
whose addresses can be found at global.penguinrandomhouse.com

First published by Bingeable Books LLC 2023
First published in Great Britain by Penguin Books 2024
006

Copyright © Bingeable Books LLC, 2023

The moral right of the author has been asserted

Map Illustration by Sarah Waites, The Illustrated Page Design
Interior Art by @samaiya.art
Interior Design by Imagine Ink Designs
Printed and bound in Great Britain by Clays Ltd, Elcograf S.p.A.

The authorized representative in the EEA is Penguin Random House Ireland,
Morrison Chambers, 32 Nassau Street, Dublin D02 YH68

A CIP catalogue record for this book is available from the British Library

ISBN: 978–1–405–96769–3

www.greenpenguin.co.uk

1
The Queen

No one had ever told my husband that too much pride was a dangerous thing.

No one had ever warned him that those he harmed would one day gather their strength—and come looking for vengeance.

And even if they had, even if the king of Eprotha had been cautioned by someone close to him…

He would never have listened.

It was his arrogance that would eventually be his downfall.

At least, that was my greatest hope.

Now, he lounged on his throne, his dark eyes bored, legs stretched out, a cup of wine in his hand. He was the picture of a relaxed, confident ruler.

But I'd watched last night. Watched his face flush purple with barely suppressed rage as he'd stalked into my chambers.

Barely half of the guards he'd taken with him to trap the corrupt were still alive. He'd returned to find his court robbed in his absence. Even the heavy jewels had been removed from around my neck.

His favorite assessor lay dead in the middle of our ballroom.

Sabium's fury was *delicious*.

Now, no one who looked at him would believe him at all distracted by the escape of more than three hundred of his corrupt—a brutal blow that ensured the court was still whispering.

Most of our court currently lined the walls of the throne room, all of them desperate to see blood spilled. They were used to being invulnerable. Protected. In one night, rebels had held their lives in their hands—all while the courtiers were frozen in time.

I kept my expression perfectly blank, the slight purse of my lips communicating the expected amount of concern.

The king glanced at me and immediately away. "How," he said quietly, "did a mere *girl* manage to align with the fae, empty my dungeon, rob my court, and *steal* from me?"

Men. So utterly predictable with their insistence on diminishing women to *girls* in an attempt to belittle us.

No one spoke.

Tymedes bowed his head, showcasing dark hair sprinkled with gray. As the man in charge of the king's guard, Tymedes would bear the weight of the rebels' achievements, freeing Sabium from any culpability.

"We are still investigating, Your Majesty."

Sabium's lip twitched, the only sign of his displeasure. "We will discuss this further this afternoon."

Tymedes paled, allowing himself to be led away.

My ladies were next. I reached for my wine, my mouth suddenly dry.

With Setella…Prisca—no, *Nelayra* gone, along with Madinia—that sharp-tongued viper—my ladies were now only four. Four was an unlucky number. Not as unlucky as five, but certainly not—

"Kaliera," Sabium addressed me, and I lifted my head. My ladies stood in front of us, ashen-faced but composed, as I'd trained them. Hopefully, the years they'd lived in this court would ensure they kept that composure.

"I don't see why you need to do this here," I said. "I've already spoken with my ladies."

"Regardless." Sabium waved a hand, beckoning them closer. "All of you have denied knowing anything regarding the corrupt's plans. But any detail could be important, no matter how small." He gave them a cold smile. "Did you ever see any indication that the corrupt and the Bloodthirsty Prince knew each other?"

Pelopia, Alcandre, and Caraceli shook their heads. Lisveth hesitated.

Sabium leaned forward. "Speak."

"Well, it's just, uh… That is, Your Majesty…"

My heart tripped. In his current mood, he wouldn't hesitate to send Lisveth down to the dungeon if he felt she wasn't telling him everything. And there were plenty of things Lisveth had noticed about my own behavior over the years that would spill out from her loose lips under torture.

I gave Lisveth an encouraging smile. "Anything you think may be relevant," I said.

"The day the Bloodthirsty Prince arrived, when he was pretending to be the *Gromalian* prince…"

"Yes," I urged, curious myself.

"It was the day you made her one of your ladies." Lisveth smiled at me, gaining confidence.

The courtiers whispered at the reminder of how much access I had given the corrupt to the palace, and I stiffened.

Lisveth's smile faltered as she glanced at the courtiers. Her shoulders hunched, and she turned back to face Sabium. "We walked into the dining hall," she blurted out. "Prisca stopped walking, and Madinia tripped into her. Madinia hissed something at Prisca, but Prisca was staring at the king's table. She told me it was because she was nervous. Because it was her first time seeing so many nobles. But perhaps…"

All of my muscles tensed at once. The fae prince had been in glamour. And the hybrid heir had still recognized him.

"Continue," Sabium snapped.

Lisveth flinched. "N-now I wonder if, if perhaps she recognized the Bloodthirsty Prince, Your Majesty."

Sabium smiled.

The questioning continued for hours. My ladies

were unused to standing for long periods of time, and eventually, Alcandre swayed on her feet. I ordered chairs to be brought to them, ignoring Sabium's narrow-eyed stare.

"Good," Sabium said. "Very good. You all did well. You're dismissed."

He got to his feet, ignoring the courtiers' low bows as he stalked from the throne room. I stayed precisely where I was.

Sabium likely believed he was the only one who had just come to a certain realization.

I lifted my own wine, hiding my smile.

The Bloodthirsty Prince had been in full fae glamour when he was in this castle. Not just the glamour they used to appear human. But the kind of glamour that required blood. The kind that was impenetrable—except in the rarest of circumstances. And yet the hybrid heir had seen through that glamour.

He knew. Without a doubt, the Bloodthirsty Prince knew exactly what that meant. But he was a man with secrets. According to my spies, Prisca hadn't even known he was fae. Which meant he was still keeping her in the dark.

If she was as clever as she'd proven to be so far, she would part from him at the first opportunity.

The Boy

The castle was silent. That was the first thing he noticed.

It was silent in a way the castle was never silent. And the boy's skin prickled with the knowledge that something was very wrong. Slowly, like the kitchen cat he'd watched earlier that day, he turned his head.

Parintha was sleeping in her chair, her knitting in her lap. The boy frowned. She could never sleep in the dark—it was one of the reasons why she was responsible for keeping the boy in his bed at night. She preferred to rest during the day, using the quiet hours of the night to spend time alone with her thoughts.

But she was lost in dreams now, her head tipped back, mouth slightly open.

Her sewing fell to the floor with a clatter, and she didn't even stir.

The boy slowly sat up, and his uncle walked into his room. His eyes flickered as he glanced at the boy. "You should be asleep."

The boy didn't bother pretending. "What did you do?"

Grief flickered across his uncle's face. He swallowed, took a deep breath, swallowed again. "I'm sorry. Sorrier than you can imagine."

The boy's gaze dropped to the amulet in his uncle's hand. And he knew.

PRISCA

"Eat."

The growled word wasn't a suggestion. I ignored it anyway, focusing on the horizon. The ship rolled, and I took a deep breath, clamping down on the urge to vomit. I just had to hold it together until we docked, and then I would find a way for Telean and me to escape.

I could practically feel Lorian bristling behind me. That strange connection still remained between us. It was an unusual kind of awareness that made it impossible to hide from his presence on this ship.

I fisted my hands. I'd find a way to sever that connection at the first opportunity.

"Fine," he bit out. "Starve."

He stalked away, and I ignored him, even as my throat tightened. He was back in his human form. As he'd been ever since we'd left the city gates. It was worse, seeing him this way—the way I'd known him before that night. It made me question my own mind, even though I knew exactly what I'd seen.

To my right, the sails swished, and the mast made a strange creaking sound. I could feel the blood draining from my face. My chest tightened, and ice-cold sweat slid down my spine.

Forcing myself to regain control, I focused on my breathing. Deep, steady breaths until it no longer felt as if I was suffocating.

I risked a glance behind me at the crew. No one else looked worried.

The sounds were likely perfectly normal.

I refused to humiliate myself by asking someone. Besides, most of the crew Lorian had arranged seemed terrified of me.

Clearly, they'd heard what had happened two nights ago when we'd led the hybrids to safety. When we'd emptied the king's dungeon, robbed his courtiers blind, and I'd left his assessor bleeding out on the ballroom floor.

He'd had it coming.

I should probably feel some kind of shame for the unhinged way I'd behaved. Something inside me had been unleashed, and I'd reveled in the blood and pain of my enemies.

Instead, all I felt was a dull sense of pride and a longing to make my remaining enemies pay.

One of the crew members was shout-whispering loud enough for me to hear Lorian's name. They were in awe of the fae prince. Meanwhile, I could barely look at him.

In exchange for Lorian's help that night, I'd stolen the amulet he'd needed so badly. I hadn't understood exactly why he needed that amulet—only that he longed for it with a desperation I'd never seen from him before.

Our bargain had relied on my delivering that amulet to him. It was the only way the hybrids would stay alive. So, I'd ridden furiously across the city with Madinia, my power drained, my body almost useless. And when I'd thrown that amulet to Lorian, I'd expected that moment to be my last. Expected the hundreds of arrows aimed at me to pierce my flesh.

Instead, Lorian had shed his human glamour and slaughtered half the king's men.

Fae. He was fae.

And not just any fae.

They called him the Bloodthirsty Prince.

He'd once laid waste to a city called Crawyth, close to the border of the fae lands. It was one of the few refuges for the hybrids. I'd been just a few winters old when I'd lived there with Demos and our parents.

The night I was stolen from that family, the Bloodthirsty Prince had turned the city to rubble.

According to Demos, there was little chance my mother had survived. She'd been too distraught at my kidnapping to use her power to protect herself when she'd gone back into our home.

Demos hadn't seen my father again after that night. He'd grown up as a rebel and spent two years in the king's dungeon, his friends slaughtered.

Fresh nausea swept through my stomach, and I tightened my hands on the rail in front of me. Lorian's words played through my mind.

"I know *you can handle it. Because I trained you to*

handle it. That doesn't mean I won't wait with my gut in knots until I see you're still breathing."

I'd thought he…cared. I'd thought we had something. That night, when I'd galloped through the city streets, I hadn't just been fleeing to my friends, my family.

I'd been aiming for *him*.

I took that thought and lit it on fire. The man I'd believed I'd known was a lie. Since he'd hauled me on to this ship, Lorian hadn't bothered to explain. Hadn't even attempted to tell me *why*. No. Instead, he paced the ship, snarled at the captain, instructed the hybrid sailors to make us travel faster, and occasionally glowered my way.

I always sneered back, my heart cracking open a little more each time.

Forcing him out of my mind, I focused on the others.

I missed Rythos. The last time I'd seen him, he'd been even taller, his ears pointed. His eyes…his eyes had been the same. Soft and kind.

"It's still me, darlin'," he'd said. But when he'd reached for me, I'd flinched.

I hadn't meant to. He'd just been so *big*. His eyes were…glowing. And those ears…

Galon had given me a disappointed look that had speared me, while Rythos had turned away. But not before I'd caught the flicker of hurt in his eyes.

My stomach writhed some more, and I leaned farther over the railing.

I especially missed my brothers. I wanted to hug Tibris. Longed to claw back some of the time that had been stolen from Demos and me. Needed to mourn Asinia's mother with her. But the deal I'd made with Lorian had been clear. I'd agreed to go with him to the fae lands, and in exchange, he'd saved Demos's life.

Lorian wasn't human. His moral compass was broken. It wouldn't surprise me if he'd allowed that bolt to pierce Demos's chest just so he'd have a way to make me bargain with him once more.

When I'd agreed, I'd thought we'd all travel together. Lorian had immediately smothered that possibility.

Rythos, Galon, and the other fae would travel in groups with Demos, Tibris, Asinia, and anyone else who was seeking refuge in the fae lands. Neither of my brothers was happy about the hybrids being split up, but they'd had no choice.

Some of the hybrids would scatter. Now that Lorian and the others had given them the blue marks declaring them as humans past the age of twenty-five winters, they had options. Many of them still had families they were hoping to find. But most seemed willing to separate into groups—some of them led by Rythos, Galon, Cavis, and Marth, the others led by the strongest hybrids. Too many people traveling together would draw attention, and if there was one thing the fae knew, it was how to sneak around beneath Sabium's nose.

Lorian had taken me straight to the dock. Apparently traveling down the coast was the safest option since he'd paid a king's ransom in bribes—killing anyone who couldn't be paid to look away. His healer was spending most of his time in the cabins beneath us. Just when I'd convinced myself Lorian was heartless, he'd ordered that healer to look after the hybrids who were too sick to be able to make the journey on foot.

As soon as we arrived in the fae lands, they'd do better. They'd have fresh air. Better food. Sunlight. I'd make sure of it.

The scent of roses mingled with the salt air. Telean. She made her way closer, leaning on the railing next to me.

"Why don't you try a little soup?" she asked.

I gagged, my head spinning.

Telean wrapped an arm around my shoulders. She was the only one Lorian had allowed to travel with us. Since she'd seen my mother wield time magic, Lorian was hoping she could teach me what I needed to know.

"Your father was the same," she said. "When we crossed the Sleeping Sea, he was in a terrible state. He refused a healer too, insisting they tend to the wounded." She nudged me with a raised eyebrow, and my mouth trembled.

I soaked up the story like the earth soaking up water after a drought.

"Why didn't you tell me? That I was the heir?" I kept my voice low. The wind whipped my hair against my face, and I pushed it behind my ear.

Telean took a deep breath, clearly enjoying the tang of the salty ocean air. "I *was* planning to tell you."

"When?"

"As soon as the hybrids were free. As soon as there weren't lives depending on you. I don't think you realize what a blow you've dealt to the king, Prisca. I wanted you to be able to enjoy your victory for a few days first. But your big-mouthed brothers let the fae learn who you were." Telean gave me a faint smile.

I sighed. I could definitely picture Tibris and Demos loudly arguing about that information.

"According to Lorian, the fae king already knew."

"Yes," she sighed. "Either way, you would have ended up in the fae lands at some point."

"Why?"

"Because once—before they left us to die—the fae were our allies."

I'd spent enough time with Rythos and the others to accept that the fae weren't necessarily our enemies...at least, not individually. But it was difficult to imagine them being our allies.

"And you're hoping they could be our allies again?"

"Your people deserve a home."

I ignored the *your people* part. I had a cousin. One I'd seen at the gates to the city when I'd first entered. I knew he had time magic, because he hadn't frozen like everyone else.

That meant he could rule.

My aunt sighed. "Nelayra."

I hunched my shoulders, at both the name and the fresh nausea sweeping through me.

"What makes you think I'd be a good queen?"

"Even before you knew they were *your* people, you were fighting for them. You got three hundred of them out of the king's dungeon."

But there were more. So many more. And now, the king knew I was alive. Alive and with the fae.

"Regner will wage a war like no one has ever seen," Telean said softly. "I know you hate Lorian for lying to you. But by the time you get to the fae lands, you must no longer see him as the man you—"

"Careful," I snarled, and she nudged me again with her elbow, unconcerned.

"You must see him and his brother as potential allies. As hope for your people."

"I don't know how to be a queen." And it was the last thing I wanted. What I *wanted* was to help the hybrids survive and then find a quiet village somewhere no one knew me and live out my life. A normal life.

"Aren't we lucky that the Bloodthirsty Prince allowed me on to this ship?" Telean's hand found mine on the railing. "It just so happens I was by your mother's side for years as your grandmother ruled. And I saw how your mother led her people in Crawyth. I'll teach you everything I know. But by the time we get to the fae lands, it will be up to you."

2
LORIAN

*D**ear L,*

Six days and no word. I'm assuming you're...unhappy that I chose not to reveal your lover was the hybrid heir.

And she is *your lover, isn't she? Or at least, she* was*. I can imagine a village girl raised to loathe our kind wouldn't respond well to your deception.*

I'm also assuming she's clamped to your side for the time being. After all, you were so insistent that she would be leaving with you.

And while I'm sure you've anticipated my needs in this matter, let me be clear: I need to speak to the hybrid heir. Bring her to our kingdom.

Your appreciative brother,

C

Dear C,

I'm sure this letter finds you well.

It finds me *on a merchant ship in Eprothan waters—nice charade, by the way. It should definitely pass inspection should Regner's fleet look our way.*

As you anticipated, I have Prisca with me. The hybrid heir. *Although I'm unsure why exactly you made sure I was one of the last people to learn this information.*

Regner will hunt her until he's dead. So yes, I'll bring her to our kingdom. At this very moment, she has absolutely nowhere else to go.

—L

I rolled up my message and attached it to the falcon's leg. I'd already been in contact with Galon and the others, but Conreth's message had only darkened my mood further.

I wanted off this ship.

Prisca had barely spoken a word to me since she'd realized who—and what—I was. But I knew her. Her fury was a wild, unrelenting thing, even if she was masking it in front of the others on this ship.

If she thought she could get away with it, she would kill me in a heartbeat.

That thought shouldn't make me hard.

The fury, I could handle. Nothing burned brighter than the two of us locked in a power struggle. But it was the misery I caught when she thought I wasn't looking that raked at me with vicious claws.

It would be so easy to hand Prisca off to my brother—directly after I gave him the punch in the face he deserved. Then, I could return to the life I'd been created for.

Killing my way across this continent.

But the thought made my gut clench. Made my mouth dry. The wildcat was mine, and I would protect her until she came to that exact realization.

So, I'd give her the time she needed—just enough time for her to understand she belonged with me.

Even if Prisca hadn't immediately loathed me the moment she learned who I was, she would have eventually loathed me when she learned the kinds of things I'd done in my brother's name.

The bloodstains on my hands would never wash off.

The thought of all that blood hadn't bothered me for years. Until I'd met Prisca and something inside me—something I'd thought was dead—had slowly come to life once more.

One of the sailors tripped on thin air, his eyes widening as he stared at me. Tiny sparks darted along my skin, and I had no doubt my eyes were glowing with suppressed power. Elemental magic occasionally leaked, and while I'd had a slight affinity for fire, wind, and water as a child, it was the lightning that slipped free when I wasn't concentrating.

Never in my life had I needed to suppress that power more than right now. The moment I'd touched that amulet, the moment I'd ripped into it with my power and released everything it was holding…

No longer did I need to reach deep for my power. No longer did I grow weaker the farther I traveled from our lands. Instead—at least in the short term—I would have to learn how to contain the power.

Unfortunately, the more I thought of the little wildcat, the more difficult it was to keep my power tucked tight inside me where it belonged.

Turning away from the crew, I made my way below deck to the galley, where I found the healer creating some kind of poultice. His eyes met mine, the deep frown line between his brows making it clear he was still holding a grudge.

I couldn't entirely blame him for the bitter twist to his thin mouth. This was the same healer I'd threatened with an excruciating death when Prisca was poisoned.

The healer certainly hadn't been pleased to learn he was coming with us, but if Regner ever learned just how he'd saved the hybrid heir's life? What the human king would do to the healer would turn even the strongest stomachs.

Our eyes met. "See that she eats something."

I didn't need to specify who I meant. Turning, I strode back toward the door.

"She can't," the healer muttered behind me. "Vomits up everything she eats."

I pivoted. The healer met my eyes and shrugged. "The queen hasn't found her sea legs yet."

If Prisca learned that people were already referring

to her as queen, she might just jump overboard.

"Fix it."

"I tried, but she insisted I turn my attention to the wounded hybrids." Something that might have been reluctant respect danced across his face.

Prisca was a natural-born queen at every opportunity. Although she wouldn't see it that way.

Prisca would refuse anything I offered her. I considered my options.

"Create whatever she needs," I said. "I'll find a way to make her take it."

I'd tie her down and pinch her nostrils shut if that was what it took.

Stalking out of the cabin, I found Telean standing on the deck, her gaze on Prisca, who was once again clutching at the rail—her hands white-knuckled as she stared at the horizon.

I'd thought her refusal to eat mere stubbornness.

My muscles uncoiled, my chest lightened, and my teeth finally unclenched.

"The healer is preparing a seasickness draught for her," I told Telean.

"She won't take it."

I just raised an eyebrow. I was betting Prisca would put her stubbornness aside. "You will make her. The hybrids are recovering, and the healer has more than enough power to treat Prisca's nausea."

"I can hear you," Prisca called. "I have no desire to spend the rest of the trip wishing to be put out of my misery. If you can guarantee the healer will have enough power should the hybrids below need him…"

Satisfaction slid through me. "I give you my word."

Prisca's face somehow turned even whiter, and she let out a sound somewhere between a snort and a laugh as she stumbled past me.

My gut clenched, and I watched her go.

"Interesting that you allowed me on to this ship," the old woman mused from behind me. "The one person who could teach Prisca enough to prepare her to negotiate with your brother."

"I care nothing for what you find interesting."

Her snort was identical to Prisca's, and I snarled, stalking after the wildcat. She moved directly to the galley, taking the vial the healer offered and gulping it down. It would be a few hours before she felt the full effects, but something in my chest unclenched as a hint of the color she'd lost returned to her face.

Prisca stepped around me, moving back toward the door. Catching her wrist, I steered her to my cabin. Surprisingly, she didn't put up a fight, although she did snatch her hand away the moment I closed the door behind us.

"What do you want?" she bit out.

"Why don't you tell me what *you* want, wildcat?"

The words were out before I realized I'd said them.

She blinked. "What do you mean?"

A strange kind of fury burned through my chest. "It's an easy question. What do you fucking want?"

Her expression became a cool mask, but her eyes burned gold. "I want to go to the hybrid camp. I want to see my best friend, who I thought was going to die. I want to see my brothers—one who almost *did* die right in front of me. I want to make decisions with Demos, who should have just as much say in his kingdom as I do. And I want to hug Rythos and apologize. I don't want to stay on this ship for another fucking minute."

She was panting when she finished, her face flushed, expression vaguely shocked.

It wasn't unlike the way she'd looked the first time I'd thrust inside her. I couldn't help my smile.

Prisca went still, eyeing me as if I were a snake about to strike. I missed the way she used to look at me. I may have lost her, but perhaps I could make her trust me like that again.

She frowned. "Whatever you're thinking…"

"I'll continue thinking it." My smile dropped, and I watched her.

I ached to give her what she wanted.

While I had no problem saying no when her safety was at risk, my instinct with her was always to say *yes*. To see her eyes light up. To make her smile. And if she ever learned just how close she was to having the Bloodthirsty Prince wrapped around her finger, she would likely laugh until she was breathless.

I'd been silent for too long. Prisca's mouth hardened, and she darted past me, slipping out the door.

PRISCA

"How many territories are there within the fae lands?" Telean prodded me over lunch a week later.

"Five," I said. Now that I wasn't continually heaving over the side of the ship, I'd spent the past few days eating and learning. It was incredibly evident that there were huge gaps in my education. The kinds of gaps that made my cheeks heat with how little I knew.

I was a barely literate village girl who now needed to understand everything there was to know about the rulers of this continent—and what they had to lose.

Unfortunately, most humans would never believe the truth. The Eprothan king, Sabium, was over four hundred years old. His real name was Regner—the man known as Sabium's ancestor. Regner had used stolen magic to stay alive all this time, faking his own death and taking his crown over and over again each time he secretly killed the human boys he pretended were his sons.

"Who are the high fae who rule those territories?"

I dunked a piece of bread into my stew. I never knew how much I'd appreciate the simple act of eating until I stepped on to this ship. "Romydan, Thorn, Caliar, Sylvielle, and Verdion." The fae only used first names.

"And who rules over all of those territories?"

I swallowed. "Conreth." Lorian's brother. And our only real hope for an alliance at this point in time.

"And his wife?"

"Emara."

"Good."

I was beginning to think clearly once more. And with that clarity came a healthy dose of fear. My friends and family were traveling down to the fae lands, but I had no doubt Regner would have deployed his iron guards to hunt them down.

Thanks to my aunt, I knew all about the iron guards.

Comprised of five hundred of the king's most vicious, loyal men, the iron guards were chosen at birth and sent to an academy where they had any spark of compassion or humanity driven from them. They were soulless killers who'd been molded for situations just like this.

Lorian had said thousands of hybrids were already living at a camp within the fae borders, but it wasn't a long-term solution. The hybrids deserved a home.

"You're distracted," Telean remarked.

"Do you know exactly where the hybrids from the castle are right now?" I wouldn't be able to fully concentrate until I knew they were all as safe as possible—even if that meant they were in the fae lands.

Telean's pause was the only indication she was surprised by the change in subject. But my aunt made an excellent spy. She spent most of her time sitting in various spots on the ship, eyes closed, face turned up to the sun, as if she was napping. I had no doubt she drifted off occasionally, but mostly, she was listening to those foolish enough to talk in her presence.

"Rythos and Galon both took their groups east through Eprotha, into the forest. They will be crossing into the fae lands near Crawyth."

"And the others?" I asked.

"Marth and Cavis are bringing their groups through Gromalia. The other groups split up and left at various times."

So that if one group were captured and killed, there was a chance some of the others would make it. My hands fisted, and I forced myself to focus. I'd gotten a mere glimpse of the groups before Lorian had hauled me away from the city gates. But I should've been there. I should be with them now.

"Where are my brothers? And Vicer and Asinia?"

She reached out and squeezed my hand. "With Marth."

"In Gromalia." Not quite as dangerous as Eprotha, but certainly not safe. Especially after Lorian had played the part of the Gromalian prince for so long.

"Yes. The Bloodthirsty Prince has contacts in the kingdom. Fae contacts."

"You are the biggest target," Telean said. "And the Bloodthirsty Prince has taken you by sea—something Regner wouldn't have expected."

I was beginning to hate how Telean called Lorian the Bloodthirsty Prince. But I couldn't understand why.

Perhaps it was merely the thought of what might have been—if Lorian and I had been different people.

"We need allies," I said.

"Yes."

I chewed on my lower lip. "What if the fae refuse?"

"They want Regner dead as much as we do. Without you, they wouldn't have that amulet back."

No, Lorian had relied on my ignorance for that. Bitterness was a taste I was beginning to become accustomed to.

"How does the amulet work?"

She shrugged. "That's a question for the prince."

I shook my head at the idea that he would tell me anything.

We ate in silence for a few minutes, until I forced myself to push thoughts of Lorian out of my head.

"I spoke to Margie when I first got to Lesdryn. She said the gods wanted to know which kingdom would survive a war. That's why they started all of this."

My aunt nodded. "They gave each ruler an artifact."

Margie's voice echoed in my head.

"Faric, god of knowledge, gave an artifact to the humans. Tronin, god of strength, gave the fae three artifacts. And Bretis, god of protection, had become reluctantly intrigued by the hybrid kingdom to the west. The people who had somehow thrived—even after separating from the fae. Bretis donated something that held such power, Tronin and Faric immediately grew jealous."

"Nelayra?"

I met my aunt's eyes. She was looking at me with that expectant yet patient look she wore so well. I glanced away. "Only one human kingdom was chosen. Why?"

She shrugged. "In the eyes of the gods, it's likely they're all considered one people."

I frowned at that, storing the information away to consider later. "What were the fae given?"

Telean smiled, and I rolled my eyes at myself. "Amulets," I muttered. "They were given the amulets, which is why Lorian didn't kill the king. He needs the other two."

"Yes."

"And the hybrids?"

"Our gift was given by Bretis, the god of protection. At least, according to myth."

"What was it?"

"An hourglass."

"To represent our time magic." My heart tripped in my chest at the thought.

She nodded. "And to make it easier for your ancestors to wield that power to keep their kingdom safe. Using your power won't always be as difficult as it is now. Once you find that hourglass, you'll be a true force on the battlefield." My aunt's eyes lit with a dark fire.

Using my power had always drained me. Sometimes, it took such a toll that my nose bled until I became dizzy. If the hourglass could help, maybe I really could help the hybrids survive. "How does it work?"

"It allows you to stretch time for longer. Allows your power to drain more naturally, instead of its being pulled from the depths of your being. The other powers are only legend—and apparently dependent on the ruler themselves."

My mind threw me back to Demos, bleeding out on the ground, and a chill rippled through me. I'd come so, so close to losing him. "Would the hourglass allow me to turn back time?"

Telean's face drained of color. "Listen to me carefully, Nelayra. You must never attempt such a thing. It would kill you. The world must be balanced."

I opened my mouth, and she held up one hand. "If you somehow lived through it, the fates would demand an equal sacrifice. The kind of sacrifice that would haunt you."

Telean was still watching me, her eyes narrowed, so I nodded. If the fates truly played with us in such a way, they'd already taken far too much interest in me. I had no desire to draw more of their attention.

If I could get my hands on the hourglass, I could practice with it until I could freeze time on the battlefield. And if we could lure Regner into some kind of trap, I could use the hourglass to kill him.

I had to find it.

We ate silently for a long moment. Telean watched me, clearly aware I was working up the courage to broach this topic. I shouldn't even ask. And yet, I couldn't seem to help myself.

Finally, I sighed. "Can I ask you something?"

"Of course."

"Crawyth. The night my parents died. When I was taken. The Bloodthirsty Prince…"

Telean watched me. I had a feeling she was seeing the tiny spark of hope that flickered inside my chest.

"You want to know if I saw him."

I nodded.

"I didn't need to, Nelayra," she said gently. "Others saw him after the attack ended."

Heat seared the backs of my eyes. But that stupid spark refused to go out.

"We will soon enter Gromalian waters." Telean sent me a sympathetic look and changed the subject. "Tell me the name of the Gromalian king."

"Eryndan," I muttered. "His son is Prince Rekja." The man Lorian had impersonated for weeks.

The back of my neck prickled, and I glanced over my shoulder. Lorian stepped into the cabin.

He might be in his human glamour, but he'd ceased any attempts to hide what he was. When he moved, it was with a speed that made my heart thrum. And when he was at rest, he was eerily still.

I slowly got to my feet. His face was expressionless… but his eyes burned with fury.

My throat tightened. "Tell me," I croaked.

"There has been an attack."

"What happened?"

"The king sent his iron guards after the hybrids."

A hole opened inside me. I should have been there. I knew I should have been there. I could have used my power. Could have given our people the upper hand.

"Who?" It was all I could say.

Lorian took a deep breath. "Eight iron guards found Rythos's group. Your fire-wielding friend was with them."

"Madinia."

He nodded. "The guards knew who they were dealing with. They'd temporarily deafened themselves so they would be immune to Rythos's power. The hybrids are still weakened."

Invisible fingers squeezed my throat until I could barely breathe. The hybrids were unused to using their powers and would've probably been more of a liability than a help for Rythos.

"Four of the hybrids died."

My gut twisted, and I suddenly couldn't swallow around the lump in my throat at the unfairness of it all. Those hybrids had gained their freedom, only to die on their way to their new lives.

"Rythos protected one with his body." Lorian's eyes turned flinty, and I knew Rythos would be on the receiving end of Lorian's wrath for that choice. "He was wounded."

My heart stuttered. "How badly?"

"You truly care?" The words were lifeless, but I heard the undercurrent of accusation.

I stared at him. "Of course I do."

His mouth twisted, and his gaze speared into mine. I knew what he was thinking. That I'd cared until I was confronted with the fact that Rythos was fae, and then I hadn't let him touch me.

Lorian had obviously seen that too.

My lower lip trembled, and I clamped down on it. I wouldn't let him see me cry. Lorian's gaze dropped to my mouth, and I glanced away.

Telean cleared her throat. "Mind how you speak to the queen."

I hunched my shoulders. Something that might have been amusement flickered in Lorian's eyes. A moment later, it was gone.

"Rythos will live," was all he said. "Your dragon turned three of the iron guard to ash. The other hybrids rallied, and Rythos dispatched the remaining iron guards with his sword."

"Dragon?"

"The fae believe those with exceptionally strong fire magic are descended from dragons."

Madinia certainly had the temper of a dragon. I tucked that information away and turned my attention back to Lorian. "I could have saved lives if I'd been there."

"This is proof that you're in exactly the right place."

"Four people are dead. Four hybrids."

He took a step closer, his expression dark. "What do you think the iron guards will do to you if they find you?"

I turned, and Telean caught my hand, ignoring Lorian. "Your people don't need another fighter on the ground, Nelayra. They need a queen."

I opened my mouth, sharp words on the tip of my tongue.

"We have company," a sailor called from outside the mess deck.

"The Gromalians," Lorian bit out.

My knees quaked, but I attempted a smirk. "Since you pretended to be their prince for so long, I bet they *really* want to talk to you," I purred. "How about you go smooth those ruffled feathers, and I'll keep traveling?"

Lorian just looked at me.

Some dark, unhappy part of me insisted I continue. "After all, we no longer need each other anymore. Your brother is the one I'll have to negotiate with. Or am I wrong?"

Lorian hadn't explained. Hadn't tried to talk to me. Hadn't bothered to *fight* for me. I'd been a distraction for him. A plaything. And once we got to the fae lands, I'd likely have continued encounters with him as I negotiated with his brother. Even though every minute I spent in Lorian's presence felt like someone had clutched my heart in their fist and was squeezing.

Telean slowly rose to her feet. She shook her head at both of us, shuffling out the door.

Lorian's gaze turned feral. "If you ally with my brother, you're also allying with *me*, wildcat."

My heart thundered in my chest. At this rate, I'd never be rid of him. Despair rose, thick and bitter.

"They're coming!" a panicked voice shouted, and Lorian gave me a long look that said we'd continue this later.

I curled my lip at him and stalked out of the cabin, winding my way up to the deck.

Sailors were running, tying ropes, turning the ship.

We'd set sail on a merchant ship. Lorian had ensured the crew were well prepared, and we'd sailed under cover of darkness as soon as we'd fled the city gates, anyone who might've stopped us already dead. But the ship that approached us...

It was a masterpiece of engineering, and my breath caught in my throat as it cut through the waves, advancing steadily toward us. The ship's hull, crafted from what looked like dark, aged oak, was intricately carved with mythical beasts. I squinted but couldn't make out much more than winged creatures that seemed to be in flight as the ship bobbed up and down with the waves.

Atop the ship's three towering masts, enormous square sails billowed.

This was a warship. My mind raced. Lorian could destroy the entire ship. But who knew how many other ships would be sent in response?

I could freeze time. But I couldn't hold it indefinitely.

"Who else has power on this ship?" I asked Lorian as he stepped up next to me.

"The crew have small amounts of various powers— most of which have been taken by Regner. As far as I'm aware, your aunt's power is defensive."

I nodded. "My aunt can cast a shield. But Regner took the majority of her power when the queen convinced him to spare her life. He ordered her continually drained every few months once she was spared." Nausea swept through me at the thought of what Telean's life had been like in that castle.

My mouth turned dry as the warship approached. If Galon and the others had been here, this would have been a different conversation. But Lorian had left them behind to get the hybrids—my people—to safety.

I knew little about ships. All I knew was the warship had clearly been designed for speed and maneuverability, with a long, narrow hull that cut through the water directly toward us. No emblems on their flags.

"What's that? At the front of the ship?"

"A ram," Lorian said. "For sinking enemy vessels."

I blinked, and I was in the river once more, the cold leeching the energy from my bones, my lungs screaming for air as the water closed over my head again and again.

Lorian was watching me. Likely seeing more than I wanted him to see. As usual.

Every time I think you're about to stop being a scared little mouse and actually reveal the woman I believe you are, you prove me wrong. Well, sweetheart, we don't have time for your insecurity and self-doubt.

"We'll find out what they want," I said through numb lips. "And if they attack, we'll make an example of them."

Lorian's gaze flickered with something that might have been approval. I ignored it, turning my gaze back to the ship in the distance.

Now we would wait. And see if whoever was on that ship attempted to kill us or wanted to talk.

LORIAN

Prisca watched the approaching warship. And I watched her.

Her face was pale, the dark circles stark beneath her eyes. It was clear she was deeply unhappy down to her bones. And that unhappiness made something in my gut twist in response.

Everything I'd done had been necessary. I held no regrets—except that she now looked at me as if I was dangerous to her. Not to her physical body, but to her heart. Her peace of mind.

Prisca was lonely. Oh, she had her aunt, and the two had become incredibly close. But often, her aunt was forced to nap, and Prisca would sit on the deck, staring at the sea, completely removed from everyone.

The crew were fascinated but wary of the hybrid heir, and their whispers followed her around the ship. Since she refused to speak to me other than the bare minimum necessary, she was hopelessly, achingly alone.

I knew the reality of such loneliness. Had spent most of my childhood lost in solitude. Not only was the wildcat alone, but she was now expected to walk into a role she had never asked for.

I never wanted her to feel alone like I had.

Loneliness could swallow you until you were nothing but misery and rage. And I refused to let that happen to Prisca.

At this very moment, I was responsible for that loneliness. I may have orders, but *I* was the one directly responsible for the weary misery in her eyes.

She turned, likely feeling my eyes on her. "What is it?"

"I've been thinking about what you said. About wanting to go directly to the hybrid camp. About seeing your family. Your friends."

She blinked. "And?"

"There are two ways to reach the camp—by sea or by land."

Prisca's eyes lit up, and something in my chest unclenched. Even with everything between us, I'd do almost anything to see hope in her eyes.

"What are you saying?" she asked, her voice low.

"It's possible that we can visit the hybrid camp first and my brother after."

"How?"

"I have my suspicions about who owns that ship." I nodded at the approaching warship. "And if I'm correct, we have room to negotiate. We would need to travel west through Gromalia to reach the hybrid camp. It will mean long days of travel on horseback. The hybrids who are still too weak to travel will need to stay on the ship and continue to Aranthon, where they can recover. Your aunt will also need to stay on this ship until you meet her in Aranthon."

"Why would you do this?"

Because I was tired of seeing the shadows beneath her eyes. Tired of seeing my wildcat grow depressed and withdrawn. I wanted to see her smile just once, even if she would never again smile at me.

"I don't think you're ready for that conversation," I said. "Do you?"

She swallowed. "What about your brother?"

I just raised an eyebrow. "Do you truly care about my relationship with my brother?"

She shook her head, her lips trembling as if she might smile. I watched her mouth hungrily, desperate for some hint that she was in there, beneath the depression that enveloped her like a blanket.

Her mouth firmed. "No," she said, turning her gaze back to the warship.

I watched it approach, our crew standing ready.

My brother hadn't specifically ordered me to travel directly to the fae capital. Oh, I knew he would be displeased. Knew he would find some way to punish me. But I had two reasons for taking this little trip.

First, I wanted Prisca separated from her aunt. I wanted her to make her own decisions, uninfluenced and unimpeded. I'd eavesdropped on some of their lessons, and Prisca's clever mind had soaked up Telean's history and information like a sponge. But her aunt had clear ideas about who and what she wanted Prisca to be.

I just wanted her to be mine.

That brought me to my second point.

I'd have unrestrained access to Prisca while we traveled completely alone. She'd be *forced* to deal with me. Just like she'd had to when we'd traveled to the city. But most of that trip had involved either attempting to ignore her or attempting to get her to wield her magic.

In the castle, we'd both been consumed by our separate tasks. Any time spent together had been stolen.

This was my chance to learn about what Prisca enjoyed. The small things that made her happy. Her habits. How she relaxed.

In my darkest moments, when I missed her the most—even as she sat right next to me—I listed what I *did* know. And I wondered if those small details would be enough to carry me through the rest of my life.

I knew she loved valeo and that the sweet fruit reminded her of her father. Knew she liked to lounge in a hot bath until the water was cool and her skin wrinkled. I knew she was one of the most loyal people I'd ever met. I knew she was cunning and clever, and that she would do anything for the people she loved.

What would it be like to be counted among those people?

It wouldn't happen. But if the coming weeks were the last we'd spend together, then I was going make them count.

3
PRISCA

Within minutes, the warship was close enough that I could see the crew and the captain—a surprisingly small man, with his hand raised to shield his eyes from the sun.

Telean approached me. "I overheard your conversation," she said. Grasping both of my hands in hers, she squeezed. "You need to be with your people. They need to see you."

My stomach swam uneasily at the thought. But I didn't want to do this alone. I could no longer trust Lorian, and I wanted to talk to the others before I saw either the fae king or the Gromalian king.

Right now, I was out of my depth. Ignorant. If I was going to help the hybrids, I couldn't remain that way.

The warship drew even with our ship. A rope ladder was slung up over the side so they could board. My palms turned damp with sweat.

Our crew were all armed with swords and knives, most of them on the deck. Several of them held their weapons like they knew what they were doing with them. Most of them were trembling, watching Lorian as if he was their only hope.

The first man made it to the top of the rope ladder, one brown-skinned hand appearing first as he hauled himself up. He wore a trim beard, his dark eyes wide and solemn as he gave us a graceful bow, then turned, holding out his hand.

My lungs burned from the breath I was holding, and yet I couldn't seem to let it loose.

The hand that slid into his was small and feminine. He lifted the woman in the way men did when they considered them precious. Her head popped up above the ship's rail, and Lorian seemed to relax next to me. Obviously, it was exactly who he'd expected.

I was reserving judgment.

Small and lean, the woman jumped onto the deck, her dark eyes pinning me in place. Her glossy black hair was worn in a long braid, while her skin had the same deep umber tone as the man who was now releasing her hand.

"Captain Daharak Rostamir," Lorian said, and she grinned at him. Her smile was wicked, full of fun. Lorian didn't bother smiling back.

"The Bloodthirsty Prince in all his glory," she purred, then turned her attention to me. I forced myself to stare back at her, and her eyes sharpened. "And you must be Nelayra Valderyn."

"You can call me Prisca," I said.

"Well now, I have use for Nelayra, the hybrid heir. In fact, I believe we can both help each other. But Prisca the village girl? She is useless to me."

My stomach clenched. She knew far too much about me. And since I knew absolutely nothing about her, the shrewd tone she used made me want to clench my teeth.

"Talk, Daharak," Lorian ground out.

The pirate queen glanced around at our crew—who were still staring at her as if she would choose to slaughter all of us at any moment.

"We'll need privacy for this," Daharak said to me. "My men will stay on our ship. And you can keep the Bloodthirsty Prince by your side for our conversation."

She was testing me, and I gave her a slow smile.

I pulled my power toward me, and time stopped. Taking a few steps closer, I let the threads of that power go. It was a trick I'd used before, and it never failed to disturb those on the receiving end.

Daharak's eyebrows shot up. The man by her side snarled, instantly transforming from a mild-mannered shadow to a true threat. Daharak raised her hand, stilling his forward motion.

"I'd wondered," she said, and her eyes danced as they met mine. "Yes, I believe we can be of great help to each other, Your Majesty."

It was the first time anyone other than Telean had referred to me in such a way, and it took everything in me to keep my expression carefully blank.

"Enough," Lorian said, his voice empty. "We'll talk below deck."

I turned, finding my aunt watching me, her eyes lit up. Daharak was murmuring with the man at her side, who was clearly unhappy with this idea, so I strode over to Telean, who leaned close.

"Daharak Rostamir," she whispered, so quietly I could barely hear her. "Pirate queen. She commands eighty thousand men and two thousand ships, and operates with a strict code of conduct, which her pirates adhere to. They have rules around how they treat prisoners. Women are often released without ransom, and other prisoners are treated with respect. Loot is distributed equally among her pirates, and all of them follow a clear chain of command within the fleet. She is fair and honorable, but she is also vicious when pushed, Nelayra. Crew members who break the rules, violate the trust of others, or act treacherously are flogged, mutilated, marooned on deserted islands, and executed. She has become such a force that neither the Gromalian nor Eprothan king knows what to do with her. She is a dangerous woman who raids merchant vessels, ransoms important people, and smuggles illegal goods."

"Don't forget," Daharak said from behind us, "I also manage to turn heads while doing it."

Gods help us if Daharak and Madinia ever met.

Daharak gave Lorian a heated look from beneath her eyelashes and swaggered toward us. From as far away as she'd been standing, she shouldn't have been able to hear our conversation.

That kind of power would have made her an excellent

spy in her younger years. We would have to be very careful about what was said within her presence.

Replaying Telean's words, I studied Daharak. I should have disliked her intensely. She was a dangerous criminal. But something about her brazen honesty and wicked grin made me willing to hear her out at least.

Besides, half this continent considered me a dangerous criminal as well.

Telean frowned at the pirate queen. "The galley will be empty this time of day," she said. "You can talk there."

Lorian stepped behind me before Daharak could follow me down the stairs. Because his brother would be unimpressed if I was stabbed in the back before I arrived in their lands.

"Whatever you're thinking…" Lorian murmured in my ear, his warm breath making me shiver.

I cast him a narrow-eyed look over my shoulder. "I'll continue thinking it," I said, parroting his own words back to him.

His mouth twitched, and I climbed down the last step.

Daharak winked at me as she took her seat at the scarred wooden table in the galley. "The fae are possessive, obsessive, and impossible to wrangle. You'd do much better with a hybrid of your own."

Lorian let out a growl so low, it was almost soundless.

Clearly, the pirate queen was looking for some kind of response from me, so I ignored that too. "What is it that you think I can do for you?" I asked.

"First, how about I tell you what *I* can do for *you.*"

I took the seat across from Daharak, while Telean sat on the outside of the table where it was easier for her to maneuver with her bad back. Lorian stood, leaning against the wall. Daharak's shadow did the same, his gaze continually drifting over each of us. She still hadn't introduced him.

"Bold move traveling through Gromalian waters after pretending to be the prince for so long." Daharak smirked at Lorian. "Of course, you didn't have much choice, given that pesky barrier."

I was watching her closely enough that I caught the naked longing that flashed through her eyes at the word. To ask about the barrier would only solidify my ignorance. Thankfully, Daharak kept talking, shifting her focus back to me.

"The Gromalians know you're here. They're on the way. At best, they will attempt to detain you—forcing you to meet with their king. At worst, they will attempt to kill you. Either option will waste precious time. Time you need to continue your travels down to the fae lands."

Again, she was proving just how much she knew about our plans. And if the Gromalians attacked…

I took a deep breath. "You're offering to help us?"

She nodded, crossing her legs at the ankles. "Most of the Gromalian fleet is currently…preoccupied elsewhere. They don't have enough ships to engage with my fleet. If we were to escort you out of their waters, you could meet the king later at your own leisure."

I glanced at Lorian. His expression was blank. If he was leaning toward trusting Daharak, I couldn't tell. Lorian could kill anyone who followed us. The problem would be what came after. I was hoping to convince the Gromalian king to see reason and to ally with us against Regner. If Lorian were forced to start killing, that would never happen. But I didn't want to talk to the Gromalian king now. Not at *his* pleasure. Not before I'd talked to the others. And especially not while I was still so unprepared.

I kept my expression carefully blank. "And what is it that you'd want in return?"

"A favor," Daharak said. "To be used whenever I like."

The pirate queen was greatly overestimating me if she thought I was capable of completing the kind of favor she likely needed. But…I may as well hear her out.

"What kind of favor?"

She just shrugged. "One of equal value."

"She's not giving you a life debt," Lorian finally spoke.

"I would never assume such a thing." She grinned.

My eyes met Lorian's. And I realized this was a test. He wasn't going to get involved because he wanted to see what I would do. As if, even now, after all that had happened, he was still trying to prepare me. To make me stronger. Something warm settled beneath my ribs, and I attempted to smother it.

I shifted my attention back to the pirate queen. There was no doubt that it was beneficial for us to meet the

Gromalian king on our terms. The alternative meant we would risk any kind of cooperation from him at best—and start a new war at worst.

"A favor equal to protective transportation," I said.

Daharak smiled. "Yes."

My mind whirled, but I forced myself to lean back in my seat, the way she had. "I have an alternate suggestion."

She raised one eyebrow. "Do tell."

"You escort us *into* Gromalian waters, help us dock safely, and provide us with security so we can move through the capital. We'll travel alone through Gromalia from there. And you escort our ship out of Gromalian waters so my aunt stays safe."

She burst out laughing. "You wish to travel through Thobirea unimpeded while the king is itching to make an example of you? Would you like me to kill Regner while I'm at it?"

"Oh no." I gave her a wide smile. "I'll do that myself."

Lorian looked deep in thought. I still didn't understand his motivations. The Bloodthirsty Prince had a task to complete—get me to his brother in the fae lands. This little trip would push his timeline back. The fact that he'd told me I could go directly to the hybrid camp...it just meant there was definitely something in it for him.

"Can you help us or not?" I asked.

"It just so happens I have one of these." She held up a silver coin, and Telean sucked in a breath.

I just nodded as if I understood the significance.

"You provide us with an armed escort to and from the city gates to the west, ensure my aunt stays safe and unharmed for the rest of her journey down to the fae lands, and I'll owe you a favor of equal measure," I said.

"It will be one hell of a favor," Daharak warned. "The magic will demand equality."

My stomach clenched at the thought. But I needed armies. Allies. Regner sending his iron guards had just been a warning. A test. And they'd still managed to kill four hybrids. People who had suffered in that dungeon, enjoyed their first taste of freedom, and been cut down just days later.

I met her eyes. "Deal."

She rolled up her sleeve. "The fae are so very interesting, don't you think? With their deals and bargains? But I must admit, their blood vows have always fascinated me the most."

I couldn't help it. I glanced down at the place on my own hand where the thin line had once scarred my palm. But it was gone, that blood vow kept. Something tickled the edge of my memory, but Daharak was already holding out her arm.

I sucked in a breath. Her skin was crisscrossed with those thin white lines from palm to elbow—too many to count at a glance. How did she keep track of all her bargains and debts?

She winked at me. "You'll need to learn to hide your thoughts much better than that, Hybrid Heir. I'm a busy woman. Now, are we doing this or not?"

Eighty thousand men and two thousand ships? Oh, we were doing this. Hopefully, this vow would be the beginning of a productive relationship for both of us.

LORIAN

The captain stared at me. "Are you certain?" he asked, his voice croaking. "Gromalian waters…"

"I'm certain," I said. "The pirate queen has guaranteed our safety."

Truthfully, our meeting with her had been a twist of fate. And I would be at Prisca's side to make sure her favor was equal to Daharak's.

Although, from the way Prisca had negotiated with her, I had a feeling she would be just fine handling that conversation alone. Pride swept through me at the thought.

The old captain nodded, although he still wore a disconcerted frown. "If you say so," he muttered. He'd likely lost cargo to Daharak's pirates more than once over the years.

Prisca and her aunt were standing on the deck, speaking in low voices. Daharak had left the wildcat some clothes that seemed to have been designed to drive me out of my mind. The leather breeches cupped her round ass, while the white blouse bared the creamy skin of the tops of her breasts. She looked entirely too sensual.

"Tell me about the coin," Prisca was murmuring as I approached.

Telean sighed. "The Gromalian king uses them to represent favors owed to him. People fight and die for those coins. Whatever the pirate queen did to receive one…"

"She's using it for this favor?"

Telean shrugged. "It may grant her safe passage infinitely until she uses the coin for the favor she needs."

I stalked closer. "As your aunt mentioned, we don't know what she did for that favor from a king."

Prisca's shoulders stiffened. "You said I could trust her."

"I don't trust her. But I trust a blood vow."

She still refused to look at me.

I clamped down on the snarl that wanted to escape my throat.

Telean glanced between us, rolled her eyes, and wandered off. I grabbed Prisca's hand and hauled her away from the crew until we had some semblance of privacy.

"Let's get one thing straight, Your Majesty."

"Don't call me that." She whirled, shoving her hands into my chest. I caught her as she rebounded off my body, hitting the ship's railing.

"*That* was embarrassing," Few things made me feel alive like seeing Prisca in a rage.

Her cheeks flushed, those amber eyes burned, and I almost groaned. My entire body turned hard, and it took everything in me not to strip her shirt over her head and show her just how incredible sex would be when she was in this mood.

I clamped my hand around the back of her neck, shoving down the urge to drag her to me. To make her *listen*.

I'd known better, and yet I'd allowed myself to be consumed by her anyway. *This* was always going to be our reality.

"Why would you do this?" she asked.

The question burrowed deep into my chest. I clenched my teeth. "Figure it out."

She let out a hollow laugh. "Because you need me cooperative. So I'll work with your brother. You only brought me with you because *he* wants me."

I wanted to shake her until her teeth rattled. Instead, I leaned even closer, my hand tightening on the back of her neck.

"You can tell yourself whatever makes it easiest for you to hate me, wildcat. But it was real. All of it."

She was quiet for a long moment. Finally, she swallowed, glancing away. "I don't understand how we can possibly sneak into the city."

Fresh pain stabbed through me at the change of subject. I'd known the moment I saw the terror on her face at the city gates that she would never accept me. But some small part of me had...

"Lorian?"

Prisca's voice was hesitant. Clearly, she didn't

appreciate admitting she was out of her depth. But she was willing to admit ignorance so she could learn.

"The Gromalian capital lies behind an island which has created a natural harbor. But the island is large enough that while the choke point helps secure the capital, the narrow passage also impedes access. It means the city is limited when it comes to trade, as larger merchant ships need to use alternative routes or smaller ports farther north and south."

"So Thobirea would be almost impossible for a fleet to take from the sea."

I nodded. "It's why the Gromalian king has been able to stay out of the conflict with Eprotha for so long. Regner can't use his ships to take the capital. If he decides to wage war, he will be forced to march his people across the border."

A faint line appeared between her brows as she frowned, clearly storing the information. "What does that mean for us?"

"It means Daharak's ships will also be too large for us to dock near the capital. So she must know of a hidden cove or inlet we can use, and another distraction ready to buy us time. And when the Gromalian king learns what she did, she will wave that coin at him. Whether she has to use it…" I shrugged. "That is between them."

"Why would she risk losing a favor from the king for a blood vow with me?"

I turned and watched her. "Clearly, she believes you'll be more helpful when it comes to whatever plans she is making next."

Prisca winced. But she glanced at her aunt, who was standing on the other side of the deck, watching Daharak's ships surrounding ours. "How certain are you that Telean will be safe?"

"The pirate queen wouldn't have risked dying an excruciating death if she thought there was even a tiny chance that your aunt would be at risk."

Her teeth worried at her lower lip, and I cupped her cheek without thinking. Surprisingly, she allowed it.

"I can't lose her, Lorian."

This was the first time we'd actually talked for more than a few moments without Prisca stalking away. Gods, I'd missed it.

"You won't, wildcat. She'll be waiting for you with my brother." My jaw clenched at the thought of turning her over to Conreth.

The reminder of my brother made Prisca stiffen. And I wasn't at all surprised when she merely nodded, turned, and walked back toward her aunt.

The Queen

I met Sabium when I was young enough to still dream of things like romance and a peaceful, happy marriage. He was charming at first. So charming, I'd fallen for his act—the innocent girl in me dreaming of the life we would have. I'd thought we would have children and finally break the curse that seemed to plague his family.

Sabium had truly thought I was so ignorant, so vapid, I would never understand just who he was.

The day we'd married, the truth was explained to me. We would never lie together. He would never give me a child of my blood. Instead, he would hand me a squalling newborn—taken from some poverty-stricken village girl. And I would be forced to raise that boy in place of my own.

I'd refused. And Sabium had sighed, as if my reaction was entirely expected and yet still unwelcome.

That was when one of his guards had taken me below. To the very dungeon that now sat empty.

They'd starved me for four days, and Sabium had visited for another *talk*. Not only would I pretend the baby was mine. If I drew suspicion in any way, I would meet with an unfortunate accident.

Now, I could forgive myself for my naivety. My parents had raised me to be a victim. If I could turn back time, I would kill them for it myself.

I studied the empty space in my mirror. The space where the fae amulet had sat for decades. I'd known what that amulet was the moment Sabium had it delivered under the guise of a gift.

Clicking sounded behind a wall, and I turned. Pelysian stepped through from the hidden passage and nodded at me, his thick black hair brushing his shoulders.

The lantern in his hand spilled light across his brown skin as he pulled the mirrored wall shut behind him.

I didn't bother asking if he'd been followed. Pelysian had come with me from my own household before I married the king. His abilities allowed him to hear information conveyed in even the lowest of whispers. There were few spies as useful, and none more loyal.

"Well?" I asked, sitting on the low sofa.

"The king sent his iron guards after the hybrids. It appears the fae separated, each taking a group to safety. The guards found a group, wounded one of the fae, and killed four of the hybrids."

"A distraction," I murmured. "Regner is planning something much bigger. And the heir?"

"My spies are still unsure. I believe she may have fled via ship."

"Leaving her people behind? Ah, but she may not have had a choice." I felt no sympathy for her. Every woman eventually understood the truth of powerful men. She had more than enough winters behind her to learn such a lesson.

Curiosity flickered across Pelysian's face. "May I ask a question, Your Majesty?"

"You may."

"You knew the hybrid wasn't who she appeared to be, and yet you allowed her access. Why is it that you wish to be informed of her every move now?"

I leaned back in my chair. "At first, I was amused by her. A hybrid rebel in my husband's castle, working under his nose…" I smiled. "Whether she was caught or not was irrelevant. It was the mere fact that she'd made it so close to the king that intrigued me."

I knew fae fire. My father had used it before it became too dangerous to do so. Still, when the maid had lit my gown on fire, I'd realized just how easily it could all be over.

Some part of me had almost wanted to burn.

But I'd seen just how few people would care. I'd watched as no one acted. And I'd memorized their faces.

So, I'd lashed out, and now, knowing exactly how dangerous the hybrid heir truly was, I felt something close to regret. Sending the maid to the dungeon had alerted the king to her transgression. Oh, I didn't regret *that*. What was the life of one maid after all? But I had unknowingly put my own life at risk with that action.

Had the hybrid heir considered ending *my* life that night when she'd stolen the jewels from around my neck? Had her hands itched to slit my throat?

If our roles had been reversed, I would have slit hers without hesitation. Would have gutted her like a pig—just as she had the assessor.

I was lucky the time-stopping queen had been too soft, even at her most dangerous.

But that had been before her fae lover's betrayal.

Nothing hardened a woman like betrayal from a man she'd trusted. And then men had the audacity to call *us* cold.

The heir had taken my favorite jewels. Many of

them priceless. The king had raged about that, even as I'd suppressed a smile.

I hoped she used them well. Hoped she waged war against Sabium. Hoped she removed his head from his neck and spiked it on the castle gates.

Just as long as she was dead soon after.

So my son could take his crown.

4
PRISCA

Leaving Telean was difficult. I hadn't realized how much I'd come to rely on her, how often I turned to her for support during the day. How many times I ran my thoughts past her. But my aunt looked exhausted—her face drawn and tight, her shoulders more hunched than usual. I was hoping she would spend most of the remainder of her journey resting.

After I'd had a good, long cry on the ship—while the horses were being procured—I'd washed my face and had a stern talk with myself.

I needed to work with Lorian. He likely had some reason for wanting me to go directly to the hybrid camp. It probably wasn't even about me—he was probably engaged in some power struggle with his brother. Either way, his change of heart would benefit the hybrids

In the meantime, I had to keep my distance from him. We might need to travel together, but I would suffocate any feelings that attempted to come back to life.

I was no longer that village girl. And he'd never been a mercenary.

Lorian had sent one of the sailors to purchase a couple of horses for us. From the long-suffering sigh as he surveyed the mounts the sailor returned with, he would have much preferred to have completed the task himself.

"This is Tilly." The sailor handed me the lead rope. He was one of the few who was brave enough to talk to me, and I smiled at him.

His skin flushed until it matched the red of his hair.

Clearing his throat, the sailor glanced at Lorian. "This is Whisper," he said.

Lorian examined the stocky horse, which didn't exactly look light on its hooves.

"Nelayra." My aunt held out her arms, and I leaned down, giving her a hug. My eyes met Lorian's over her shoulder. He stared steadily back at me, and I attempted to mimic his calm demeanor.

"She will be fine," he murmured, and for once, neither of us was hissing at the other. *That* was unlikely to last.

"And the hybrids?"

"The healer is remaining. They will recover better on the ship where they can rest."

Sailors called to one another on the ship. The pirate queen was waiting to escort them out of Gromalian waters, and they needed to depart. Since Lorian had been correct about the hidden cove, we'd decided it made the most sense for Lorian and me to slip into the city like any other travelers. Hopefully, by the time the Gromalian king learned we'd docked in his city, we would have made it out of Gromalia.

"Stay safe," my aunt ordered.

I nodded. "I'll see you soon."

And then she was gone, and Lorian and I were riding through the streets of Thobirea and toward the western walls of the city.

I was wearing the clothes Daharak had left me. Any pants of hers would have hit me several inches above my ankle, so she must have borrowed them from someone else. She'd also found me a cloak, which would help hide me from anyone who knew to look out for the hybrid heir.

"I need to stop for a few minutes," Lorian said.

Glancing at him, I made sure he saw my knowing smirk. "Ah. So this little side trip wasn't a gift for me at all."

"I would have returned to the city myself after I left you with Conreth," he replied tonelessly. "This is simply a more expedient choice."

I wrinkled my nose at the reminder of who he was and what his plans were for me.

"Fine. I need to send a letter to my brother anyway."

"To which brother?"

"Don't you worry your bloodthirsty little head."

His eyes flashed. "You want my help? You'll tell me exactly what you're up to."

"I'm *owed* your help," I hissed. "But if you think I'm trusting you with my plans after the way you lied to me, you're dreaming."

Lorian slowed his horse and grabbed my own reins. My skin prickled, the way it always did when he was within touching distance.

"You need to assert your independence, wildcat? Fine. But don't forget you're here thanks to my goodwill. My task was to take you straight down to my kingdom. Something *you* agreed to. I'm allowing you this little trip as a courtesy."

The world narrowed, until all I could see was his face.

I shifted my upper body, leaning close and giving him a cool smile. "I don't remember any blood vow at those gates. Do you?"

Right now, Demos was already healed. I'd overseen that healing myself at the city gates. And he was also currently out of Lorian's reach. I might have traveled this far with the fae prince, but he'd been too distracted to insist on a blood vow that night.

It had only been when I'd studied the numerous marks on Daharak's arm that I'd realized I had none left of my own. And thanks to my little deal with Lorian, I should've had one.

He went still. And something that might have been appreciation gleamed in his eyes. I had a feeling Lorian secretly enjoyed it when I outmaneuvered him.

But not as much as I enjoyed it.

Lorian crossed his arms. "You would go back on your word?"

I laughed. "My word to *you?* Without a second

thought. You try to take me anywhere I don't want to go, and I will disappear. You know I can do it."

I could, too. I could burn myself out, dig deep into the very dregs of my power if I needed to. For now, it benefited me to stay, but I'd survived alone before when I'd had no idea how to use my power. I could do it again if I had to.

Lorian's mouth curved in a wicked grin. "It makes me hard when you defy me, wildcat. One day soon, I'm going to make you suffer for every snide comment you've said. For every moment you refused to listen."

I curled my lip at him. "Threatening torture? And you wonder why I don't trust you?"

"Oh no," he purred. "You know I'd never *torture* you, wildcat."

Our conversation from the castle played through my head.

"I thought we'd moved past threats of torture."

"I wouldn't need to torture you. A few hours in my bed and you'd answer any question I asked."

Despite my loathing of him, heat pooled in my body at what he likely meant. Lorian knew exactly how to make my body respond.

"A pigeon from Gromalia won't make it to your brother once he's in the hybrid camp," Lorian said. "The fae magic will confuse it. And it's likely the iron guards are watching the sky closely along all roads and trails from Lesdryn to the fae border."

I closed my eyes. "Fine." I wanted to know my

friends and family were safe, but not enough to risk them.

We fell into a tense silence. Well, I was tense. Lorian just looked thoughtful. Around us, the Gromalians went about their day, the city a tapestry of colors and sounds—almost overwhelming after being confined to the ship. The narrow, serpentine streets were packed with timber-framed buildings, the scent of freshly baked bread drifting out of a bakery to our left.

Artists sat and sketched on corners, beggars called out from side streets, and the clang of a blacksmith's hammer reverberated from an alleyway as we continued through the city.

Eventually, Lorian directed his horse down a side street. I followed him, and he dismounted outside an inn.

Handing my reins to a groom, I slid off my horse, my boots crunching on gravel as I trailed after Lorian. Even though it was the middle of the day, laughter poured out as we stepped into the tavern. On one side, a young man played a fiddle, while heat spilled from the fire near the door.

Lorian walked over to the fire, nodding at me to sit in one of the stuffed chairs. "Wait here."

I ground my teeth at the order but sat. Lorian strode over to a table close by and slipped into a chair across from an incredibly beautiful fae woman.

A barmaid clunked a cup of ale on the table next to me, and I thanked her absently, still staring at the fae woman.

She was in human glamour, of course, but when she

leaned close to greet Lorian, it was evident she wasn't human or hybrid. She moved with that fae grace Lorian had attempted to suppress for all those weeks. Her skin was a little lighter than Rythos's, her eyes a bright green, and her high cheekbones, lush mouth, and pert nose made it clear some god had taken an interest in her when she was born.

Lorian smiled at her.

If I'd been born with Madinia's power, I could have set her hair on fire.

I immediately spun and faced the fire, taking a drink of the watery ale.

It was absolutely none of my business how close any other woman got to Lorian. Our relationship had been dust from the moment I learned he'd spent weeks lying to me.

My mind helpfully provided me with the image of Lorian and the fae woman naked together, and I took a deep breath. I was practically trembling with the urge to get to my feet and stalk outside for some fresh air, but the overbearing fae behind me would simply follow me out.

Then he'd know just how dark my mood was. And he'd likely assume it was about him.

It wasn't. I was merely tired.

"You're far too beautiful to be frowning into the flames," a deep voice said.

This day just kept getting worse. I kept my gaze on the fire. "Leave me alone."

Of course, the man moved closer. I dragged my gaze away from the fire and looked up.

The stranger was remarkably handsome. Tall, wide-shouldered, with blue eyes that laughed at me. His nose was straight, his face clean-shaven, and he projected an air of trustworthiness that made suspicion tighten my gut.

I opened my mouth, right as a huge hand clamped down on the back of my neck. I slashed out with my knife, and Lorian's other hand caught my wrist.

"Wildcat," he growled.

I'd almost unmanned him. My mouth twitched, and my gaze met the stranger's. He grinned at me.

"We're leaving," Lorian said.

"Goodbye, *wildcat*," the stranger said.

Lorian went still in that eerie way of his. I got to my feet. Clearly, the man had overimbibed and decided to pick a fight with Lorian. It wasn't about me.

When it came to men and their need to display their egos in public, it was rarely about women.

Lorian's gaze had turned predatory as he watched the man. The man just stared back, his blue eyes no longer twinkling. No, now they looked dead.

Lorian angled his head, his eyes flat. I knew that expression. He was contemplating murder.

Cold dripped down my spine. As much as I insisted I didn't believe in fate, all of my instincts were telling me I would see this man again. I took a long moment to memorize his face. Those blue eyes met mine again, and I barely suppressed a shiver.

Turning, I stalked toward the door.

Lorian was behind me a moment later. "Why are you

in such a bad mood?" he snarled into my ear.

The stable hand nodded at us, turning to find our horses. A group of men in dusty, travel-worn cloaks strode toward the door of the inn, and Lorian nudged me to the side, placing his body firmly between mine and the men. I ground my teeth. "I don't know what you're talking about."

"Ah. You're jealous."

My heart raced in my chest, but I managed to give him a flat look.

"I'm glad you're jealous," he continued, voice dripping with satisfaction. "It's about time you stopped pretending not to care."

I peered at my nails. Where was the stable hand? "I'm not jealous. Simply reflecting on the fact that while I have many, many good qualities, the past few weeks have proven my judgment of character is supremely lacking."

"Keep telling yourself that, wildcat."

The clip-clop of hooves announced the arrival of our horses, and Lorian turned. I took a deep breath, mentally bracing myself for the long days of traveling next to the man I'd almost given my heart to.

Despair rose, so sharp and sudden, I almost groaned.

Lorian whirled, eyes feral, lips pulled back from his teeth in a vicious snarl. It was the first time I'd seen any true emotion from him since we'd left the ship, and I jolted.

"I'm almost done with these games."

Staring him down was one of the hardest things I'd

ever done. "I have no idea what you're talking about," I said, my voice carefully neutral.

"I thought you were a fighter."

"I am," I said. "When I find something worth fighting for."

Stepping past him, I walked over to my horse, checking the girth. The mare liked to puff up her belly while being saddled, and I tightened the girth another notch, giving her a pat. Lorian dropped a coin in the stable hand's palm and swung himself up into his own saddle, waiting as I mounted.

I followed him back to the road. I had a faint ringing in my ears. A numbness sweeping through my body. Any time Lorian forced me to talk about the ruins of our relationship, it was all I could do not to flee.

It was simple. I needed to bury every feeling I'd ever had for him somewhere deep where I'd hopefully never need to look at it again. And I'd pretend he was a stranger. A smart, knowledgeable man I'd hired to escort me to the border.

Later, when I was alone—when he'd returned to whatever he did when his brother sent him on his little journeys—I could fall apart at my leisure. Then I'd build myself back up and never think of the fae prince again.

Pulling the hood of my cloak over my head, I steered my horse around a vendor selling roasted nuts from a cart. We were traveling through the outskirts of the slums now, and the musky odor of an unwashed street stuffed itself up my nostrils—fruit, exotic spices, urine, stale beer, horse shit. Someone was cooking something meaty and heavy with garlic.

"Who's going to do the cooking now that Rythos isn't here?"

Lorian steered his horse to the right. "I'm perfectly capable of skinning and cooking a rabbit."

The thought made my stomach turn. But Lorian continued talking, as if starved of conversation. "Rythos enjoys cooking. The only one of us who does."

I nodded silently.

"I can teach you if you'd like," Lorian said.

I glanced at him, but his gaze was on the city gates in the distance.

Tamping down my natural instinct to deny him, I thought about it. It hadn't been all that long ago that I'd been running for my life, wondering how I'd survive. Just like the other skills I'd picked up from the mercenaries—I refused to think of them as fae nobility—it made sense to learn this too. Even if it meant talking to Lorian.

He was waiting for me to speak. His expression was perfectly bored, but I could sense his attention. I took a deep breath. "I'd like to learn how to cook over a fire."

Was I imagining the triumph that flashed through his eyes? I reached for a change of subject. "Tell me when I should use my power."

He nodded, turning his gaze back toward the gate in the distance. It was just as heavily guarded as the Eprothan gate.

"Now," he said, and I tugged on my magic.

In the end, the crossing was uneventful. We spent the entire day on horseback, until my body ached and I was more than ready to eat and sleep. Lorian built the fire, lit it with a single look, and then went hunting. I placed our bedrolls on opposite sides of the fire, fed the horses, and then sat, staring sightlessly into the flames.

When he returned, he showed me how to cook two rabbits over a spit. From the faint amusement in his eyes, I'd turned green.

Lorian waited until my eyes were heavy and I was buried under a blanket, lying on my bedroll. The bastard dragged his own bedroll just feet from mine, trapping me between his body and the fire.

"What are you doing?" I hissed.

He cast me a disinterested look. One I'd seen so many times during those first days when we'd traveled together. One I'd never thought I'd see again.

Obviously, we were in agreement about exactly how this trip would go. And our relationship as acquaintances.

It was what I'd wanted, but it stung that he didn't even care. He'd never attempted to explain…

"You can tell yourself whatever makes it easier for you to hate me, wildcat. But it was real. All of it."

I stabbed that little memory until it was dead. Lorian closed his eyes. "Protecting you, Nelayra."

It was the first time he'd called me Nelayra. The word did what he was likely hoping for. I rolled over, curled myself into a ball, and closed my eyes.

But I could feel his gaze on the back of my neck.

My skin prickled. If there was one thing Lorian had, it was patience. He was used to biding his time—after all, he'd done exactly that while he'd waited for the perfect opportunity to get close to Regner.

And my instincts were screaming at me that he was simply biding his time once more.

LORIAN

I'd dreamed again last night.

I didn't often dream anymore. It was Prisca who woke with choked screams dying in her throat. And each time it happened, I wanted to wrap her in my arms and force her to accept what little comfort I could offer.

Today, she was the one casting me the occasional searching look.

I ignored those looks in favor of gazing at her instead. Each time she tucked a blond curl behind her ear, she revealed a sliver of skin at her neck. I knew just how soft that skin was. Knew how she tasted.

"If you don't stop staring at me, I'm going to push you off your horse."

Her snarl was enough to pull me from my darker thoughts. "Good luck with that, wildcat."

Since it was annoying her, and I'd gladly take that

annoyance over her insistence on pretending I was a stranger, I continued to stare. Now that I had her alone, I would no longer allow her to continue to build walls between us.

Giving her space hadn't worked. So perhaps it was time to do the opposite.

She licked her lips, her amber eyes narrowing as she deigned to glare at me. Her mouth had always fascinated me, even when we'd first met—when I was determined to ignore her existence.

Her cheeks flushed, her eyes sparked, and I ruthlessly suppressed the urge to crush my mouth to hers.

I wanted to haul her off that horse and roll her beneath me.

I'd thought I could tolerate her cold silence. Thought I could swallow down the hurt in her eyes each time I spoke. Thought I could deal with the way she'd refused to even ask me to explain.

I'd given her time. But I could see now just how I'd erred. My wildcat had clearly decided that the time I'd allowed was a signal I was giving up.

She was going to learn differently.

"We need to water the horses," I said, and she nodded, reining in her horse and following me off the trail.

Prisca dismounted, wincing a little.

"Do you need some healer's balm?"

She slid me a cool look. The same kind of look a woman might send someone she didn't know. Someone she had no intention of knowing further. "No thank you."

That was enough. She'd turned to walk away, but I caught her wrist, pushing her up against the closest tree.

"Let go," she ordered, baring her teeth as she leaned close, her voice shaking with suppressed wrath.

Fury carved a hole through me, until I lowered my own head, leaning close to her ear.

"Hate me, rage against me, refuse to admit what you feel. But don't you *dare* treat me like a stranger."

Those were tears sparkling on her lower lashes. Tears she refused to shed.

"You *are* a stranger."

I raised my head just enough to catch the way she stuck out her chin.

"Keep pushing, wildcat, and see what happens."

Her eyes fired. "If you hurt me, your brother will—"

Gods, this woman knew just how to cut at a man. Taking her shoulders, I gave her a gentle shake. She raised her knee, but I blocked it with my thigh.

"You know I'd never hurt you. Who and what I am haven't changed that."

"I don't want to talk about it."

Slowly, I released my hands, stepping away from her. "Enjoy your silent treatment. Because it's ending soon."

5
PRISCA

How *dare* he?

Attempting to keep my expression blank, I mounted my horse. Lorian knew exactly what I was doing. If I raged at him the way I wanted to, he'd know just how much he'd hurt me. He'd know exactly how much I'd cared. So my only choice was to treat him with cold disdain.

Unfortunately, he could see through it.

"Enjoy your silent treatment. Because it's ending soon."

His arrogance truly knew no bounds. As if he'd *tolerated* my ignoring him so far, and now he had the right to demand I engage with him.

I'd engage with him, that was for sure. I'd freeze time, and when he unfroze, it would be to find me choking him with his own blanket.

Staring at the back of Lorian's neck, I lost myself in a murderous haze. He glanced over his shoulder at me, and his lips twitched.

Of course he would find it amusing. He'd gotten exactly what

he wanted. I was shaken from my apathy and vividly picturing his death. Why he somehow thought this was better than my ignoring him, I'd never understand.

Wings flapped, and a pigeon landed on Lorian's shoulder. He took the message, gave the bird a stroke, and unrolled the parchment.

His shoulders stiffened.

"What is it?" I asked.

"None of your concern, wildcat."

Oh yes, it was. That bird wasn't from his brother. No, the fae king used a falcon, and Lorian had once told me he used a hawk named Aquilus. Terrible possibilities ran through my head, one after the other. Someone I loved had gotten sick. Or died. A travel party had been attacked, and *no one had survived*.

Lorian slowly turned his head. "Everyone you love is fine," he said, slowly and clearly.

I nodded, but my mind continued to race. Something else, then. All of my instincts urged me to read that letter, and I watched as Lorian shoved it in to the pocket of his cloak, turning his horse.

My thighs, ass, and calves burned when we finally stopped for the day. We were both quiet as we made up the camp, and Lorian cooked dinner. I couldn't bring myself to interact with him, so I simply watched silently. He didn't attempt to make me talk, just handed me slices of meat and a waterskin.

I'd spent most of last night awake and the rest of it caught in dreams. During the day, I'd been refusing to think about the woman I'd called Mama. The woman who'd taken me from my birth mother and set off the chain of events that ensured my birth mother had died that night. But last night, Mama had appeared in my dreams, her last words playing over and over.

"I knew you had to live, so you could save us all. But first, you must find the prince. Find him and meet your fate."

Was Lorian the prince she had meant?

Or did she mean Regner's "son," as I'd assumed at the time? The son I'd never seen during my time at the castle, because Regner wouldn't allow him home?

I finished my food and glanced at Lorian. We were sitting across from each other, and he'd been watching me for the last few minutes, a contemplative expression on his face. After a long moment, he got to his feet. "I need to wash," he said.

Taking off his cloak, he laid it on his bedroll. He didn't so much as look at it again, wandering away toward the river. For once, his steps were loud. In fact, Lorian was clearly annoyed, because he was almost stomping. I counted his steps until they faded.

And then I pounced.

I rounded the fire and slipped a hand into the pocket of his cloak.

Wrong pocket.

Silently cursing myself, I plucked the message from the other pocket and unrolled it.

L,

C's spies have learned of the hourglass. His suspicions were correct. C advises caution and silence for now. It is possible the hourglass will soon be moved.

—P

I didn't know who P was. But that hourglass…

It belonged to the hybrids.

Lorian's footsteps sounded once more, cutting through the silence of the night. I didn't bother moving, just raised my head until my eyes met his.

He was shirtless, drops of water still dripping down his chest. He angled his head and swept his gaze over me, still poised on his bedroll, his private correspondence in my hand.

I waved it like a weapon. "None of my concern?" I hissed.

Something that might have been satisfaction gleamed in his eyes before it was replaced by annoyance. "Didn't anyone ever teach you not to snoop through other people's belongings?"

"Where is it, Lorian? Where's the hourglass?"

"I don't know. And if I did, I couldn't tell you."

Fresh betrayal flooded me. My hand trembled. He watched me, his expression coolly patient. "My loyalty will always be to my people, Prisca. To my brother."

Some tiny spark inside me—one I hadn't realized was still burning—went out. Lorian's gaze just fell to the letter I was holding.

"Think, wildcat."

"Fuck you, Lorian." Getting to my feet, I stuffed the stolen message into my own cloak pocket and stalked past him toward the river.

Caution and silence.

Telean had told me the hourglass had made it easier for my ancestors to wield their power and protect their kingdom. If I could find it, I could truly help the hybrids. That hourglass had been given to them by the gods. How dare the fae attempt to keep it from them?

Caution and silence.

I kicked out at a stone, watching it fly into the water. It splashed, and the sound tickled something at the edge of my memory.

Lorian was fae. When he wanted to be quiet, he didn't make a sound.

And he didn't leave his personal belongings behind. Given our current relationship, he would never be stupid enough to leave his cloak near me once I'd seen him slip that message inside his pocket.

Even as he'd warned me that his loyalties would always lie with his brother, he'd wanted me to read that letter.

Pulling out the note, I read it again.

He'd said he *couldn't* tell me, not that he *wouldn't*.

I was forgetting that while he was a fae prince, he served at the pleasure of his king.

Blowing out a frustrated breath, I began to pace.

I had to start thinking like one of them—the men who ruled the continent. The men who'd been wielding their power since before I was born.

If I were a fae king, I would take one look at the "hybrid heir" and see her as a symbol. I'd want her to be just powerful enough to rally her forces to kill Regner, but never powerful enough to present an actual threat if she decided to turn on me. If, say, she decided to make me pay for the way my people had abandoned hers.

If the fae king saw me as a symbol he could control as he saw fit, he wouldn't want me to give the hybrids that hourglass. No, he'd want to make sure the fae got their hands on their amulets and the hybrids were left to rely on fae benevolence.

I snarled.

"You're finally thinking it through." Lorian's voice was a rough growl behind me. This time, he'd moved the way he usually did.

Silently.

I slowly turned. "You didn't have to do this. Why did you?"

He shook his head. We weren't going to discuss it.

I'd work with what I had.

"You can't tell me where the hourglass is. But who else knows this information?"

Pride flared in his eyes, although his face remained

expressionless. "Your brothers will be in the fae lands by now. I'm due for a message from Marth tomorrow, so I suggest you add a message for him to give to your brothers."

Because they might be able to learn the information Lorian couldn't tell me. Not without betraying his brother.

My chest had tightened, and I forced myself to take a deep breath. "I will."

"You need to get some sleep," Lorian said, still studying my face. "We're training in the morning."

"What do you mean?"

"Galon won't be pleased to learn you haven't been training. It's time you got back to work. I'll take over for now."

I didn't want to be that close to him. If I told him that, Lorian would only laugh at me. Or give me that blank stare, perhaps with a raised eyebrow that invited me to ask him if he cared.

"Fine."

He nodded, turned, and stalked away.

I watched him go for long enough that he could probably feel my eyes on him. My gaze slid down to his ass, and I spun, facing the water once more.

Figure it out.

It wasn't the first time he'd said those words. He'd said the same when he'd agreed to pretend we were already allies before we met the king. And when I'd asked him why he'd chosen to take me directly to the hybrid camp, he'd told me I wasn't ready for that conversation.

I could accuse Lorian of many things, but I could never accuse him of wanting me to be weak. Time and time again, he'd insisted I learn to wield my power, train to defend myself physically, and conquer my fears. He'd continually pushed me to do better. *Be* better. And even now, with the ashes of our relationship dusting the ground between us, he was still ensuring I had every scrap of information I needed to make the best decisions for my people.

My eyes burned. And then I was striding back to our fire, back toward the fae prince who still made me question *everything*. I didn't want him. Had come to terms with the fact that he was poison to me. And yet.

He lifted his head, and his gaze pinned me in place. His eyes…gods, his eyes were glowing with repressed power, and tiny sparks jumped from his skin. I could feel that power from here, brushing against me like a well-fed cat.

"Why, Lorian?"

His eyes shuttered. "My people owe yours."

"Is that the only reason?"

Silence.

Shaking my head, I opened my mouth to press him further.

The sound that came from him was guttural—part growl, part groan. In one of his too-fast-to-see movements, he was suddenly standing in front of me once more. He buried his face in my neck, and I shivered as the stubble along his jaw scraped my skin.

More. I wanted more. I always would when it came to this man. And that was what made him so fucking dangerous.

I swallowed around the lump currently burning a hole through my throat. "This is never going to work. You and I. We're doomed. You know that."

He sighed, and I closed my eyes, basking in the feel of his breath against my neck.

"I know." He slowly drew back. "But that doesn't mean I won't wish for you with every fucking breath for the rest of my life."

The Boy

The servants thought the boy couldn't hear them whispering. Thought he couldn't hear the things they said.

"He shouldn't have survived," they murmured.

"Perhaps we should count ourselves lucky that most of his power was taken," a man whispered. A man who had once been the boy's father's friend.

The boy slowly turned his head and allowed him to see he had heard. Just so he could watch the fear flicker through the man's eyes.

"Perhaps we should," another muttered, and one of the boy's pointed ears twitched—enough to make it clear

he was listening. The group of courtiers strode away.

Within days, he was all alone. His nanny hadn't forgiven herself for falling asleep that night and had become listless and withdrawn.

And then one day, as he was sitting beneath the table in the kitchen, petting the kitchen cat, he heard two words that made the breath catch in his throat.

"Your Majesty," one of the cooks said.

The boy sucked in a breath. His father was alive. They'd been wrong after all. He'd told them. And if his father was alive, his mother was alive too. His father would have protected her with his last breath. His chest expanded, and his cheeks tightened as an unfamiliar expression overtook his face.

A smile. This was what a smile felt like. It had been so long, he'd forgotten.

Scrambling out from beneath the table, he let out an exultant laugh. "Papa!"

The room went silent. Conreth stood in front of him. And the servants were bowing. Not to the boy's father, but to his brother.

The new fae king.

The color drained from Conreth's face, even as his eyes glistened. "No, Lorian. It's me. It's just you and me now."

PRISCA

Lorian received his letter from Marth the next morning, and I sent a letter of my own to Tibris, carefully written in our code. In it, I asked him to decode the letter for Demos, and for both of them to do whatever they could to find the location of the hourglass.

The hybrids were loyal to both Demos and Vicer, and many of them were powerful. Hopefully, they could figure out just where the hourglass was, and we could get to it before the fae king did. I refused to let the hybrids be at the mercy of yet another foreign ruler.

Lorian stood with his hair tied back, his sword on the ground a few feet away. We were up early—Lorian eager to make it to the forest along the border. He'd refused to allow me to take watch last night, but he still looked alert and rested.

This morning, he'd told me we were deep in bandit territory and far too visible on the plain. The thought made the skin on the back of my neck prickle.

"Are you ready?" He focused on me as if nothing else existed. That look was predatory, patient, possessive.

I frowned. We'd packed up the camp, and the fire was dampened, the horses saddled. "You want to train now?"

One dark brow rose. "You'd prefer to wait until you've been riding all day?"

I was still dealing with chafed thighs and an aching back after each long day of riding. I was sore now, but it would be much worse later. "No," I sighed, rolling my shoulders. "Let's get this over with."

He crooked his finger.

"You want me to attack?"

"Galon's been training you to be defensive. But there may come a time when you need to take someone by surprise. And that means learning how to hit hard and fast before they get a chance to put you down."

"That's not really my—"

"Prisca."

Lorian's voice was hard. I sighed, taking a single step closer. His stance was loose, his hands by his sides. As if I wasn't even a threat. Annoyance rumbled in my chest. He smiled as if he knew.

"I'll even let you have a knife," he said, throwing me a dagger. I somehow managed to catch it by the hilt, and his smile widened.

Annoyance turned to fury, and it got very quiet inside my head. I could do this. I refused to let him see how my body responded when he was close.

I circled him. He moved with me. I had to be fast.

"Anytime," he taunted me. "We don't have all—"

I struck, taking the distance between us in a long jump. He caught my left wrist in his hand. Fuck.

I slashed at the back of his hand with my dagger. He sucked in a breath but didn't let go, so I attempted to pull him off-balance with my left arm, aiming my right elbow at his face.

My elbow glanced off his chin. Not good.

He tensed. Using his hold on my wrist and my own unbalanced body, he threw me over his hip.

I gaped at him like a fish on land, winded.

"What have you learned today?" he asked, reaching into his pocket and pulling out a bandage, which he tied around the shallow cut I'd given him. The bastard would probably heal it within minutes.

And me? I *still* couldn't breathe. I gasped uselessly for air.

Lorian leaned down, taunting me once more. "I would hope you've learned that you don't attack those bigger and stronger than you without a plan in place."

I managed to roll onto my belly, weakly getting to my knees. Since I was able to keep my breakfast down, I counted it as a win.

He'd goaded me into this attack. I groaned, stumbling up to my feet. "You're a bastard."

"And *you* should never attack without using your power first."

My lower lip stuck out before I could stop it. Lorian's gaze dropped to my mouth, and his expression tightened.

"Using my power would be cheating," I snapped.

Lorian slowly raised his gaze, until it felt as if he was caressing every inch of my face. When our eyes met, he stepped closer, his eyes burning into my own.

"When it comes to your survival, you cheat," he snarled. "You cheat and you lie. You fight dirty. And you do whatever else it takes to stay alive."

"Even with you?"

"Even with me. You can work with Galon on your physical training. Your aunt can help you with your power. But when you train with me, you use both together."

He seemed to be waiting for me to agree. "Fine." I wasn't stubborn enough to say no to the kind of training that could save my life.

Since he'd already humiliated me enough for one morning, Lorian taught me how to lash out with my front leg to dislocate someone's knee. I'd get more power from using my back leg, but he wanted me to be able to strike fast.

We switched to knife work, and he showed me interesting techniques that included dropping down and slashing my blade across leg muscle, tendon, even hamstrings. It was brutal, necessary training. And hopefully, if there ever came a time when I couldn't use my power, it would help.

When I was leaning over and panting, hands on my knees, he just angled his head. "Defensive training next."

"Are you—"

He launched himself at me. Since I'd seen him spar with Galon and the others, I knew he was moving at about half speed. And yet I still barely darted out of the way in time.

He attempted to grab my arm again, but this time, I was onto his tricks. He kicked out, at quarter speed for him.

I barely dodged it.

Lorian grinned. He was having fun. My temper sparked, but I refused to let it get the better of me once more. I dodged the arm he swept toward me, kicked him in the knee, and sidestepped, jabbing my elbow into his gut. Triumph roared through me.

He let out a pleased laugh. Despite my annoyance, something warm took up residence in my stomach. No one pushed me to be better like this man. So I let a hint of my power out. Just enough to slow his speed. I turned, and there was my opening.

I slapped him across the face.

I wasn't dumb enough to punch him. I'd probably break my hand—at least bruise my knuckles on his hard head, and I needed to be able to use my hands. The shocked, heated look Lorian gave me made my heart stutter.

Enough that I lost my grip on the threads of my power.

I was flat on my back and staring up at him a moment later.

"A good start," he said, his voice tight.

I wiggled, attempting to push him off me. He played with one of the curls that had slipped free from my braid.

I was panting. That was the only reason I couldn't seem to stop breathing in the scent of him. My body was reminding me of what it had been like the last time we'd been in this position, lying on soft sheets.

My mouth had gone dry. "Let me up."

His gaze dropped to my lips. I tensed. If he kissed me, I didn't know if I would have the willpower to stop. I might bury my hand in his hair, urge his head closer, wrap my legs around him...

He was gone a moment later, hauling me up next to him. My head spun.

"We need to get moving," he said.

I attempted to give him back his dagger, and he shook his head. "Keep it." Unbuckling a leather sheath from his arm, he handed it to me.

I'd lost my weapons that night when I'd freed the hybrids. It felt good to have a knife again. The leather was still warm from his body, and I waited until he'd turned back to his horse, stroking it.

The sheath was far too large for my arm, so I slipped it around my thigh. It slid a little against my leather pants, but it worked. Lorian turned back to me, his gaze dropping to the sheath, and his eyes darkened.

"Let's go."

I nodded, enjoying the feel of his gaze on me despite myself as I strolled toward my horse. I swung my leg over her rump, took the reins from Lorian's hand, and gave her a nudge. He caught up to me, and we rode in silence for the next couple of hours as our horses plucked their way across the plain toward the forest in the distance. I was tired of traveling across the scrubland, which offered little shelter and made me feel as if there were eyes on us.

The back of my neck itched. Someone *was* watching us. From the hard expression on Lorian's face each time I looked at him, he felt it too.

"How much longer do we need to travel?" I asked.

"A few days once we hit the forest. We'll enter the fae lands from the Gromalian border. The Gromalian king has problems in this part of his kingdom."

"Problems like what?"

He gave me a faint smile. "Problems like rebels of his own."

"Hybrids?"

"Both hybrids and humans. The rebels welcome all. They've managed to take control of an area to our north, near the intersection of the Gromalian and Eprothan borders."

"I thought that was where some of our people were crossing from Eprotha? Would the rebels attempt to stop them?"

"There's still a large expanse that is a kind of no-man's-land. The rebels aren't stupid enough to attempt to cut the fae off from our kingdom."

"What do they want?"

He gave an elegant shrug. "What every rebel wants. Hope, freedom, and safety for themselves and their families."

I contemplated that for a while. Perhaps we could convince the Gromalian rebels to join us. It would mean more mouths to feed, but if the Gromalian king refused to ally with us, perhaps they would be interested in an alliance instead. I began making a list in my head.

We needed the hourglass.

We needed weapons.

We needed allies.

We needed...

I pondered Lorian. "If I asked you for a favor, would you grant it?"

He gave me a dark smile. "The fae aren't known for our favors. We are, however, known for our bargains."

I ground my teeth. "I'm not doing another blood vow with you."

"Tell me what you want, Prisca."

"I want you to send a spy to find my cousin. The man who was at the city gates when we first crossed into Lesdryn. Don't make contact. Just watch him. I want to...I want to know what kind of man he is."

My cousin was the only other option for the throne. He could be a good, strong man who would make an excellent king. I needed to know.

Lorian's green gaze seemed to spear straight into my soul. "Are you sure about this?"

We were no longer close enough for me to trust him with my inner thoughts. So I gave him my best hard stare. "Will you help me or not?"

"I will. But you'll owe me."

I rolled my eyes. "I'd expect nothing less."

His face was expressionless, but I got the distinct impression he wanted to roar at me. "It will be done."

My throat ached, and I glanced away.

This was the best choice.

If Lorian's brother died and he had to take the

throne, I had no doubt Lorian would make an excellent king. Because he knew basic things about our world like what the *barrier* was. And why warships couldn't dock in Gromalia. And what made the pirate queen so dangerous.

If not for Lorian and Telean, I would have made numerous mistakes so far. Mistakes so grave, they would have cost me people I loved. The hybrids needed a ruler who knew what they were doing. Not someone who was fumbling her way through this due solely to some accident of birth.

There were real repercussions to my ignorance.

And…even if I were to learn everything I needed, even if I were to rely on those around me who knew that information, the fact remained that I would make a terrible queen. I'd never wanted power. All I'd ever wanted was a quiet life. A happy life. The hybrids deserved someone who *wanted* to rule.

That didn't mean I was washing my hands of them.

Oh no, I was going to fight. I was going to find this hourglass and hand it over to my people. I'd ally with anyone I could—at least while the term *hybrid heir* carried any weight. And I'd make sure the hybrids had their own hope, freedom, and safety before I was done.

We finally passed into the forest, the shade a relief after riding beneath the sun for so long. Not only was it warmer the farther south we traveled, but the seasons were already changing. My heart raced at the thought of the time that was passing.

I had no doubt Regner was planning something

terrible. And the longer he had to plan, the worse it would be.

Goose bumps broke out over my arms, and I went still. Lorian glanced over his shoulder and gave me a single sharp nod.

We were being followed, and he wanted me to pretend I didn't know. They must have been lying in wait. We would have noticed them while we were traveling through the plains.

I hissed out a breath. This trail was narrow. Between the horses and the trees, we'd have little room to fight.

The path widened ahead, just enough for me to ride up next to him. I held out my waterskin, attempting to make the movement look natural. As if I was just taking advantage of the increased room.

Lorian took it. "We're surrounded," he ground out, his voice so low I could barely hear. "We're at a disadvantage here, so we need to get to a clearing. I want you on my horse."

He leaned over, and I was suddenly in his arms. He'd plucked me off my horse like I weighed nothing. Lorian slapped my horse on the rump, and she took off. I managed to get my leg over the saddle just as he kicked his own horse into a gallop.

It was dangerous—riding this fast along such a narrow path. But a male shout rang out behind us.

"What do we do?" I yelled into the wind.

"I'm going to hide you somewhere and take care of them. I'll come back and find you once they're dead."

"No, you're—"

"Duck!"

I was already hunched in the saddle, and Lorian clamped me to him, curving his huge body around mine.

An arrow went whistling past our heads. It lodged itself into the tree next to us, and Lorian cursed as his horse bucked.

"The iron guards," he snarled.

"How do you know?"

The arm around my waist somehow became even tighter. "I recognize those fucking arrows."

6

PRISCA

Another bolt flew far too close for comfort. I sucked in a breath. Ahead, the trail curved to the right. Perhaps we could lose them.

Or perhaps I was being far too merciful. If they lived, they would continue to hunt us. And they'd continue to hunt the people I loved.

"Kill them, Lorian. I know you can do it."

"If I use my power in a wide arc, there will be no survivors. We need at least one of them alive for questioning. I want to know how they found you."

My heart raced at the thought of his being hunted. Instant denial shot through me. "Lorian."

"I'm going to drop you off the horse. You'll hide. Freeze time, and I'll circle back."

It was a good plan. I pulled at the threads of my power as the path veered to the right.

Crippling pain burst through my arm. I let out a choked scream, and behind us, someone *cheered*.

Lorian cursed. "Fae iron. I can scent it. You're fine. You're fine, wildcat. But you won't be able to use your power until I get the iron out."

His voice was very calm. But I knew him. And I could hear the wrath buried beneath the calm.

The horse was still galloping, jolting my arm with every movement. In the corner of my eye, I could see the bolt, straight through the flesh of my upper arm. My vision darkened at the edges, and fresh panic coursed through me. Powerless. I was—

"*Breathe,* Prisca." Lorian curved his body even tighter around mine.

I complied, sucking in deep, steadying breaths. They cleared my head enough that I no longer wanted to pass out.

"That's it," Lorian crooned. "I don't know how many of them there are. I need a better visual. There's another curve coming up. You're going to jump."

I nodded. I'd jump, pull the arrow out of my arm, and circle around from behind. Then I'd help him hunt these bastards down.

We were just foot-spans from the curve of the path when Lorian let out a strange grunt. A gurgle.

Terror punched through me. My limbs turned numb.
"Lorian!"

He slumped against me. I grabbed the arm he'd wrapped around my waist and held on with all my strength.

He didn't say a word. But I knew. They'd shot him in

the back. The arrow hadn't hit his heart, or he'd be dead already.

"Jump," he ordered, his voice tight.

Their bolts contained fae iron. Lorian couldn't use his powers now either. He was planning to lure the iron guards close, kill whoever he could with his sword, and go down swinging while I ran.

I slowly unwound his arm from my stomach.

"Good girl," he muttered.

Condescending bastard. If he lived through this, I'd kill him myself. Instead, I swung the horse wide and threw my arm behind me. It only worked because Lorian weighed so damn much and because he hadn't expected the move. He cursed as he fell off the horse, his body immediately swallowed by a tangle of trees and cluster of shrubs next to the trail.

Gods, I hoped that arrow hadn't just found its way to his heart. But this was our only chance.

The horse tossed her head. I wrestled for control, and the path split. I had a choice to make. Left or right.

I steered left, my arm screaming at me as I pulled the reins. The horse was faster without Lorian's weight, and we practically flew down the path. I drew her to a stop, and she bucked, refusing to cooperate as I attempted to guide her off the trail and into the forest itself.

The horse was panting, wild-eyed. I slipped off her, gently guiding her off the trail and behind a huge tree. She snorted, clearly unhappy. I couldn't blame her.

"Come on, beautiful. Just for a few moments."

Finally, she took a couple of steps, right as more shouts sounded behind me. I ducked, hoping the horse was hidden well enough.

Five or six iron guards charged past us. I had moments at most before they realized my hoofprints had disappeared. Taking a deep breath, I looked at the arrow in my arm.

This was going to hurt.

I had to push it through my arm, or I'd rip through too much flesh. Tibris had taught me enough about veins and arteries to know I had to be careful. I could practically hear him screaming at me.

"Projectiles stay in *the body, Prisca!"*

Unfortunately, if I did that, I was dead. I had to take my chances and hope the arrow hadn't hit anything important. At least if I could access my power, I had a chance at survival. Slipping a hand into the saddlebag closest to me, I groped around until I found a long bandage.

Hooves sounded. The iron guards were coming back this way.

I grabbed the shaft of the arrow with my other hand. Just that much jostling made me want to pass out. Sliding down, I leaned against a tree, panting through my teeth as I shoved a short branch between them, biting down.

My hand shook, but I snapped the end of the shaft, groaning around the branch in my mouth. My vision dimmed, and I forced myself to push the arrow through my arm, breathing deep.

If I passed out, I was dead.

"She's over here!" one of the iron guards yelled. "I can see tracks."

Live or die. This is it.

A muffled scream left my throat as agony blazed through my arm, but I kept pushing until the arrow popped free. Grabbing the bloody arrowhead, I pulled the rest of the arrow and shaft free, throwing it on the ground. My head turned lighter than air, my vision blurred, and I leaned over, bracing my good arm on my knees.

My other arm was drenched in blood.

Fae iron didn't affect hybrids as much as it did the fae. But it still weakened us. And reaching for my power felt like crawling through mud.

Please...

I didn't know who I was begging. The gods had forsaken hybrids long ago.

My heart cracked at the thought of dying here. Alone. At the thought of not making it back to Asinia and Tibris and Demos and the others. But it was Lorian's face that flashed through my mind, his lips pulled back in a vicious snarl.

I yanked my power with everything I had. Blood streamed from my nose.

The forest went silent. I choked out a sob. It had worked. My head ached, my body rebelling at the use of my power. Winding the bandage around my arm, I stumbled back onto the path where the iron guard waited just foot-spans away.

He wore some kind of strange black armor, his

helmet slung over his saddle. The bloodlust and triumph frozen on his face made me want to vomit. Instead, I used my good hand to grab his boot in an attempt to pull him down.

The huge man didn't so much as move. My hold on my power was loosening already. My breaths came faster, my throat so dry, each inhale burned.

My hand hit something. The hilt of a knife, sheathed in his boot. I slipped it free and buried it in his thigh, where Tibris had taught me the largest artery was located. I stabbed once more, and my head spun. Moments. I had moments.

Yanking the knife out of his thigh, I slipped back off the path and behind a tree, time resuming without my input. The iron guard groaned, slumping, his horse continuing to move until the guard fell to a heap on the ground.

I darted forward, took his sword, and ignored the terror in his eyes as he gazed up at me.

"Did you cheer when you heard me scream?" I hissed.

He flinched. His stare turned glassy. He was already dead, although it would take a few minutes for him to succumb completely.

But his friends were on their way.

My head spun. I stumbled back into the forest, waited until the next horse galloped along the trail, and reached for the dregs of my power.

A hand slapped onto my mouth. I clawed at it and

stilled. I knew that scent.

"Don't fucking move," Lorian hissed. "Stay here, or I swear to all of the gods, I'll make you regret it."

My mouth dropped open, and he released his hand. I whirled, but the Bloodthirsty Prince was already moving, his sword swinging.

He was in his fae form. The sight made my heart trip—memories of the castle gates merging with the sight of him now. He was even taller, moved even faster, but his shirt was wet with blood. Wet because...

Three arrows impaled him through the back. He'd taken three arrows. And yet he stood on the dirt path, arms folded, a dark scowl on his face as if he was annoyed by the *inconvenience*.

The iron guards arrived from both sides. Obviously, the other path had looped around. Lorian merely raised an eyebrow. "Where are the rest of you?"

The closest guard pointed at the unconscious man on the path. "The hybrid bitch is going to pay for that."

I scowled. The hybrid bitch was ready to get this over with.

I opened my mouth. Lorian must have sensed it somehow, because his eyes shifted almost imperceptibly toward my hiding spot, gleaming with warning. His dark hair seemed to fly back from his face, his green eyes almost glowing above those razor-sharp cheekbones.

The iron guards leaped from their horses.

Lorian watched them, his expression speculative.

And then he struck.

I sucked in a breath.

I'd miscalculated. And I'd never truly seen Lorian fight. His sword flashed too fast to see, and he moved as if I'd frozen time just for him. The first guard fell to his knees, and Lorian kicked his body off the blade of his sword. The second guard lost his head before he realized Lorian was in front of him.

The third managed to swing his sword at least, but his scream as Lorian thrust his sword into his chest…it made me want to clamp my hands over my ears.

"Stop playing with them," I hissed.

Lorian flicked me a glance. His eyes were frigid. "They would have done unspeakable things to you before they killed you."

I reached for my power. It hurt, but I pulled anyway, my nose trickling blood. Time stopped. Including Lorian. I stepped onto the dirt path and slit the throat of the man closest to me. I was standing next to the one in front of Lorian when time resumed without my input. I thrust my knife into his back.

Lorian's eyes turned feral, and he caught my wrist, dragging me behind him as the guard groaned.

"That was dangerous and reckless."

"Says the walking pincushion currently beheading people."

"I could have swung my sword before I knew you were there," he growled. "I could have fucking beheaded you."

I ignored that. His reaction time was lightning-fast.

"If you're going to question him, you should do it now."

"We're having a conversation about this later."

I just sighed, gesturing to the man who'd fallen to his knees. The guard paled as Lorian stepped closer. "How did you know where we were?"

"Fuck you."

Lorian glanced at me. "Look away, wildcat."

I shook my head. If I was going to partake in murder, I wouldn't avert my eyes like a coward. Lorian's jaw tightened, but he turned his attention to the guard.

"I can make your death quick, or I can make it long and excruciating."

"I didn't know. I just follow orders," the guard snarled. His face was ashen now, and he glanced at me as if for mercy. My breath caught in my throat.

"Don't look at her," Lorian breathed. "Look at *me.*"

The guard ignored him, his expression hardening. "You're going to suffer," he told me. "King Sabium has big plans for you."

Fury twisted my gut. Lorian swung his sword, and this time, I did look away.

"We need to go now," I said tonelessly when it was done.

"We'll talk about this," he promised darkly. He didn't mean the guard. He was still annoyed about my getting involved. Turned out I could still freeze him after all—even with his power.

I planted my hands on my hips. "Where's your horse? We need to get out of here."

PRISCA

I was getting really tired of the men in my life taking arrows for me.

Especially when they refused to use any kind of sense.

"You're being ridiculous," I hissed.

Lorian nodded at the brackweed salve. "Give it to me."

"I can do it," I snapped.

He held out his hand.

Since Lorian was a stubborn, unreasonable man, he still hadn't allowed me to pull the arrows from his body. Under his watchful gaze, I'd already boiled water, rinsing out the wound on *my* arm. And while I'd silently ground my teeth against the pain, Lorian had acted like I was twisting a knife in his own wounds, his expression thunderous.

Meanwhile, I could scent his blood. It was making me nauseous.

"What happens if you bleed out because you're being a stubborn bastard?"

He gave me a cool look and took the salve. "It will take more than a few arrows to kill me."

"What *would* it take?" I asked, curious despite myself.

"Given your wicked temper, I think I'll keep that information to myself, wildcat." His mouth curved, and I hated how much I enjoyed the sight.

Lorian slathered the salve on my wound, his hands achingly gentle. A muscle ticked in his jaw. "You'll never do anything like that again."

I ignored that. I was too busy lost in the scent of the brackweed and the memory of the last time I'd used this salve—when I'd first decided to stay with the mercenaries. Rythos had insisted on cooking for me that night.

"Prisca."

I ignored that too. "Turn around."

He gave me a look that promised we'd be having this conversation later, but he turned.

I examined his pointed ear. It was so different from mine, and yet something about it made me want to touch.

Shaking those thoughts from my head, I got to work using my knife to cut away his shirt.

Lorian didn't so much as grunt when I snapped the shaft of the arrows and pushed them through his back until they came through his chest. I had to lean my head down twice when my vision speckled, but he just waited me out.

"It's all right," he eventually told me when I raised my head the second time. "I promise."

"I should be the one saying that to you," I muttered, getting back to work.

I would *not* be distracted by all that lean muscle and smooth skin. I refused.

Perhaps talking would be a better distraction. "If you can't use your power, how come you're in your fae form?"

"This is my natural form. It takes power to use a human glamour." He glanced over his shoulder at me. "When you pushed me off that horse, it was one of the worst moments of my life. All I could think about was how you were alone, hurt, and unable to access your power."

I raised my gaze from the wound I was cleaning. "Lorian..."

He turned his attention to the flames. But it was my turn to be irritated. "Why didn't you kill them all when you first noticed them following us? I saw what you did at the city gates. You didn't need to be hurt this badly."

"I'm powerful, but I'll never be quite as powerful as I was in that moment when all my power returned to me in a rush. Besides, we needed one of them alive."

And yet he'd killed him instead of torturing him for that information. Was it because I'd been watching?

"But you could have killed some of them at least."

His eyes met mine, and this time, they were lit with a predatory light. "You would have tolerated that, would you, wildcat?"

I frowned. "What do you mean?"

"You've only just begun to let me near you again. Forgive me if I wasn't willing to watch you look at me like I was a monster once more."

"This is about the city gates?"

He caught my chin with his fingers. He was so close,

I could see the silver flecks in his eyes. Close enough that my body instinctively responded, my stomach fluttering.

"This is about all of it. What would have happened if you'd found out I was fae in that castle, wildcat? You've been raised to fear my people. To hate us. And even though you were learning that everything you thought you knew was wrong, you were still holding on to that last piece. You and I both know that you would never have trusted me with the hybrids. Instead, you would have attempted to do it alone. And without my help, you wouldn't have gotten those hybrids free."

My gut twisted. "Because I was busy finding your fucking amulet."

His fingers tightened warningly. "If I hadn't been the very creature you've been taught to loathe, the king would have slaughtered all of us that night. Your precious hybrids would have burned. And you would have burned with them. So yes, I hid my secret for my people. And because I didn't want to see the terror in your eyes when you looked at me. But I also did it *for* you."

I gazed up at him silently, processing everything he'd just told me. He was right. I could admit that much to myself.

He must've thought I was going to deny him again, because he released my chin with a shake of his head. "I'm not stupid. I'm not someone you would have chosen to be with. I'm someone you were intrigued by and attracted to despite yourself. I'll never be safe, Prisca. I'll always be the monster who slaughters anyone who attempts to hurt you. I don't know how to be anything else. My mistake was attempting to shield you from the sight of that monster."

My chest had tightened until I could barely breathe. "At the city walls—"

He snarled. "I can still be the man you laughed with. The man you allowed to touch you, to *taste* you. Just as I can also be the man who will kill viciously when provoked. And nothing provokes me more than the sight of you in danger."

This conversation was overdue, and yet I wanted to block out his words. Because thinking of what we'd almost had…it *hurt*.

"It wasn't just that you killed the king's guards the way you did, Lorian. It wasn't your pointed ears or the lightning. It wasn't the fact that you were suddenly bigger or sparking with power. I had no power of my own left. I was completely drained. Madinia barely got me to the city walls. Getting through the city was… It was…" My throat locked, and I took a deep breath. "Parts of the slums were burning. People were fighting in the streets. The streets we chose were blocked over and over again. And the whole time, I knew something was wrong. I knew we should have seen the king at that ball, and the fact that he wasn't there meant that everyone I loved could be dead. When I arrived, I thought I was about to die. I was willing to if it meant you'd save the hybrids. But then I heard them call you that name."

"The Bloodthirsty Prince."

My eyes stung, the painful ache spreading through my head, down my tight throat, and into my heart. "I didn't think you were a monster because of the way you slaughtered those guards, Lorian. I thought you were a monster because I'd heard all about your reputation. So, tell me the truth. Did you destroy Crawyth? Are you the one who killed my parents?"

My lungs burned, but I couldn't seem to loosen the breath I was holding. Couldn't take my eyes off him. Couldn't let go of the hope that dampened the burning fires of my rage. The fires I'd stoked every minute of every day since we'd left the city gates.

Lorian leaned even closer. His scent danced toward me, and I was instantly assaulted by the memory of the way I'd basked in that scent, rolling around in his sheets. Silence stretched between us, and a chill broke out along my skin at the feral gleam in his eyes.

"Tell me one thing first, wildcat," he said. "Tell me you'll believe the words I speak. Tell me you won't instantly assume I'm lying."

I couldn't. My lungs screamed, and the air slowly shuddered out of me.

"You spent weeks lying to me, Lorian."

"And if I tell you I didn't do it?"

I opened my mouth, but any words I could've said got stuck in my throat. Lorian's expression drained of all life.

"As expected," he said.

I glanced away. Everyone in my life had lied to me. Vuena and Papa had lied for years. Even Tibris had pretended he didn't know what I was, when he'd really been working with the rebels. The king of Eprotha's lies had killed thousands. Asinia and I had lied to each other, pretending we were human. Even Demos and Telean had kept the fact that I was the hybrid heir from me until the last possible moment.

When I'd traveled with Lorian, he'd been so open about the world. About the way things worked. He'd never softened anything he had to say—even to spare my feelings. By the time I'd let him into my bed, I'd begun to trust him. And he'd been lying to me for weeks.

His lies had hurt the most.

So how could I trust him now when he said he hadn't attacked Crawyth?

Everyone lied. *Everyone.*

Lorian got to his feet. The life was slowly leaving his expression, Masking the pain the movement must have caused.

I hadn't realized just how withdrawn he'd been on that ship. How he'd reverted to the coldhearted mercenary I'd first met. The one who'd left me for dead without a second thought. But I could see him doing it now.

Even during our power struggles, when we'd had to cooperate, we'd always worked well together. And trusting each other to survive the iron guards had cracked open that hard shell of indifference he'd once again built around himself. Now that shell was back.

I wasn't exactly sure why I cared.

He turned, heading toward the river. "Go on," I

snarled, frustration coursing through me. "Walk away. Why would I expect any different?"

His shoulders stiffened, and I fisted my hands as he slowly turned his head. "You keep pushing, and I'm going to lose control." He turned fully to face me, and a cruel smirk curved his lips. "But perhaps that's what you want. You want me to take you in anger, wildcat? To make you moan my name while you writhe beneath me...all while you loathe me for every second of pleasure? I'll do it. But you won't get it by taunting me. You want hate sex? You'll have to *beg*."

I stared at him, cheeks blazing. His eyes cooled, and he turned, strolling away as if he didn't have a care in the world.

"I hope you drown in that river," I called out. His low, taunting laugh trickled out from the forest. The sound seemed to caress my skin. Skin that was suddenly much, much too sensitive.

The Queen

"What news do you have of Jamic?" I demanded as Pelysian stepped through the hidden door and into my room. I'd sent my remaining ladies away, ordering the maids to give me privacy.

They thought I was mourning my lost jewels.

Idiots.

"He has been moved again, Your Majesty."

I stalked to the window. Staring sightlessly down at the gardens, I could practically see my son as he'd been, just two winters and toddling naked across the path, having somehow escaped the maids responsible for him.

I hadn't touched the boy since the day Sabium had put him in my arms and instructed me to play my part.

It wasn't unusual for a queen to have nothing to do with the actual child-rearing of her son. The court believed me cold, uninterested, and that was acceptable.

I opened my mouth to call for the maids, but it was too late. The boy slammed into my legs, tiny hands clutching at my skirts as he stared up at me.

"Mama," he said.

Fury blazed through my body, until I knew if I'd had the power of fire, the child would have been turned to ash.

I would never have children of my own. Would never hear my own child say such a word. Instead, I'd rot in this castle, forced to fall in line with Sabium's schemes.

Courtiers were staring. A noblewoman whose husband was close to the king smiled at the sight of us, and I had no choice but to lift the boy into my arms. His little body was still so light in mine. He had a dimple that appeared when he smiled at me.

His hand cupped my face, warm and sticky. "Mama," he said once more.

"No," I murmured, barely moving my lips.

A nanny appeared, paling at whatever she saw in my eyes as I smiled at her. "He needs a nap, I think," I said cheerfully. As if I would know what a child of that age needed.

"That's exactly right," the nanny said, surprise in her voice, as if she believed I knew enough of the child's schedule to understand such things.

A guess, that was all it had been, and yet the maid was smiling at me as if we were...friends.

She glanced down at the boy, who chortled, babbling up at her.

"A nap. And no more running naked through the castle," she laughed. Clutching the boy tightly, she turned. The boy waved solemnly at me from over her shoulder.

Since there were eyes on me, I waved back.

"There's something else," Pelysian murmured, jolting me from my memories.

Truthfully, I'd forgotten he was here.

"What is it?"

"There are...concerning rumors about the king. We know he has lost one of the amulets. The most powerful. That loss should have proved a fatal blow. And yet, Sabium immediately used the tunnel from his room and traveled via carriage out of the city."

That was my husband. Always planning. Always scheming. And always three steps ahead.

"Where did he go?"

"Lyrishade."

"The granite mine?"

"Yes. It's where he's keeping the second amulet. And it's where he's using the magic in that amulet to breed strange, lethal creatures. Creatures he will turn on the fae."

"How is he breeding them?"

"Long ago, before the fae and humans were truly at war, Sabium's ancestor attacked a fae settlement. The winged, monstrous creatures had left their young to go hunt, never imagining they would be attacked. The king had the young taken and hidden so our people could experiment on them. Those creatures are still alive. But Sabium has been using the amulet to manipulate them. To make them not only more powerful, but loyal only to him."

Sharp pain stung my hands. Glancing down, I found myself twisting them. An old habit. One I'd banished as a little girl with the *help* of a nanny who was fond of the cane.

If the fae were going to have any hope of winning this war, they needed to take that amulet back, before Sabium found more creatures to transform with his stolen power.

I took a deep, shuddering breath and forced my hands down by my sides, straightening my shoulders. The time had come. I could no longer sit idly by and wait.

It was time to act.

7

LORIAN

As soon as my wounds healed, Prisca mostly returned to ignoring me. We would reach the hybrid camp before nightfall. I had only a few hours left with her before she would be able to avoid me once more. For once, I wished *I* had the ability to slow time.

Today, it seemed, Prisca was finally willing to talk to me. Likely because she was tired of the strained silence. I'd caught her glancing at me again and again since we'd begun traveling for the day.

"What is it, wildcat?"

"Nothing."

I narrowed my eyes at her, and she finally shrugged. "I was just wondering why you started traveling with Rythos and the others."

The first interest she'd shown, and it was about Rythos.

Prisca glanced at me, her eyes widening at whatever she saw on my face. "Forget it," she muttered.

"No," I said, unwilling to return

to stiff silence. If Prisca was asking me questions, I would answer them all day simply to hear the sound of her voice.

"Rythos…that's a long story, and some of it is his to tell. But I can tell you how I met some of the others. Galon was once friends with my father. He led a secret military cadre and took care of threats to fae security—from both within and outside of our lands. Eventually, he and my father no longer saw eye to eye when it came to the threat Regner presented. Galon began training those who would one day attempt to enter the cadre, and when I was old enough, my brother sent me to him."

I'd been used to fighting the servants' children and "training" with my brother's guards. And yet, Galon had been remarkably patient, considering my puffed-up self-importance.

"How old were you?"

"I had seen nine winters."

Prisca's eyes flashed. Clearly, she had thoughts about that, but she was keeping them to herself. I watched her. "What is it?"

"Nothing. Tell me about the others."

I'd get it out of her eventually. I loosened my reins, giving my horse her head. "When Regner took the amulet from the city near our border, his men also targeted a village called Jadynmire, which was just a few hours' ride from the city. The village was decimated, and the fae family in charge of the amulet couldn't bear the shame. The patriarch covered up the theft of the amulet and made it seem as if the attacks were just a way for Regner to test our security. Cavis was from Jadynmire. One of Galon's men found him wandering alone and barefoot in the forest. He was the only survivor."

Something that might have been devastation gleamed in Prisca's eyes. "How old was he?"

I sighed. "Six winters."

She chewed on her lower lip, and I understood. Demos had been the same age when she was taken.

But she inhaled sharply as we rode over the invisible line marking the fae territory. "What was that?"

My skin prickled at the familiar magic. "The ancient wards my people set. They prevent those who are not fae from entering our lands without permission."

"The same wards that locked the hybrids out once Regner had the hourglass." Her voice was bitter.

I couldn't blame her for that bitterness. "Yes."

Prisca took a look around. This part of the fae lands looked relatively similar to the landscape across the border. She would only begin to understand some of the differences if she traveled deeper within the fae kingdom.

"I don't understand," she murmured. "Where is the camp?"

I smiled. "You'll see."

It took us another hour to reach it on horseback before I gestured for her to stop. Prisca looked at the vast empty space near the Solith River. Slowly, she turned her head, her eyes promising murder.

I wanted to pull her off her horse, tumble her to the ground, and—

She scowled. "Lorian."

I sighed, angling my horse until I was next to her. "Come here."

She allowed me to take her face between my hands. I ached to take her mouth with mine. "Close your eyes," I whispered.

Surprisingly, she did that too. Perhaps she was finally beginning to trust me once more. I murmured in the old fae language. "Open."

Her eyes were more gold today, luring me closer. I lowered my head.

She yelped, drawing back, and I sighed as her mouth fell open, her gaze on the camp behind me. "This is… this…"

"It's hidden by the ward," I confirmed. "Those who wish to send and receive messages from this camp must travel closer to the border to meet with messengers."

I turned my head reluctantly, far more interested in Prisca's reaction than the camp that had suddenly appeared in front of us. But it had been years since I'd visited the area, so I surveyed the tents of every size and scale, the cooking fires billowing smoke into the air, the large arena where hybrids and fae trained—currently under Galon's command, and the hybrids using the rope and pulley system to collect water from the river and transport it to the cooking tents. That system was a last resort if hybrids or fae with an affinity for water had drained their powers.

Prisca's attention had turned to the tents, which stretched into the distance—significantly more than the last time I'd visited.

"How many?" Prisca asked, her voice low.

"With the three hundred you freed, the numbers will be around ten thousand or so. Of course, that doesn't count any children who have been born. Your people are much more fertile than mine."

"How?" she asked. "And why?" Her horse shuffled beneath her, clearly picking up on her roiling emotions.

I knew she wasn't talking about fertility. "Once... once my father learned of the attack—and how your people had been forced to flee—he convinced his council to open our borders. It was too late. Thousands had died attempting to get here, assuming we would help." My gut twisted at the words. And at the horror in Prisca's eyes. But I wouldn't lie to her.

"After Crawyth, they had few options available to them. Most disappeared, hiding among the villages. They were so good at hiding, in fact, that Regner began requiring the priestesses to use the blue mark." I tapped the skin between my temple and my eye.

"But the fae helped."

I sighed. "It took too long. By the time the fae learned of what had happened and ceased arguing about the correct action...by the time they lowered their wards and managed to provide a place for some of the hybrids to find safety, most hybrids no longer trusted us. Our people had already split once before—the hybrids becoming increasingly insular. And they saw this as another reason to distrust us. To hate us."

She swallowed, still gazing at the camp in front of us. "This is one of the places Vicer was helping smuggle the hybrids to, wasn't it?"

"I don't know your friend's plans, but it's likely. There are hidden hybrid camps across Eprotha and Gromalia, but Regner makes an example of them each time he learns of one."

And if our wards ever failed...if we lost the war to come, and Regner managed to find this place...

Prisca was silent for a long moment. When she turned her head, I caught the despair in her eyes. "They truly have nowhere to go. I knew it, but it took seeing this camp to make me understand."

I nodded. "The hybrids are proud. They don't want to be here, and yet they have no way of crossing to their kingdom without drawing Regner's attention. And even if they made it across the Sleeping Sea, they have no idea what's waiting for them on the barren continent."

"It's not barren," she reminded me.

"No," I said softly. "But there are other things that live there. Vicious, wild things."

"How do you know?"

I opened my mouth, but someone had broken away from the camp and was running toward us.

Asinia. The friend Prisca had risked everything for. The reason she'd never gotten on to a ship and had instead walked into Regner's castle.

Prisca leaped from her horse, and the two women threw their arms around each other, embracing as they rocked. I couldn't tell if they were laughing or crying. Wasn't sure if they even knew themselves.

I sometimes forgot. That for Prisca, all of it had been for this woman—her sister by choice, if not by birth.

In the distance, Galon raised his hand in greeting. Safe. I'd known it, but it was a relief to see it with my own eyes.

Now, we would prepare to deal with the consequences of disobeying my brother.

PRISCA

I tried to let Asinia go three times, pulling her close again each time. Tears streaked her face, but eventually, tears turned to relieved, slightly hysterical laughter.

"You made it," she said when we finally separated.

I nodded at Lorian, still waiting on his horse behind us. He'd snagged the reins of my own horse, and he was watching both of us with a faint smile on his face.

Some of the color left Asinia's face. I sighed, but I could understand why she was afraid. The last time she'd seen him, Lorian had been spearing the king's guards with his lightning—his entire body aglow with the power he'd finally had returned to him.

"Are you…well?" Asinia asked me, and I bit my lip,

conscious of Lorian's sensitive hearing.

"I'm fine, I promise. We have a lot to talk about."

Asinia smiled at something behind me, and I whirled as Tibris pulled me into a hug. We clutched each other for a long, long time, holding tight.

I never wanted to be separated from him like this again.

"I heard what happened," I said when Tibris finally released me, his dark eyes glinting. "About the attack."

Something shifted in his face. "We're all right, Pris. The mercenaries…the *fae"*—he corrected himself—"have been good to us. Rythos saved lives that day."

I nodded, and then Demos was there. Relief spread wings inside me as my gaze dropped to his chest. The last time I'd seen him, he'd been barely healed.

Demos threw an arm around me. "None of that," he growled, dragging me close.

My throat burned. I hadn't realized just how badly I'd needed to see them all safe until just this moment. "You're—"

"I'm fine," he said, and I pushed back out of his arms just enough to sweep my gaze over both him and Tibris.

Tibris looked tired, his dark eyes hooded. He'd lost some weight—likely from the travel. He also needed a shave.

Demos looked almost too alert by comparison, and since I'd seen him last, he'd packed on muscle. Freedom was doing wonders for him. But he had a hard glint in his eye when he flicked a glance at Lorian behind me.

Asinia reached out and squeezed my hand. "I kept them in line for you."

I laughed, the sound more of a choked sob. Tibris ruffled my hair. "We missed you too, Pris."

Demos grinned at me, threw his arm back around my shoulders and steered me toward the camp. I glanced back at Lorian, who nodded at me, his gaze returning to Galon—currently strolling toward us.

It was the first time I'd been parted from Lorian for weeks. As strange as it felt, it was a good thing. Truly.

"Now, there are a few things you should know about this camp," Demos said.

"She doesn't need a tour." Asinia rolled her eyes next to me. Tibris looked like he was barely suppressing a smile.

"Of course she does, Sin."

She let out a low hiss.

Demos's grin widened, and he steered me to the right. "As you can see, that's the training arena," he said. "Unsurprisingly, the prisoners who chose to come with us are in pretty bad shape. We're feeding them and they're slowly building up some stamina, but it's going to take a while."

"You know who's not in bad shape?" Asinia muttered darkly. "Demos."

"So I've noticed," I said. The arm he'd slung around my shoulders was heavy with muscle. It seemed as if he'd been away from that dungeon for a year rather than a few weeks.

He smirked at me. "We'll talk about *that* later."

"I can take a tour later as well. We need to talk. Somewhere private."

Demos's arm tensed for a moment, but he nodded, his expression immediately serious. "Who do you want to attend?"

"Just us for now." I had no doubt Lorian would be meeting with Galon and the others too. "And Madinia."

Tibris winced. "Seriously?"

"Yes. Don't tell me you've just been ignoring her since you got here?"

"She was one of the queen's ladies," Tibris muttered, and Asinia nodded.

I sighed. "She saved my life twice that night. She's the reason we managed to get the amulet to Lorian. And she's now all alone, which means she has just as many reasons to hate the king as we do."

Tibris sighed. "Fine. Anyone else?"

"Vicer. We keep it small and figure out who we need from there. But let's gather quickly before any of the fae wonder what we're doing."

I could feel eyes on me from every direction as we walked through the camp, and I fought the urge to hunch my shoulders. Tibris met my gaze. "They're just curious," he said.

Movement in the arena caught my attention. Cavis was training with one of the hybrids. From the way the hybrid's arm trembled as he swung his sword, he was one of the prisoners we'd rescued from Regner's dungeon.

The hybrid sidestepped, and I grinned as I recognized his face. "Dashiel. How is he?"

Demos shrugged. "Like all of them, he's got a long way to go. Some of them…their only goal was to get free. And now that they're free, they don't know what to do with themselves."

More heads were turning as the hybrids from the prison called out greetings to me. Lina raised her hand, and I smiled back at her. I hoped we would get a chance to talk.

Asinia linked her arm through mine. "We've appropriated an extra tent for meetings. I'll show you where it is."

"I'll go find Madinia and Vicer," Tibris said, wandering away.

I had to suppress the urge to grab his hand and ask him to stay. Now that I was back with Asinia and my brothers, I didn't want to let any of them out of my sight.

Demos nodded toward the huge fires to our left. "I'll get some food. You must be hungry."

Asinia steered me to the left, past the huge cooking fires and the men and women hard at work. The tent Asinia had *appropriated* was close to the cooking area, at the edge of the sprawling city of tents.

"What's that?" I asked, nodding at a huge building behind us.

"The armory," Asinia said. "I haven't been inside, but Demos snuck in and took a look around. He didn't seem pleased." She sneered, and I suppressed a smile.

Obviously, being neighbors in the prison, escaping together, and being forced to work together in this camp still hadn't thawed their frosty relationship.

"Prisca." Madinia approached from the left, Tibris next to her. She had dark circles beneath her bright-blue eyes, and her wealth of red hair was tangled.

"Madinia." I smiled at her. "Were you taking a nap?"

Madinia just shrugged. Clearly, she wasn't doing well. She gestured to the tent. Made of some kind of heavy-duty canvas, the entrance was high enough that we didn't need to duck our heads as we stepped inside.

A large, circular oak table dominated the inside of the tent, surrounded by eight chairs.

Madinia took one of the chairs as Tibris stepped inside with Demos and Asinia.

I studied both my brothers. Considering how antagonistic they'd been toward each other in the castle, they both seemed to be...tolerating each other well.

I sat, Asinia planting herself on my left, Demos on my right. Within a few moments, we were sitting around the table, snacking on roast lamb, flatbread, and fresh vegetables.

Tibris had a faint smile on his face as he watched me. "The food is good here," he said.

"Yes." Demos's mouth twisted. "The fae have been very *benevolent*."

Vicer stepped inside and claimed a chair, giving me a nod. "Good to see you alive." His cheekbones looked sharper, and a new line had appeared between his brows.

But his skin had tanned beneath the sun, and he smiled at Asinia when she handed him a plate.

"You too," I told him.

There was an expectant air in the tent, and all eyes turned toward me. I took a deep breath.

"What do we know about the hybrids left in Eprotha?"

Silence. I glanced at Asinia, who dropped her gaze to her plate.

My stomach churned. "Tell me."

"We knew there would be retaliation for emptying Regner's dungeon, Prisca," Vicer said gently, and I nodded, but my throat was suddenly too tight to speak.

"How bad is it?"

"Daily executions."

My lungs seized. Asinia reached out and took my hand. "The hybrids prepared for this as well as they could, Pris."

Vicer rolled his shoulders. "We had to be careful before the prisoners were free. We couldn't afford even a rumor to reach Regner. But the night we left, I sent messengers to each part of the city. I warned anyone who'd ever had a family member imprisoned to hide—no matter how distant the blood tie. We knew it was only a matter of time before our headquarters were discovered, so we cleared it out and set it alight."

I smelled burning. Smoke rose from Madinia's hand on the table, and I reached for my own power, ready to intervene if necessary.

"Prisca nearly turned her horse toward your

headquarters that night," Madinia hissed. "She was half dead but ready to sacrifice herself for the hybrids she thought were trapped inside."

Vicer ignored the threat in Madinia's voice, but his gaze jumped to mine. "I'm sorry."

"It's all right." A chill slid over me at the memory of those moments. Of the helplessness. Fire and rioting, and the knowledge that something had gone terribly wrong.

"Pris." Asinia squeezed my hand, and I squeezed back.

"I'm fine. How many are dead?"

Tibris winced. "Maybe we should—"

"How many?"

Vicer's gray eyes were dark with grief. "A few hybrids a day. According to rumor, the king remarked that if he couldn't burn the three hundred in his dungeon, he would make up the numbers from Lesdryn."

Chains of fae iron were squeezing my lungs. Surely that was why I couldn't take a full breath. My skin turned clammy, and I gave in to the urge to lower my head until the tent stopped spinning around me.

"We made it worse," I managed to get out, my voice muffled.

"No," Vicer said, the word carefully neutral, and I wanted to hit him for the tonelessness of his voice.

I lifted my head, ready to rip into him, and Asinia squeezed my hand again. Her face was ashen, but she glanced around the table, and I followed her gaze.

No one in this tent was neutral. All of us felt the

helplessness. The rage. Including Vicer. Years of spying had allowed him to control his voice, his expression, but with us, he let the banked rage in his eyes free.

Taking a deep breath, I attempted to slow my racing heart. "What can we do?"

Demos sighed. "According to the message we received yesterday, Regner is getting careless. He's so committed to his daily burnings, he proceeds with them even based on rumor and malicious gossip. After you killed his favored assessor, he summoned another to the castle, but he refuses to risk more hybrids being undiscovered in the villages—which means not enough assessors for the city."

Assessors were rare. It took power *and* training to be able to determine whether someone else had their power—and what that power was.

"Humans have been burned," Madinia said.

Demos nodded. "The populace is becoming uneasy. It was one thing to learn that their neighbor was harboring a hybrid—and that her child had been arrested, her entire family slaughtered. It's quite another when you could get mistakenly caught up in the same hunt."

Would that be enough to shake the humans from their apathy? I'd like to believe so, but we definitely couldn't rely on it.

"We have to do something," Asinia said, and it was my turn to squeeze her hand.

"We will."

Vicer picked at his food. "We're attempting to

smuggle as many hybrids to this camp as we can. But the iron guard is keeping watch, as are the border guards."

"I need to see a map," I said. We had to figure out some kind of distraction. Some way to get as many hybrids free as possible.

"I'll have one brought in here," Vicer said.

In the meantime… "What have you learned about the hourglass?"

Tibris took a bite. "At first, we weren't sure who P was, but Vicer here knows someone with a talent for getting in and out of places undetected."

I glanced at Vicer. I was pretty sure I knew who that person was. He just smirked at me. "P stands for Perrin— one of the fae king's generals. Conreth has a few thousand fae training here. Apparently it's also a strategic point for them to stay when traveling for various duties. It's also a way for him to keep an eye on things."

Something twisted my stomach, but I nodded. "What did you find?"

"They're being careful. Perrin knows where the hourglass is, I'm sure of it. If we can't find out what we need to know, we'll have to get it out of him," Demos said.

I blinked at him. Was my brother casually discussing torture?

Asinia shook her head. "Pris will never go for that."

"You obviously didn't hear what she did to the king's assessor in the castle," Demos said, a proud gleam in his eyes.

A hard life. My brother had lived a hard life. The same life I would have lived if I hadn't been taken that night. Of course, our parents might have survived if they hadn't spent so long looking for me. The hard lump of guilt in my stomach would likely be with me always.

"Torture needs to be our last resort," I croaked, and Tibris sent me a concerned look. I just shook my head at him. "We torture a fae general, and we're declaring war on the people we're hoping to ally with. What would that mean for the hybrids who've made this place their home?" No one replied, and I turned my attention back to the human king. "I don't understand why Regner wouldn't have made sure the hourglass was in his possession already," I said.

Demos's mouth twitched. "It's in his possession—after all, he has hidden it in his kingdom. But the hourglass does strange things when it's held by those without time magic. Regner may have been able to keep it in the castle for a few years, but eventually, he would have noticed weird occurrences. Time speeding up in some places, slowing down in others. I heard rumors there were pockets of land around his castle that had differing seasons."

Madinia's eyes gleamed at that. But she dropped her gaze to her nails, her voice carefully neutral. "You won't be able to steal it alone."

No, I wouldn't. But I also couldn't allow Lorian to learn about it. Oh, he knew I was attempting to find the hourglass. But once we found it, I had to keep that location from him. Otherwise, Conreth would learn that not only did I know about the hourglass, but that I refused to stay ignorant and rely on fae *goodwill*.

"If we can't take Lorian and the others, we need to keep this quiet."

Vicer nodded, his expression grave. "No one will say a word."

I could feel time trickling through my fingers like sand. "Anyone who is traveling with us needs to be ready the moment we know where we're starting the search."

"They will be," Demos said. "We've been training, and I heard Galon has some plans for you to join us."

He must've seen the grim acceptance sweeping through me, because he grinned. Meanwhile, Asinia looked like she'd tasted something terrible. I raised one eyebrow, and Demos smirked at me. "She's been putting off training with a crossbow. But tomorrow is the day she starts."

Her eyes fired. "Who put you in charge?"

Tibris looked like he wanted to agree with the sentiment, but he cleared his throat. "Unfortunately, Demos's power makes him the best option. The hybrids also know he's the hybrid prince, and they follow his orders."

My curiosity pricked. "Are you actually going to tell me what your power is?" I asked Demos.

"Don't get too excited," he said. "I'm only useful on the battlefield."

Vicer angled his head. "I'd say you're useful for slightly more than that."

I'd forgotten—before Demos was imprisoned, the two of them had worked together.

Demos smirked, and his eyes met mine. "I'm difficult to kill—when I haven't been starved and imprisoned for two years. I heal quicker, move faster, and hit harder than most. When I train, my body adds muscle much, much more quickly than anyone else. I can wield any weapon, and when I'm fighting, my mind allows me to see tactics that others wouldn't see."

My mouth had gone dry. "What do you call that kind of power?"

"Death," Madinia remarked idly. "You call it death."

Demos's expression turned hard. "Or you call it life."

Time for a change of subject. I reached for the next question on my list. "What's the status on the jewels we stole from the castle?"

Demos and Vicer glanced at each other, and my heart tripped in my chest. "Please tell me we still have them."

"We do," Madinia said. "They're in my tent. Under my cot."

"Sounds secure," Asinia remarked.

"Where do *you* suggest?" Madinia asked.

"Maybe not where anyone could wander in and—"

"What about our food stores?" I changed the subject as Madinia snarled. "Our weapons and armor?"

Demos sighed. "Food isn't a problem. The fae have been feeding our people for decades now, likely their attempt to overcome their guilt. But most of the weapons are old, blunt, only useful for training. We need armor as well."

"The jewelry we stole from the castle... How do we turn all those jewels into weapons, food, and armor for our army?"

Vicer shifted in his chair. "There's a fae town several days south. The fae love glittering things. We can take the jewels and sell them there."

Word would definitely reach Conreth, but we needed resources.

Madinia's face had turned cold. It was clear she didn't trust the fae. Of course, she'd seen her father beheaded in front of her the night she'd learned just who Lorian was.

Vicer went still. "Someone is coming."

"We'll meet again as soon as we hear anything about the hourglass," I murmured.

The tent entrance shifted, and Margie poked her head inside, her gaze instantly meeting mine. "Is this a private meeting, or can anyone join?"

8
The Boy

The boy's brother didn't know what to do with either a crown or a child.

The crown, at least, he had advisers to help him with. His father's court hadn't been perfect, but most of the infighting had been resolved long before the boy was born.

The boy was given to nannies, who attempted to console him each time he woke screaming for his mother.

One of them lasted longer than the others. Each night, Darielle would rock him, humming a lullaby as he shuddered in her arms.

Eventually, she began to mutter to the other servants.

"A child needs a family," she said. "The poor thing has already lost his parents, and the king hasn't seen him for weeks. Weeks!"

One day, when the boy grew so inconsolable he couldn't be reasoned with, Darielle scooped him into her arms and took him from the nursery.

"His Majesty is asleep," a low voice said.

"How nice for him," Darielle spat, *and a hint of fear took up residence in the boy's gut even as he sobbed.*
"Wake him."

Silence.

"He instructed he is to be woken in the event of any emergency concerning Lorian," Darielle said.

"The child looks fine."

"Based on your extensive experience with such things?"

The door opened. A few minutes later, it opened again. "What is the problem?" *Conreth asked.*

"He does not sleep, Your Majesty. Every night, as I've mentioned. But tonight is the worst. He needs his family."

Strong arms reached out and took the boy. Conreth gazed down at him, and his eyes lightened. The king turned and carried him into his rooms without another word.

PRISCA

"It's good to see you, Margie." I scanned her, taking in the softened lines around her mouth. It had taken some convincing for her to leave Lesdryn—the city where Regner had murdered her daughter. But Vicer had managed to make it happen.

"You too." Margie smiled at me. "Let me find you a tent."

I got to my feet, my gaze finding Asinia's. She gave me an encouraging smile. "Dinner tonight?"

"Yes. Just you and me," I promised. We were well overdue to spend some time together. Just a few uninterrupted hours.

I followed Margie out of the tent, turning left. "This is the main thoroughfare," she told me. "If you continue walking along this path and follow it as it curves to the right, you'll eventually end up at the arena. Keep walking, and you'll be back at the camp entrance, and then at The Hearth. The Hearth is close to the cooking fires, and it's where anyone is welcome to sit and eat together throughout the day."

This time as we walked, the staring wasn't so bad. Sure, curious gazes clung to me like blood to a sword, but when those gazes shifted to Margie, hands raised in greeting, mouths stretched in smiles, and people called out to her.

"Now, don't you go training on that ankle before you see the camp healer," she scolded one boy, who looked like he'd only seen around fifteen winters. Tall, thin verging on scrawny, he had shoulders wide enough that he might carry some serious muscle one day. The boy stuck out his chin, turning his attention to me.

"You're the hybrid heir."

My mouth turned dry, but I nodded.

His expression was almost accusatory. "Are you

going to help us?"

Margie's hand tightened on my arm. "Now, Silas, I *know* you're not being rude to the woman who saved your brother's life."

He glanced behind him. "My brother is crippled from the iron guards."

A weight pressed on my chest. My eyes met Margie's. "Has Tibris—"

"Yes," Margie said softly. "We need more healers. There are only three hybrid healers with enough power to tend injuries like broken bones and infection, and they must see to the entire camp."

I blinked. "There's no fae healer here?"

"He tends to the fae. The hybrids refused to tolerate his ministrations."

Silas wandered away.

I ground my teeth as Margie continued to lead me down the main thoroughfare. "So, they desperately need a fae healer, but they won't allow one because they don't trust them."

"That's right." Margie slid me a cool look. "After everything you heard about the fae your entire life, would you trust them in their position? If you hadn't fraternized with the Bloodthirsty Prince?"

Hurt warred with shame, and I slowly unwound my arm from hers. Margie's mouth tightened. "Forgive me. That was rude."

"No," I said softly. "Speak your mind."

She sighed, suddenly seeming much older than her

years. "I don't begrudge you your relationship with him," she said. "Without his powers, we would be dead. But you have to understand what kind of message it sends when you're seen with him here, among the hybrids. Some of them lost family members who were locked out of this kingdom when they fled. The oldest among them remember slamming their hands against those wards themselves—and then watching as their friends and family were cut down. You represent our hope. He represents our death. And the people living here watched as you conversed easily with him at the camp entrance."

It made my skin itch, the thought of people watching my every move and judging accordingly. I wasn't a symbol of hope—some days I could barely make a decision without questioning it for hours. And Lorian would stand between Regner's iron guards and anyone in this camp without a thought.

Margie sighed, patted my shoulder, and continued walking along the main path until we were directly across from the arena. Only a vast, grassy space separated the tents from the hybrids currently training.

"There are more tents behind the arena," she said. "That's where the fae sleep. Many of them train here for months at a time. And others use the camp as a convenient rest stop on their way into Eprotha and Gromalia."

I had no doubt Demos and Tibris were both keeping an eye on those fae.

"It will probably be noisy here during the day," Margie said apologetically, and I jolted back to the present.

"I'm sure I won't be spending much time in here during the day anyway." I offered her a smile. "Thank you, Margie."

She smiled back, opening her mouth.

"There you are." Erea threw her arms around me. "You're all right!"

"Can't. Breathe."

She grinned and released me, flashing her chipped tooth. Behind her, Daselis nodded at me, reserved as always. But her usually fair skin had gained a golden glow from the sun, and her ash-blond hair was no longer twisted into an unyielding bun. Instead, it hung over her shoulders, making her appear much younger than her years.

"How is your niece?" I asked her.

Her lips curved slightly. "Hanish is doing well. She enjoys working in The Hearth whenever possible and has been learning how to cook."

Margie pushed open the flap of my tent and gestured for us to step inside. The tent was larger than it appeared from the outside. To my right, a narrow cot waited next to a small bedside table that held a jug of water and a basin. To my left, a large chest was currently open—and empty.

"We'll find you some clothes," Erea said. "The camp seamstress will be so excited to know she is sewing for the queen."

I shifted on my feet. "I would really appreciate if we could tone down the whole 'queen' thing. Let's just refer to me as Prisca."

A tiny line appeared between Erea's eyebrows. Behind us, Margie and Daselis gave twin snorts.

I slowly turned, narrowing my eyes. Both of them wore placid expressions.

"I'm no different from anyone else in this camp," I said. "I just want to help."

Daselis only shrugged, clearly unimpressed. Margie looked like I'd disappointed her. An awkward silence claimed the tent.

"We'll give you a few minutes alone," Daselis said. "We can arrange for a bath later if you'd like."

"Oh gods, I would *love* that."

Her mouth twitched, and she nodded, leading the others out. Margie turned and gave me a long, searching look before ducking her head and following her.

Silence. I was alone for the first time since I could remember. I'd thought I would enjoy it, but instead, my mind roiled with the kinds of thoughts I didn't want to look too closely at.

I sat on the cot and buried my head in my hands.

Daily burnings in the city.

Walking through the city had already been terrifying. I'd watched again and again as the city guards had cornered the poorest residents, searching them for contraband, taunting them, beating them…

What would it be like now?

I couldn't let it all be for nothing. I had to get the hourglass so I could give it to the hybrids. I had no doubt losing the hourglass would prove a vicious blow to

Regner's reputation. Perhaps…perhaps those who were loyal to him out of nothing more than fear would begin to feel some kind of hope again.

"Prisca?" a voice called, and I shot to my feet, darting out of the tent. Rythos was walking toward me.

He smiled, but there was something restrained in that smile. He was in his human form, moving slowly, as if I was a particularly high-strung horse he didn't want to spook.

A choked sob exploded out of me, and I launched myself at him.

His dark brow creased as I jumped into his arms, burying my head in his chest. I'd thought I'd never get a chance to make things right.

"Hey now, darlin'. What's wrong?"

"I'm sorry," I mumbled against his shirt. "For the city gates."

Strong hands clasped my shoulders, and Rythos gently nudged me back, frowning down at me. Distantly, I could feel more eyes on us, and I attempted to block them out.

"What are you talking about?" Rythos asked.

"I was…afraid of you." I dropped my gaze to the ground, unable to even look at him. Rythos had always been my friend. He'd been gentle, slowly coaxing me into that friendship from the moment we'd met. And the moment I'd learned he was fae, I'd—

"Do you think I would hold that against you?" Rythos let out a booming laugh, and I raised my head as a group of hybrids stopped in their tracks, watching us closely.

I wanted to bare my teeth at them.

Instead, I turned my attention back to the man in front of me. "When I heard you were attacked, I thought I'd never get a chance to apologize…"

"Prisca." Rythos's voice was gentle. "No one could blame you for reacting in any kind of way that night. You'd just had your world turned upside down—just watched your brother almost die. And Lorian had made you agree to another one of his bargains." He rolled his dark eyes. "No apology necessary."

My chest lightened. "Do you want to come in?" I asked instead, gesturing at my tent.

Rythos slowly shook his head. "I don't think I need to be explaining to Lorian why I was in your tent. He's not exactly reasonable when it comes to you."

I sneered, and he grinned at me again. "Cavis wants to introduce you to his daughter," he said. "And I know Marth and Galon want to see you too. Lorian's mood has been getting progressively darker since he arrived, so he probably needs to see you're in one piece as well."

Shaking my head, I slipped my arm through his. Margie's words about the fae ran on a loop in my head.

Perhaps the hybrids' natural fear of the fae was half the problem here. If they were going to be staring at me constantly, perhaps it was good for them to see me and the others interacting with the fae.

After all, if I managed to ally with the fae king, there was a good chance we would all be going to war together.

The hybrids and fae would need to fight side by side.

So I strolled through the camp, smothering Margie's warning and listening to Rythos regale me with stories of his travels—leaving out the attack. Curious eyes and whispers followed me everywhere, and by the time we were on the fae side of camp behind the arena, I was clasping his arm as if I were drowning.

"You sure about this?" he asked me, flicking a glance over his shoulder. I could feel hundreds of eyes burning into my back, but I nodded, raising my head.

Rythos led me to a tent so large, it would have encompassed ten of my own. Instead of a table, Lorian and the others were stretched out on comfortable-looking stuffed chairs close to the ground.

My gaze met Lorian's, and he ran his eyes over me, as if checking I hadn't been damaged in the few hours since we'd seen each other. I opened my mouth, but I was instantly wrapped in Marth's arms.

It was like being smothered by an overly muscled giant. I pushed against his chest, and he released his hold slightly, grinning down at me. His blond hair was cut shorter than when I'd seen him last, hitting just below his shoulders now. The scruff along his jaw was longer in its place, reminding me of one of the pirates I'd glimpsed on Daharak's ship.

"Let her breathe," Galon growled, shoving Marth aside.

I swallowed, studying his face. Was he still disappointed in me? I didn't know why I cared—only that I did.

Galon ran his gaze down my body. "You've lost muscle. Training tomorrow."

My lips twitched. "I'll be there."

A wail sounded, and I jolted, peering past Galon. Cavis lounged at the back of the tent, soothing the bundle in his arms, a stunningly beautiful woman next to him. She smiled at me, flashing pearly white teeth that contrasted sharply against the dark skin of her face. She was also in her human form. Were they…worried about being in their natural form around me? After my reaction at the city gates, I couldn't blame them. But I wanted them to feel comfortable…

"Prisca," the woman said, getting to her feet. "I've heard so much about you."

The fae were huggers. I'd learned that much already. She pulled me in for a quick embrace and then released me, gesturing at Cavis and the tiny bundle in his arms. "I'm Sybella, and this is Piperia."

Cavis beamed up at me, and my heart suddenly felt too big for my chest. Leaning over, I used one finger to push the blanket aside. The baby was sleeping, long eyelashes brushing against her cheeks. Her tiny ears were pointed and currently far too big for her head. My lips twitched.

Sybella laughed. "She'll grow into them."

"She's adorable."

"You can hold her," Cavis offered.

"Uh, maybe later. I haven't had much experience."

And Piperia looked far too small and breakable.

Cavis gave me a knowing look. His eyes were no longer dreamy, his gaze no longer focused on the distance. Instead, he seemed alert, those eyes sharp, his attention on the love of his life and his tiny daughter.

Lorian's words came back to me. Cavis had been found wandering alone in the forest as a child. He didn't have a family, so he'd built one himself.

Cavis pressed a kiss to the baby's forehead, and she chortled up at him. Sybella grinned at them both, and something in my chest wrenched.

Mama's gaze was on me while I watched the happy couple, a grin stretching my face. "I'm going to get married one day. Here in the village."

"No, you won't, Prisca. Such things are not for you."

My eyes burned, and my throat ached until I could barely swallow.

I was just tired. That's all this was.

I could feel Lorian's gaze clinging to me, with that strange connection between us. I refused to glance at him, taking one of the low, plush seats next to Rythos instead.

By some silent agreement, no one spoke of the war, of Regner, or of anything that would kill the lighthearted mood. Someone brought in more food, and I watched the others eat, listening to Marth brag about a sea creature he'd once had to kill to prevent it from overturning his ship. Rythos caught my eye and shook his head, and I suppressed a grin.

I must have drifted off, because the light was low

when I opened my eyes once more.

I yawned. "I need to go meet Asinia." I glanced at the bottles of some kind of fae alcohol that had appeared while I'd been napping. "Don't drink too much."

Marth belched, and Galon slapped him upside the head. Rythos sent me a bleary grin. I sighed. "Clearly, that warning is coming in late."

Lorian looked perfectly sober, although the bottle in his hands was half full. "Want a taste?" His voice was a low taunt, but his eyes gleamed with that feral light.

I shifted my attention to the others. They suddenly got busy looking elsewhere. Sybella grinned at me from where she was pacing back and forth with Piperia.

Taking a step toward Lorian, I raised my eyebrow at him, even as my cheeks flushed.

"Pass," I said, and several sniggers broke out.

"Pretty Prisca," Lorian murmured. "Why don't you come sit over here and—"

Sybella strode over and placed Piperia in his arms. I'd expected Lorian to freeze, the way I would have done. Instead, he cradled the baby close, expertly holding her as he pressed a kiss to her tiny head.

The sight did something disturbing to my heart. I ducked out of the tent, wishing I'd never seen the fae prince looking entirely too comfortable with a baby in his arms.

That image was now imprinted on my mind forever.

The cooler air helped wake me up a little as I walked toward The Hearth. While The Hearth was supposed to be the center of life—the meeting place where community was built, according to Margie—I'd already noticed that the fae and hybrids ate in shifts. Never together.

I found Asinia sitting at a table, drinking a cup of ale. She grinned at me, and I slipped into the seat across from her.

"I fell asleep," I admitted.

"I just got here. Your brother insisted on going through security protocols for the hundredth time."

I didn't need to ask which brother she was referring to. "Is everything okay between you and Demos?"

She groaned. "He makes me crazy. I had to listen to his cynical theories about life every day when I was in that cell. Some days, I swear I would've rather been tortured."

She looked so put out, I swiped my hand over my mouth in an attempt to hide my smile. Asinia's dark eyes narrowed, and she shook her head at me. "Suddenly, it's not so surprising that you two are related."

I burst out laughing. After a moment, she joined me. The hybrids at the table next to us were staring, and my laugh trailed off. I attempted a smile. One of them smiled back, while the others simply continued to stare until his friends whispered something into his ear.

Asinia glanced at them. "I could eat again. Let's get some food and take it to my tent."

We loaded up our plates, and a few minutes later, we were sitting in her tent. The meat was tender, the root vegetables flavorful, and the bread fresh.

"I never thought we'd get to do this," Asinia said, taking a bite. "Just sit and eat together. When I saw you that day in the dungeon, I was so fucking angry at you. Because I thought you'd end up burning right next to me. But you did it, Pris. I know I've said it before, but…thank you."

I grabbed her hand. "You never have to thank me for that. *Never*. At no point did it cross my mind to leave you there. And I know it wouldn't have crossed yours either."

Her eyes filled, but she blinked the tears away. "Do you remember when you'd just turned thirteen winters and we snuck up onto the bakery roof?"

My mouth trembled. "That roof desperately needed to be repaired. We're lucky we didn't fall through it."

Asinia grinned back at me. "We'd just learned about fae blood vows."

I winced. "And we decided we would make a vow of our own."

"Sisters of the soul," Asinia said. "Sisters by choice, if not by blood. No matter where life took us."

I reached out and squeezed her hand. "Neither of us knew the other had power. Do you think we…broke our vow?"

"No. I think sisters protect each other, no matter what. If one of us had been caught and a truth-seeker used on the other…at least one of us would have been safe."

"It's only looking back now that I can admit I was in such a dark place. I thought about telling you, you know. Then I wondered if you'd ever forgive me for my dishonesty."

"Put it away, Prisca. It doesn't matter anymore. All that matters is what we do next. So, why don't you tell me everything that's happened since the city gates."

I filled her in. I told her about Daharak and my blood vow. Mumbled darkly to her about the fae woman who'd practically sat in Lorian's lap in that inn. Explained just how difficult it had been traveling with him, and how the iron guards had found us.

"You're lucky you escaped."

"Lorian had three bolts in his back, and he acted like it was nothing."

Her lips twitched. "For a woman who swears she no longer wants him, you certainly sound...admiring."

I gave her a mock scowl. "I was admiring his *form*. The way he swung his sword."

She smirked. "I bet you were admiring his *form*. And his *sword*." Her expression sobered. "Are you ever going to forgive him, Pris?"

"I don't know." It was difficult to hate him when I saw how he risked his life for me. When I saw just how committed he was to protecting his people. And I'd... wanted to believe him when he implied he wasn't the one who'd killed my family. But there was too much at stake for me to risk being wrong.

Asinia nodded. "I'm here when you're ready to talk about it."

For now, a change of subject. "Tell me about what it has been like here."

She pulled her knees into her chest, her brow furrowing. "I've been talking to the other hybrids. Some of them have no real hope left. They believe they'll live and die in this camp. Others think it's only a matter of time before Regner finds a way to break the fae wards and they're all slaughtered. But some of them…some of them remember what it was like."

"What it was like?"

"Our kingdom, Pris. The hybrid kingdom. At night, the hybrids sit around their fires and tell the younger ones stories of children laughing in the streets. Of magic and peace and strange creatures…"

A memory flitted through my mind. A tale my father had once told Tibris and me before bed.

"Once upon a time, there was a kingdom soaked in magic. And in that kingdom lived all kinds of creatures. Strange, terrifying, beautiful creatures."

"Did they eat people?" Tibris asked, shifting closer.

"Yes," Papa said. "But they ate the weak of character."

"What does that mean?" I asked, sticking my thumb back in my mouth.

"These creatures could see into the heart of all—humans, fae, and hybrids. And they judged them accordingly."

Tibris frowned. "So, if you're mean, the creatures won't like you?"

Papa smiled. "It takes humility, bravery, and true strength to be able to bow before such creatures. If you ever see one, do not run. "

"Pris?"

"Sorry, I was remembering a story Papa told me about some strange creatures. Now, I wonder if he was telling me what he could about the hybrid kingdom."

"We'll see it one day, won't we?" Asinia asked.

I studied my best friend, and my heart clenched at the desperate hope in her eyes.

She was asking if it would be worth it. If everything we'd suffered—and the suffering that was sure to come— would be worth it one day. If she would be able to find some kind of meaning in her mother's death. If we would go *home.*

"We're not just going to see it, Asinia. We're going to live there. You're going to have an incredible life. A life of peace and joy. I promise."

9

PRISCA

The next morning, I splashed water on my face in an attempt to shake the dregs of sleep from my mind. Last night after dinner, I'd spent my time wandering through the camp. Lorian had joined me for some of it, giving me a tour of the fae side of camp.

He'd been completely sober, almost reserved. We were both being very careful with each other. In fact, he'd almost treated me like a stranger. Just as I'd insisted I wanted.

My gut twisted, and I forced myself to shove that thought deep down into the depths of my mind.

The fae who'd spotted Lorian had treated him with respect and a little awe. He'd spent time talking with anyone who approached, and they'd watched me curiously until I finally began introducing myself.

I had a feeling the number of fae here was due to the surge in hybrid numbers over the past ten years. Something told me the fae king would prefer to have enough fae here to take care of any potential uprising and to prevent groups of hybrids from deciding to explore the fae lands further.

For the hybrids, this camp was a sanctuary, but it was also a prison. We would change that. One day, the hybrids would be able to travel without fear. And it would all start with the hourglass. Telean had said I could wield its power on the battlefield. And I would wield that power as many times as it took to free the hybrids.

Thoughts of my aunt made my shoulders tense. I missed her steady presence. By now, she'd be in the fae capital, waiting for me to meet her.

But she understood exactly why I needed to be here. She'd wanted me to visit this camp first. I clung to that thought as I braided my hair. Today, I'd start training. But I was also hoping to talk to Galon.

If Lorian hadn't destroyed Crawyth, I needed to know why everyone thought he had. I needed to learn the truth—and soon. Because the more time I spent with him, the more difficult it was to picture him slaughtering my people. I was afraid that with him, I lost all judgment. All semblance of reason seemed to abandon me.

My parents—who'd died protecting me—deserved more than that. The hybrids deserved more than that. And *I* deserved more than that.

A man let out a howl of laughter outside my tent, yanking me from my thoughts. I pulled on my boots and stood.

Before I'd gone to sleep last night, I'd found training clothes on my bed. I wore a pair of tight leggings and a simple, knee-length tunic with a wide leather belt around my waist. Taking the knife Lorian had given me, I slid it into my sheath.

"Pris?" Tibris called, and I stepped outside. He surveyed me. "You look ready."

"I don't think you can ever be truly ready for training with Galon."

He gave me a crooked grin and slung his arm over my shoulders. "How are you?"

"Fine."

"Pris."

"I'm better now that I'm here. With everyone. You and Demos seem to be working well together."

His sigh told me he'd noted the change of subject, but he let it go. "We wouldn't choose to be friends if we'd met each other under different circumstances. But we can tolerate each other for your sake. And for the sake of the hybrids."

I studied him. My brother could have gone on to live a normal life. He was human. He'd received his allotment of his power back. He could have married, moved somewhere warmer.

"What are you thinking?"

I told him, and he rolled his eyes. "If you hadn't been a hybrid, and you'd learned that I could have saved Papa's life if Regner hadn't stolen my power, what would you have done?"

"I would have vowed to make him pay," I said without hesitation.

Tibris nodded. "I'm still working on forgiving our father for what he did. For the way he changed our memories. Part of me wonders if that was why he stopped fighting at the end. But his life wasn't meaningless. None of our lives are. Regner is playing at being a god and taking what doesn't belong to him. Even if I ignore everything I know about what he has done to your people, he has still stolen from the humans in his kingdom too."

"He has." Humans who might have had different lives. Easier lives. *Longer* lives.

Tibris elbowed me. "I know you like to take an absurd amount of responsibility for everyone in your life, but rest assured, I would have always been here."

I sniffed. "You say absurd amount of responsibility, I say a strong level of oversight."

He just shook his head. "Let's go before you're late."

We wandered toward the arena. The weather was warmer this far south—which would make it tough to train during the middle of the day. But the mornings were still cool and crisp.

I glanced at my brother. His gaze had landed on a hybrid walking toward the arena. Blond and built, the hybrid looked back, his smile welcoming.

I smirked. "And just what is happening there?"

A hint of color touched Tibris's cheeks. "Nothing," he muttered.

Tibris was notoriously closed-mouthed about his romantic life. I studied the hybrid. Tibris elbowed me again. "Don't even think about it."

I shifted my gaze to the arena. Encircled by a thick wooden fence, the open-aired enclosure was both inviting and daunting. According to Demos, hybrids trained in the morning, while the fae trained in the afternoons. But a crowd had gathered today, leaning against the fence with an air of expectation.

I left Tibris's side and walked into the arena. The ground was a hardened mixture of compacted soil and sand. Likely, it was designed to cushion falls, but it bore the imprints of countless boot-clad feet.

The rhythmic clashing of steel rang out as two hybrids lunged at each other, both blindingly fast. The sound melded with the dull thuds of wooden swords striking padded dummies close by, and I recognized several of the hybrids hitting the dummies from Regner's dungeon.

On the other side of the arena, Asinia stood next to Demos, who was handing her a crossbow. From the way her mouth twisted, he'd said something to annoy her. I sighed, making my way over to Galon, who was watching the sword-wielding hybrids closely. He looked away long enough to run his gaze over me clinically once more. He was right—I'd lost the little muscle I'd managed to gain when I was traveling with him and the others. I hadn't eaten well at the castle, my anxiety crippling my appetite. And then, of course, I'd been stuck on that ship.

"You know what I'm going to say," he said as I approached him.

I nodded, and he turned his gaze back to the two hybrids. "I want you eating past the point of fullness while you're training at this camp. Your stomach has become smaller. You also need to be eating much more meat and fish than usual."

My appetite had already returned with a vengeance. "I will."

He let out a whistle, and the hybrids both froze, instantly stepping back. Both of them turned, listening intently as Galon gave them feedback on their defenses and footwork. When he was done, one of them glanced at me, his gaze lingering on my face.

"You're the hybrid heir," he said, his tone somehow caught between accusatory and awestruck.

I nodded.

His friend snorted, spat on the ground, and walked away. After a long, awkward moment, the first man followed him.

Galon ignored them both. "Sword or knives?"

It felt like a trick question, and I shrugged. "I'm used to knives."

"Because you're used to fighting up close."

"Well…yeah. Tibris taught me to fight with a sword, but it's not pretty."

"You'll continue up-close defensive training with Lorian. So, we may as well start you on the sword," he said.

More up-close training with Lorian. Perfect. Galon would only growl at me if I whined about it.

He angled his head. "No comments?"

"Nope. Tell me what to do, and I'll do it."

Galon narrowed his eyes, and I couldn't help but grin. "I need to learn."

After another long moment, he prowled away to find me a practice sword. I allowed my gaze to wander. The instructors—both fae and hybrid—stalked across the arena, scrutinizing every movement, demonstrating techniques, correcting stances. The air was already heavy with the scent of sweat, and I sucked it into my lungs.

We would fight on a battlefield. Soon. I needed to learn how to wield a sword, because my power would only last so long, and eventually, I'd be forced to fight against people who were larger and faster than me. I had to take advantage of this time. Every minute of training would count.

Galon returned, and I shifted on my feet as he handed me the wooden sword. I could feel eyes on me, and I ground my teeth, loathing it.

Galon swept his gaze past me to the fae and hybrids gathered along the outside of the arena. A moment later, most of the eyes had disappeared.

"Effective," I said.

He led me to the dummy. "That sword will be a little heavy for you, but you need to build muscle and quickly."

I nodded, already feeling the weight of it.

"Show me," he said.

I swung. I couldn't remember the last time I'd wielded a sword, and it felt awkward in my hands. But I remembered the last combination Tibris had taught me. Cut, cut, thrust, slash. Horizontal, diagonal, vertical, stab.

"Good," Galon said. "Your grip is too tight, but some of that is the weight of the sword. It'll ease up as you get used to it."

He had me continue basic cuts and thrusts on the dummy until my arm was shaking, and then he made me switch to my left hand. By the time we moved to footwork and he let me drop the sword, I was trembling with fatigue.

"Take a break and get some water," he instructed.

I wandered over to the water station, finding Demos and Tibris watching me, wearing twin looks of approval. Demos handed me a cup. "You've got work to do, but at least you know how to move, and you've got the foundation in place."

I nodded at Tibris. "He built that foundation."

Tibris's eyes crinkled. His shirt was damp with sweat. The sun was now high above us.

I gulped at the water, watching Asinia and Madinia shooting at the wooden dummy. Asinia managed to hit it in the chest. When Madinia missed, the dummy burst into flames.

"Put it out," Demos snarled, stalking toward her. I hid a smile, and Tibris nudged me.

"Galon is trying to get your attention."

My muscles screamed at me, and I heaved a sigh. "Don't make me go back."

"Prisca," Galon growled from across the arena, and I trudged back toward him.

Thankfully, we were moving on to stretches next. The arena began to clear out as the hybrids headed to lunch.

"Straighten your back," Galon said.

I complied, leaning over my leg and stretching my hamstrings. "Can I ask you something?"

He nodded.

"Crawyth."

Galon angled his head, clearly waiting for me to continue.

"Lorian implied he wasn't responsible for the slaughter."

He just shrugged one shoulder. "Because he wasn't."

I narrowed my eyes at his flippancy. "Why didn't he tell me earlier?"

Galon leveled me with a hard stare. "You were certainly eager to believe the truth."

"All I've heard my whole life is how the Bloodthirsty Prince destroyed Crawyth. Demos was there, Galon."

Galon gave me an impatient yet amused look that was as good as a pat on the head. "Your brother was a child. Find a witness who can state without a shadow of a doubt that they saw the so-called Bloodthirsty Prince destroying the city. Because I swear to you, he didn't do it."

I thought of Demos as he'd been in my memory of that night. Furious and traumatized and so, so young. "What happened, then?"

"That is not for me to tell you. I love that boy like a son," he said, and I almost smiled at the thought of Lorian as a boy. "And yet, I'm not blind to his faults. His temper is as bad as yours. Only, when he rages, people die. But of all the accusations you can level at Lorian—and I'm sure there are many—you can't accuse him of indiscriminate murder. Ask yourself what reason Lorian would have had to attack Crawyth. And then ask yourself if, after everything you've seen from him, after everything you've learned, it seems like something he would do."

"Then why didn't he defend himself when I accused him that night?"

"Would you have listened? You'd just learned we were fae. You're more open-minded than most humans or hybrids, but you'd just seen him grow taller, seen his ears change, and seen him wield that power. Can you honestly say you would have listened if he told you he didn't kill your parents?"

"He lied to me about who he was." And yet, I knew deep in my bones he hadn't been lying when he'd told me he didn't attack Crawyth.

"He had to. That doesn't mean everything between you was a lie." Galon shook his head. "You make me feel ancient. Why is it that the young like to take one piece of information and use it to change everything else their instincts tell them to be true?"

I couldn't answer that. He shook his head at me. "I suggest you talk to him, Prisca."

The Queen

The hybrid's screams were giving me a headache. I wished more than anything that someone would put him out of his misery just so I could soak in some silence.

Sabium's guard leaned down, and I shifted my gaze to the courtiers gathered in the throne room, forced to watch the torture.

No, not just forced to watch.

Forced to cheer. To *rejoice*.

One woman had swooned and was currently being held up by several ashen-faced friends near the back of the crowd.

It was clear Sabium was giving up any pretense of being the levelheaded ruler he had pretended to be for so long. And yet, according to my spies, there weren't yet any whispers questioning Sabium's sanity.

None of the courtiers had fled, all of them confident they would not be targeted.

It was almost amusing. Those who believed they were safe because they stood with the tyrant were only fooling themselves. In the game of power, everyone was a pawn, and no one was exempt from sacrifice.

My ladies were shadows of themselves. Sabium continued to insist we all watch his little torture sessions, and he had refused to allow me to excuse them from the throne room. It was just another way for him to prove I had no true power here.

My hands fisted in my lap—the only indication of my fury. I was loyal to few. And any loyalty I did have would only go so far. Still, those women had been at my side for years. I owed them any scrap of protection I could provide.

If the circumstances were different, I would have enjoyed watching Sabium unravel.

The choices he'd made over his long life had ensured both the hybrids and the fae would not rest until he was dead. There was no way for him to back down. His only option was to continue his attempts to eradicate them and to steal their power to use it against them.

The loss of the amulet had shaken him to his core.

Even as he refused to admit it.

"He knows something," Sabium hissed. "All of them are working against me."

The hybrid was mostly dead now, his screams little more than weak moans. A waste. Lisveth's eyes met mine, wide and filled with tears. Fury clawed at me, and I stared her down until she dropped her gaze.

Why would I risk myself to protect these women when they couldn't even control their own reactions?

I took a deep breath. "I believe if he'd known something, he would have told you already, husband," I said.

Sabium slowly turned his head, pinning me with his gaze. I raised an eyebrow at him, my heart racing in my chest. With a flick of my gaze, I indicated the courtiers watching us.

He took a deep breath. That crazed light slowly faded from his eyes. "Oh, very well." He waved his hand through the air. "Everyone out."

The courtiers were silent, but they didn't hesitate. There was no pushing, but the throne room was empty within moments.

Silence stretched. I took one moment to appreciate it, even as I steeled myself for Sabium's rage.

"You forget yourself, my *queen*," he hissed.

A strange kind of recklessness bubbled within my chest. I angled my head. "I believe you are the one who is allowing your emotions to cloud your judgment. My *king*."

Surprise flashed through his eyes. "You dare—"

The door slammed open. I let out the breath I was holding. Sabium turned toward the door with a snarl.

"Forgive the interruption, Your Majesty. There has been a development."

I glanced at the guard. Not one of mine. Hopefully, one of my spies would be attending this meeting.

"Fine," Sabium said. He slowly uncurled himself from his throne and leaned close to me. I refused to lean away.

"Be very careful," he murmured. "We both know you have more to lose than I do."

He turned and strolled away, leaving me trembling.

The child had green eyes. And somehow, whenever I was walking the castle grounds, he would be there.

Always having escaped some maid or nanny.

I would ignore him when I could. When there were eyes on us, I would do the bare minimum required to avoid the worst of the rumors.

Each time I saw him, fury burned through me, and a headache pounded behind my eyes. I would hand him back to whichever nanny was chasing him with a close-lipped smile and retreat to my rooms, where I would lie in bed for hours.

Eventually, I stopped my walks outside, furious that my one joy had been taken from me.

And then he began finding me inside the castle.

He was two winters. I knew he wasn't hunting me himself. That was ludicrous. Either Sabium was playing games—taunting me with this slow torture—or there was someone else responsible.

If it wasn't Sabium…whoever had decided to play with me this way would die screaming for mercy. In my quiet moments in that bed, I lost myself to fantasies of a body swinging from the gallows, turning to ash in flames, or dragged behind my favorite horse.

Perhaps there was some accident the child could have. I could plan for it to happen while I was away from the castle. A quick fall, a snapped neck, and I would finally be able to walk the grounds once more.

Sabium would know. He always knew. And he wouldn't grant me a quick death. No, he would make sure my death lasted for weeks.

The only solace I had was my library. I would spend

hours in there each day, in my favorite chair, ignoring the courtiers who attempted to gain my favor.

And hiding from a child.

Until one day, I heard a familiar sound.

Chortling.

Tiny feet padding on wood. Irritation warred with rage. He rounded the corner, steadying himself on a shelf, and his face lit up.

"Mama."

I closed my eyes and fought not to hurl my book through the window.

"Mama?"

Closer now.

I opened my eyes to find him staring up at me, his tiny, round face filled with joy. He held out his arms in the way such children did, expecting to be lifted onto my lap.

I leaned down.

"I am not your mother," I hissed.

His face scrunched up. He opened his mouth and wailed.

Someone let out a choked gasp, and I raised my gaze. The same dark-haired nanny as that first day. She was responsible for this. Had been responsible every time.

I would see her dead.

Our eyes met. Her mouth was open, expression horrified. As if I were the monster.

Sabium was the one who was the monster. He had done this to me.

Launching herself forward, she pulled the child into

her arms. He wound his arms around her, pressed his little face to her neck and sobbed.

Bitterness exploded in my mouth.

Turning, she hurried away. The child lifted his head, his cheeks streaked with tears.

He didn't wave.

10

PRISCA

"*I suggest you talk to him, Prisca.*"

Galon's words played through my mind, and I absently waved at Lina as I walked toward my tent. I'd seen something vulnerable in Lorian's eyes when I'd asked him about Crawyth. And the moment I'd made it clear I couldn't—or wouldn't—believe him, he'd shut down.

I couldn't exactly blame him.

But I didn't know where to go from here.

I missed him. Missed his hands on my body. Missed his sarcastic humor. Missed simply talking to him.

I was still furious with him. And yet, my instincts urged me to hear him out.

Deep down, I was afraid the real reason I was so angry was because I'd let Lorian in, and his deception had proven I was still that sheltered village girl who didn't have any true understanding of the world. It had proven I still hadn't learned my lesson. That I was naive, gullible.

I needed to push those kinds of thoughts out of my mind. Soon, I would go after the hourglass, and Lorian's brother would likely send him on some other dangerous excursion. As much as the thought of separating hurt, it was for the best.

The camp was quiet at this time of the day, most people grabbing dinner or chatting in groups. Asinia and I had found a private spot to wash in the river, enjoying the cold water on our overheated skin after training. She'd spent the time naming the best-looking men in the camp—both fae and hybrid—and for a while, it was as if nothing had changed and we were still in our village.

I stepped into my tent, and my instincts screamed at me. My hand dropped to the hilt of my knife, and it was immediately snatched from my grip.

"You'll have to be faster than that, wildcat."

My heart hammered in my chest. "Gods, Lorian. What are you doing here?"

He loomed over me, and yet my traitorous body wanted to snuggle into his chest.

"Waiting for you. The better question is, why are you so distracted? I could have been anyone."

I glowered at him. "There's only one man who would dare wait in my tent, knowing I could pause time and castrate him."

He gave a low, taunting laugh. The sound seemed to caress my skin. Skin that was suddenly too sensitive.

"I missed you." He said it simply, unashamed. As if it were simply a fact. "Have you missed me, wildcat? Have you thought about the feel of my hands on you? My mouth on you?"

I sucked in an unsteady breath.

His eyes darkened. "I thought so."

"That doesn't mean anything."

"That's where you're wrong. It means *everything*."

"Lorian..." My voice cracked.

His jaw tightened. "Do you think I want to be here? I'd stay away from you if I could."

"So do it," I choked out. Perhaps if we just avoided each other for long enough, I'd stop longing for him constantly. I'd stop imagining his hands on me. Stop dreaming of him every night.

He stepped closer, and I watched him, fisting my hands so I wouldn't reach for him.

"You're still angry."

"I'm..." I didn't know what I was. Furious that we couldn't turn back time to the way we'd been in the castle. Devastated that I'd found a man I wanted more than anything, only to learn we could never be together. Hurt that he hadn't told me. And he'd let me fall.

His mouth slammed down on mine, and I breathed him in, a sob hiccupping in my chest. This was what I'd wanted, even while I was attempting to hate him with everything in me. And it *hurt* wanting the man who'd betrayed my trust. The man I still couldn't trust.

Wouldn't *let* myself trust.

He was loyal to his brother first. He'd made that clear.

"Turn it off," he muttered against my mouth. "Just fucking turn off that busy mind and *feel* me."

I *could* feel him. He was currently nestled against my belly, thick and hard. I breathed in the scent of him and wished I could freeze time just like this. Wished we could stay here forever. He tore his mouth away from mine and kissed his way up my throat.

Heat pooled in my stomach. Too many clothes. I was wearing too many clothes.

"I know, wildcat."

Had I been speaking those words?

Lorian leaned back and stripped my shirt over my head. The flexible material around my breasts was gone next, and I shivered at the air on my bare skin.

He groaned, his gaze dropping, but I was already pulling off my boots. "One time," I got out. "Only once."

"Hmm." One of his hands had found my breast, and he gently brushed my nipple with his thumb. I let out a strangled groan, my stomach tumbling.

"I'm serious, Lorian."

"I know you are."

His mouth brushed mine, and the rest of the world disappeared. A moment later, his lips were gone as he pulled off his shirt, and I instantly caressed his chest. His busy hands were working on the fastenings of my leggings, and I slid my own hand down, finding his hard length.

Lorian sucked in a sharp breath that made my thighs clench. His gaze met mine as he pried my hand off him long enough to push my leggings and underclothes down my thighs. My legs were trapped and I wiggled, but he shook his head, turning me until my back met his chest. He slid one of his big hands to my stomach, holding me still.

"Did you miss me?"

I could feel him, hard and thick against my back, and I pushed back against him. "No," I lied, and he nipped the lobe of my ear, sliding his hand down to the wet heat of me.

"Do you remember the way I made you feel?" His voice was a low taunt. His finger brushed my clit, and I was instantly on edge. Fury burned through me, tempered by pleasure.

"I hate you!" I hissed, riding his hand. "I wish I'd never met you."

The lies stung my throat, and Lorian's hoarse laugh told me he knew.

"Do you think *I* wanted this?" He turned me, until he was staring down into my eyes. My breath caught at the sheer *want* in his gaze. At the tenderness that flickered across his face. He was showing me too much.

"This changes nothing."

His smile was bitter. "Fine. If this is all we'll ever have, then I'll take it."

My head whirled as I was suddenly in his arms, as he stalked toward my bed, laying me down and stripping off my leggings.

His leathers disappeared, and I sucked in a breath. Lorian naked was a glorious sight, and I let my gaze run over his huge shoulders, down his chest, over his abs, and down to the full length of him, erect and ready.

"Gods, the way you look at me," he said, and my breath caught as he prowled closer, his gaze burning with a possessive light.

He leaned over me, his mouth finding mine, and despite my frustration, I sighed against him. His touch was proprietary as he dragged his hand over my breast, down my stomach, and between my legs.

"Mine," he told me, his mouth catching my instant denial.

Then he was gone, pulling me down until my ass was on the edge of the bed. He knelt between my legs, pushing them apart and kissing his way along one thigh. Sensation rippled across my skin. My head fell back, and I arched, urging him on.

He swiped his tongue over me, and my body ignited, desperate for more. My hands found his hair in an attempt to keep him in place. He lifted his head, and I let out a pathetic moan.

"Beg me, Prisca." His cheeks were flushed, his eyes almost glowing. And yet his mouth was firm, unyielding.

My mouth fell open. I sucked in a breath, ready to tell him exactly what he could do with that suggestion...

And his tongue swiped along my clit once more. Sparks of pleasure danced from my core, through my belly, and I dropped my head back onto the pillow with a groan.

His words echoed through my mind.

You want me to take you in anger, wildcat? To make you moan my name while you writhe beneath me, all while you loathe me for every second of pleasure? I'll do it. But you won't get it by taunting me. You want hate sex? You'll have to beg."

"You bastard."

He chuckled against me. The vibration made me groan, and he immediately lifted his head. "That doesn't sound much like begging to me."

"I'll kill you."

His chuckle became a laugh. "Neither does that." He turned and nipped my thigh. I attempted to kick him, but he held me still. My traitorous body turned languid, reveling in his dominance.

"What. Do. You. Want?" he growled.

"You know what I want."

"I've been burning for you since we left the castle. And I'm feeling mean. You'll beg me, Prisca."

He lowered his head and swiped his tongue over my folds, teasing my clit. I gasped, attempting to lift my hips, but he held me still, lifting his head once more.

"I can do this all night."

I was desperate for him, and he somehow had all the control. Frustration roared through me, and my words came tumbling out in a rush. "You don't want to fuck me? I'll find someone else who will."

"Now *that* won't get what you want." His voice was a dangerous croon, and I shivered.

One large finger slid inside me, and that clever mouth found my clit once more. I moaned.

He stopped.

I was burning up, my skin too tight, my body on the edge.

He'd asked if I remembered how he'd made me feel. Some days, it was the only thing I could think about.

"Please," I said quietly.

"I didn't hear you."

I attempted to wrench my legs out of his grasp, but he soothed me with a sweep of one hand. "I suppose it will do."

He dropped his head, pushing my thighs wider, and I arched my hips, rocking against his face, desperate as he devoured me. Within moments, I was begging once more, only this time, it was because I was so close, my entire body trembled.

"Gods, the way you fall apart for me."

His clever tongue stroked, his fingers thrust, and I clenched my teeth, shuddering through a climax so intense, the pleasure turned my muscles weak.

The moment I was wrung out, he was standing, holding me in place as he nudged against my entrance. He leaned down, his mouth finding mine, and I twined my arms around his shoulders, holding him close.

"Missed this," he mumbled against my lips.

I'd missed this too. I was still trembling with

aftershocks, and yet I needed more. Needed *him*.

He slowly pushed inside me, and we both sucked in a breath as I tightened around his thick length. He leaned back, his eyes lust-darkened as he moved deeper. I gasped as he hit just the right angle on his next thrust, and his eyes narrowed. He hit the same spot again. And again.

I tensed, my breath shuddering out in a moan. His gaze met mine. "Missed *you*."

My chest tightened. I'd missed him too. So fucking much. Lorian slipped his hand down to my clit, a hoarse laugh leaving his throat as the brush of his thumb over my sensitive nerves made me clench around him.

I lifted my hips, demanding more, and he increased the pace, each thrust deeper than the next, until I was whimpering, dissolving, quaking.

"Lorian…"

"That's it. Only me, Prisca. Only ever me."

He drove our bodies together, and I wrapped my arms around him, nails digging into his back. He let out a groan, and my thighs shook.

"Lorian…"

"I know that tone. Come for me, wildcat."

I sucked in a breath, the edges of my vision darkening as my climax swept over me, bathing me in pleasure. Lorian let out a growl as I ground my hips up into him, his green eyes feral.

He cursed, flooding me with heat, and I blinked until I could focus once more, find him staring down at me. I was limp, still panting, spread naked beneath him.

His grin was very male. And very smug. That grin said he was certain I was his once more.

I groaned, reaching for a pillow to throw at him. He caught my hand, pressed a kiss to my fingers, and pulled me close, rolling until I was sprawled on his chest.

"What is it, wildcat?"

"Nothing." Gods, what had I done? The camp was quiet, the tent dark except for one of the strange glowing orbs the fae used in place of lamps. I attempted to sit up.

"Prisca."

"You need to go."

He just watched me, his expression patient. "Is that truly what you want?"

No. "Yes."

He chuckled, pulling me close, and I sighed, nestling into him. His masculine scent surrounded me, and I reveled in the feel of his hard body. I'd never felt safer than when I was wrapped in his arms.

Gods, I was stupid. And I was making life a lot more difficult for myself. But I couldn't seem to help it.

We dozed off and on, and when I finally startled awake for the third time, Lorian caught my hand. "It'll be better if you talk about it." His mouth twisted. "I promise not to see your sharing as a craving for true intimacy."

My cheeks heated, but he watched me, still waiting.

Hands shaking, I pushed my hair off my face. "I was dreaming about Vuena."

My thoughts and emotions around her were so mixed up. I'd known her as my mother my entire life. But ever since she'd died, I'd begun remembering things. Horrific memories that came to me as nightmares.

Lorian nodded, waiting for me. I chewed on my lower lip.

"When I was a young girl, we went to a celebration in one of the villager's homes. Papa and Tibris were there too, and I remember thinking how…happy everyone was. And then the assessor came and slaughtered the family who owned that house. He took their son to the city to burn. He was Tibris's age."

Lorian took my hand, and I drew in a shaky breath. "The last words Ovida said were accusing Mama. She said…she said, 'You're a seer! How could you not see this?' I guess…I guess I'd blocked the memory out, because it came to me when I recognized the king's assessor in Regner's castle."

"You think she *did* know," Lorian said, squeezing my hand lightly.

I nodded, my chest tightening. "I think she knew, and I think she used that experience to terrify me. She insisted I watch most of it. And before they died, she said to me…" My throat closed, and I sucked in a breath.

Lorian wiped at my face. I hadn't realized I was crying. I'd been so determined not to let Lorian see my weakness, and yet some part of me knew…I could trust him with this.

"Tell me the rest," he murmured.

"She said, 'Watch, Prisca. Watch closely. See what happens when a child is caught using forbidden magic.'

And then she let it happen. She let that entire family die, Lorian. Their son was so young. And she did it to teach me a lesson. To make sure I never forgot what would happen if I was caught using my power." I raised my head, catching the pity in Lorian's eyes. That pity would usually infuriate me. But I knew he was pitying the young girl I'd been. And I also knew him well enough to know exactly why that muscle was ticking in his jaw.

"You're angry for me."

He pressed a gentle kiss to my cheek. "Sometimes I wish *I'd* been given time magic. And that I could use it to turn back time and get you out of there. I would have protected you."

"I know." I could never doubt Lorian's protective instincts. I lifted our linked hands, pressing a kiss to his knuckles. Surprise mingled with pleasure in his eyes.

"She could have saved them, Lorian. I'll never understand it."

"And you never will," Lorian said. "You're not like her, wildcat. We'll probably never know why she made those choices. But…if you'd been caught as a child…if you'd burned, you never would have saved three hundred hybrids."

"You think that's why she did it?"

"I think she was a seer, and she was shaping forces she had no business shaping. She knew you were the heir to the hybrid kingdom. What she did was inexcusable, but I believe she justified it, because in her mind, you had to live. So you could save your people."

The Boy

Each night, when the boy woke screaming from nightmares, his brother came. Eventually, he had the boy moved in to his chambers so he could hear him screaming in the room next to his.

The king sat on his bed silently at first, clearly at a loss. And then he began reading from his favorite books. Ancient fae tomes so dry they would sometimes send the boy straight to sleep.

When that didn't work, he told him of the great battles of fae history. This was when Conreth would come alive. Through his stories, the boy learned of tactical warfare, weapons, and the great sieges of the fae lands. He learned of magical creatures and the power his parents had once had.

And so, the boy found solace in the tales of valor and heroism that his brother recounted. The vivid stories wove themselves around the boy's dreams, chasing away the nightmares, until occasionally, he could sleep through an entire night.

But it was the days that turned darker. Panic would clutch at his chest, and the boy would scratch at his throat, unable to take a full breath. The world would turn quiet and still, except for the screaming in his head. The screams that never ended.

11

PRISCA

The next morning, I woke with aching muscles and a tight chest. Lorian had left when the sun came up. I'd felt him kiss my forehead and feigned sleep, although I was sure he'd known I was awake.

So much for staying away from him. He still hadn't told me why so many believed he'd destroyed Crawyth, he'd spent weeks lying to me, and I'd rolled right back into bed with him.

"My loyalty will always be to my people, Prisca. To my brother."

I sat up. Maybe…maybe it didn't have to be a big deal. We were both stressed, and we'd used each other. I'd made it clear it was a one-time occurrence, to combat some stress. I'd…slipped. That was all it was.

Yes, you slipped right onto his cock.

Shoving my hands against my burning cheeks, I groaned. It didn't matter. Lorian knew where we stood. And the moment I found out where the hourglass was, I would be leaving. From there, I would need to work on finding allies for the hybrids. I wouldn't even see Lorian for months. Perhaps—if we ended up fighting on different battlefields—even for years.

My heart slammed into my ribs at the thought, and I took a deep, steadying breath. One mistake. I was allowed one mistake.

And what a mistake it had been.

My body heated at the way my muscles ached as I swung my legs out of bed, slowly getting to my feet with a wince. I'd kill for a bath, but first, I had training.

I washed with the basin of water by my cot and dressed quickly, finding Demos waiting outside my tent. I smiled at him, wishing we had more time to spend together. Every time I searched for him, he was training the hybrids, meeting with the hybrid leaders, or murmuring quietly to Vicer.

"Heading to training?"

"Yeah. Galon is attempting to whip me into shape. He's made some kind of decree to the cooks. They insist on giving me extra meat, and then they stare at me to make sure I'm eating it."

Demos grinned. "He's trying to help you build muscle. I want to train with you at some point too."

Hadn't I just been thinking about how I wanted to spend more time with Demos? I had no doubt he would be just as hard on me as Galon—if not harder. Perhaps I should be careful what I wished for.

I sighed. "It's difficult being this popular."

Demos smiled, but his gaze was distant.

"What is it?"

"Madinia left, Prisca." Demos's mouth tightened. "And she took the jewels with her. I searched her tent."

My gut churned. I closed my eyes in an attempt to shield myself from the blow. It didn't work. We needed those jewels. Needed them to hire mercenaries, to buy weapons and armor for the hybrids. I'd known Madinia was unhappy, but she'd seemed committed to the cause.

"Do you want me to find her?" he asked.

I opened my eyes. "She could be planning to return."

"Perhaps." From Demos's tone, he didn't think so.

Madinia's face flashed through my mind. She'd saved my life twice. She had no family left. Nowhere else left to go.

"Send our best tracker after her. To *watch*. If they spot her traveling from the fae lands, they can intercept or report her movements back to us."

Demos nodded. "We'll give her one week," he said. "Any longer, and I'll go after her myself."

One week was more than enough time for her to sell those jewels and flee. Even if he found Madinia, she could have hidden the coins she received for them anywhere.

I hadn't taken the jewels back. Hadn't ordered them secured elsewhere. Because I'd never expected Madinia to leave with no warning. Once again, I was proving that I had no idea how people behaved outside of my small village.

A headache pounded at the base of my skull. We

needed weapons desperately. We couldn't rely on the goodwill of the fae. How could I look the hybrids in the eye when I was still allowing these kinds of situations to happen?

Demos lingered, his mouth becoming a grim line. "There's something else."

I fisted my hands. "What is it?"

"Your friendship with the fae has been noticed."

"And?" If I was honest with myself, some part of me had known this conversation would be coming.

"I'm not sure you understand who they are, Prisca. Your friend Rythos is practically royalty himself—his family is from an island located off the coast between fae and Gromalian lands, and the only reason he didn't stay to rule was because he was the second-born son. Galon? He's old enough that he was friends with Lorian's father, and he once led the Bazinith."

"The Bazinith?"

"Think the iron guard, only much smaller, much more powerful, older, and fae. Like it or not, but who you spend your time with sends a message. I just want to make sure you're aware of the message you're sending."

"They're good men, Demos. They kept me alive. They kept *all* the hybrids alive and got them down here to this camp. Doesn't that count for something?" My tone was sharp with frustration.

Demos merely nodded. "It counts for everything to me. But I've spent my life in Eprotha, making difficult decisions and seeing exactly how the world works—and all the shades of gray. Thousands of the hybrids in this camp haven't left since they arrived. Hundreds were born here. If you want to continue your friendship with the fae, I just need you to know what those hybrids are saying."

"And what are they saying?"

Demos's mouth tightened, and I leveled him with a hard stare. "Tell me."

"They're saying you're a fraud. That you're not truly the heir, and you don't have time magic. They're saying you have no rightful claim to the throne and you shouldn't even be here."

I waited to feel something. Some kind of instant denial. The problem was, I agreed with everything they were saying.

Except for the time magic part. At least I knew I had that.

Demos was waiting for me to speak. "What do you advise I do?"

He shoved a hand into his dark hair. "You need to send a message. Something public. There's one man who is saying this shit the loudest. A man named Roran. He was one of the few who managed to make it here when the fae finally dropped the wards after our kingdom was invaded."

"So, he's had to rely on their mercy and *hospitality*, all while remembering how little they helped when we were attacked."

"Yes."

My stomach churned uneasily. I was beginning to

understand how my brother thought. "You want me to make an example of him."

"Nothing that would make people hate you. But if you could demonstrate your power publicly…"

I cringed. Demos just gave me an expectant look.

"Like it or not, you're the hybrid queen."

"I'm the heir," I muttered. "It's not the same thing."

I didn't want to disappoint him. Gods, that was the last thing I wanted to do. My brother had suffered for his people. Had bled and starved for them. But…

Using my power felt like taking off my clothes and stalking through this camp. And the worst part of that was what using my power would mean to these people. I would be offering them proof that I was who some of them thought I was. A queen. I would be lighting the spark of hope, only to douse it when they realized I would never be a ruler worthy of them.

"Shouldn't you be at training?" a deep voice boomed behind us.

Rythos. I grasped at the distraction. "I should." My gaze found Demos's. "You arrange for the demonstration, and I'll do what I need to."

A hint of pity darted through his eyes. But it was gone a moment later. "I'll meet you after your training."

"Fine."

I made my way to the arena, finding Lorian leaning against the fence, sharpening his sword. He towered over most men, even wearing human glamour, but it was his eyes—hard, cold, and a little feral—that drew attention.

I knew him well enough now to know he was deep in thought, likely pondering how best to strike at Regner, but I could see why the hybrids were giving him a wide berth, their gazes darting to him as they whispered.

Some of those eyes were filled with curiosity, but most were filled with fear or apprehension. Lorian either didn't notice the hushed silence around him or he didn't care.

His gaze found mine, and I felt my cheeks heat as memories from last night assaulted me. Those eyes darkened as I walked toward him.

"What happened?"

I shrugged. "It's nothing."

A muscle ticked in his jaw, but he let it go. For now. I had no doubt he would bring it up later when we were alone. I'd messed up by assuming I could climb in and out of his bed and pretend nothing had happened.

Lorian was indeed a patient man. He was slowly chipping away at my defenses, and I'd gotten too close.

"Where's Galon?"

"Galon is busy," he told me. "We'll work on your sword work this morning and switch to knives later this afternoon."

My stomach fluttered uneasily. I hadn't planned for this. No, I'd planned to spend the day avoiding him and rebuilding my defenses. I narrowed my eyes, watching him pick up a couple of training swords.

Was Galon truly busy, or had Lorian convinced him to step aside?

I took the wooden training sword he handed me, the hilt scraping against the new blisters on my palm.

He was still watching me too closely, and I swung the sword, stretching my neck. The hybrids were going about their own training now, although they'd left us a training space that was far larger than we needed.

I raised one eyebrow. "Let's see what you've got."

The notion was ridiculous, of course. I'd seen the way he'd moved when the iron guards had attacked us in that forest.

He gave me a slow smile. A smile that told me he was picturing me naked. My cheeks heated, and I sent him a killing look.

His smile widened, but his nod told me he would behave. For now. My heart jumped at the thought of finding him in my tent again.

"If I didn't know any better, I'd think you were trying to distract me from the way you've been sneaking around," he said.

I went still. "I have no idea what you're talking about."

Lorian lunged at me, his sword aimed for my chest. I parried, conscious of the fact that he'd slowed his speed to a crawl.

He shook his head, dropping his sword to his side.

"You're trying to match my strength. That will hurt your hand, tire your muscles, and eventually, you'll drop your sword." His expression tightened as he finished speaking.

This was why I generally preferred daggers. But they would require me to be fighting up close. "What should I do, then?"

"Timing, technique, and leverage. You already know you need to work on your footwork, but you're quick and agile. That means your goal should always be to avoid the full force of your opponent's attacks. You need to learn to anticipate their swing and react just before the strike would land, using their momentum to deflect the blow. And you'll need to learn your angles so you can redirect with the strongest part of your blade." Lorian lifted his sword and tapped the section closer to the hilt. "Then, you'll learn counterattacks and how to exploit weaknesses."

"I'll never be good enough to hold my own in time."

"You don't need to be," Lorian said. "You're going to learn how to fight with a combination of your sword and your power. If there ever comes a day when your power fails you and I'm not there—" a dangerous light entered his eyes "—you'll at least know enough to stay alive until I can get to you."

Something wrenched in my chest. He spoke as if the idea of his not being by my side was ludicrous. And yet, we'd be separating. Soon.

Lorian was watching me closely. Probably reading far too much on my face. I managed to make my expression blank, and he swung his sword once more.

This time, I attempted to redirect it. But he dropped his wooden sword and stepped behind me, his hand sliding to mine where it gripped the sword. "This would be easier if we had someone to attack so I could show you. Perhaps I should ask one of the hybrids."

His voice was amused, but I could sense weariness beneath it. I opened my mouth, but he was already leaning over my shoulder, adjusting my sword as his hand found my hip. My skin tingled, my breath caught, and I had to prevent myself from closing my eyes and soaking in the feel of him. Instead, I stepped to the left, following his motion, and he nodded, drawing back.

"Again. Slowly."

He swung, his sword aiming for my head. This time, I changed the angle of my strike, darting right as I parried. When I pushed his sword aside without my arm howling at me, I let out a pleased laugh.

Lorian went still, staring at me. "It's been a long time since I heard that sound."

I shrugged. "I haven't had much to laugh about."

We began to circle. "What are you up to, Prisca? Why the meetings?"

Our swords clashed, and I attempted to dodge. He was relentless, pressing me with a series of swift strikes.

I panted, blocking another blow. The impact shuddered up my arms, and I understood why he wanted me to improve my footwork. "Is that your strategy? Tire me out until I tell you what you want to know?"

His laugh was a low taunt. "If I wanted to tire you out, I wouldn't do it in an arena."

My thighs clenched as my mind helpfully provided

me with an image of last night, tangled in his arms. "Your arrogance is astounding."

"Pris."

Lorian stepped back, allowing Demos to walk toward us. He nodded at Lorian, and our eyes met.

My palms went damp. It was time.

"I have something I need to do," I muttered.

"Fine. I need to meet with Rythos," Lorian said. His gaze found mine, his expression set in unyielding lines. "We'll train again later." Clearly, our little conversation wasn't over. I'd need to find some way to distract him. My heart tripped at the thought.

I pushed strands of sweat-soaked hair off my face, pulled the leather tie from the end of my braid and began rebraiding it. Lorian studied me for one last moment and then turned, prowling out of the arena. The moment he was gone, much of the tension drained from those who were still training. Conversation picked up, someone laughed, and even the sounds of swords clashing against each other seemed to grow louder.

"I want you to fight him," Demos said.

I frowned. "What? Who?"

"Roran."

I froze, the end of my braid still clutched in my fist.

"That's the worst idea I've ever heard. Did you not see me waving my wooden sword around?"

His lips twitched. "Hand-to-hand. Like you're used to. One dagger each. Fight to first blood or until I call it."

"First blood?" This was getting out of hand. "He

could gut me, Demos."

"You're going to be using your power, remember?"

Just the thought made black dots appear at the edges of my vision.

"Demos, I don't think I can do it. I don't think I can use my power publicly like this."

My brother's eyebrows lowered, and he angled his head. Clearly, he didn't understand. *I* didn't even fully understand. Yes, I'd used my power at the castle, but this felt wildly different. It felt as if someone had taken one of the targets from across the arena and stuck it to my back.

Silence stretched. Finally, he sighed. "All right, Prisca. You should know, though, the rumors are likely to get worse. It's difficult to build morale like this."

I wished Lorian hadn't left.

Just the thought irritated me. I couldn't rely on other people to carry the weight of my decisions. To prop me up because I was unable to deal with the reality of my life.

That was what I'd been asking Demos to do. He was doing the best he could in this camp, but now my brother was asking *me* for something. Something he thought we needed.

I had to put on a good show. Because I sure as fuck wasn't good for anything else.

I took a deep breath. "I'll do it."

He leaned against the arena railing. "Are you sure?"

"Yes."

My mouth was dry, and I stalked to the water station, taking a cup the attendant handed me and gulping down the cool liquid. It didn't help.

"My sister needs to practice her knife work," Demos announced loudly. "Who wants to help?"

The heavy weight on my chest instantly lifted, even as the backs of my eyes burned.

His sister.

His sister, who he was counting on.

I wouldn't disappoint him.

A man jumped the rail, stalking toward us. Dark-haired, bearded. The same man who'd been fighting when I'd arrived at the arena to train with Galon. The one who'd spat and stalked away when he'd learned who I was.

That weight reappeared. I'd watched him fight and admired his speed. What was Demos thinking?

Roran handed his sword to his friend and pulled a knife, eyes glittering as he waited for me. He wasn't thin, but he wasn't bulky either. No, he was light on his feet, moving gracefully as he stepped into position.

"First blood," Demos said as I made myself approach. "You know the rules, Roran. We don't have enough healers to go around, so don't do anything stupid."

My hand trembled, and I squeezed the hilt of my dagger tighter.

A crowd was gathering, and I glanced behind Demos at where Asinia was clutching the railing, Tibris next to her. He shook his head at me, clearly unhappy. At least he was close if Roran decided to gut me like a pig.

I'd fought for my life on more than one occasion—and won. But that wasn't what this was. This wasn't about brutal tactics and doing anything to keep breathing. This was about demonstrating skill, self-control, and, of course, power.

"You shouldn't have come here," Roran said, so quietly I could barely hear him. "You're giving false hope to people who deserve better."

Perhaps that hope was all I could contribute until someone else came along. Someone who would be able to lead the hybrids home. Maybe…maybe that would be enough, and one day, when this was all over, I could stand in front of a mirror and look myself in the eye. Roran was wrong. Hope was worth everything.

"Are we doing this?"

He rolled his shoulders.

And then he attacked.

He slashed out with his knife, and I darted right, circling him. Several laughs broke out. It looked as if I was running from him.

Roran swung his other hand, and I felt the wind shift next to my face. My kick was more of a stomp, but I slammed my foot into the side of his knee.

He let out the tiniest noise. Triumph roared through me. Oh yeah, that had hurt.

He swung again and again. I dodged each time. My own knife slashed out, but his arms were longer. My power slipped free before I realized I'd reached for it, giving me enough time to bat his arm away and sink a punch into his gut.

Roran grunted, and his backhand caught my jaw.

Stars burst in front of my eyes. The pain hit a moment later, exploding through my face. I dropped to my knees, and Roran's eyes lit up with victory. I yanked on the thread of my power, giving myself enough time to get to my feet and take a breath. And then he was on me.

His knife whistled past my head. Demos yelled something, but it was too late. This fight had become more than just training.

I dodged, right, left, right, using my power to freeze Roran at key points. To keep myself just out of his range. My power worked in sync with my movements. Pure joy danced along my spine, and for the first time, I understood what Lorian had meant. I was still overusing my power, immediately feeling the drain, but I would get better.

Roran bared his teeth, obviously frustrated. He was better than me, and we both knew it. But he couldn't work out why he couldn't land his hits.

I pulled the tiniest thread of power free, and Roran froze again, just long enough for me to evade a wicked slice that would have slashed open my throat.

"Finish it, Prisca," Demos called.

I knew what he was saying. No one could tell what I was doing. Right now, I just looked like I was moving incredibly fast. As fast as the fae. Roran lunged at me again, and this time, I pulled harder at my power, ensuring time only stopped for him.

Shocked gasps sounded, and I fought to ignore them, rounding Roran and placing my knife to his throat.

When time resumed, he almost slit his own throat on

my blade. I winced, moving it just in time. He froze, and I repositioned it.

He was slightly taller than me, but I was studying him closely, so I saw him swallow. Saw the slight tremble in his shoulders.

"I think this means I've won," I said.

"You really do have the power."

"If I remove this knife, are you going to do anything stupid?"

"No, Your Majesty."

I jolted at the words, almost stabbing him again.

Fuck.

Demos stepped forward, casting me a warning look. He flicked a glance to the other side of the arena.

Telean was here, practically glowing with pride as she watched me. Our eyes met, and something in my chest unlocked. Safe. She was safe. Next to her stood a man with long, white-blond hair and pointed ears. Like all of the fae, he was beautiful. But it was a cold beauty. I half expected him to turn me to ice.

Since he was surrounded by guards and wearing a breathtakingly lovely crown of some indeterminant white metal that glittered with pale blue jewels, it was obvious who this was.

The fae king had gotten tired of waiting.

And he'd come here instead.

PRISCA

Demos stepped up next to me. "That's—"

"Yes," I breathed. I needed to handle this very, very carefully. Hybrid lives were at stake.

I wished for Lorian again. And that thought was enough to make me move. Striding toward the fae king, I frowned as his guards pulled their swords. My gaze dropped to the knife in my hand, and I slid it into my sheath. I'd need to clean it later.

"Nelayra Valderyn," the king mused, those pale eyes studying my face.

I wasn't sure what he was seeing—or how much of the fight he had witnessed. I would have liked to have been prepared to meet him—not bruised and sweating, with damp strands of my hair stuck to my face.

"Your Majesty," I greeted him. My gaze found my aunt's, and she gave me a nod. She looked no worse for wear. In fact, she looked rested. Behind her, several of the hybrids who had been sick and wounded on our ship also now looked strong and healthy.

"Please," the fae king said. "Call me Conreth."

Whispers sounded around us, and I ignored them. "This is my brother Demos."

Conreth bowed his head. "A pleasure."

Demos nodded. I was beginning to learn that nothing fazed my brother, and few people impressed him—

including fae kings.

"Thank you for bringing my aunt with you."

Conreth cast her an amused look. "I'd suggested she stay behind, but she refused."

Telean merely gave him a thin-lipped smile. I took a deep breath. The fae king had wanted me to be unprepared, and he'd gotten what he'd wanted. But that didn't mean I had to let him see just how much it had shaken me.

"I'm assuming you're looking for Lorian?" I asked.

"No," Conreth said. "I will speak with him at a later date. But you and I have much to discuss."

In other words, he wanted to talk to me before Lorian knew he was here. Interesting, and not entirely unexpected. I gestured awkwardly at my sweat-soaked tunic, and Conreth's pale brow winged up. "Believe it or not, but I do train with my people. Your appearance doesn't offend me."

My lips twitched, and he seemed to realize how that had sounded, because his eyes thawed. "Forgive me. We traveled quickly. If you've finished training, would you meet with me now?"

Oh yeah, he definitely wanted to figure out who and what I was without his brother around. Lorian was going to lose his mind when he found out the fae king was here. I'd bet that was exactly why Conreth had appeared at this exact time—when Lorian was nowhere to be seen.

But Conreth needed to learn that I wasn't his subject. "Please allow me to freshen up, and I will be right with you. It won't take long."

Conreth nodded. "I'll have one of my guards escort you to my tent."

"Of course," I said. While I'd usually climb over the arena railing, I strolled toward the gate instead. Telean met me, wrapping me in her arms. I breathed her in.

"I missed you."

"I missed you too. Now let's get you cleaned up." Knowing my aunt, she also wanted to make sure I was as prepared as possible before my little chat with Conreth.

I glanced back, searching for Demos. He was currently speaking to the fae king, his voice low. He glanced back at me and nodded. He'd keep him occupied and learn whatever he could. Although I had no doubt Conreth was a cagey bastard, given what I'd seen from him so far.

Telean and I walked toward my tent. "Can I take Demos into the meeting with me?" I murmured.

She shook her head. "Demos is acting in the role of the hybrid general. You can only bring him if Conreth's general will also be in attendance."

I hated these rules. My stomach fluttered, and Telean took my arm. "We don't have much time," she said. "Tell me what you remember from our lessons about Conreth." She glanced over her shoulder. "Quietly."

I took a deep breath, reaching for everything she'd somehow managed to stuff into my head. "He rules with Emara, his queen. He's over one hundred years old and the eldest son of the last fae king and queen, Alaricel and Celandine. While he is exceptionally powerful, he has an affinity for ice magic. On the battlefield, before he became king, he was known for freezing his enemies and shattering them into millions of pieces." My stomach roiled uneasily at that visual, and I stepped into my tent.

Telean cast her gaze around the small tent as I threw open the trunk of clothes, searching for a clean dress. "Good. And who is in his inner circle?"

My aunt hadn't been idle while working as the queen's seamstress. No, she'd kept up-to-date with as much information as she could.

I threw the dress onto my cot and stripped. I couldn't do anything about my hair, but I could at least wash with the basin next to my cot.

"The two advisers he trusts the most are named Horastir, and Meldoric. Horastir grew up with the king, while Meldoric gained his trust later in life."

"And his military?"

I dried myself and forced my mind into submission. "The vanguard is trained in combat, including elemental magic, archery, and swordplay. They're the first line of defense if the borders fail. The enchanters specialize in protective magic, wards, illusions. The rangers patrol the fae lands, gather intelligence, and slip into Gromalia and Eprotha when necessary. Each division reports directly to the high general Hevdrin—Conreth's highest-ranking military officer. Hevdrin reports directly to Conreth."

"Very good."

I pulled on the dress, and Telean sighed. I winced as I took in the wrinkled, slightly threadbare fabric. I'd worn leggings and tunics since I'd arrived and hadn't exactly expected to be meeting with the fae king. I had no doubt Telean had plans to fix my wardrobe, though.

"Well," she said after a long moment. "There's nothing much you can do about it now."

"Prisca?" a voice called, and Erea poked her head into my tent. It had taken a while for her to stop calling me Setella. "I heard you might need someone to do your hair." She took in my sweaty braid and winced.

"We don't have time."

"We do," Telean said firmly.

Erea carried a large satchel, and she gestured for me to sit on the cot, reaching in and finding some kind of powder. Unwinding my braid, she shook the powder onto my hair, combed it through, and murmured a word I didn't recognize.

My scalp tingled, and I jolted.

"That's better," she said, and I could hear the smile in her voice. "I'll just put it up. It won't take long."

Telean handed me a mirror when she was done, and my mouth dropped open. My hair was clean. It even *smelled* clean. Erea pulled it into a simple bun, leaving a few strands free.

"Thank you so much. What is in that powder?"

"It's enchanted. Incredibly expensive, but I stole it from the queen when I knew we were leaving." She winced, and I grinned at her.

"Of all the things to steal from that woman, this was what you chose?"

She grinned, flashing that chipped tooth, and gestured

to the satchel. "Oh no, that's not all."

My aunt studied Erea, and I could tell she was pleased. "We will find you new supplies when necessary."

Now probably wasn't the time to tell my aunt that all the jewels we'd taken had gone missing. I was still hoping Madinia returned before I had to make *that* admission.

Getting to my feet, I slipped on a pair of shoes and rolled my shoulders.

"You can do this," Telean said. "Remember, you are equals."

The thought was so ludicrous, I almost snorted. Telean shook her head at me and waved at me to leave.

"Can you please find a tent for my aunt?" I asked Erea.

"Of course. Good luck, Prisca."

"Thank you."

One of Conreth's guards was waiting outside my tent. Broad and stocky, with the kind of shoulders that made me picture him swinging an ax, he nodded at me, instantly turning to lead me in the direction away from the arena. Ah. Conreth didn't want to draw attention from the fae yet, so he was spending his time on the hybrid side of camp. Since the hybrids weren't exactly best friends with the fae, it would take some time before Lorian learned he was here. I thought back to my training this morning. Galon, Cavis, and Marth hadn't been there, but neither had Rythos. Come to think of it, other than Lorian— who'd only trained me for about an hour—none of the fae instructors had been in the arena. Had Conreth arranged that? The thought made my skin itch.

I nodded at the guard as he waited in front of the tent and gestured for me to enter. I hesitated, well aware that the guard would be watching me and reporting my every action back to the fae king. But I took a moment to collect myself anyway. My heart hammered against my rib cage, bringing a surge of nausea with it.

Several deep breaths later, I stepped inside the tent.

Conreth's retinue had been busy. My feet sank into a thick rug, and several orbs of light hovered in the air around the tent, giving it a warm glow. A map of the continent had been hung on one of the canvas walls, and I longed to study it. In front of the map, a small table had been set with two plates, a platter of meats and cheeses between them. Conreth sat at the table, his expression distant. His pale gaze met mine, and he nodded at the seat across from him.

I surveyed him, looking for any similarities between him and Lorian. Where Lorian was dark-haired and built like he'd been born to rage down a battlefield, Conreth was slightly shorter, with longer limbs and those cold eyes. Despite their differences, I could see the family resemblance in their high cheekbones and the shape of their eyes.

"Please." The fae king nodded. "Eat."

I sat, but there was little chance of my eating unless he wanted to watch the hybrid heir lose her stomach.

"I was hoping to meet you sooner," Conreth said, stretching out his legs. The movement was casual, as if we were two friends catching up. But I had no doubt that everything he did was purposeful.

"I'm grateful to Lorian for bringing me here. To my people." The words tasted like ash on my tongue, but Conreth was expecting to talk to the hybrid heir. So that was who I would give him.

Conreth studied me for a long moment. "You're a very beautiful woman," he said, although there was no heat in his eyes. He was looking at me clinically, as if attempting to see beneath my skin. "You helped return a great amount of power to the fae with your actions in Regner's castle. And of course, you freed the hybrids in his dungeon. But I admit, I'm unsure exactly why Lorian would choose to commit treason for you."

I swallowed, my mouth suddenly bone-dry. "Treason?"

Conreth reached for his plate with a nod. "Our kingdom has long had strict laws when it comes to defying the will of either the king or the generals. The fae are powerful, often wild, and so must be ruled accordingly, with a firm hand."

A dull ringing sounded in my ears. Lorian had committed *treason* for me? "And the punishment for treason?"

He spread soft cheese onto bread. "Consequences vary from imprisonment to death."

I felt the blood drain from my face. I hadn't seen Lorian for hours now. Had Conreth had him arrested?

Getting to my feet, I reached for my power, holding it ready.

"What did you do to Lorian?"

12
PRISCA

onreth angled his head. "Lorian is fine. At least, he was last time I had my men report his whereabouts. But your reaction is interesting." He took a bite of his food. I tamped down the urge to slam my fist into his face and fought to keep my expression blank.

I knew better than this. And yet I'd played right into Conreth's hands. "Is there a reason you'd choose to imply otherwise?"

"Merely determining your relationship. My brother lied to you, and yet it seems all is forgiven."

"With all due respect, Your Majesty, my relationship with Lorian is none of your business."

He slowly shook his head. "That's where you're wrong. You're young, unused to ruling. Your first lesson is that everything your enemies, allies, and potential allies do is your business."

"And which category do I fall into for you?"

He merely gave me one of those

cold smiles. "I have a suggestion. For the remainder of our talk, you will vow to answer my questions honestly, and I will vow to do the same." He nodded at the knife on the table.

I stared at it, uncomprehending. Then it hit me. "A blood vow?"

He gave a languid shrug. "One way to keep us both honest."

If either of us lied—breaking the vow—we would die an excruciating death. Clearly, there was something Conreth wanted to know, and he was convinced I would otherwise lie about the answer.

And yet, when else would I have the fae king at my disposal to answer all of my questions honestly? Conreth may be a passive-aggressive, patronizing prick, but he knew the history of both his people and mine. He knew where I was most likely to find allies. And his people had been at war with Regner for centuries now. Conreth's brain was a wellspring of knowledge. Knowledge I desperately needed if I was going to be able to help the hybrids.

"Fine."

Conreth's expression didn't change, those cold eyes didn't thaw, but I was studying him closely enough that I caught the way his shoulders relaxed the tiniest amount.

I needed to be very, very careful.

I sat back down and held out my palm, wincing at the sting of the knife. Conreth sliced his own hand, murmured the fae words, and agony slithered up my arm as the vow locked into place.

The fae king gestured for me to speak first. "Please. Ask your questions."

"Why was it so important that you met me now?"

"I'm currently determining whether allying with your people would be a help or a hindrance. My decision needs to happen sooner rather than later."

Conreth wanted to watch my reaction to that, so I refused to give him one. "What makes you think it will be a hindrance?"

"You're naive, untested. You don't truly wish to rule, and this is obvious to anyone who interacts with you. You have no allies. The Gromalian king could perhaps be convinced to turn on Regner, yet you have not arranged to meet him. There are powerful creatures in the hybrid kingdom, yet you haven't attempted to visit. Instead, you came here first, because you wished to see your friends and family."

I sucked in a deep breath. Conreth didn't know we were training for a specific purpose or that we were looking for the hourglass. It benefited us that he thought I was merely in this camp hiding from what he saw as my duties. Yet his judgment stung just the same.

"And what exactly do *you* bring to the table?" I asked, my voice carefully level. "Your people turned their backs on the hybrids and now expect them to kiss your feet for offering them this swath of land to squat on while their families and friends die in Eprotha and Gromalia. The fae were this continent's only chance when the hybrid kingdom was decimated, and instead of fighting, you did *nothing*."

I'd expected Conreth to make some kind of denial. To at least become angry. He merely angled his head, raising his goblet to his mouth and drinking deeply. "My people made mistakes," he said, placing the goblet down. "One of our biggest was waiting for allies from across the seas."

I glanced at the map. The hybrid kingdom was located to the west of this continent, across the Sleeping Sea. Conreth shook his head. "You're looking in the wrong direction." Getting to his feet, he reached into a satchel and handed me another map, this one much smaller, the edges of the parchment yellowed with age. To the east of our continent, there were indeed other continents. Other *kingdoms*.

I stood and leaned over the table, studying the map. "Why don't we ever hear of them?"

Conreth turned to study the map from his side of the table. "Before both his son and grandson died, Regner found an ancient text. It predates humans on this continent. The text was written by one of the dark gods. And Regner learned dangerous information. One of the pages of that book provided instructions to create a barrier so long and impenetrable, he must have realized how it could be used."

This was the same barrier the pirate queen had spoken of, her eyes dark with longing.

"And then Regner's son died," Conreth said. "Regner decided he wanted complete control of this continent, and he wouldn't achieve that control if we could receive help from other continents. And if the humans in Eprotha learned that across the seas, fae, hybrids, humans, all lived together—along with other creatures they'd never even learned of…it would threaten his ability to control the population."

Those other continents sounded magical in more ways than one. I couldn't imagine so many people with varying backgrounds and cultures and magic all living together as one.

"Nelayra?"

I met Conreth's eyes. "Are there any humans who would help us?"

He gave an elegant shrug. "Even if they would, it's unlikely my people would trust them. The humans never seem to remember our shared history, and yet the fae never forget."

We sat in silence for a long moment. If we could achieve such a thing, we could ask the other kingdoms for help. There had to be some kind of deal we could strike in return.

Finally, I sighed.

"How do we take the barrier down?"

"That is a conversation we should have when others can join us. I have a feeling it is only a matter of time before this conversation is cut short. You should ask your other questions now."

Was this because he wouldn't be under a blood vow the next time I asked the question, or because we truly were running out of time? Either way, I recognized the stubborn set to his jaw. I'd certainly seen his brother wear it more than once.

Fine.

"Tell me about the amulets."

Conreth angled his head. "I'm assuming Lorian hasn't told you about the loss of our family's amulet."

"No."

He sighed. "He will be…angry that I interfered. But—" a faint smile touched his mouth "—I'm currently angry at him too. And perhaps one day he'll thank me."

He paced, as if it was taking everything in him to resist his memories. Finally, he took his seat once more, gesturing at the chair in front of him. "This will take some time."

I sat. Conreth's gaze grew distant.

"My people don't often talk about this time. Especially Lorian. Of all of us…" His voice trailed off, and he pinned me with his stare, his eyes hard. "But I want you to understand just what Regner did to the fae. It wasn't only the loss of our amulet that did so much damage to our people. It was the loss of our ability to trust those we loved. The loss of some of our most precious souls."

Several men walked past the tent, voices loud, weapons clanging. Conreth raised his hand, and it was suddenly entirely quiet, our tent encased in some kind of silence ward.

"The amulets allow my people to share power. To

bolster our forces when necessary, to heal our sick, and to take power from those of us with more than enough to spare and share it during lean times. Our father wore his amulet every day, conscious of what had happened to the other two amulets. Of how they had been stolen from us—and how our people had been too arrogant to see Regner as a true threat until it was too late."

So, the first amulet we'd found was actually the last to have been lost.

"Can anyone free the power from the amulet?"

"Regner has been slowly leeching power from the amulets, but they require fae blood in order to release all the power at once. This is perhaps the only reason the human king hasn't yet laid waste to this continent."

A fine tremor took up residence in my hands, and I shoved them into my lap. I had no doubt that if Regner ever found enough power, he would completely eradicate the fae and hybrids from this continent. He had to be stopped.

"What happened when Lorian took the power from the amulet? Did he take it all?"

Conreth's lips twitched. "No. My brother would never take what isn't his. The power automatically dispersed to those it originally belonged to."

That meant Lorian was naturally that powerful. It was difficult to reconcile that knowledge with the man who'd been in my bed in his human form last night. And yet I knew deep in my bones that Lorian would never become like Regner. He didn't thirst for power.

"What do you know of the sleeping spiders?" Conreth asked.

I blinked at the sudden question. "They're believed to be a myth. We play...played King's Web in my village. According to legends, one of Sabium's distant ancestors broke the minds of children and slipped them into foreign courts. They were called sleeping spiders, and when a specific phrase was whispered in their ear, they were awakened...completely under the king's control."

Conreth shook his head. Perhaps at the fact that humans had made a card game out of a myth so horrific. "They're not just stories. And before we were at war with Regner, his grandfather did, indeed, learn how to slip his so-called spiders into our courts."

"How?"

"Some believe he used the same ancient text Regner used to create the barrier, passing the knowledge down to his son, who eventually passed it to Regner."

When precious children couldn't be trusted not to grow into adults that would kill and maim for a foreign court...what did that do to a culture? Especially one with fertility rates as low as the fae, where every child was celebrated.

"My father was the eldest of two," Conreth said. "He ruled as king, and his brother Astraus was his best friend."

My heart stuttered at the horror that gleamed in the fae king's eyes.

"My uncle used to say he fell instantly in love the first time he met my aunt. She was a hybrid. When the fae love…we love deeply and unreservedly. Our emotions are stronger and *wilder* than either humans or hybrids, and my uncle adored my aunt with everything in him. When the first amulet went missing…the king wasn't told until far too late. The family responsible for keeping that amulet safe was humiliated by their failure, and instead of alerting my father, they covered it up. But by the time the second amulet was stolen, my father knew what was happening. He would have done *anything* to protect the third amulet. So Regner had to try something new."

Conreth's words were flat, almost bored. But his hand tightened around the arm of his chair.

"He got to your uncle."

"No. He got to my aunt. We didn't know this, but he'd ensured Eirathia was kidnapped as a child. Your people were already in ruins—scattered and hiding. No one would have noticed yet another hybrid missing. There are…ways to see the future. To learn who she would marry. He used a powerful seer."

"He knew she would be married to your uncle."

"Yes. And he took her when she was still small enough that she could be shaped. Molded. Created into one of his *spiders*."

Bile burned up my throat. "He waited," I choked out. "He must have waited years, until they met."

Conreth's eyes met mine. "He waited until they had children. Until even while the war raged, they were *happy*. And then he unleashed her."

"What happened?"

"There are herbs that cause madness, even for the fae. Eirathia began lacing my uncle's food with those herbs, along with the barest amount of fae iron. He began to weaken. His mind began to break. He could sense something was seriously wrong with his wife, and that knowledge pricked at him, pushing him even closer to madness. Regner knew it wasn't Eirathia who would be close enough to my father to kill him and take the amulet. It was Astraus. My father—so distracted by Regner's continued attacks—didn't notice."

I couldn't understand what this had to do with Lorian. Conreth gave me a faint smile. "To truly understand Lorian, you have to know our history." He stretched out his legs. "My aunt continued to work on my uncle. But there was something Regner hadn't counted on."

"What was it?"

"They weren't just husband and wife. They were mates. An incredibly rare occurrence, but one that meant Eirathia eventually managed to stop lacing my uncle's food—Regner's dark magic unable to override the soul-deep love she had for him. And that was when Regner struck. He had their children taken. My cousins were young, even by fae standards. Regner told my aunt and uncle they would get their children back when they gave him the amulet."

"He would never have returned them," I said.

Conreth nodded. "But my uncle's brain was muddled. He believed this was his chance. He would take the amulet and use the power to kill Regner once and for all."

"Fuck."

Conreth nodded. "Exactly. My uncle was trusted, so when he began visiting various courts throughout the fae lands, they believed him when he said he wanted to ensure a unified response to the threat Regner presented."

No wonder the fae refused to trust one another now. They couldn't communicate, and when they did, that communication was based on a lie.

"What did he do instead?"

"Regner had used the book to magically alter many oceartus stones. So they would slowly drain those around them of power. He sent the stones to my uncle, and Astraus placed them in each of the courts.

"Then came the night of his betrayal. Astraus used a heavy sleeping tonic to lace all the food in the castle. He stole the amulet from around his brother's neck and used a forbidden spell to activate the oceartus stones, draining some of the most powerful fae in our lands. That power was transferred to the amulet, as was my father's power. My uncle then went from fae to fae in that castle, the amulet taking everything we had to give. When he got to Lorian, my brother woke."

My heart thundered in my chest. Even knowing Lorian had survived that night and so many more didn't help.

Conreth sighed. "He'd skipped dinner, choosing to play-fight with one of our nanny's children instead. When he opened his eyes, his uncle was standing over him, the amulet in his hand."

I pictured the Taking ceremonies I'd witnessed in the villages and how the babies had screamed and screamed. The blood drained from my face. "He was awake when his uncle took his power."

"Yes. Lorian loved Astraus. And my uncle had a soft spot for the boy who reminded him of himself—the second-born son. It must have killed him to look Lorian in the eye and take his power. I know it hurt Lorian. But he never spoke a word about it."

My heart ached for that young boy, who'd been conscious and aware when his uncle betrayed him.

"He learned young that no one was to be trusted," Conreth said, clearly following my thoughts. "My uncle took the amulet to Regner, my aunt at his side."

"The children?" I whispered.

"Already dead." Conreth's eyes glinted. "Regner displayed their broken bodies for all to see."

I closed my eyes, attempting to block out the image. It didn't help, and my hands shook with my rage. "Your uncle attacked."

"Yes. But he was weakened—the herbs and fae iron had worked, making him slow, ensuring he couldn't trust his own mind. Even with all the power in that amulet, it still takes someone strong, with enough power of their own, to wield it. And even though my aunt had managed to cease poisoning him, much of the damage remained. They fought on the outskirts of a city called Valtana. What my uncle didn't know, was that Lorian had followed them."

Even knowing Lorian had survived didn't help. My heart still pounded in my chest. "He saw your cousins."

Conreth nodded. "Lorian saw everything. He saw my uncle, bloated with power but out of his mind. He saw my aunt, immediately killed by a bolt of fae iron to the heart. And he saw Regner use the power of the other two amulets to kill my uncle and take the final amulet.

"My father had woken to find the castle asleep as if dead, the amulet gone, and Lorian nowhere to be found. He managed to rouse my mother, and they tracked the amulet to Valtana. But it was a trap. Regner's men had created a device filled with fae iron. When it exploded, my parents perished—already weakened by the loss of their power and the sleeping draught."

My eyes stung. "And Lorian?"

"Our father shielded him with his body, but it was still somewhat miraculous that he survived. When residents of Valtana finally approached, they found nothing but the dead—and a young fae boy still sparking with lightning. Lorian had tried to attack Regner, you see. And even with most of his power gone, he was still a force to be reckoned with. Regner and his men had used most of the power they could drain from the amulet and had been forced to flee."

"And anyone who arrived from Valtana found the Bloodthirsty Prince waiting, unharmed."

Conreth sighed. "Yes. Regner made sure to encourage those rumors. He made it seem as if Lorian—who was still a boy—had come to the city of his own accord, simply to destroy it. And Lorian didn't exactly help himself—

he was furious at the residents of the city for not coming sooner. For not helping his family. He roared at them until my father's best friend arrived and carried him away."

My eyes burned. Lorian had faced all of this as a small child. I opened my mouth, but Conreth sighed, his gaze on his hands.

He lifted his gaze. "I believe it is your turn to answer some of my questions."

I nodded.

"Who did you believe Lorian was when you first met him?"

I frowned. "No one. I believed he was a mercenary. I thought they all were."

He angled his head, as if even with the blood vow, he still couldn't quite believe it. "You had no idea he was fae?"

"No." My mouth opened, and I continued speaking, the vow demanding more. "I spent my life in small human villages. Lorian didn't look much like a merchant—and he didn't travel with a caravan of goods to sell. All of them looked dangerous and heavily armed, leading me to believe they were mercenaries."

"And in the castle?"

"I'm not sure I understand your question."

He narrowed his eyes at me. "When you realized Lorian was also in the castle, what did you believe he was doing?"

"At first, I believed he was there to kill someone close to the king. Perhaps to discover some information.

When I learned he was looking for something, I decided it must be incredibly valuable."

He seemed to accept that, folding his hands together on the table in front of him. "At what point did you realize he wasn't a mercenary?"

I thought back. "I don't know," I told him honestly. "But I didn't think he was fae."

Conreth's eyes widened almost imperceptibly, and he waved his hand, gesturing for me to continue speaking.

"Truthfully, I was mostly focused on finding a way to save my best friend. And then on freeing all of the hybrids in that dungeon. When I gave it any thought—which wasn't often—I assumed Lorian was also one of the corrupt. Like I was. And that he was working for someone with an interest in protecting the corrupt."

The look Conreth gave me made it clear he wondered how it was possible to be that stupid. I refused to allow my cheeks to heat. I didn't give him permission to make me feel small. In fact, it was to my benefit if he underestimated me.

"And tell me, how do you feel about the fae now?"

I chose my words as carefully as the vow would allow.

"In Eprotha, we're told the fae are vicious and that you want us dead or enslaved. But that's not what I've seen. Your biggest problem when it comes to my people hasn't been outright cruelty. It has been indifference and a failure to act."

Conreth's mouth opened slightly, and our eyes met.

"You don't hold back, do you?"

I pinched the bridge of my nose, suddenly tired. "No. Was it your father or grandfather who decided not to help the hybrids?"

"Our wards were open to your people, provided your queen still had the hourglass in her possession. A loophole one of my ancestors had created and no one had noticed. When Regner took the hourglass, your people were unable to get through our wards. They scattered. Once the fae realized what had happened, it was too late."

I let that sink in. I could see it. Could imagine the hybrids running for their lives, only to realize they had nowhere to go.

"Mistakes were made," Conreth said into the silence.

"And when the fae began to realize what had happened to the hybrids?"

"We took who we could, but...some of the fae remember a time before the hybrids separated from us. Many of those fae are now powerful, half-wild, and can't be trusted not to attack based on old wounds. Hence why this camp was created."

Taking a deep breath, I raised my gaze.

"And Crawyth?"

He smiled. "The question," the fae king said, "is why you didn't listen when Lorian told you he didn't destroy the city?"

Ah. So he knew I'd been asking about that. My mind raced as I attempted to figure out who had overheard me talking to either Asinia, Galon, or Lorian himself.

"That is between Lorian and me."

Conreth held up his hand, still stained with blood. "No, it's not."

The vow tightened around my throat, and I sucked in a breath. "He lied to me about who he was. I need proof he's not lying to me again. Because it's more than just me at risk if I'm wrong about him."

Conreth merely nodded. We were likely running out of time.

"What will it take for you to ally with me?" I asked.

"Show me your people have rallied behind you. That they'll fight in your name. Including those who are still hidden in your kingdom. Find a way to make the Gromalian king turn on Regner, and we just may have a fighting chance. But I will not risk my people in a war we cannot win. If necessary, I will find a way to get the two other amulets, shore up my borders, and wait."

I stared at him, my stomach churning at the horror of it all. "You would do that?"

"A ruler's first duty is to their own people. This is something you will need to learn—and quickly."

I swallowed down the vicious response waiting on the tip of my tongue.

"I will be sending Lorian away within the next few days," Conreth said casually.

Every muscle in my body seized up in instant refusal. "Why?"

"He has rested. But it is time for him to get back to work. I have a task for him elsewhere in my kingdom."

Did he truly? Or was Conreth separating us because it pleased him to do so?

Conreth watched me, a warning glint in his eyes. This was why he'd told me Lorian had committed treason. So I would know exactly what Lorian would be risking if he ignored his brother's order and came with me.

And while Conreth might forgive his brother once, it was unlikely Lorian would escape repercussions a second time if he were to choose me.

I needed to travel to both the hybrid kingdom and Gromalia. I needed to find the hourglass and give it to our people. And I would have to do it without Lorian. I thought I'd resigned myself to that fact, and yet knowing there was absolutely no way Lorian could come with me...

It turned out I hadn't truly accepted it. But I was going to have to.

Dare I ask Conreth about the location of the hourglass while he was compelled to tell me the truth? If I did, he would know I knew about it. He'd know I was going after it and that I knew the fae were aware of where it was and yet hadn't told me.

No. It was too risky. When we went for the hourglass, we had to do it without any warning.

"It is my turn to ask questions now," Conreth said. "What is it you're keeping from me as you sit there so quietly?"

My throat closed up, the mark burned into my palm, and I only had a single moment to reach deep.

"I'm thinking you're incredibly condescending—verging on patronizing. I'm wondering if it's a trait you were born with or one you grew into as you ruled for so long."

Conreth stared at me, as if I were a new kind of bug he'd never seen before.

My cheeks burned as if they'd been set alight.

He threw his head back and laughed. I hadn't expected it from the cold king, and I jolted.

"I can see why Lorian is so amused with you," he said. I watched him.

I had to study these men who had ruled this continent for so long. I had to analyze their every move, understand their actions, their mistakes, their *thoughts*.

And I had to learn how to beat them.

I gave Conreth a sweet smile. "It really annoys you that Lorian cares for me, doesn't it?"

All humor disappeared from his expression. "What makes you believe that?"

"You've gone out of your way to make it clear I'm nothing more than a passing fancy to your brother. Nothing more than an *amusement*. It makes me wonder why—if this is the case—you feel the need to share it with me. That's a question, by the way. Why *are* you so irritated by my relationship with your brother?"

Conreth looked like he'd tasted something bitter. Clearly, the blood vow was now making him answer too. I was small enough to enjoy that.

"Because in all these years, my brother has been

committed to two things. Our people and my crown. Within days of knowing you, he was making decisions that prioritized you—whether he would admit such a thing or not. Never before has he disregarded an order the way he did when he brought you here. That makes you dangerous, Nelayra Valderyn. Dangerous not just to my brother, but to my people."

We stared at each other for a long moment. I could see the truth in his cold eyes. The fae king had decided I was a threat. And our conversation had shed plenty of light on what Conreth did to those he considered threats.

A huge body burst into the tent, breaking whatever Conreth had done to block out the noise of the camp. I jerked, sucking in a breath. Lorian's hand slid to my wrist, and he hauled me out of my chair, wedging his body between mine and Conreth's.

He was in his fae form, his power twisting around him like a living thing. I stepped to the side, taking in his expression—pure, unrelenting wrath—and his eyes—cold and empty. Lorian looked at his brother as if he was the enemy.

Conreth merely held up his hand as several guards burst into the tent. One of them was covered in blood, and the fae king gave his brother a long-suffering look.

"Really, Lorian?"

"This conversation is over," Lorian snarled, and I sucked in a breath as the blood vow mark disappeared from my palm.

Lorian spun on me, his gaze dropping to my hand.

He slowly turned that gaze to the knife on the table. With another deadly look at his brother, he wrapped his arm around my shoulders and pulled me close, herding me toward the tent exit. The guards stayed in place for a long moment, and the scent of lightning filled the air.

"Lorian," I choked out, but Conreth must have given some signal, because the guards parted.

"We will speak later, brother," Conreth said. Lorian ignored him, and fresh fear shuddered through me.

13

The Boy

*D*uring *the day, the boy would escape the keen eyes of whoever had been tasked with watching him and would roam the castle instead, finding each hidden corridor and secret tunnel.*

There, he would listen as the adults discussed what to do. As they whispered about plans Regner had been willing to wait centuries to put into action, and what the loss of the last amulet—and so much of their power—meant for the fae.

Slowly, the boy came to understand just what had happened.

He was still mourning his family. His father with his booming laugh. His mother with her gentle hands. His aunt and uncle and cousins, all of them dead.

But the fae were planning for war.

They spoke of villages slaughtered, of a human king who had somehow tricked his people, stealing their power.

So, he asked his brother just how

the human king had achieved such a thing.

Conreth had sighed. "Eavesdropping, were you?"

The boy just stared sullenly at him, waiting.

"Regner has been paying close attention to the way people behave. To their thoughts and fears. Particularly when those people are struggling to survive."

The boy frowned, confused, and Conreth waved his hand. "The way someone worships their gods—and the gods they choose to worship—is a personal choice for most. But a clever ruler will use religion to play on their emotions. Their desires. And their fears. They will promise either eternal happiness or the avoidance of suffering— here or in the afterlife. You will find it is surprisingly easy for someone to use a population's fear of the unknown— and their poor education—to control them with lies."

"But I don't understand. We're not hunting humans. And the gods aren't keeping us from their borders. The humans came for us."

"Humans have always been wary of fae. We're stronger, longer-lived, more powerful. They've always wondered when we would become a threat. And Regner used this wariness, stoking it into fear to confirm that they should be afraid."

"It's not fair."

His eyes flashed. "No, it's not. But it won't be forever, Lorian. One day, the humans will understand."

Time dragged on. The boy reached seven winters, and then eight. The small amount of power his uncle had left him continued to grow as he matured. He was big for his age. Fast and clever. While the court had a natural cautiousness of the prince—and his wicked temper—they also began to respect him.

Others his age were drawn to him. He was often found brawling with everyone from the courtiers' sons to the stable hands. He cared nothing for propriety or rules about who he should be spending time with, and the fae loved him for it.

Lorian reached nine winters. He didn't see his brother as often anymore. And when he did, Conreth was often watching him with a strange look on his face.

Until one night, when Conreth came to his rooms. Something that hadn't occurred for years.

"You're sending me away," the boy said. He wasn't stupid. He'd heard the whispers.

"It's for your own protection," Conreth said.

"Father would never have sent me away."

Shame flickered in the king's eyes, but it was gone in an instant. "Father isn't here. I am, Lorian. And this has to happen."

"Why?"

"You're too fast and too strong to be trained here. Your power is dangerous. If you stay, you could hurt someone. But there's someone who can help you."

All the boy heard was that he was too much. Too much, and yet not enough.

"You're special, Lorian. You could do incredible things for this kingdom. For me. But you need to be trained."

"Who will train me?"
"His name is Galon."

PRISCA

Lorian hauled me with him, marching away from the tent.

"I'd ask what you were thinking, but you can't have been thinking at all if you'd meet with my brother alone under a blood vow," he snarled.

I threw out my foot and tripped him. Even with his natural fae grace, Lorian stumbled, shot me an irritated look, and regained his footing. At some point while he'd charged out of the tent, he'd regained his human glamour. Part of me mourned the loss of his true form.

"You shouldn't have gotten involved," I muttered. Conreth had already made it clear he wasn't happy with whatever Lorian felt for me.

Incredulous silence. I waited him out.

"I owe my brother everything," he finally growled. "But that doesn't mean I'll tolerate him playing his games with you."

I opened my mouth, but Tibris and Demos fell into step with us, clearly eager to hear all about Conreth.

"What happened?" Demos demanded.

I glanced around. There were too many people this close to the tents, and I jerked my head toward the wide, grassy expanse near the camp entrance—far enough from the guards that we wouldn't be overheard.

All of us were silent until we were gathered in the empty space, forming a loose circle. "We discussed the continents across the sea, the fact that I haven't yet convinced the Gromalian king to join us or visited the hybrid kingdom, the reason Regner was able to get the last amulet…" I let my voice trail off and glanced at Lorian, who looked as if he'd swallowed something bitter. We'd talk about the rest of that discussion later.

All three of them were watching me expectantly, and I cleared my throat. "We'll meet with Conreth and his people again to discuss the barrier."

"The barrier?" Tibris asked.

Demos glanced at him. "I'll tell you what I know of it," he said. "I want to get something to eat anyway."

A fae woman I didn't recognize was walking toward us. Everyone turned quiet. She sidled up next to Lorian, murmured a few words too low for me to hear, handed him a note, and slipped away.

He opened the message, and his eyes met mine. Despite his dark mood, I caught the hint of sympathy.

My gut clenched. "Tell me."

"The spy I sent to watch your cousin was killed. Your cousin left a note on the body. A note addressed to you."

My hand trembled as I reached out and took it.

Demos stared at me. "You sent someone looking for

our cousin? The only other contender for the throne? Are you mad?"

"You didn't want to talk about him at the castle. I needed to learn what I could."

"I didn't want to talk about him because his parents are the reason our kingdom was lost!"

My lungs seized, and Demos bared his teeth at me. "They wanted the throne, *Prisca*. And once their precious son was born—with time magic—they figured they could take it. So, they worked with Regner. They lowered the wards surrounding our kingdom and left the hybrids to die. And they're the reason why our people are dead."

He was talking about the actions of our cousin's parents. Our aunt and uncle.

"How old was he?"

Silence.

"How old, Demos?"

"Twelve winters."

"And you'd immediately judge him as the same as his parents?"

"He's the only challenger to your throne!" His expression turned cold. "But that's the point, isn't it? You're hoping he'll be the backup. That your people will prefer him. And you can hand the whole royal situation over and disappear somewhere."

"That's not what this is."

Not anymore. At least…not exactly.

The look Demos gave me cut to the bone. "I don't believe you." He turned and walked away, his shoulders stiff, and I pressed the heels of my hands to my burning eyes.

Demos was right. The man had murdered Lorian's spy and used his body to send a message. Clearly, he wasn't an option. I ripped open the note and went still.

Dearest cousin

Spies are unnecessary. If you'd like to talk, I'm more than willing to meet.

- Zathrian

That was it? He killed a man and offered a meeting?

I lifted my gaze and handed the note back to Lorian, letting my eyes wander over the bustling camp surrounding us. "If he'd noticed the spy, Zathrian could have simply used him as a messenger to get this back to me. Killing him is a threat. Demos was right."

Tibris angled his head. "You couldn't have known that without all the information."

"And now a man is dead. Can you…check on Demos?"

Just weeks ago, my brothers had loathed each other. Now, Tibris nodded. "It'll be all right, Pris." He wandered away, and I met Lorian's eyes.

I'd gotten one of his people killed. "I'm—"

"You couldn't have seen this coming. I didn't see it coming," he said, rage burning in his eyes. "If I'd judged the situation accordingly, I would have sent someone with offensive magic." He crumpled the note. "What else did you talk to my brother about, Prisca?"

"He told me about what happened to your aunt and uncle. About the amulet."

His expression shuttered. "Did you learn everything you needed to know?" His voice was blank, but I didn't miss the bitterness coating his words.

"I'm sorry, Lorian." I was sorry for what had been done to him as a child. For the fact that he'd woken up to find his uncle taking his power. And that he'd seen his family slaughtered. I wouldn't…couldn't be sorry for the fact that I'd asked.

He just nodded. Then he turned and walked away.

LORIAN

"You're angry," Galon mused, his sword slicing through the air. I met his swing and turned into it, aiming a kick at his gut. He neatly sidestepped. "Too slow. Do you resent Prisca for needing to know exactly who she's dealing with?"

I bit down on my tongue—and the bitterness that still lingered there.

"Ah," Galon said, moving brutally fast. "You wish for blind trust, even as you refuse to give the same to *anyone*."

His sword sang through the air. I slid back just in time, watching several locks of my hair fall to the ground. Galon sent me one of his rare smiles.

"It's none of your business."

"It is my business when you look like you swallowed something foul and Prisca is drifting around this camp like she's sleepwalking."

"This is the most you've spoken in years. And my personal life is what you choose to waste your words on?"

Galon raised an eyebrow. "Your piss-poor mood tells me everything I need to know."

"And what would that be?"

"Prisca is asking too many questions. You know she asked me about Crawyth, and she obviously asked your brother about the amulet. You're displeased that the hybrid heir would choose to make sure you weren't the one who attacked that city—even if her heart believes you—so she can confidently tell her people that the Bloodthirsty Prince she's currently allied with wasn't the one to kill her parents."

Displeased? I wasn't *displeased.* Galon took my inattention as an opportunity to stomp on my foot and slam his elbow into my face.

"Fuck!" My nose exploded with pain. Broken. Again. It would need to be set.

My vision narrowed, my hand tightening on my

sword. Galon merely waited. "You're fighting sloppy," he said. "I haven't caught you with that trick since you'd just seen twenty winters." He threw down his sword and stepped close. "You would *never* blindly trust someone with the fate of your people—let alone someone rumored to have killed them in the past. So why would you expect it of her?"

Galon jerked his head to my left, and my gaze met Prisca's. She was pale—even her lips drained of color as she watched us, her hands clenched on the rail in front of her. My gut twisted. There was nothing I loathed more than seeing her hurt.

Several hybrids and fae were glancing between us. Some of the color returned to Prisca's face, and she turned, walking away.

Galon leaned close. "You've been doing everything you can to prepare her so she can take that throne if she wants it. Punishing her for stepping into that role is unfair."

"You're right."

"I know." Galon nodded. "Now go do something about it."

I let out a huff of laughter. Prisca had just been wounded by both me and her brother. I'd walked away, assuming that if I needed time, she likely did too. But she may have assumed I'd abandoned her instead.

I needed to make it right.

A quick stop to a healer to get my nose fixed—my wildcat would be *displeased* otherwise—and then I went searching for her.

Unfortunately, Prisca wasn't in her tent. She wasn't training, and Asinia claimed not to know where she was, although from the narrow-eyed stare she sent me, she likely knew and wouldn't break, even under torture. The dull edge of panic sliced at me.

I located Demos's tent, but he was sitting on his cot, idly handling a dagger. Tibris stood in front of him, arms crossed. Clearly, I was interrupting some kind of argument.

"Where's Prisca?" I demanded.

They both glanced at me. Demos's eyes were still hard, while Tibris managed to offer me a shrug. "I don't know," Tibris said. "Do we need to be concerned?"

She wouldn't leave. It was likely she just needed some time alone. "You need to be careful what you say to her," I addressed Demos softly. "She worships you."

Demos gave me a cold look. "Stay out of my relationship with my sister."

I showed him my teeth, and he bared his own in a challenging smile. "Seems like you can't find her. What did *you* say to her, Bloodthirsty One?"

Prisca already had one brother. She didn't need a spare. I took a step toward him, and Tibris slapped his hand against my chest.

"What Demos doesn't understand," Tibris said, giving the other man a dark scowl, "is that Prisca was raised to be terrified of her power. She was raised to never tell anyone what she could do."

"We all were," Demos bit out.

"Not like Prisca," I snarled.

Demos let out a low growl. Tibris ignored him, speaking directly to me. "She told you about the family?"

"Yes."

Demos went still. "Which family?"

Tibris filled him in while I paced the tent like a caged animal. When Tibris was finally done, Demos cursed. "The woman she called *Mama* allowed a family to die in front of her? As a warning?"

"That was just one example," Tibris said, his voice tight. "Prisca doesn't remember most of them, but they're there, buried and waiting. She only remembered that family because she recognized the assessor. And it's likely that my father was working on her memory, attempting to mitigate what my mother had done."

I closed my eyes, wishing I could strangle both of her parents. "So she would forget most of the worst memories, but the terror would remain." This was why Prisca craved normalcy almost as much as I craved *her*.

"Yes," Tibris said, turning to Demos. "So you may not understand why she needs stability. Why she's so afraid of people knowing about her power. Of being a leader. But you don't get to hold that against her. My mother was working on Prisca for almost her entire life."

Demos buried his head in his hands. I could spare the tiniest drop of sympathy for him. Although I still wanted to slam my fist into his jaw.

Enough of this. Closing my eyes, I attempted to think

like my wildcat.

Considering her discomfort with water, she loved staring at it. Whenever we'd argued while traveling, I'd usually found her near a lake or river.

Turning, I stalked out of the tent.

"Good luck," Tibris muttered.

I found Prisca sitting on an overturned log by the river. She was alone, her shoulders hunched, her chin resting on one fist. She looked fragile. Breakable. My chest clenched.

"I thought it would be easier if I asked your brother," she said, still staring into the water. "You clearly didn't want to—or couldn't—talk about it. Don't worry, he didn't tell me anything about Crawyth."

I bit back the words that wanted to flood from my mouth. But she must have sensed them, because she still refused to look at me.

Enough.

Grabbing her shoulder, I swung her toward me. I caught her chin before she could pull away. Tears caught on the ends of her lashes, and my gut twisted. "Don't cry. Gods, don't cry."

She sniffed, glowering up at me. "Why? Are my *feelings* too much for you?"

"No. Because I want to gut anyone who made you cry. And I don't want to have to impale myself on my own sword."

Her mouth curved into a reluctant smile. "You're not as amusing as you think you are."

I leaned down and nuzzled her cheek. Surprisingly, she allowed it. "I don't like to talk about that time."

"I know. I'm sorry."

"Stop apologizing. Even though I don't talk about it…I'm glad you know. About my uncle."

"What did you mean when you said you owed your brother everything?"

I pulled back enough to look at her. "After our parents were murdered, he kept me at the castle with him. My nightmares were so crippling, eventually he allowed me to sleep in his chambers. He'd tell me stories until I fell asleep. When he sent me away to train with Galon… it was difficult for him."

Prisca's gaze was steady on mine. Her usually expressive face was carefully blank. For once, I had no idea what she was thinking.

"What is it?"

She attempted a smile. "Tell me about that time."

I shrugged. "The training camp was brutal. Galon had already seen one hundred and twenty winters. I was young, cocky, and certain that fighting his students would be just like brawling with Conreth's guards."

She smirked at me. "I'm guessing it wasn't."

"No. The camp was located in the foothills of the Minaret Mountains—a freezing, dangerous place. I didn't exactly make any friends the first few winters. I was targeted for multiple reasons—the fact that I was the prince, and the rumors of my actions the night my parents were killed. Each time I was close to giving up, when all I wanted to do was hide beneath my bed, something would arrive from Conreth. Something small. A letter. Perhaps a new knife. Encouraging words."

Her face had gone pale. I studied her. "What is it, wildcat?"

"Nothing. I just don't like the thought of you being there so young. How old were the others?"

I shrugged. "Most had seen at least fourteen or fifteen winters. I knew young my power and speed were both a blessing and a curse. It had to be harnessed so I could protect our kingdom."

Prisca cupped my cheek with her hand. She was touching me again, and the tension inside my chest began to unwind. I caught her hand with mine, holding it in place.

"I want to tell you about Crawyth." My gut burned at my own words, but Prisca stroked her thumb over the tops of my knuckles. And the invisible rope around my throat loosened slightly.

"I'm sure you've asked yourself what reason the fae would have to attack Crawyth?"

She nodded. "It never made sense to me. It never made sense to anyone. What happened?"

"Regner happened. He learned that the hybrids had made it a sanctuary of their own—your mother had made that happen. Even the priestesses were hybrids, and all of this was happening in his own kingdom. After the events the night my family was killed—and the way residents had found me on the outskirts of Valtana—Regner had been sure to keep rumors of the Bloodthirsty Prince alive.

"He fed stolen power to one of his own people who could harness lightning. It didn't matter that Regner's puppet couldn't use other elements like I could. Those who lived in Crawyth just saw buildings exploding. They saw the sky lit with lightning, and they saw a man who appeared to be fae, riding a dark horse. It was easy for them to believe it was me. But we had our own spies. One of them had warned Conreth of what Regner was planning."

Confusion flickered across Prisca's face. "Why didn't Conreth send his people?"

I'd asked myself the same question. And it killed me that I had no answer to give her. Once again, our people had failed hers. And even if I wasn't directly responsible for her parents' deaths, the fae could have prevented it.

Prisca's lips thinned at my silence. But she waved her hand at me to continue.

"I got there in time to witness the last of the destruction. The destruction happening in my name. Regner had used the reputation he'd created over and over, until I was known as a monster. A butcher. I found the impostor dressed like me, wielding less power at his best than I could at my weakest. We...fought. I attempted to shield the buildings around us from the worst of it. I could hear screaming. I knew the people were fleeing. I killed him." Satisfaction coated my words. I would kill him a thousand more times if I could. But he hadn't been the only one I'd killed.

Prisca squeezed my hand. I raised my head. It felt as if she was very far away. Her face was wet, and that jolted me back to the present moment.

"Don't cry."

"Shh. Tell me the rest, Lorian."

"When I pierced the impostor's wards, he threw his power out in a wide arc. He died, but I'd dropped my ward. Regner still had most of my power, and I was drained. I couldn't hold the ward and attack. There was a child nearby." I could still see his face. It was burned into my memory. Into my nightmares.

"Oh, Lorian."

"He died instantly."

"It wasn't your fault."

Her instant denial grated on me. Prisca wasn't seeing me for who I truly was. It was one thing to be the kind of monster who hunted other monsters. Who shed blood so others didn't have to. But I was a monster who'd ended an innocent life.

I pulled my hand from hers and got to my feet. "He was about Demos's age, Prisca. If he'd been the one to die, would you still say the same? It could have been you that night, if you hadn't been taken." Just the thought made bile burn up my throat.

Prisca was silent for long enough that I finally turned back to her. Her eyes held such misery.

My chest was so tight I could barely breathe. "I'm sorry. The choice to go that night wasn't entirely about your people. It was also about ego. My reputation. And making Regner pay. Your parents died…"

"No, Lorian. I'm crying for *you*. You've held this for almost as long as I've been alive. And it wasn't the first time. Let me guess, once Regner's lackey was dead, people came out. They saw you. The real Bloodthirsty Prince."

I nodded.

"And it looked like you'd destroyed the city. Again. You didn't try to deny it."

"Conreth…he attempted to protect me when our parents died. But he was my brother. No one truly believed him. Eventually, it was decided that it was to our kingdom's benefit that our enemies believed I was truly the Bloodthirsty Prince."

"Who decided?"

"What do you mean?"

"Conreth decided, didn't he? He liked the idea of making you into a monster and pointing you at his enemies. He didn't care about what it would do to you to have everyone tremble at the thought of you coming for them."

I sighed. "It was a strategic move, wildcat. Regner likely regrets the reputation he created. Over the years, we've found his spies, stolen his most trusted advisers, and my reputation has given us access to information we wouldn't have otherwise had."

She glowered back at me. "I don't care."

"Prisca."

"I don't *care*, Lorian. His job was to protect you.

Instead, he sent you away at just nine winters old, all alone, throwing you the occasional treat to keep you loyal. Gods, I wish someone had saved you from him."

I stared at her. Strange emotions were warring inside me. Tenderness, fury, confusion. I wanted to block out her words, and yet I could also see the logic she was using. "That's not what he did."

She bared her teeth. "That's *exactly* what he did. He was your brother, and it was his job to put you first."

I sighed. To Prisca, the people she loved were everything. She couldn't comprehend making strategic decisions that would make their lives more difficult, even if it benefited her and her people. I would do everything I could to protect her from those decisions, even as I knew, by the end of this war, she would have to make them anyway.

The strange sickness that had been burning in my gut disappeared, and I pulled her into my arms.

I'd been my brother's monster for my entire life, for the good of our kingdom. I didn't regret it, but some part of me had mourned the man I might have become. A man who was gentle and tender and patient. A man who didn't burn to possess this woman.

She knew the worst parts of me, and instead of running, she was trembling against me. Trembling with rage. If she could, she would make my brother pay. He was her only hope for an ally, and she would hold this grudge. She would nurture it until the time was right. I knew her well enough to know that much.

My heart warmed. Prisca didn't understand my brother's actions because she was made of loyalty. If she chose to take her throne, those around her would try to change her. They would try to harden her. To make her into a monster like me.

I would do whatever it took to protect her from that.

"Who and what I am was solidified that night. I was the vicious Bloodthirsty Prince who destroyed Crawyth. And I've never cared about that title before now. I've used it to make my enemies cower, to make those who would threaten the fae lands run for their lives. I've never worried about the look of horror on a woman's face before. Until now."

She watched me, her eyes seeing more than they should. As they always did. "You cared. You just shut out that part of yourself."

I pulled her close and held her for a long moment. Eventually, I lifted my head. "The sooner I talk to him, the sooner he will leave." I wanted to get it over with, so I could spend more time with Prisca, just like this.

My hand found the back of her head, and I held her in place, taking her mouth. Gods, I'd missed this. She allowed it, opening for me, allowing my tongue to delve deep as my other hand pulled her close.

I pressed a kiss to her neck, enjoying the way her pulse thundered against my lips. "We'll continue this later, wildcat," I promised.

First, I needed to have a serious conversation with my brother.

14

LORIAN

My brother rarely wore his crown. And yet, he'd arrived at this camp in full regalia. That crown sat on the table in front of him now as he crossed his arms, surveying me with a frown.

"You seem changed."

"I haven't seen you for three years."

He shrugged. "We have gone longer without meeting."

He wasn't wrong. Conreth preferred to keep me away from the castle as much as possible. He said it pleased him to have his court wonder where exactly I was and what secrets I could be learning—both in his kingdom and elsewhere.

"You ignored my order." His voice was carefully neutral.

I just raised my eyebrow. "You told me to bring Prisca to the fae lands. I did."

He frowned, likely attempting to remember the exact wording in his letter. "I hadn't realized I would need to state my orders so plainly," he said coolly. "I've never needed to be exact before."

A reference to Prisca. I just waited.

"Tell me, what is it about this woman that makes you prioritize her? Why are you spending so much time training her?"

I needed to choose my words carefully. But by now, Conreth already knew how I felt about Prisca. "My priority remains our kingdom. But Prisca is fierce and brave and so incredibly loyal, that loyalty is going to get her killed one day, unless I can teach her how to stay alive."

Conreth stared at me. "I already give you more freedom than anyone else," he said. "If certain people were to learn you were ignoring my orders, they would expect consequences. And I would have no choice, Lorian. None."

Of course he would have a choice. "If your rule is so precarious that you're that reliant on *certain people*, you have greater problems than my choice to bring Prisca here first."

I saw the moment he decided to drop the subject. Not because he considered it closed, but because he wanted to change tactics.

"Where are we with the amulet?"

"My spies are still searching. There are rumors Regner has built several new residences—in an attempt to encourage us to split our attention. I believe we will find it in the north."

"Why?"

I shrugged one shoulder. "My instincts urge us to prioritize that location."

"Interesting. Instruct your spies to focus their attention to the north, then. In the meantime, I have a task for you," he said.

Now that we weren't discussing Prisca, Conreth's body language had relaxed. But his eyes were still hard. "What kind of task?"

"A group of wildkin has begun acting strangely in the southeast, close to the Gromalian border."

I took a seat across from him. "They're ancient, vicious fae who wrestle with insanity. Exactly how do you define the term 'acting strangely'?"

"Reports indicate a few of them have wandered across the border into Gromalia, only to return hours later."

I cursed. If the wildkin were leaving our lands, they were up to no good. Chances were high they were hunting humans, and if the Gromalian king found out, it would end any chance of an alliance with him.

"They have also been venturing into our villages. Several children told their parents they saw Xantheros when they were playing in the forest near their homes."

"They saw Xantheros, and he didn't decide they'd make a tasty snack?"

Conreth pinched the bridge of his nose. "The children were out of their minds with terror, Lorian. Something is going on with the wildkin, and we need to fix it. Since you're almost as savage as they are and they seem to respect you, I'm delegating the task to you."

I had no doubt there was a problem with the wildkin. Conreth wouldn't lie about that. But his timing was interesting. "And when do you want me to leave?"

"Two days from now. You may take your little friends with you."

I couldn't help the grin that stretched my mouth. Truthfully, it was more of a baring of teeth. "My *little friends* are the reason you're still wearing that crown," I said mildly. Together, we had fought off any challengers to Conreth's throne.

He waved a hand, but I knew him well enough to know when he was uncomfortable. Conreth had never understood the relationship between Galon, Marth, Rythos, Cavis, and me. For the first time, I felt truly sorry for him. How could he understand such brotherhood when those around him were little more than sycophants?

"Cavis will stay," I said. "I won't pull him from his family so soon."

"Take whomever you like. Just find out what is making the wildkin act so oddly."

He was waiting to see if I would announce I was taking Prisca. But I wouldn't drag my wildcat on a perilous journey simply because I wanted her with me. She could continue training with her brothers and the other hybrids. Could continue working on whatever plans she discussed when she met with them while I was busy. She'd be safe here. Cavis would watch over her. As would her brothers.

And Asinia was also becoming deadly with a bow and arrow.

"Fine," I said, getting to my feet. "Will that be all?"

Conreth swept his gaze over me. "You're different. I don't like it."

I'd spent a lifetime itching for his approval. And his words had the effect he was hoping for. Ignoring the sting of them, I turned, stalking out of his tent.

I found Prisca walking toward her own tent, an apple in her hand. Colors were suddenly brighter. The air smelled sweeter. I was beginning to loathe it when she was out of my sight. Especially with Conreth here.

Her brow creased. "What did Conreth say?"

"He needs me to go take care of something for a few days."

She didn't look surprised. But that might have been a flicker of disappointment in her eyes. Still, my instincts were roaring at me.

"What are you hiding from me, wildcat?"

She rolled her eyes. "This is going to shock you, Lorian, but not everything is about you."

And she went on the offensive. Definitely hiding something. Unfortunately, since we were in public, I couldn't exactly turn to my usual methods of finding the truth—as much as I enjoyed the thought of stripping off those tight leggings, bending her over the closest surface, and—

"Lorian?"

My gaze met hers, and she flushed, even as her

amber eyes heated. I herded her toward her tent. I needed to take a new approach. "Keep your secrets," I said. "I'm choosing to trust you, wildcat."

She instantly looked like I'd stabbed her in the gut. Oh yes, whatever she was keeping from me was something I wasn't going to like at all. So I twisted that knife.

"If there's one thing I know, it's that you would never betray me."

Her face turned ashen, and something dark wound through my gut. Whatever she was up to, she was practically radiating guilt. But her mouth firmed, and she rolled her shoulders, leveling me with a hard stare. "That's right," she said. "Don't try to manipulate me, Lorian. You won't like the outcome."

Just like that, I turned as hard as stone.

PRISCA

Lorian followed me into my tent. I dropped my apple on the empty plate on my small bedside table, no longer hungry.

He crowded me with his body, and I instantly responded to the furious energy radiating from him. My nipples hardened, and he caught me around my waist, lowering his head to whisper in my ear.

"Have you been keeping things from me, wildcat?"

I sucked in a shaky breath. "You've been keeping things from me too. It will always be like that between us." I hadn't meant for my voice to sound so mournful, and behind me, Lorian tensed.

"That's where you're wrong." He nipped at my earlobe, and I attempted to turn to face him. He merely slipped one arm around my waist, easily holding me in place. And my traitorous body responded to that too, enjoying the fact that I couldn't move. That he had all the power, and for just a little while, I had none.

I couldn't keep him, but I would enjoy this while I could. No longer would I push him away. Instead, I'd soak in every moment. Because one day, these memories would be all I had.

"My brother is dangerous, Prisca. If he has made some kind of deal with you…"

Distraction was my best choice. Besides, it would lead to somewhere pleasurable for us both. "Do you really want to talk about your *brother* right now?"

He chuckled, the sound dark, and I pressed my thighs together.

"Something you want, wildcat?"

I clamped my mouth shut, and he stripped my tunic over my head. The band holding my breasts in place disappeared a moment later, immediately replaced by his hands. I sighed, arching my back, silently begging for more.

"Filthy girl."

Heat pooled in my core. Lorian's fingers found my nipples, and he squeezed until I sucked in a breath. He slid one hand down my belly, beneath my leggings, and it was his turn to inhale. "Hmmm," he said, his voice hopelessly amused.

My cheeks blazed. I was still discovering new facets of my sexuality, and the fact that I enjoyed his orders, enjoyed his playing with me this way...

"I love how wet you get for me," he murmured in my ear, as if reading my mind. "Some days, it's all I can fucking think about."

Lorian removed his hand, pressing a gentle kiss to my cheek when I let out a mewl of disappointment. But he was already stripping my leggings from me, lifting me into the air so I could push them off my feet.

"I want to make you feel good," I said.

He shook his head. "I'm in a dangerous mood."

"I don't care."

"Another time, wildcat."

"No. Now." I met his eyes and watched that feral light enter them.

"Get on your knees."

I'd dropped before he finished speaking. His gaze blazed into mine.

"Open your mouth."

I raised my hand to undo his pants, but he shook his head. "No."

I'd never been filled with so much lust in my life. I squirmed, rubbing my thighs together in an attempt to get some relief, and he smiled. "You're perfect. Now open your fucking mouth."

I complied. He made me wait, mouth open, while he slowly pulled his pants down just enough for him to free his cock.

"Lick," he said.

It was difficult, not using my hands. From the lust burning in Lorian's eyes, that was exactly what he wanted. I had almost no experience with this, but it didn't seem to matter to him. He just waited, and the moment my tongue caressed the tip of his cock, he growled. I moaned at the taste of him, running my tongue along him, enjoying the low curse that rumbled from his throat.

I might enjoy handing him the power when we were together like this, but right now, *I* had the power, and it felt good.

So good, I slipped my hand down my stomach.

"No," Lorian said, burying his hand in my hair. "Suck."

He *was* in a dangerous mood. But I took a long moment to sweep my gaze over him—from his thick, muscular thighs, over the length of his cock, the slab of muscle he called a chest, and to his face.

Gods, that face.

Sometimes when I looked at him, my breath would catch in my throat. One moment, we would be fighting or traveling or laughing, and the next, I would stop, staring, hoping he wouldn't catch me entranced by the way his eyes gleamed in the sunlight or the sharp jut of his cheekbones when he scowled.

His gaze had turned strangely tender at whatever he saw on my face.

"The way you're looking at me is very interesting, wildcat," he murmured, and I blinked, my cheeks heating. If I wasn't careful, this man would see far too much.

So I lowered my head and took him into my mouth.

He stiffened, and I opened wider. He was large enough to make my jaw ache, but I slowly slid down him, my core heating as he let out a pleased, male sound. He pushed my hair away from my face, and I glanced up to find him staring at me.

Lorian's eyes heated, and a low growl rumbled from his chest as I took him deep. He sucked in a breath. "That's it."

He thrust gently at first, his hand in my hair holding me in place for him. "Eyes on me," he demanded, and I met his gaze, my eyes watering. His next thrust bumped the back of my throat, and I gagged. He did it again, hissing as I swallowed around him. "You're so fucking perfect."

I lifted my hand, using it with my mouth. His thighs tensed, and my own arousal burned hotter. My nipples were hard points, my legs shaking, and his eyes practically glowed with possessive hunger as he watched me take him deep.

"Enough," he snarled, and I blinked.

My head spun, and then I was in his arms as he bent me over the cot, urging me to my knees. His hand slid to my clit, gently caressing, and my muscles tightened.

"Already close, wildcat?" He removed his hand. I let out a string of curses, and he laughed.

"You're hiding something from me. Perhaps you shouldn't get to come."

I lost the ability to speak, and he laughed again. The wide head of his cock pushed inside me until it was all I could feel, my body stretching to accommodate him. Would I ever get used to his size?

I'd frozen, and he slipped his finger over my clit once more, the momentary pleasure allowing him to thrust fully inside me.

My breath caught, my body began to tremble, and he swept one hand down my back soothingly, before sliding it around to cup my breast, his thumb scraping over my nipple. I arched my back, and he made a pleased sound as the angle changed.

He hit something inside me that made my thighs clench. I was groaning now, my head hanging low as he pounded into me with long, rough strokes.

"More," I demanded, and he gave me more. More and more, until all I could do was bury my hands in my blanket and push back against him, begging in low groans.

"You make me insane," he growled in my ear, his huge hand sliding down to tease me, stroking my clit in time with his thrusts.

I sucked in a breath. "Don't stop."

"Never. It will be like this forever, wildcat," he rasped.

It wouldn't.

Lorian seemed to hear my silent thought, because he nipped my neck, stroking over my clit as his thick cock drove into me.

"Come," he demanded.

And I did. On and on it went, my climax sweeping through me as I shuddered in his arms. Distantly, I was aware of him growling his own pleasure, his hands holding me still as he spilled inside me.

PRISCA

I sat in The Hearth, chewing absently. As usual, there were eyes on me, but it felt as if there were fewer than usual. Lorian had left to find Galon, and I'd taken a quick detour to the only female healer in camp. She'd provided me with a tonic that would prevent conception, along with a handful of herbs. "One leaf a day," she'd told me.

"Prisca." Demos stood in front of my table, offering me a strained smile. "Can we talk?"

My stomach tightened, but we needed to clear the air. Still, I wasn't looking forward to the moment Demos realized the queen he hoped I'd be had never truly existed. All my potential had been snuffed out the night I was taken.

I nodded, taking my final bite. One of the cooks plucked my plate from the table with a smile.

Demos led me back toward the river. Only, instead of finding a rock to sit on, he kept walking until we were surrounded by a copse of trees. He'd obviously visited earlier, because a wide blanket was laying over a patch of grass in the shade. He gestured to the blanket. "Sit," he said.

I complied. My heart hurt when I looked at my brother. Something inside me fractured when I attempted to come to terms with the fact that I would never be who he wanted. I'd never be the queen he'd envisioned when he'd thought of the hybrid heir. I'd been his sister for weeks, and I was already failing at it.

"I'm sorry," we both said at the same time. My eyes stung, and Demos sat down next to me, close enough to touch.

"No, Prisca. Listen."

The name lay between us like a dead animal, and I opened my mouth, but he was already speaking.

"I talked to Tibris. Not just today, but while we were traveling. I was…desperate for stories about you. And he was kind enough to tell me what it was like growing up with you. I listened to what he said, and I listened to what he didn't say."

My mouth had turned dry. "And?"

"And I'd never really thought about what it was like for you—to be shown so clearly what it meant to use your power publicly. And then to need to use that power to save so many lives. I'd assumed that after what you did that night in the castle, you'd conquered any fears or reservations you might have had. But that's not how grief and terror work."

"You spent two years in a dungeon, Demos."

He pinned me with a hard stare. "And before that, I understood who and what I was. I knew about the king's lies, and after our parents died, I was brought up in relative safety with other hybrids."

Demos took my hand. I shook my head. "I don't think I can be who you need. I'm trying. I swear I am. But—"

"Stop. I never want you to feel like you're not enough for me. Gods, you were enough the moment you took my hand in that dungeon while Tibris was healing me. You're all heart. You'd die for the people you love, and in your mind, you're helping our people more by stepping down. I understand that, even if I don't agree with it."

Something fluttered in my chest. Something that felt a lot like hope. But I didn't trust it yet. "So, where do we go from here?"

"I'm your brother, and I'll always love you. I'm also your general, and that means I'm looking out for the best interests of our people. I believe *you're* in our people's best interest. But when all this ends, and our people are finally home, if you want to step down, I'll support you."

The lump in my throat was so large, I could barely breathe. "You will?"

His jaw was tight, but he nodded. "I'm planning to

show you that you can be an incredible queen," he warned me. "But if we get to the end of all this and you still want a quiet life, I'll do whatever it takes to make that happen for you."

My mouth opened, but I couldn't make a sound. Demos pulled me into his arms. "It will work out," he told me.

I let out a shuddering breath, and something inside me settled. "I'll do everything I can," I promised, my voice muffled. "No matter what it takes, we'll kill Regner."

"I know."

I pulled back and wiped at my face. This was the first time I'd been alone with Demos since I'd arrived. "There's something else I wanted to talk to you about."

"What is it?"

"They should be training together, Demos. The hybrids and the fae."

He nodded. "Agreed."

I hadn't expected that. But Demos was a constant surprise.

"And living together," I said.

He gave a rueful shake of his head. "That's unlikely to happen."

I angled my head. "When I met Lorian and the others, I thought they were vicious mercenaries. Living and traveling with them allowed me to see them as real people. I got to see Rythos's gentleness, Marth's humor, Galon's bravery. I've seen the way the fae and hybrids interact. They look past one another, as if the others don't exist."

"And you think forcing them to spend more time together will help?" Demos looked unimpressed, but I *knew* this was a good idea.

"Fae and hybrids who aren't in a family group are currently sharing tents with someone around the same age, is that right?"

"Yes."

"I want them sharing tents with one another."

Demos raised an eyebrow. "It's not going to go well."

"No. In the short term, it's going to be bad. But if the hybrids and fae end up as allies, they need to be able to trust one another. I want them living and training in mixed groups. No more split training sessions unless they're split by ability." It was going to be terrible. No one was going to like it. But if the hybrids and fae learned to trust one another, it could make a difference. It could be the deciding factor in whether we won this war.

"The order can't come from you," Demos said. I opened my mouth, and he held up his hand. "It will be bad enough that you allow it to happen once the order goes out. But we need the order to come from me and Hevdrin—Conreth's general."

I nodded. It made sense. I was still an outsider. Distrusted by most, and idolized by the rest. "Fine."

Demos studied me for another long moment. "This will be terrible in the short term." He gave me a sudden grin. "It's a good thing we won't be here to put up with the whining."

I let out a laugh, and his mouth twitched. "You're already thinking like a queen," he told me. "This is going to be easier than I thought."

I rolled my eyes at him, and he pointed at the blanket beneath us. "Lie down."

Raising my eyebrow, I did as he said. He lay next to me, and we stared up at the clouds. My heart twisted.

"I love the clouds," he'd told me once. *"I used to lie on the grass and watch them for hours. Especially when the sun was right about to set."*

When he'd taken that arrow to the chest, all I'd been able to think about was that he'd never get to do this again. That I'd never get to experience it with him. This was one of his favorite things to do, and he was sharing it with me.

We lay in silence, staring up at the wispy clouds. The sun, poised at the edge of the horizon, cast a warm, golden light, the clouds reflecting a soft gradient of colors. Shades of pink, purple, and orange intertwined, and a gentle breeze rustled the leaves of the trees nearby, their branches swaying.

I could suddenly breathe freely again. And I understood why Demos loved this so much. The sweet, earthy scent of the grass tickled my nose, while the sky turned ablaze with color and the sun slowly lowered.

"I love you," I said solemnly. "And if anyone tried to hurt you again, I would kill them."

Demos burst out laughing, the roar of it silencing the birds nearby.

I frowned. "I'm serious."

He let out a choked gasp, and I turned my head to scowl at him.

"I know you are," he chuckled. "I love you too." His hand reached for mine and squeezed.

The Queen

Sabium had chosen to take his dinner in his rooms each night recently. And he'd insisted I attend. This was my punishment for speaking during the hybrid's torture.

Thankfully, we ate in silence. He was reading a stack of parchment, while I numbed myself with wine.

A knock sounded on the door, and I suppressed a frown. These days, interruptions at dinner were rarely good news.

"Enter," Sabium said, his eyes on whatever he was reading. I itched to leaf through his messages.

Tymedes approached with a bow. I'd thought he would be dead by now, but he'd somehow managed to convince Sabium he was still worth keeping alive. "Ships from Daharak Rostamir's fleet have been seen approaching the Frosthaven Isles, Your Majesty."

Sabium went still. "How many ships?"

"At least one hundred."

"That pirate bitch is up to something," Sabium muttered.

"Excuse me, Your Majesty?"

Sabium pinned Tymedes with a hard stare. "Has the pirate *queen* been seen?"

"Not yet, Your Majesty."

"I want her dead, and I want her fleet flying under my banner. You told me this would happen months ago."

Tymedes swallowed but bravely raised his gaze. "Her fleet is large enough that it rivals ours. Her pirates know the waters surrounding our continent better than anyone else. This allows them to evade capture. She has also formed strategic alliances with smaller pirate groups, along with local military leaders and officials. Each time we are close to capturing her, someone tips her off."

"She was seen in Gromalian waters recently. Why did Eryndan not capture her?"

"According to rumors, they have an agreement of their own, Your Majesty."

My lips didn't curve. No amusement was evident on my face. I was much too experienced for that. And yet Sabium slowly looked at me anyway, as if he could *feel* such amusement.

I just stared back.

Sabium was likely wishing he'd understood just how much of a threat Rostamir would be before he created that barrier. Perhaps he was beginning to learn just how little most women appreciated being caged.

If *I* had planned in his place, I would have ensured

the pirate queen was either dead or tricked into traveling just outside of the barrier before I created it. The resulting chaos and lack of leadership would have ensured her pirates turned on one another. Then, I would have waited until they were at their weakest and taken the remainder of her fleet for myself.

"Dead," Sabium said. "Make it happen."

"Yes, Your Majesty."

I could almost feel sorry for Tymedes. The pirate queen hadn't gotten where she was by being an easy target.

He bowed and walked out. Sabium met my gaze. "You have something to say?"

"I want to see him."

He didn't bother asking who I was talking about. Instead, he threw back his head and laughed. "A stray cat would have been a better mother, and now you choose to be invested in the boy's life?" Getting to his feet, Sabium ignored the servant who pulled out his chair. "You should focus on your own position, *my love*."

He strolled away, leaving me with my wine.

"Out," I said. The servants disappeared.

The nanny didn't say a word. The boy was kept away. I could come and go as I pleased. And as I strolled the grounds, I focused on the small freedom I'd gained.

Not the sick, twisting shame that cramped my stomach.

A tiny child. I'd frightened a tiny child. Made him

cry. If I could have gotten away with it, I might have killed him.

What had happened to me since I'd come here? Was it Sabium's poison? Or had this place just brought exactly who I was to the surface?

Months passed. I no longer studied each courtier's face, waiting for the whispers to begin. No longer waited for Sabium to darken my doorway and demand to know why people were talking. Why they said I'd denied the child was mine.

My thoughts returned to escape. To murder. One day, I would find a way to end Sabium. It wouldn't be this year. Or the next. But it would happen. I would make him pay for what he had done to me.

And then the nanny appeared.

In my *library.*

She had pale skin, dark hair, and sharp eyes. And she was in my territory. Alone. The only person with the power to make my life even more difficult.

My smile must have been a terrible thing to witness. She didn't flinch.

"Your son is sick, Your Majesty. He needs you."

The nanny held my gaze, and I saw the unspoken threat in her eyes.

"If you're thinking of killing me, you should know I have an attack power," she murmured. "It's one of the reasons I was chosen as your son's nanny. To protect him."

Her audacity might have been impressive if she

weren't blackmailing me.

"What is your name?"

"Orlissa, Your Majesty."

"And what exactly is it that you want, Orlissa?"

"I want you to see your son."

"He is not *my son," I hissed.*

"Regardless." Her gaze was still steady. "You are all he has."

I weighed up my potential actions. I believed her when she said she had an attack power. My own power was...lacking. It was just one of the things Sabium liked to taunt me about. "I do this, and you swear to keep your silence. Forever."

"I'll swear it."

"Ten minutes," I said through numb lips. "I will see him for ten minutes."

She nodded, turning and leading me to the nursery.

The nursery was quiet. Peaceful. I hadn't stepped inside this wing of the castle since I'd been that girl who thought she might have a child of her own. My heart slammed into my ribs.

Orlissa's neck was very white. Her pulse throbbed evenly. I could likely slit her throat before she could reach for her power.

"He's had a fever for two days," she whispered, leading me close to the bed.

The boy was so small. I'd forgotten just how small he was. When he was toddling through this castle as if he owned it, that laugh bubbling from his chest, he seemed larger-than-life.

"*Where are the healers?*"

"*They have visited and tended to the worst of it. If they were to heal every childhood fever, his body would not learn to heal such things itself. He will have to endure it for a little while longer.*"

"*Perhaps it is better to put him out of his misery.*"

A simple twist of the wrist and his neck would snap. Life was suffering. Ending his would be a mercy.

Orlissa paused. "I'm going to pretend I did not hear that," she said.

Despite the situation, my mouth twitched.

She seemed to be waiting for me to do something.

"*Speak.*"

"*You should sit on his bed, Your Majesty. Try to comfort him. Can I trust you to be alone with him?*"

"*If I kill him, I will die in agony directly after,*" *I informed her. "Regner will ensure it.*"

Her lips thinned, but she nodded.

"*Do you need anything?*" *she asked.*

I'd forgotten his name. If I asked it now, Orlissa would make me pay somehow.

"*No,*" *I said. "You may leave.*"

After a moment of hesitation, she whirled and strode out the door.

I examined the sleeping child. He had ludicrously long eyelashes. His face was pale, except for his cheeks, which were flushed. And he let out a whimper in his sleep.

Turning my attention to the rest of the room, I surveyed it.

It seemed...large for a boy so small. One corner held a box of wooden toys, with several of them sprawled outside. As if he had been playing before he fell ill. I peered into the darkness, reading a carved word on one of the toys.

Jamic.

He shifted, letting out a cry, and I glanced toward the door. Green eyes opened and met mine. His eyes were bleary, confused. His little face scrunched up.

"Mama?"

I sighed. If I denied such a thing, he might wail, and that busybody nanny would make me pay for it somehow. I knew she would.

So I said nothing. And we watched each other.

Orlissa had told me to comfort him. I should have told her I had no idea what that meant. He shivered, and I tucked the blanket closer over him. My hand brushed his warm cheek, and before I knew what I was doing, I was pushing his hair off his forehead. His eyes grew heavy-lidded.

There was a tiny cup of water on his bedside table.

"Are you thirsty, child?"

He nodded, and I helped him sit up. His clothes were damp with sweat. Was the fever breaking? The boy took several gulps of water.

I took the cup back, waiting for him to lie down.

Instead, he climbed into my lap.

I froze. My arms came around his tiny body almost of

their own volition.

"Mama."

I looked down into his green eyes—so different from mine.

My rotten, black heart cracked open.

"Yes," I croaked. "Yes, I'm your mama."

My son had seen his twentieth winter as a prisoner, and I hadn't been allowed to visit. Sabium had refused to allow him home for the recent celebrations. And his reaction tonight had confirmed my worst fears.

Jamic wouldn't be coming home.

My hands shook with rage.

I knew more than Sabium could imagine.

I knew his real name was Regner. I knew he was alive due to stolen magic and dark knowledge. And I knew he was planning to kill my son.

It didn't matter what "Sabium" did. He could torture as many people as he liked—could horrify the court, could terrify our entire kingdom. Because he'd simply fake his own death, and the people would gladly embrace him when he pretended to be a levelheaded, shy young ruler unexpectedly taking the throne. When he pretended to be my son.

I would do whatever it took to make sure that didn't happen.

PRISCA

That night, while Lorian met with Conreth's general, I met with Tibris, Asinia, Demos, and Vicer. I'd made my decision—I'd go to the hybrid kingdom, and I'd leave this camp as soon as we had a plan in place. Now I just had to convince the others this was a good idea. I'd enjoyed spending time with my friends and family. Enjoyed training and avoiding thinking about whatever Regner could be planning next. But it was time to begin making our moves.

I'd barely seen Vicer, but he looked tired. Apparently, he'd been continually traveling to the fae border to welcome new hybrids and send messages back to his remaining rebels in Eprotha with various plans to help smuggle them down here.

"We need to talk about what comes next," I said. "What do we know about the hourglass?"

Demos paced the tent. "Nothing. I don't think we're going to find what we need here. I need to go search in Eprotha."

The thought made my lungs constrict as sweat broke out on the back of my neck. "It's not safe," I croaked.

Tibris sent me a sympathetic look. "We always knew we couldn't stay here, Prisca. You're about to tell us that you're not staying here either, so don't expect the same of us."

"Us? You want to go too?"

Demos didn't look pleased at the thought. "I work best alone."

"And I'm a healer," Tibris said mildly. "Knowing you, you'll need one of those."

Despite my fear, my lips quirked.

"I need to visit the hybrid kingdom," I said quietly, looking at Demos. "I thought you'd want to come too."

He looked tortured, but he shook his head. "My skills mean that I'm of better use searching for the hourglass. As soon as we know where it is, we'll send a message to you."

Vicer cleared his throat, his gray gaze on my face. "We have enough hybrids willing to help with the search that we can split them into several groups."

"Isn't that too dangerous?" Asinia asked. "The iron guards are looking for hybrids."

"All of us have the blue marks, thanks to the fae prince," Vicer said. "That will give us some level of protection. Either we act soon, or war will eventually come to this camp. And to the children living here."

"I need to travel across the fae lands and through the Asric Pass. And we need a ship to make it across the Sleeping Sea," I said.

Demos shook his head. "If you're judged worthy, you'll be taken across the sea."

"And if I'm not?"

A muscle ticked in his jaw. "You will be."

Asinia glanced at me. "I'm going with you."

Demos looked like he'd argue, but I shook my head at him before studying Asinia. "Are you sure?"

"You know I am."

"Fine," I said. "We need to keep this from Lorian. If he finds out, he'll come with me. And Conreth has made it clear that can't happen."

Demos gave me a hard stare. "I don't care what repercussions he faces for it. I want him there."

Because Demos knew Lorian was rabid when it came to my safety and would thrust his body directly between me and any danger that came my way. I narrowed my eyes back at my brother.

"I care. It's not happening."

Demos raised one eyebrow. "Your Bloodthirsty Prince will make you pay for trying to protect him like this," he said.

"Don't call him that," I said. "He's not responsible for what happened in Crawyth."

Demos looked unconvinced.

"He was set up," I said, and then I explained the bare minimum about what had really happened. Lorian could fill in the details in the future if he chose to.

When I was finally finished speaking, there was a long silence.

"I believe him," Asinia said. "The fae had no reason to attack Crawyth. And Regner had every reason to."

"He may not be responsible for Crawyth, but he's done other things," Vicer said. "Reprehensible things."

"I know."

The bearded man he'd killed at the inn flashed in my mind.

"I'm not someone you would have chosen to be with. I'm someone you were intrigued by and attracted to despite yourself. I'll never be safe, Prisca. I'll always be the monster who slaughters anyone who attempts to hurt you. I don't know how to be anything else. My mistake was attempting to shield you from the sight of that monster."

"We will all do terrible things before this is over," Demos said. I sent him a grateful look and changed the subject.

"I'm going to meet with Conreth again. I want to learn about the barrier. If there's a chance we could somehow bring it down, we might be able to convince other kingdoms to help us."

"Barrier?" Asinia asked.

Since Tibris and Demos already knew, and Vicer didn't look at all surprised to hear about it, I filled her in.

Asinia looked like I'd dumped a bucket of icy water over her head. "There are more continents?"

"Regner had the information struck from the history books. I'm sure there are people in the cities who knew of the other continents, but villagers like us…"

Asinia's mouth twisted.

"I'm leaving too," Vicer announced. "I'm returning to Eprotha."

I gaped at him. "Why?" We'd all barely escaped Eprotha with our lives. He would be at the top of Regner's kill list.

"There is a hybrid camp located in the foothills of the Normathe Mountains. I've been communicating with them for years now, attempting to convince them to join us—especially now that so many hybrids are making their way to this camp. They've had a hard winter. The area is at constant risk for landslides and flooding, not to mention Regner's iron guard is always looking for these kinds of camps so he can destroy them."

"Why don't they want to join us?" Asinia asked.

"They're isolationists. They want to be left alone to raise their families. Which is understandable. But Regner will learn of them eventually and wipe them out. It's only a matter of time."

"You're going to try to convince them to travel down here?" Demos asked.

"Yes. Their leader is a woman named Kaelin Stillcrest. We've met twice over the years, and she refuses to see reason. But I'm hoping she will understand the increased risk and choose to join us."

All of us were separating. A wave of anxiety washed over me. Was this the right decision? We would be far apart, with no way to help one another if any of us were attacked or captured. Or...worse.

Asinia nudged me with her leg beneath the table, and I rolled my shoulders. It had to happen. We were lucky we'd had the luxury of spending this time together. Luckier still we'd all managed to do some training. It would have to be enough.

"What do we know about the fae amulets?"

Demos leaned back. "Not much. I've been spying on their spies, but they don't have anything so far. What are you thinking?"

Asinia smirked and then turned her attention back to Demos. "She's thinking if Conreth takes our hourglass, she'll take something of his."

Tibris's mouth dropped open, and he stared at me like he'd never seen me before. Demos gave me a pleased grin.

"If Conreth wants to double-cross us, we will do the same to him." He nodded. "I like it."

"Hopefully we won't need to," I said. "We all have the same goal—to kill Regner. We need to fight together. But if he wants to neuter us, and to force us to rely on his goodwill…"

"At least we'll have something to trade," Asinia said

15

PRISCA

Lorian stood in front of me, eyes hard, expression blank. In his arms, Piperia batted at his chin with her fist. Lorian's eyes lost some of their sharpness as he caught her tiny hand. He kept his gaze on me, though, watching me thoughtfully.

It was time for him to leave. Galon strode over, holding out his hands for the baby, and Lorian scowled at him, whispered something I couldn't hear into the baby's ear, and handed her over.

I rolled my eyes at them. Cavis's daughter was going to grow up entirely coddled with this group of murderous mother hens fighting over her attentions.

Galon wandered away with Piperia, and Lorian turned his attention back to me, his expression contemplative. I kept my own expression carefully blank. He was going to lose his mind when he returned and learned I'd traveled to my kingdom without him. But at least

Conreth couldn't accuse his brother of treason.

I had no doubt that when I finally saw Lorian again, we would have a glorious fight about it.

But it was my turn to protect him for once.

"Tell me what you're thinking, wildcat." Lorian leaned close.

My throat tightened, my eyes burned, and I had to resist the almost overwhelming urge to bury my face in his chest.

"Safe travels," I said instead, attempting a smile. Above our heads, Lorian's hawk circled. According to Lorian, he'd had an injured wing and needed to recover at camp, which was why he hadn't traveled with Lorian to Regner's castle.

He studied my face. "I'll see you in a few days."

I nodded. For some reason, I *loathed* lying to him.

Lorian stepped back, his eyes cold. He knew something was wrong.

For one wild second, I almost told him everything.

But he was already turning away, mounting his horse. I memorized this moment, along with his face—eyes sharp, expression vaguely irritated. The scent of dew-covered grass and damp soil filled my nostrils as a fresh breeze played over my skin.

The others were waiting, and I lifted a hand as Rythos grinned at me. Galon pinned me with a hard stare. "Keep up with your training."

"I will," I promised. I would train every morning as I traveled to the hybrid kingdom.

Marth winked at me. He'd just given one of the fae women a lusty kiss, and she stared at him as if he were made of gold, before sauntering away toward the fae tents.

Cavis stepped up next to me, Piperia back in his arms. I held out my finger, and she clasped it with her tiny hand. Her father practically radiated contentment as he watched the others leave without him.

"You don't wish you could go?" I asked.

He shook his head. "I've spent too much time away from my family recently," he said. "Lorian doesn't even need the others with him. They probably just want to find something to kill."

I winced and he laughed. "Ready to hold my daughter yet?"

I sucked in an unsteady breath. "Soon," I promised. "Let me work up to it."

Cavis nudged me out of the way as Lorian and the others turned their horses toward the camp entrance. Lorian's eyes met mine. "Keep your secrets, wildcat," he called. "I'll learn them soon enough."

My stomach swooped at the thought of just how he'd likely attempt to learn those secrets.

Marth let out a low laugh, while Rythos rolled his eyes. Galon was already steering his horse toward the entrance, one hand raised to shield his eyes from the sun.

"Safe travels," I said, and Lorian just gave me a wicked grin filled with promise. Moments later, they were gone.

Cavis wandered away, and I turned my face up to the sky.

The sun was warm on my skin, and within hours, it would be blazing, ensuring we gulped cups of water while we trained. It was early enough that most of the camp hadn't yet roused, and the distant sound of the river teased my ears.

"Prisca."

My aunt stood behind me, hands on her hips. Sometimes it was difficult to believe we weren't blood related—especially now when she lowered her brows, giving me her I-dare-you look. I'd worn that same expression myself more times than I could count. And Demos practically woke up wearing it each day.

I walked toward her.

"I'm going with you," she murmured beneath her breath.

My eyebrows shot up. We hadn't kept our trip a secret from her, but she hadn't expressed that she'd wanted to travel with us. Still, I should have talked to her about it.

"Telean—"

"I know what you're thinking. The old lady will slow you down." Her mouth twisted, and something that might have been shame flickered through her eyes. "But I may be helpful. Don't forget, I used to live in that kingdom—"

"Telean. You're more than welcome to come. I'm sorry I didn't ask you sooner."

Her scowl deepened, another argument clearly already on the tip of her tongue. She opened her mouth and seemed to realize I'd agreed.

"Well, then. When will you leave?"

I scanned our surroundings, but other than Demos and Asinia slowly walking toward us, no one else was around. "Within a few days. But we need to keep it quiet."

"I still don't believe you should be going without your fae bodyguard."

I shook my head. Calling Lorian a bodyguard was a little like calling a lion a house cat.

Asinia sent me a concerned frown as she approached. I just shrugged at her. "Telean will be traveling with us tomorrow," I told Demos.

He surveyed our aunt. "You sure you can haul that bag of bones you call a body through the pass?"

I shook my head at him.

"Demos," Asinia hissed, but Telean gave a hoarse chuckle. "Just you wait, boy. We'll see if *you* can keep up."

I was surrounded by people with egos larger than their brains.

I opened my mouth, but my attention was caught by someone dismounting a horse, pulling a huge sack from its saddlebag, and striding through the camp entrance as if the entire camp belonged to her.

Madinia's long legs were encased in leather, her red hair loose around her shoulders, and that massive sack was slung over her back. She looked nothing like the woman I'd met in the castle.

And she'd returned.

She spotted me, sauntered toward us, and dropped

the sack at my feet. "Your coin, Your Majesty." She grinned at me.

My mouth had fallen open. I snapped it shut. "How…?"

"If there's one thing I know, it's jewelry. I was raised to look pretty, remember? I knew how much every piece was worth and negotiated accordingly." She seemed to pick up on the undercurrents and glanced around, raising her eyebrow.

"Something wrong?"

"No," I said, before anyone could speak. "Nothing's wrong. This is amazing. Thank you, Madinia."

She ignored that, glancing at Demos, who was still looking at her speculatively.

"Ah," she said, and that beautiful face turned cold. "You assumed I'd taken the jewels and run. Because I'm not just useless with a bow and arrow, I'm a thieving coward too."

Demos's gaze never flickered, even as she bared her teeth. I reached forward and laid a hand on her shoulder. "I didn't think that. I swear."

She glanced at me. Some of the color had returned to her cheeks, and her gaze dropped to the sack of coin at her feet. With a shake of her head, she shrugged my hand off her shoulder and stalked away.

I sighed. "That went well."

"She should have told us what she was planning," Demos said, his expression hard.

I wanted to talk to her, but something told me she

wouldn't welcome me approaching her right now. I was beginning to learn just how much Madinia valued her own space—especially when she was upset.

Demos nudged me with his elbow. "Come with me. Vicer has some people he wants you to meet."

PRISCA

Vicer nodded at me as I entered the tent, and several people looked up from where they were poring over a map of Eprotha.

"Prisca," Vicer said. "You remember Ameri."

I nodded at her. "It's good to see you again."

She smiled at me—a much warmer welcome than the one I'd received when I'd first met her. "Nice work at the city gates," she told me.

"Ameri has a power which helps her divert attention," Vicer said. "She's excellent at getting in and out of places most people couldn't access."

"I'll be traveling with Vicer back to Eprotha," she said.

Vicer nodded at a boy who looked like he'd only seen around sixteen winters. But the steady gaze he turned on me told me he was older.

"This is Finley," Vicer said. There was something

almost smug about his tone.

"It's nice to meet you," I told Finley. I could practically feel Vicer waiting for me to ask, so I did. "And what power do you have?"

"Perhaps a demonstration is in order," Vicer said. "Give him your dagger, Pris."

Frowning at Vicer, I slowly reached for my dagger, handing it to Finley. He closed his eyes. Goose bumps rose on my skin as something changed in the air. Next to me, I could feel Demos watching intently.

One moment, Finley's other hand was empty.

The next, he held another knife. It was exactly the same as the one I'd given him.

I let out a shocked laugh. "That's incredible. You're the one with replication magic."

He nodded, a hint of pride in his gaze. But his face had drained of color, and Vicer pulled a chair toward him, gesturing for him to sit.

"Your documents allowed Tibris and me to get into the castle," I told Finley. "You helped save over three hundred lives."

His cheeks flushed, but his eyes had widened slightly when they met mine.

"Thank you," I said.

"Welcome," he replied gruffly. Not a big talker, Finley.

"He's also coming with me," Vicer said.

I looked at him. Perhaps now, he'd tell me what his power was.

Vicer shook his head. "Not yet," he told me.

I just nodded, and he sent me a grateful look. I understood what it was to be uncomfortable with your power. And whatever Vicer could do, it hadn't allowed him to save the woman he'd loved.

He'd been punishing himself ever since.

We spent the next few days training, eating, and solidifying our plans. Demos had taken over most of my training, and he was just as brutal as Galon. He insisted on training in the forest, away from prying eyes, taking away my weapons and attacking me over and over, while pointing out all the "natural" weapons I had at my disposal.

I became excellent at throwing dirt into his eyes, slamming fallen branches into his gut, and throwing rocks at his head. Unfortunately, I'd had to haul him to Tibris after the rock incident.

Tibris had laughed and laughed when he'd healed him. But he'd nodded approvingly at Demos. The next day, he'd shown up too, and when my brothers had finally agreed I knew instinctively to use *anything* I could as a weapon, they'd moved on to restraints.

Knots, ropes, even handcuffs. Demos taught me to pick a lock, but it wasn't a skill that came naturally to me. He insisted I walk around with a hairpin and a set of iron handcuffs, practicing whenever I had a few moments free. When I'd mastered that, we moved on to using the tip of a dagger, a belt buckle, even a hardened quill.

Finally, in what he likely believed was a show of

good faith, Conreth came to the hybrid side of the camp for our meeting. I'd kept myself busy, suppressing the urge to stalk into his side of the camp and demand he end his power plays.

We gathered in the tent we'd used to meet when I'd first arrived—Demos, Asinia, Tibris, Vicer, Madinia, and Telean, along with Conreth and his general, Hevdrin.

Hevdrin was a tall man who liked to clean his weapons when he was deep in thought. He didn't speak often, but when he did, people listened.

Madinia was still in a terrible mood. I'd attempted to talk to her twice now, and she'd shut me down. I was relatively sure the only reason she was attending this little meeting was because she hadn't otherwise left her tent since the moment she'd dropped a king's ransom of gold at my feet.

"You're traveling to your kingdom the day after tomorrow," Conreth remarked.

"Yes," I said. "As you suggested." I was just a poor, silly young girl, here to be led by rulers much older and wiser than me.

He smiled, as if he'd expected nothing less.

I smiled back. One day, I would make him pay for everything I suspected he had done to Lorian.

That day wouldn't be today. Pasting on my most placid expression, I took a deep breath. "I'd like to know about the barrier."

Conreth sighed. "This isn't the first time your people or mine have attempted to receive help from other continents. Almost four hundred years ago, when the human king learned an army was finally coming to challenge him, he gifted the boy then known as his son with stolen power—so much that his body could barely contain it. With his most loyal men, Regner traveled out into the sea, until he could glimpse the armada from the continent on the horizon."

My stomach churned. Part of me wished I could hide from whatever I was about to hear.

"He followed the book's instructions, used its ancient magic, and slit the boy's throat," Conreth said, and for the first time, his eyes glinted with sorrow. "The explosion of power allowed him to create the barrier."

My heart hurt. The boy hadn't been his son, but he'd been treated as Regner's child just the same. And yet Regner had slaughtered him like a pig. "Why didn't the fae take it down?"

"We have…enemies in other kingdoms. Ancient discords that ensure we always have to be wary of threats."

"And you decided the barrier could benefit you."

"Not at first. I was not yet king then," he reminded me. "I hadn't even been born. The fae will never be ruled the way of humans. There are wild creatures in these lands—creatures so old and so powerful that to kill them would be a challenge even for me."

I'd be willing to bet Lorian could do it.

Conreth smirked, as if reading my mind. "My brother would never admit it, but he adores the wildkin. They're brutal and arrogant, cunning and wicked."

Just like Lorian.

Conreth left the words unspoken, but he gave me a knowing look.

Demos cleared his throat. "So, the barrier would protect you from your enemies across the oceans."

Conreth's expression tightened. "Yes. If the fae could only be convinced to fight as one, we would lay waste to any who attempted to harm us. But that will never happen. At best, we cooperate only when necessary to prevent catastrophic bloodshed."

Conreth met my eyes. "You remember I told you one of the amulets belonged to a powerful family who hid the disappearance from the rest of the fae."

I nodded.

"They should have notified the king immediately. Instead, they chose to hide their shame, ensuring the fae didn't know the amulet was missing until too late—when the barrier had been in place for several days. A century later, we learned another boy would be sacrificed."

"The fae tried to stop the sacrifice?" Asinia asked.

"Yes. But Regner had learned how to make the most of his sacrifice. He ensured the boy he called son was exposed to more and more power over the years, building that power up—including his tolerance. This made the sacrifice even more powerful."

I rubbed at my temple, where a headache had begun throbbing. "So, wherever Regner's false son is now, it's likely he's trapped, brimming with power his body can barely hold, and about to be sacrificed so Regner can reinforce the barrier, pretend to die, and take his place."

We had to find Jamic. The boy who'd been raised as the king's son. Not just because he was the only way we'd have a chance to bring that barrier down...

But because he'd been used by the king. Would be killed by the man he called father.

Did he know it was coming? Or did he truly think he would rule one day? Would he believe that right up until the moment Regner slit his throat?

The horror of it crushed my chest until I could barely breathe. But I forced myself to gaze at my family and friends gathered in this tent. All of them willing to go to war with me.

If I wanted to make the best decisions, I had to strip away the emotion. I couldn't think of Jamic as an innocent man. I had to think of him as a potential ally— one who was saturated with power. And if we were able to convince him to join our cause...

"Where is he being kept?"

Conreth sighed. "My spies located the boy three months ago. By the time my legion arrived, he had been moved, and Regner's iron guards were waiting to meet them. We've continued looking—following every rumor we can, but Regner has been careful. We'll find him," Conreth said, his icy eyes darkening. "But unless we find him soon, it will be too late."

And Regner would reinforce the barrier, leaving us with only the allies we could gather on this continent. Who knew if they would be enough? Not to mention,

Regner could continue his atrocities until he eventually "died," stepping into Jamic's shoes. I was willing to bet that Regner would ensure he died a martyr to the humans. And it would all continue.

"We will listen closely for any information regarding his location," Demos said.

Conreth angled his head. "I'm afraid it's unlikely you will find such information while navigating the Asric Path."

"Demos, Tibris, and Vicer are traveling to various hybrid camps and shelters in an attempt to convince them to travel to this camp." My voice was casual. Almost bored. I'd practiced with Asinia before this meeting.

Conreth's pale eyes met mine. And my heart thumped. Did he suspect we were looking for the hourglass? I kept my expression blank, and he finally nodded.

"There is something else I wanted to discuss, Nelayra."

My heart stuttered in my chest, and I wondered if his fae senses allowed him to hear it. I had no desire to make an enemy of Conreth—at least not *now*, but if he took that hourglass from the hybrids…

Tension was thick in the room. Conreth leaned back in his seat, folding his hands on his stomach. "I wanted to apologize for my actions while you were at the castle."

"Excuse me?"

"When Lorian told me of your power, I instantly knew who you were. I asked him to bring you to me. I should have communicated with you directly."

My chest tightened, and I forced myself not to shift in my chair. Because I knew exactly what Conreth was doing.

With a few sentences, he'd reminded everyone here that just weeks ago, I had been a sheltered villager, completely unaware of my heritage. He'd also reminded us that Lorian had brought me to the fae lands only because Conreth had ordered him to.

He was implying that anything Lorian and I had shared in that castle—any relationship we had built—was worthless, and if not for the fact that I was the hybrid heir, I never would have seen Lorian again.

I wished it were only fury that rampaged through me. But the fae king had known exactly where to strike.

Satisfaction glimmered in Conreth's eyes at my silence. I tilted my head. "Apology accepted," I said coolly, keeping my gaze steady on his. "I trust you won't make such choices in the future."

Silence stretched between us. Finally, Conreth gave me a chilly smile. "Of course." Getting to his feet, he nodded at us, stalking from the tent.

"Pris?" Asinia murmured.

"I'm fine. I don't want to talk about it."

I spent the rest of the day preparing. Before Lorian had left, Hevdrin and Demos had announced the new living arrangements. To say they weren't popular was an understatement. Several fights had broken out, which left Demos and Hevdrin busy as they put a stop to them.

The hybrids and fae had been moving in to new tents

as ordered. And while Hevdrin and Demos had taken joint responsibility for the decision, it was clear everyone knew it had come from me.

I could no longer walk anywhere in the camp without facing mutters and dirty looks from both the hybrids and fae.

At least they could all agree on one thing, even if it was how much they hated me.

It was a start.

I was now in the perfect mood to talk to Madinia. This time, I'd wait her out until she listened. Funny how dealing with the fae king had made verbal sparring with Madinia seem easy in comparison.

Madinia let out a low growl when I walked into her tent. She was lying on her cot, her head buried in her pillow.

"Leave me alone, Prisca."

How had she known it was me? I chewed on my lower lip as the answer to that question made my stomach clench. She'd known it was me because absolutely no one else here cared enough to check on her.

I swept my gaze around her tent. Weapons and clothes were strewn across the ground. A crossbow sat balanced against her narrow cot. I sat on the edge of that cot. "I like what you've done with the place."

She snorted. "Out."

"Look, I wanted to thank you."

Her shoulders tensed. "I'm not interested."

Gods, she was hard work. I put on my haughtiest

voice. The one I'd learned directly from her. "Too bad. I'm the hybrid heir. That means you have to listen to me."

She lifted her head, teeth bared, and then caught the smirk on my face. "Cute."

I'd known that would work.

I sighed. "Look, Madinia, one of the reasons I was so desperate to get to this camp was because I wanted to thank you for what you did that night. I wouldn't have made it to the city gates without you. I wouldn't have gotten that amulet to Lorian…"

"And that's a good thing? The fae are *threats* to us, Prisca." She used that imperious tone that never failed to make me grind my teeth. The tone she'd used so often in the castle when she was implying I was the stupidest person alive.

But I knew enough about wounded animals to know they often lashed out at whoever was closest.

I wouldn't ask how she was handling her father's death. Instead, I fought to keep my voice even.

"I made a deal with Lorian when I was at the castle. I had to get him that amulet if the hybrid prisoners were going to stay alive. He trusted me to find it, and in return, I trusted him to get them to the gates."

She sneered at me. "And then you learned who he was."

"Yes." But we weren't going there. "I know it was the worst night of your life. After what happened with Davis—"

"I don't want to talk about that," she hissed.

"And your father," I continued as if she hadn't spoken. "Yet you're still working to keep the hybrids safe and to further our cause. Thank you for exchanging the jewels."

She stared at me. Emotions danced across her face, too quickly for me to follow. Finally, she swallowed. "You're welcome."

"What can I do for you, Madinia?"

She didn't hesitate. "Get me out. I want out of this fucking place. Send me somewhere else."

"Done."

She blinked. "Truly?"

"You're clever, vicious, and you were one of the queen's ladies for years. I'd be a fool not to use you."

She didn't smile, but some of the tension left the corners of her eyes. "What do you need?"

"The prince. Before Conreth finds him."

Satisfaction gleamed in her eyes. Clearly, she liked the idea of outmaneuvering the fae king. Something untwisted in my gut. She still had some spark left.

"Why do you let him patronize you?" she demanded.

"We need him to underestimate me. Let him think us weak. I hope we're both there to see the expression on his face the moment he learns otherwise."

Madinia smirked, getting to her feet. Some of the color had returned to her face, and those incredible blue eyes were blazing. "Twenty summers," she murmured, returning her attention to the prince. "Jamic has been away from the castle for a while now. Long enough that people are asking questions. No doubt, they're forgetting exactly what he looks like."

"Regner's hiding him somewhere, Madinia. We have to find him and take him."

She frowned. "You want to use him too."

"Regner has been slowly bloating him with stolen power over the years. He's a human and not created to hold that much power. It will be driving him insane. We find him, and maybe we can figure out how to release the power before he loses control of it—or before Regner ensures none of us can ever get off this continent."

Madinia stared into the distance for a long moment. "I have a few people who may help me." Her eyes met mine. "I'll find him, and we'll take that barrier down."

"In that case, follow me."

She didn't argue, merely hauled herself off the bed and strode after me as I led her toward the river.

We couldn't risk meeting in our tent. Not with Conreth paying close attention to what we were doing. Tibris, Demos, Asinia, and Vicer were already waiting when we arrived. The river would help mask the sound of our conversation. I gestured to Madinia. "She's going after the human prince."

Demos studied her. "You think you can do this?"

She swept him with a cold look. "Of course."

"Try not to set him on fire," Asinia teased her.

Madinia opened her mouth, clearly about to threaten to set *Asinia* on fire.

Vicer cleared his throat. "Everything is prepared.

There's just one more thing." He reached into his pocket and placed a handful of what looked like small coins onto the grass between us.

"What are they?" I asked.

"If any of us are caught with no way out…"

"They're the way out," Demos said softly.

It took me several seconds to understand what he meant. The air left my lungs in a rush.

"Suicide?" Asinia's voice cracked. Demos's expression tightened.

"If it comes down to a quick death or one that includes days or months of torture—and giving up your friends and family—you'll choose the quick death."

Their eyes met, and something strange passed between them. Demos had seen Asinia at her weakest. Clearly, their days in those cells had given him some insight into her.

My mouth went dry at the thought of one of us being forced to choose that option. "How does it work?" I asked.

"The magic feels your intention. You just put it in your mouth and tell it what you want, Pris," Tibris said gently. "It's fast."

Madinia didn't hesitate. She grabbed one of the disks. "How do we hide them?"

"They stick to your skin. They were created with fae magic, and they were formed in such a way that the fae can see them, but hybrids and humans can't. You'll be able to feel the edge if you run your hand over your own skin, but no one else will."

The way out. I wanted to scream a denial that any of us would ever need such a thing. And yet, I'd promised myself I would face reality and make the difficult decisions.

Madinia pulled her hair up and pressed the disk to the back of her neck. It disappeared into her skin.

Asinia slowly reached for a disk, adhering it to the inside of her upper arm.

If I were ever in chains, I'd have a limited range of motion. After a moment of deliberation, I chose the side of my neck, just above my collarbone.

Demos, Tibris, and Vicer took their disks.

"Well, that was suitably morbid," Asinia muttered. "Are we done here?"

I nodded, getting to my feet. "I have something to show you."

We left the others behind, and I led her along the river, into the grove, picking my way to the spot.

My heart fluttered. I knew Asinia like I knew myself. But still, I hoped I'd made the right choice.

It was peaceful here, next to the river. One of Demos's hybrid friends had owed him a favor. He'd shaped the headstone out of rock so white, it looked almost like marble. And I'd asked him to etch Asinia's mother's name and birthdate on it.

Asinia would never have a body to bury. But Cavis had warded this place, promising that for as long as she lived, Asinia could visit.

I linked my arm through hers, and her breath caught.

"You can add anything you like," I said.

She looked at me, her eyes gleaming with tears. "Thank you, Pris." She hesitated. "What about…"

"I can't yet. Vuena kidnapped me. She let people die to teach me lessons. I know there were good times and she did what she thought she had to, but…"

"It's complicated," Asinia finished for me.

I nodded. My birth mother had never been buried either. Her remains were likely still in the ruins of Crawyth.

Asinia looked at me. Her face was wet with tears. She took my hand, pulling until we were sitting on the ground in front of the headstone.

And together, we mourned her mother.

16
LORIAN

Five days of dealing with the wildkin. They would always be a threat, but I'd at least managed to warn a few of them against straying out of our territory. Hopefully, word would spread. The last thing I wanted to do was go back and swing my sword, and most of the wildkin were at least reasonable enough to know that was exactly what I'd do if I had to.

I was desperate for a hot meal, a warm bath, and my woman. Although I'd take Prisca first if I could convince her to overlook my rough appearance. I ran one hand over my unshaven jaw and pictured her lost in pleasure and grinding on my face.

The ward at the camp entrance shivered along my body, and I swept my gaze around, keeping an eye out for the wildcat. My entire body groaned as I dismounted, allowing one of the stable hands to lead my horse away.

Prisca wasn't in her tent.

She wasn't sitting at her spot near the river.

She wasn't in the arena.

In fact, I couldn't see any of them. Not Demos, Tibris, Asinia… I kept my eyes peeled for Vicer and Madinia, but they were nowhere to be found. Neither was Telean.

Fear wasn't an emotion I was used to. But it slithered through me now, oily and cold.

Cavis strode toward me, his daughter snuggled into his neck.

"Where is she?" I demanded.

"Prisca left, Lorian."

Fear turned to panic, sharp and unrelenting. "Left to go where?"

"Conreth encouraged her to visit her kingdom. To attempt to find allies." Cavis's eyes were hard. "I only learned of her trip once she had already been gone for hours. I stayed because I needed to make sure someone let you know."

She'd gone alone. Alone and unprotected.

The other hybrids didn't count. They didn't know the fae lands.

I turned with some vague idea of heading back to the stables, only to find Conreth waiting for me. His shoulders were squared, his head high. This was how he looked when he stepped into an arena to spar with his guards.

I met his eyes, letting him see the fury that blazed through my body. "You allowed her to leave without me?"

My brother held up a hand. "I sent five of my most trusted guards. She will be fine."

I let out a strangled laugh. "Fine? That woman could find mortal danger in an empty, freshly plowed field. How could you do this to me, brother?" I attempted to step past him, with no thought other than to find her.

He moved to the side, blocking my way. "As your king, I forbid you to leave."

Blood pounded in my ears. I leaned forward, into his space. "As your brother, you can go fuck yourself."

An icy calm came over his face. "King overrules brother this time, Lorian."

The betrayal was almost incomprehensible. He'd done this. He'd made it clear Prisca needed to bring something to the table in order to receive his help. Then he'd sent me away. He'd risked her life for his own games.

"Why?"

"I like your wildcat, Lorian. She's brave and fierce and loyal, and all the other things you told me about her. But you also need to be honest with yourself. Your relationship is doomed. She's the hybrid heir, and you're the Bloodthirsty Prince, and even without that between you, how do you expect to have a future? At some point, your paths will diverge, and it may as well be now, before it's more painful later."

"So you were *protecting* me then, were you?" I let out a bitter laugh. "How did you convince her to go along with your plan?"

"I reminded her that you'd already committed treason once by not following directions."

And my little wildcat had reacted just as Conreth

knew she would. She'd left to protect me.

Something in the region of my heart melted. It wouldn't stop me from roaring at her just as soon as I found her alive.

Several guards stepped close to my brother. I smiled at them, and one of them reached for the hilt of his sword, his hand shaking.

"I'm leaving," I said.

Conreth's eyes widened. "Excuse me?"

"I've never asked you for anything. I've protected you, Emara, and this kingdom since I was old enough to swing a sword. And the first chance you had, you lied to me, terrified Prisca, and separated us."

The blood drained from his face. "I won't let you leave, Lorian."

I let out a low laugh. "You believe you can stop the *Bloodthirsty Prince,* brother? How many men do you have who will line up to die? Not the guard to your right. He's barely holding his bladder."

Color swept up the guard's face, before an icy look from Conreth made it drain away once more.

"You would make an enemy of your king?"

"No. But you will listen carefully when I tell you this—if you try to keep me from Prisca again, it will become your biggest regret."

Was that true hurt in his eyes? I couldn't even tell anymore.

His expression turned blank once more. "You have

three weeks, Lorian. And we will discuss this once you have returned."

I stalked toward the stables. An endless fury swept through me, even as a line of cold sweat ran down my spine. She was fine. I would know if she weren't. Somehow, I would know.

"Lorian."

Rythos strode toward me, his expression tense. "I know you're not trying to leave us behind."

My breath shuddered from my lungs, and I attempted to think clearly.

If I was taking Prisca through the fae lands alone, I wanted Rythos and the others with me. I was powerful, but even I could be overpowered if enough wildkin surrounded and attacked us. Around half the time, it was possible to travel through wildkin territory and merely feel their eyes on you. The other half, you would end up fighting for your life simply because the ancient creatures were bored.

"Tell Cavis he doesn't need to—"

"I'm coming," he said from behind me. I turned. He stood next to Galon and Marth, his daughter in his arms. Sybella slid me a narrow-eyed look but took the baby from him. "Bring Prisca back safe," she said.

PRISCA

As much as I hated to admit it to myself, traveling wasn't the same without Lorian. Conreth had advised us to head east, staying within the fae lands as long as possible until we reached the Asric Pass. We'd left Tibris, Demos, Vicer, Ameri, and Madinia close to the fae border, and I'd memorized their faces—some part of me wondering if I'd ever see them again.

The thought cut my heart open, and all my fears came spilling out.

As the day crawled by, I grew paralyzed by that fear, until all I could do was sit stiffly in my saddle and force myself to take deep breaths.

My aunt rode next to me, her brow creased in thought as she stared into the distance. Asinia was also quiet, and the five fae men Conreth had sent with us weren't speaking except to direct us when necessary. Apparently, we would eventually come to a vast lake bordered by fae villages. Within the forest behind those villages— the forest we would ride through—we would likely be watched by wildkin.

Hopefully, they would let us pass. However, according to one of the guards—a rather solemn fae named Cadrus—the wildkin may decide to play with us first.

We'd fallen into a routine. We'd wake, I'd train with

Asinia while the fae pulled down the camp—we'd both offered to help and been ignored—and then we'd travel all day. Lunch was usually comprised of dried meat, fruit, and nuts, and eaten in the saddle. Conreth's men seemed very interested in getting us to the pass as quickly as possible. Almost as if they were on some kind of schedule that involved Lorian not finding out where we were. Shocking.

Since that worked just fine for me, I woke with the sun each morning, readying myself for the day ahead. Telean, Asinia, and I slathered so much healing cream on our inner thighs, we were beginning to smell like brackweed.

We'd passed a few merchants at the beginning of our journey, before Cadrus had steered us off the paved road and toward a much narrower trail. Now, we saw no one but one another.

Telean had continued my lessons, and she stuffed my head full with history, protocol, and political alliances, quizzing me as we rode. And of course, I'd asked my own questions.

"I know what the hybrids and the fae received from the gods," I'd murmured earlier today as we clopped down the trail. "But what did the humans receive?"

She'd stretched her back, already looking weary after a few days of travel. "A mirror. That mirror allowed Regner to spy on us. He'd already become jealous, and when his son died, he vowed to wage war until he was more powerful than both the hybrids and the fae. That mirror allowed him to learn all about the fae amulets—including how the fae used them and where they were kept. And he learned of the hybrid hourglass. The hourglass your grandmother wore on a chain around her neck."

Was that the mirror I'd seen in the queen's rooms? It seemed unlikely that the king would allow such an important artifact out of his sight. The amulet, I could understand since Lorian would never have known it was in the queen's rooms if not for my position as one of her ladies.

By the third day, the forest had thickened, huge canopies blocking out the sun until I huddled in my cloak, skin chilled. This forest was ancient in a way my mind could barely comprehend. It felt as if the trees themselves were watching us.

Thoughts whirled through my mind. There was so much still to do. Even if Madinia found Jamic, we would need to learn how to take down the barrier so we could beg for help from across the seas. And if we didn't mobilize our people soon, we would have no chance at receiving that help before Regner waged war.

Hybrids were still dying daily in Eprotha. Vicer and Ameri would smuggle out as many as they could, but no hybrid would be safe until Regner was dead.

And then there was my cousin. I'd hoped…

It didn't matter now.

"Pris?" Asinia murmured.

"Hmmm?"

"You've got a strange look on your face. Like you might vomit."

"I'm just thinking about everything we need to accomplish. And at some point, I'll need to do that favor for the pirate queen."

Asinia snorted. I'd told her about the blood vow with Daharak. "With our luck, she'll choose the most inconvenient time possible."

We had to do all of this without Regner learning of our plans or attacking while we were still unprepared.

My limbs turned numb, and I suddenly couldn't breathe. "Pris?"

I stuffed the list back into my cloak pocket and attempted a smile. From the grimace she sent back, it hadn't worked.

The birds weren't singing.

The breeze had stilled.

Everything went silent.

Asinia's eyes widened, and I nodded. She was on my left, and without a word, she steered her horse until my aunt was riding between us.

The fae guards were alert, swords in their hands. I drew my own sword, although on horseback I was just as likely to stab myself as I was anyone else.

An arrow flew through the air, hitting the blade and knocking my sword from my hand. Several other swords dropped behind me. I reached for my power…

And Lorian stepped into our path.

Rythos, Galon, Marth, and Cavis melted from the

forest, surrounding us.

My heart was still racing, a metallic taste in my mouth. My lungs had turned to stone, and my body took a long moment to come to terms with the fact that we *weren't* under attack.

Lorian looked at me, lightning dancing in his eyes. My breathing slowed, my muscles loosened, and awareness thundered through my body.

He flashed his teeth in a grim smile. "Imagine my surprise when I returned to camp and found you'd left without me."

Lorian's voice was pure seduction, but also a strange comfort. It was a hot bath after a long day. The feel of a thick blanket on a cold night. It was familiarity and newness all at once.

His expression, on the other hand, was terrifying.

His eyes were frozen green pits, while his jaw was clenched so tight, a white line had appeared along each of his cheeks.

He *radiated* menace.

"We have orders from His Majesty," Cadrus said.

Lorian kept his eyes on me. "I'm overriding those orders."

The fae guards moved their horses closer to mine.

"Your Highness…" Cadrus began.

Lorian winced at the address. If the situation hadn't been so serious, I might've laughed.

"Let me be clear." Lorian smiled grimly at Cadrus. "I'll be taking the wildcat. If you have a problem with that, you're welcome to challenge me for her."

Of all the overbearing, possessive, *arrogant*... "Did you lose what little sense you had left?"

His gaze drifted back to me. "I'll deal with you later."

"Stab him," I ordered Cadrus. "We'll leave him bleeding out right here."

Rythos roared with laughter. Galon just shook his head at me.

No one infuriated me more than the fae prince currently sending me a patronizing smile from the trail in front of us.

Everyone stayed still. I glanced at Telean, who gave me an impatient look. Clearly, she was expecting me to do something. "Let me try to talk some sense into him," I muttered.

Asinia snorted. "Good luck with that."

I sighed and dismounted, darting out of reach as one of the fae guards attempted to grab me. "Don't push the crazed man any further," I advised him.

The moment I was within a foot-span of him, Lorian clamped his hand around my wrist. I allowed him to pull me farther down the path.

"What were you thinking?" he growled.

"I was thinking I had to travel to the hybrid kingdom and you were needed elsewhere."

"Don't play with me."

I threw up my hands. "Do you think I *wanted* to go without you and the others? Of course, I couldn't *wait* to travel through the fae lands with *Conreth's* men, whom

I don't know and don't particularly trust. I was trying to *protect* you, you fool."

His lips pulled back from his teeth in a vicious snarl. "Yes, my brother was very detailed about how he'd manipulated you."

Shaking my head, I slammed my hands into his chest. "And now you've ruined it. You've committed treason, and Conreth will punish you. Because of me."

"Stop trying to protect me."

"I can't!" My voice cracked, and I covered my face with my hands.

Lorian caught my hands, pulling them back down. He'd gone very still. "And why is that, Prisca?"

I shook my head. When I raised my gaze, his eyes were blazing with triumph. He pulled me closer, and his mouth was suddenly on mine. Gods, I'd missed him.

I didn't realize I'd said it aloud until he smiled against my mouth. "Missed you too, wildcat." Lorian lifted his head, and his brow creased. "You want to visit your kingdom? I can save you a week of travel."

An entire week? "How?"

His mouth twisted into a grim smile. "First, we negotiate."

"Lorian…"

"No leaving without me. Ever."

"I'm not agreeing to that." I'd be lying, after all. The moment Demos and Tibris found the hourglass, I was going after it. And Lorian couldn't come. My chest ached.

Lorian let out a low growl. It was a sound I'd only

ever heard when he was dealing with me.

"How will Conreth punish you?" I demanded.

"That's not relevant."

I took a step back. "It's entirely relevant. You want to negotiate? Then be honest with me. What would he do?"

"It's not what you're thinking, wildcat. Conreth won't kill me, and he won't imprison me. Not only would it be terrible for morale, but he needs me. The wildkin won't respond to anyone else, and he'll need me for this war. I had some personal time owed to me. I took it."

I let out a hollow laugh. "With no warning? And to help *me*? And you don't think he'll punish you for it?"

Lorian stared back at me, but a muscle ticked in his jaw.

I didn't understand him. He'd only brought me with him to the fae lands because his brother had demanded it. Now, his brother had ordered him to let me go, and he'd done the opposite.

"We need to talk about this."

"It's happening."

This wasn't the end of this conversation. My instincts insisted Conreth was holding something over him. But I also knew that stubborn expression. Lorian was coming with me. I might as well accept his help. But I'd find out how Conreth would punish him.

"Fine," I said. "You may join me on my trip."

Lorian gave me a wicked smile. "Don't choke on it, wildcat." His smile widened, and I knew he was thinking about what he'd prefer for me to choke on. I narrowed my eyes at him, but a smile tugged at my mouth.

He lowered his head, his mouth caressing mine, and I sighed against him. His lips left mine, and he kissed a trail down my neck until I was gasping, my head spinning.

He stiffened, slowly lifting his head. "What is that?"

I raised my hand, finding the ridge of the disk Vicer had given us. "Uh…"

"Prisca."

I sighed. He was fae. He recognized fae magic. Which meant he knew exactly what it was.

"It's in case I'm ever captured. If there's no other way out…" My voice trailed off at the dangerous glint in his eyes.

"Who gave it to you?"

"Vicer determined it was best if we all—"

The disk was in his hand a moment later, and he threw it into the forest. I lunged, but he snared my wrist, holding me tight.

"Lorian!"

"What have I told you, Prisca? You never give up. Not you."

I kept my voice even. "You know me. You know I'd never do it unless there was no other choice."

He showed me his teeth. "If you're ever taken, I will find you. No matter how long it takes."

"And if you're dead or captured?"

"Galon and the others will find you."

"You're being entirely unreasonable."

I'd find Vicer and ask for another disk. Not because

I was suicidal. But because I knew I was unlikely to hold up well under torture. And I refused to put my friends and family at risk.

Lorian was watching me closely, and his expression hardened. "You ever do such a thing, and I'll find you. Wherever you are. Even if you're in Hubur. I'll make my way to the underworld, and I'll drag you back."

I studied him, taking in the obstinate set to his jaw, the unyielding glint in his eyes. This reaction wasn't normal. Even from my possessive fae prince.

"Who did you lose?"

He *flinched*. It was quick, but I caught it.

Oh, Lorian.

"Pris?" Asinia called.

I kept my gaze on the stubborn male in front of me. "We'll be right there," I called back. "We're talking about this later," I promised Lorian.

He glowered back at me.

"How are *you* the one who is irritated right now?"

"What can I say, wildcat? You bring it out in me."

I squinted at him. "That's funny. You do the same to me."

He pulled me close. "You terrified me. Don't do it again."

I would have snarled at him, except this time, the words weren't an order. This time, he said them almost as if pleading with me.

I sighed. How I could go from wanting to punch him in the gut to wanting to jump into his arms within the span of just a few seconds, I would never understand.

"I'll try. How big of a threat is Conreth to you, Lorian?"

He cupped my face in both of his large hands. "I'll let you in on a little secret, Prisca. I'm more powerful than my brother."

"That's not exactly a secret. But…he has an entire army at his disposal."

"To kill me would risk a fae war. He wouldn't take that chance. But I don't want you alone with him."

He watched me until I nodded. He knew his brother better than I did. Knew exactly what he was capable of. I could live with that. "Fine. Don't think I don't know you're avoiding the real question. He's keeping you in line somehow. And I want to know how."

Lorian just pressed a kiss to the tip of my nose, linked his fingers through mine, and guided me back toward the others. I stepped onto the trail and frowned. Conreth's guards were gone.

"Where are they?" Lorian asked.

Galon scratched his cheek. "It seems they decided to leave without a fuss."

Lorian nodded. "Good."

"This means they're going straight back to Conreth," Asinia pointed out. "Isn't that a bad thing?"

"He already knew where we were going," Rythos said. "This won't surprise him."

Marth leveled me with a long look. "You cost me a hot bath with a beautiful woman."

I rolled my eyes. "My apologies."

He just shook his head and ducked off the path to go find his horse.

Asinia grinned. Meanwhile, my aunt was staying very quiet. She had the hint of a smile on her face, and something told me everything had worked out just the way she was hoping. I surveyed her, and she waved her hand.

"What are we waiting for, children? We're losing the light."

Lorian spared Telean a glance and then nodded back toward the way we'd come. "We need to turn around."

I frowned. "We'll lose time."

"Trust me, wildcat. We're heading back toward the lake."

I didn't understand how that would get us closer to the hybrid kingdom, and Rythos grinned at me as Marth returned with his horse.

"You're going to see where I was born, Prisca."

LORIAN

Just weeks ago, I'd wondered what it would be like to be one of Prisca's inner circle. To be someone she cared enough for that she would do anything for them.

Now I knew. It was incredibly inconvenient, and yet it made me want to grin with pride.

Her natural urge to protect clashed with my own plans. And even as she'd fought to protect me from my brother, she refused to admit that she'd done such a thing because she had feelings for me.

Oh, she knew. Deep down, Prisca knew she wanted me. But my wildcat was nothing if not stubborn.

I studied her as she rode, laughing at something Marth said. She'd been pleased to see me. She'd admitted it herself. But I'd caught the wariness in her eyes. That wariness remained each time she looked at me. Obviously, she was furious I'd ignored Conreth's orders—just as I was furious she'd left without me. But...

I scanned the group. Asinia's eyes met mine, and I gestured for her to join me.

She arched one eyebrow and waved her hand imperiously, gesturing for me to join *her*.

I was beginning to see exactly why Asinia and Prisca were so close.

Glancing meaningfully at the others—who were riding closer to her than to me—I pointed at the spot next to mine. She rolled her eyes but slowed her horse.

"What did Conreth say to Prisca when she met with him while I was gone?" I asked.

She narrowed her eyes at me. "Why?"

"Because Prisca is acting strangely."

Not just strangely. Something in the way she looked at me told me I'd hurt her, and she was preparing for me to do it again. I ground my teeth.

Asinia snorted. "Your brother reminded all of us that he'd sent a letter to the castle, instructing you to bring her with you when you left."

Her words at the city gates ran on a loop through my head.

"This is because people believe I'm the hybrid heir, isn't it? You and your brother...the fae king... You want to use me somehow."

I should have felt satisfied. This was, after all, proof that Prisca cared. Instead, fury burned in my gut. Conreth was still playing his games. I'd told Prisca he couldn't truly punish me—at least not now, while we were on the brink of war. But he knew to strike where I was weakest.

I refused to allow this any longer.

Asinia nudged her horse, trotting back to the others. I watched as she said something that made Prisca laugh some more, her head tipping back in the dappled sunlight.

I wasn't entirely sure when this woman had become as necessary to me as the air in my lungs.

Maybe it was when she finally understood how to use her power—and used it to freeze me in place so she could kick me in the balls.

Perhaps it was the moment I realized she'd never gotten on that ship. And she was instead in the most dangerous place she could possibly have been as she fought to free her best friend.

It might have been when I saw her dying in that fucking castle and realized I was so completely out of my mind, it might as well have been me who was poisoned.

Maybe it was the way her voice had shaken with rage when she'd learned of my life in that camp when I'd only seen nine winters. Her fury that she couldn't turn back time and rescue the boy I'd been.

There were so many moments that had shown me who she was. Had demonstrated her bravery, loyalty, and cunning.

I was tired of fighting it. It was time to make sure my wildcat knew I'd wanted her from the start. And I would want her until the end.

PRISCA

That night, we made camp in a small clearing. Lorian and the others were much more vigilant than the guards Conreth had sent with us. When I asked him why, he said it was because they'd spent years traveling through the fae lands, and they knew just what kind of creatures hid in the forests, waiting to prey on unsuspecting travelers.

"We need to talk," Lorian murmured in my ear after dinner. I shivered at the feel of his warm breath on my skin, even as I slitted my eyes at him.

"What about?"

"Do you truly want to do this here?"

I glanced around the clearing. The others were gathered in small groups, eating and chatting, but I caught more than a few interested looks directed our way.

"I talked to Asinia," Lorian rumbled.

"And what did you talk to Asinia about?"

His eyes hardened. "About how Conreth told you I only brought you to the fae lands because he had ordered it."

"What is your point?"

He watched me, his green eyes bright. "Check my saddlebag, wildcat."

I didn't move. "Why?"

"Scared?"

Annoyance flickered through me, and I stalked over to his saddlebag, riffling through it until my hand brushed parchment. I pulled the letters free.

They were dated. And they were from the time we were in the Eprothan castle.

I glanced over my shoulder, but Lorian was just watching me. So I scanned the first letter.

It was from someone named C. Conreth. He was... berating Lorian for the way he'd threatened the healer when I was poisoned.

The memory rose up. The way Lorian had ordered me to live. And how he'd stayed by my side. When I'd finally started to recover, he'd even carried me to the bathing room.

"You can tell yourself whatever makes it easier for you to hate me, wildcat. But it was real. All of it."

I pulled out the next letter. And my heart skipped a beat.

Dear C,

I'm taking the wildcat with me when we leave. She won't be pleased by this, so I'm afraid you're unlikely to meet her at her best—although, you've always enjoyed seeing me with my hands full.

And I have no doubt that she will make me pay.

Yes, she has the power of time. And has even kept me frozen for several moments.

Everything else is going according to plan. Apart from the fact that I still can't find what we're looking for.

L

Lorian had written this before he knew who I was. He'd told his brother I had the power of time, but he'd said it as if he was...*proud*. Not as if he was planning to use me.

On the back of the letter, Conreth had scrawled a quick note back to his brother. Likely the only reason Lorian still had the original letter.

I whirled, the letters still in my hands.

Lorian grabbed my wrist, and I let him pull me out of the clearing, away from the others. When we were close to the river, he let me go.

"You were planning to take me with you," I said.

"Even before your brother knew who I was."

One sharp nod.

"Why?"

"I told you why. Because you're mine."

He said the words as if he were commenting on the weather. As if they were simply *fact*.

Ignoring the way my traitorous heart thumped harder, I turned away. "You don't get to decide that. You don't—"

"Prisca."

His voice was so gentle, I flinched. A callused finger brushed my throat.

"Wildcat."

He took my shoulders gently, turning me to face him. My stomach tightened, my heart tripped, and my eyes inexplicably filled.

"Gods, don't do that."

"I'm fine." I swallowed. "It's just been a long day."

"Talk to me."

I gazed up at his face. The sharp cheekbones, strong jaw, those green eyes. Those eyes were dark now, concerned. But his expression shuttered as he watched me watching him. "You latched on to my brother's words because you knew you needed something to help you keep your distance, didn't you?"

I turned away, but he just crowded my body until my back hit a tree. "And if I did?"

"You can raise all the walls between us that you like. I'll knock them down one by one. In the end, it will be *us*, wildcat."

He spoke with such a deep certainty. A *knowing*. It would be easy to get wrapped up in that if I didn't remind myself of reality. "You know that's not what's going to happen here."

"So, you'll give up? I expected better from you."

I shoved my hands against his chest. When he didn't move, I attempted to kick him in the shin. He waited me out, until I glowered at him. "You've always been like this. Always pushed me until I wanted to break."

He let out a low growl. "You think I didn't want to be soft with you? Didn't want to guide you gently with sweet, encouraging words? Perhaps I could have done such a thing if you weren't a queen. If you weren't going to be in danger over and over again. If I didn't know you'd eventually see me for who I was and *leave*, and my only hope was that I'd taught you enough to survive without me." He eyed me. "Now, why don't you tell *me* something, wildcat. Give me one thing to hold on to."

I hesitated. Moments passed, until the life began to eke from his eyes, his expression becoming blank. Cold.

I dropped my gaze. He caught my chin in his hand. "Look at me," he demanded.

I lifted my gaze to his face. I'd expected to see triumph. But...it was tenderness in his eyes now. Tenderness and stubborn expectation.

I sucked in a deep breath, and the words came out in a rush.

"I've gone my whole life feeling like I'm holding my breath. Like my lungs are burning. Like I'm desperately fighting for each gasp of air. But when you're around, I can…breathe. And I'm furious at you, because when that ends…when we're forced apart, I don't know how I'll take a full breath without you."

I caught the dazed pleasure that flickered across his face before he could hide it. My eyes stung.

He slid his hand into my hair, right as his lips caressed the side of my throat. I angled my head to give him more room. Gods, he was good at that.

"So, wildcat," he murmured against my ear. "Just how much did you miss me?" The question was a low taunt. Heat pooled in my lower belly.

"A little," I said. "Hardly at all, really. If anything, I barely noticed you weren't here."

He nipped my earlobe, and I laughed. His lips caught my laugh, his mouth hot and possessive against mine. His hand slipped to my lower back, urging me closer, and I breathed him in.

My hands ripped at his shirt, desperate to feel his skin against mine. He groaned, and then he was stripping me with methodical precision, his gaze hot as he watched me. I shivered at the promise in those green eyes.

My head spun as he lifted me into his arms, stumbling toward a fallen log. He sat, and I slid my hand into his leathers, stroking the hard length of him.

Moments later, he was sliding inside me. I gasped against his mouth, and he nipped my lower lip, his hands cupping my ass.

"You feel so fucking good." He took my mouth,

swallowing my moans, and I tightened around him. "There are so many things I want to do to you. With you."

I rode him slowly, getting used to his size in this position, groaning at the feel of him inside me.

"That's it," he urged me on, and I threw my head back as he kissed his way across my breasts. The feel of him angled right where I wanted him most...

I needed more.

His hands moved to my thighs, easily lifting me up and down, and I ground against him as he hit the spot inside me that made me tremble.

"Yes," he hissed, pulling me down harder, going deeper. Even in this position, I was at his mercy, and I clutched at his shoulders, my nails digging in as he brushed his thumb over my clit.

He growled when I clamped down around him. "There you go," he said. "Give me your pleasure."

I shuddered, panting as my climax poured through me, unfurling slow and long. Lorian watched me, his eyes burning into mine, before following me over with a low groan.

17

LORIAN

Two days later, we stopped to water the horses just a few hours from the largest fae village on this side of the lake. Traveling suited Prisca. Her cheeks were flushed, her eyes bright, and she constantly swept her gaze over the landscape, as if drinking in everything she could.

Was it any wonder I'd felt the first stirring of reluctant interest when we'd been forced to travel together all those weeks ago?

"What are you thinking?" Prisca asked, and my lips twitched. I told her, and she scowled at me. "You did *not* behave like a man who was finding it difficult to keep his hands off me."

"Believe me, wildcat, I've always found it difficult to keep my hands off you."

She sent me an unimpressed look that made me want to haul her into my arms. "Tell me about where we're going."

"I think I'll keep the location a

surprise. But you'll get to see Rythos's people."

Behind us, Asinia sat on an overturned log next to Telean, discussing some kind of seamstress technique with fabric. Marth's deep laugh sounded from the river to our right. Likely, he was regaling Cavis and Galon with an entirely untrue exploit.

"Rythos's people?" Prisca's eyes lit up with interest. And I clamped down on the urge to pound his face into the dust.

I knew Prisca didn't think of Rythos that way. But did she have to look so delighted at the mere mention of his name?"

"Lorian?"

Was that amusement in her voice? Yes, her amber eyes were laughing at me.

"Rythos was a spoiled second son with no purpose when I met him," I informed her.

"Mm-hmm," she grinned at me. "Do tell."

"Your fondness for him is going to get him hurt one day."

The grin left her face, and she gave me a narrow-eyed stare. Unfortunately, the wind ruffled her curls, and she looked adorable rather than threatening.

"I think of Rythos as a brother," she said.

"Don't you have more than enough brothers by now?" I muttered.

She sighed. "So, Rythos was a spoiled second son," she prompted.

"Did I hear my name?" Rythos called, and Prisca grinned at me.

"You did," she called back. "I was asking Lorian about your people."

Rythos tied his horse to a tree branch and nodded at her. "My people are known as the Arslan. They're solemn—primarily scholars and engineers, known for their incredible minds and magical inventions."

Prisca was studying him. "Why did you leave?"

"My parents urged me to give my life some meaning. Some way that would help my people or the fae in general. I'd imagined I might find a way to bring down the barrier to discover if we could trade with other continents. My brother was centuries older than me, and he was unenthusiastic about getting to know his loud, charming younger brother." Rythos winked, but it wasn't difficult to hear the tension in his voice.

"And then I arrived," I said, and Rythos cast me a grateful look. "Rythos's father was unimpressed. He didn't see how we could possibly find a way to steal back our magic, unite the fae lands, and win the war."

"Lorian was cold and arrogant," Rythos said dryly, making Prisca laugh. "But he truly believed in something, and he was willing to do whatever it took to free his people. I decided to join him. My father told me that if I was going to leave, not to bother returning. I saw that as a sign that I would only ever be accepted if I was who my father wanted me to be, and I left anyway. I was young, selfish, and rebelling against my father because I had nothing better to do. But when I began traveling with the Bloodthirsty Prince—"

"Don't call him that," Prisca snapped.

Surprise flashed in Rythos's eyes. My heart strained, my throat locked up, and for a long moment, I couldn't speak. I reached for Prisca's hand and pressed a kiss to her wrist.

She didn't need to defend me to Rythos. But the fact that she would…

Rythos met my eyes. Then he gave Prisca a fond look that almost got him stabbed. "When I began traveling with *Lorian*," he continued, "and saw what was happening to the fae and hybrids away from Arslan lands, what started as a second-son's rebellion became something…more."

It had become his reason for breathing. And now, Rythos would return to the people who had disowned him. And he would steal from them—likely removing any chance of a reconciliation.

Prisca's expression tightened. "Should I talk to your father?" she asked. "How do I convince him to help us?"

"What do you usually do in these situations?" Rythos asked.

She chewed on her lower lip. "Well, I'm very new to this, but usually, I find a weak spot and poke at it. Eventually, the other person grows so enraged, they say something they didn't mean to."

Rythos laughed. "That tactic could use some work. Thankfully, I'm not planning to let you loose in my father's court just yet."

"Then what are you planning to do?"

"You'll see."

The Queen

"What do you mean, they're rioting?" Sabium snapped.

The messenger bowed his head. "It is confined to the slums so far, Your Majesty. One of the humans who was…arrested was the son of Caddaril the Cleaver."

Elation bubbled in my chest. Sabium's expression was stone.

"The crime lord. You arrested the son of one of the most notorious crime lords in this city."

This messenger was a brave one. He flicked his gaze toward Tymedes, who was closely watching this conversation. The commander stiffened at the silent implication.

"Is the son still alive?"

"No, Your Majesty. As usual, he was burned with the dawn."

Sabium's eyes flickered as he processed this information. "The Cleaver is responsible for the riots."

"Yes, Your Majesty. He is making some outrageous claims. Usually, those claims would be ignored. Yet…he is not the first human parent to lose a child in the past month."

This messenger wasn't just bold. He was practically daring Sabium to have him hauled away.

"And?" Sabium's voice was pure ice.

"And he is claiming that the corrupt have not been rejected by the gods. He insists they fled their kingdom after it was invaded, and…"

"By all means," Sabium crooned. "Continue speaking."

The messenger went silent. Sabium pinned him with an expectant look, and the messenger took a deep breath.

"He has said you are a thief who has stolen your people's power. His son was human and was killed due only to mistaken identity—as were many others."

My hands tightened on the arms of my throne as Sabium considered his next move. If he ordered the slums to be burned to the ground, he would have a full-scale rebellion on his hands. And he knew it.

As much as I would wish otherwise, Sabium was far too smart for that.

"Invite Caddaril to the castle. I will have dinner with him, and we will talk through our differences. I'm sure we can come to some arrangement."

The messenger nodded, bowed, and escaped out the door before Sabium could change his mind.

I hid my smile. And there, Sabium had erred.

He had no understanding of the true depths of love a parent could have for their child. He truly thought he could pay Caddaril off, perhaps offer him more power or agree to have his guards look the other way when it came to Caddaril's crimes against the crown.

Sabium didn't comprehend the truth. That the crime lord would see him dead if he could.

"And the slums?" Tymedes asked.

"Send in the guard. Tell them to keep deaths to a minimum and offer food and coin to those who agree to return to their homes."

Frustration gnawed at me. Tymedes bowed, and I waited until he'd made his way out of the room before slowly getting to my feet.

"And where are you going?"

I raised a brow at Sabium's tone. "I wish to rest."

He watched me with those dead eyes. Finally, he nodded. *Dismissing* me, as if I were one of his subjects.

Through sheer willpower, I controlled my expression, walking slowly to the door, head held high. By the time I reached my rooms, I was trembling with rage.

"Your Majesty?"

"Not now, Lisveth. Everyone out."

My ladies filed out of the room, leaving me in blessed peace. I paced, almost desperate for my meeting with Pelysian. When I could wait no longer, I whirled, striding toward the mirror.

Truthfully, few things terrified me like the thought of transporting myself through this mirror to its twin. But impatience rolled up my spine, and I squared my shoulders.

I could do this.

Pelysian stepped into the room, suddenly so close,

we were almost touching. His eyes widened, and I took a step back.

"Forgive me, Your Majesty. Were you…"

"No. I was merely waiting."

He eyed me but said nothing. I turned to pace. "You said your mother couldn't locate my son because of the wards surrounding him."

"That is correct."

"Could she find the hybrid heir? Or her friends?"

Silence. I turned back to him.

"If Sabium's best locators cannot—"

"Do not lie to me," I hissed. "Your mother's power is different."

"Her power requires great sacrifice, Your Majesty."

"Speak to her. I will do whatever it takes."

PRISCA

The empty wooden boat was practically a dinghy. Fashioned from timeworn wood—without a sail or oars—it drifted eerily across the placid lake toward us. I stood on the wharf and watched it approach.

"It looks like it's being sailed by ghosts," Asinia murmured next to me. The boat bumped up against the wharf, and we both eyed it.

"Not ghosts," Galon said. "Just magic. In you get."

The wharf groaned beneath us, the wooden boards slick under my boots as we piled into the boat, one by one. Galon held out his hand, steadying us as we stepped inside, following Rythos's directions for seating to keep the small boat balanced. I ended up wedged between Lorian and Asinia. And then we were moving once more.

The boat rocked gently as we glided across the vast lake, the warm glow of the late-afternoon sun reflected on water. It was so still, if I looked down I could see the gold and crimson of the sky mirrored below us.

A breeze cooled the back of my neck, carrying the scent of wild flowers, and I sighed, closing my eyes.

Lorian leaned down until his mouth was right next to my ear. "You're so fucking beautiful."

My eyes popped open, and just like that, I wanted to find a quiet spot somewhere and climb on top of him.

"We need to work on your timing," I said breathlessly.

"You've never complained about my...timing before."

I laughed.

Marth rolled his eyes. "I think I liked it better when you were actively planning his murder," he told me.

Seated on the other side of the boat, Rythos was quiet. Brooding. I wasn't used to seeing Rythos unhappy. He was the one who cheered everyone else up. Perhaps I could do the same for him.

When Tibris brooded, distraction was the best approach. Perhaps Rythos was the same.

"Tell me more about the Arslan," I said.

Rythos pulled his attention from the horizon and cocked an eyebrow. "What do you want to know?"

"Everything."

That at least earned me an almost-smile. "Let's just say, if you're impressed by this boat, you'll enjoy your visit. Our territory is known as the island of Quorith. When the gods gave the fae our amulets, our territory was too small for the fae king to consider giving one to our people. Now, it is the second most populated region outside of the capital. Many of the fae have been attracted to Quorith over the centuries, making it a diverse, welcoming place."

"Do you miss it?" Asinia asked.

"Sometimes. Not enough to go back, even if my father would allow such a thing."

Rythos nodded at the lakeshore as we approached. "You'll enjoy this next part."

I'd expected the boat to dock once more, but instead, it seemed to increase its momentum, until we were almost flying toward the shore. My lungs turned to stone, my heart slammed against my ribs, and fear punched into my gut.

Lorian threw his arm around my shoulders, squeezing me to him. Rythos called out a fae word that seemed to rip through the air, echoing over and over.

The boat moved faster. Telean looked as peaceful as if she were in a carriage traveling through some lush park.

Asinia had turned pale, but her chin stuck out stubbornly. She'd decided to trust the fae, and once she gave someone her trust, she didn't take it back lightly.

The boat cut to the right. And Asinia let out a squeak as we hurtled *through* the shore. The breath was still frozen in my lungs, or I might have made the same noise myself.

And then it was over, and we were surrounded by trees on all sides, navigating a winding river through the forest.

"How?" I croaked out.

"We're traveling toward a bay," Lorian said. "This river leads into the bay, but the Arslan warded it centuries ago as a way to increase security. Only those of their blood can see the ward and unlock it."

The river narrowed, until low-hanging branches almost brushed against the tops of our heads. But within minutes, the river spat us out into the bay, and the scent of salt water drifted up my nostrils.

The bay was narrow, and nestled at the mouth of it was the mere suggestion of an island. Blurred and indistinct, it was almost difficult to look at, my attention continually diverted by some kind of ancient magic.

Quorith.

Rythos let out a shuddering breath but stood, easily keeping his balance as the boat rocked back and forth along the waves. He said another word, and I gasped at the explosion of light fifty foot-spans ahead of us. He'd taken out another ward.

Awe washed over me as I took in the island. From here, I could only see the main dock and the buildings in the distance—their elegant spires stretching toward the sky—but there was *something* about this island that made my heart beat faster in my chest.

Lorian led us off the boat, while Rythos had what seemed like a strained conversation with a fae in uniform.

"Wildcat?"

"One moment."

Lorian chuckled, but I was barely paying attention. I was too busy soaking in everything I could see.

"I want to live here," Asinia breathed.

I could see why this island called to someone like Asinia, who adored color. Lush green foliage sprouted from every corner, vivid blossoms dotting the landscape like precious jewels. Flowers hung in baskets from balconies and streetlamps, while the buildings themselves were painted in bright colors that seemed to glow as the sun set behind us.

I breathed deeply, drawing the scent of wild flowers and salt deep into my lungs. It was much warmer here, and the air was heavy, humid. It was the kind of place that would come alive after the sun had set each night.

Lively chatter and laughter reached my ears. Across from the dock, several taverns were open, the fae sitting at tables outside. Most of the Arslan were as dark-skinned as Rythos and all of them in their true forms. It was a shock seeing so many pointed ears after the last few days. Lorian and the others had been wearing their human glamour most of the time, although when I glanced at him, he was back in his fae form. Larger, taller, with his pointed ears, the sharp jut of his cheekbones, and, of course, those green eyes which seemed to glow. And yet, the look in those eyes was so familiar, it removed any lingering fear I might have had from the first time I'd seen his face form at the city gates.

His eyes met mine for a long moment, as if he was waiting for something. When I stared back, the ghost of a smile curved his mouth, and he leaned down, pressing a kiss to my forehead.

He moved away to speak to Cavis, and I caught sight of a huge building in the distance at the edge of the city. The building was a sprawl of towers, connected by bridges and passages of marble and stone hanging in the air. Was that where Rythos's family lived?

Two women with long, dark hair approached from across the street, hand in hand. One of the women was all lush curves, while the other was tall and muscled, a dagger in the sheath at her hip.

Rythos handed the uniformed fae a heavy purse. Clearly, we were bribing our way through this part of our plan. The taller woman narrowed her eyes at Rythos, and both women picked up their pace, until they were standing close to him. Did they know Rythos's plans? Were they here to stop us?

The taller woman could have been his sister, with the same dark skin and a dimple in the exact same spot when Rythos muttered something that made her crack a smile.

"There's something about them," I murmured, staring at the women. They were in love, yes, but they looked at each other with something deeper.

"They're mates," Cavis said, strolling toward us.

"Mates?" Conreth's words came back to me. He'd said his aunt and uncle were mates. But his tone hadn't invited me to ask exactly what it meant.

"It doesn't happen often," Lorian said, stepping up next to Cavis. "For those in power, it is often ignored. My brother's mate was a serving girl he met in a tavern before our parents died. When he took over the throne, he knew he had to marry, and he needed a match that would cement him on the throne."

"He could do that? What happens if you don't choose your mate?"

Lorian sighed. "Meeting your mate, knowing who they are—this is seen as fate tapping you on the shoulder and pointing you toward the one who would be your perfect match. Sometimes, that timing doesn't work. Besides, it's incredibly rare for fae to find their mates. And just because fate has chosen for them, does not mean they need to go along with her whims." He gave me a look, and I smirked back. He knew my thoughts about fate interfering with our lives.

"Do you think Conreth regrets it? Leaving her there?"

Lorian shrugged. "I can't see how he wouldn't. He had the opportunity to live his life next to the one person who would bring out the best in him—in all ways. Who would understand him deep in his soul. And he chose a political match instead. He has to live with that for the rest of his life."

A horrifying thought intruded, clamping around my throat. My voice came out low and hoarse. "Have you ever met *your* mate?"

The thought of him knowing another woman had been designed by the gods for him made me want to vomit.

Rythos stalked over to us. "We need to go." His expression was harder than I'd ever seen it. "That was my cousin Miric and her mate Janea. They know what we're doing."

18

PRISCA

"What's the plan?" I murmured to Lorian.

"Steal a particular ship before anyone notices."

"That's the entire plan?" I asked. Behind me, Asinia chuckled.

"The best plans are simple, wildcat."

Rythos led us toward the other end of the dock. A symphony of groans and creaks sounded around us as we walked, whispering of the countless journeys the docked vessels had taken.

I shaded my eyes against the sun glinting off the water, nodding as Asinia pointed to a strange ship adorned with majestic wings. It wouldn't surprise me if the ship could actually fly, although Lorian shook his head when I sent him a questioning glance.

To our right, a sleek, sinuous ship seemed to undulate like a snake on waves, its hull shimmering like iridescent scales. The ship on our left boasted billowing sails that appeared so delicate they might have been gossamer, giving the impression of the finest lacework.

The ship Rythos led us to was much less whimsical. If anything, it more closely resembled the pirate queen's warship, the streamlined black hull drinking in the sun. Carved into its prow, a majestic sea serpent was caught in mid-motion—its intricate scales so realistically wrought, it was as if it was preparing to dive into the depths of the ocean at any moment.

I wanted these ships.

I could practically see them, filled with powerful fae and cutting Regner off from his own fleet.

Rythos jerked his head, gesturing for us to board. I shifted my attention back to the ship, stomach clenching. If only I'd saved some of the concoction the healer had made for me the last time I was in this situation.

I sighed, resigning myself to weeks of leaning over the ship's railing. Lorian gave me a questioning glance, and I shook my head, following him on board.

Rythos's cousin had trailed after us, and she was standing on the dock, watching closely, although she didn't seem to be planning to alert whoever was in charge. Instead, she surveyed us with that strange half smile on her face, Janea by her side.

Rythos and Galon seemed to know what they were doing, because they threw out orders to Cavis and Marth, ignoring the rest of us. Within moments, we appeared ready to depart.

Masts creaked overhead, and a glittering pattern

sparkled in the sun. "What are they?" I asked.

"Glyphs. They harness the essence of the winds. This is just one ship in the fastest fleet you'll find anywhere on this continent," Lorian said.

He leaned forward, caging me against the railing, and pressed a kiss to my neck. I arched for him.

"I hope you weren't planning to steal this ship without me," a voice said. My heart jumped into my throat, and I wiggled out of Lorian's arms.

A man stood behind Rythos, his head canted. While he boasted the usual fae beauty, he was short and slight, his fair skin barely flushed. But his eyes were surprisingly dark, and they glinted with fun.

Rythos tensed, slowly turned, and took in the other man. "Fendrel."

"You left me behind last time, you bastard."

"You'll be staying behind this time too," Rythos said. But a slow grin spread across his face, and he crossed the deck in three strides, pulling Fendrel into a hug.

The two men embraced, but Rythos pulled back quickly. "You need to go."

Fendrel's face fell. "That's the first thing you're saying to me after you left me last time?"

Lorian cleared his throat. "If I remember correctly, your father threatened to disown you as well if you went with him."

His unsaid words hung in the air. Rythos had been disowned and left. Fendrel had chosen to stay.

Fendrel waved that away. "A mistake. I've wanted

off this island ever since, and clearly, fate has stepped in if you're stealing my father's ship."

"His father's ship?" Asinia asked.

Fendrel gave her a wide grin. "Aren't you a beauty? And yes, my father's ship. Rythos has obviously just learned that his own father's ship is currently in use."

"You can't come with us," Rythos murmured. "We're heading into dangerous waters."

"Dangerous waters are my favorite."

Next to Lorian, Marth rolled his eyes. "The most dangerous waters that man has experienced were in his bathtub."

Fendrel shot him a glare.

Galon reappeared from below deck. He shook his head at the sight of Fendrel, but his gaze was already flicking to Rythos. "We need to leave now," he said.

Rythos took Fendrel aside and murmured quietly to him. It didn't seem to go well. A dull flush swept up the back of Fendrel's neck, and he stomped from the ship. Was he the kind of man who would lash out? Report us for this theft? Rythos didn't seem overly concerned, although he watched Fendrel leave, heaved a sigh, and stalked to the ship's helm.

He nodded back at Lorian, who stepped out from behind me and lifted one arm.

It started with a slight breeze against my skin. And I shivered at the feel of Lorian's power caressing me. I shot him a look and he grinned back at me, a tendril of his power dipping lower, beneath my shirt.

Lorian's grin widened. Something warmed inside my chest at seeing him have *fun*.

The wind picked up. The ropes securing the ship to the dockside loosened, slithering back to coil neatly upon the deck. Slowly, the ship began to inch away from the dock, the water beneath us frothing and churning.

More wind. The air around us grew charged with energy, the glyphs above our head stirring until they glowed. We pulled away from the dock even more quickly than I could have imagined. Behind us, shouts rang out, and my stomach churned.

Rythos's expression was stony. His family had already disowned him, and he'd done this anyway. For me.

A ward appeared in front of us. Someone was attempting to stop us. Rythos waved his hand, and it broke with a twang.

Lorian's wind pushed us on. I was so used to seeing his lightning, I'd forgotten he could control other elements. His brow was slightly wrinkled in concentration, those green eyes a little blurred. The wind wrapped around him, until I could see the outline of his chest muscles beneath it.

My heart thumped erratically, my stomach tumbled, and my knees went a little weak. I wanted to drag him below deck and have my way with him.

Would it always be this way between us?

His eyes met mine, sharpening with dark promise, and I forced myself to glance away.

We were in the open water now, and Lorian's winds began to calm, the glyphs taking over and wielding the natural winds.

Across the ship, Rythos was staring into the water, his shoulders hunched. He was surrounded by friends and family, and yet in this moment, he looked alone. I knew what that was like. I'd spent my life feeling alone in my village. Taking stumbling steps across the ship, I made my way to him, my stomach already churning.

"Lorian told me you get seasick," he murmured. "This part won't last long."

I had no idea what he meant by "this part" since we were days from the hybrid kingdom. But I nodded anyway. The others wandered away, while Lorian stopped to speak quietly to Galon.

"You could have used your power on everyone who saw you arrive at that island," I said.

"You could have as well."

I reared back. Should I have…

He put his hand on my arm. "Relax, Prisca. I would have asked if I thought we needed your help. I was prepared to involve you if the worst happened. My cousin would have warned us."

I thought back to her strange smile and the way she'd just watched us, as if fascinated by our stupidity. "Truly?"

He laughed. "Yes. Oh, she would have made me pay for it. But my cousin is still loyal." His smile faded. "Think about what you would do if we were all captured by Regner. How you would do anything to keep your friends safe."

My heart pounded at the thought, and Rythos nodded at me. "That feeling is what I can create. It's not just that people *like* me. It's that they think I'm their friend. And when I pull that power away, it's as if they've suddenly lost a deep, trusting friendship. As they come to their senses, they feel the betrayal that one feels when they realize they never really knew their friend at all. And that friend has been lying to them from the moment they met."

"I'm sorry."

"For what?"

"That your power doesn't feel good to use."

He looked vaguely amused. "Your power rips your body apart. I've seen your face covered in blood when you stretch time for too long."

"Yes, but it's different. There are no long-lasting effects…unless I leave someone dead, of course."

He laughed at that. We were silent for a long moment. My stomach twisted, and I took a moment to focus on the horizon and breathe through it.

"It helps that I've experienced that feeling," Rythos said into the silence. "I've lived with that emptiness. When my father disowned me, most of my so-called friends turned their backs on me. All except Fendrel. I was no longer close to power in their eyes anymore."

"They didn't deserve you."

He wrapped his arm around my shoulders. "Thank you."

He said the words, but I could tell he didn't truly believe

me. His family and friends had turned their backs on him all those years ago, and he was still wounded from it.

I met his eyes. "I think the true measure of someone is not how much power they have, but how they choose to wield that power. You choose not to make anyone feel the way you felt. If you'd been a small person, you could have lashed out. You could have used your power on them and then left."

"Don't think I didn't consider it. Besides, most of our power was also taken when Lorian's uncle…"

"Something tells me you would have wielded whatever you had," I said wryly, and he laughed.

I watched him. I hadn't realized until today just how much power Rythos had. "Your father didn't just disown you because you chose to go work with Lorian, did he?"

"No. Even with the little power I had left, I was a threat to his rule. And to my brother. It didn't matter that I didn't want to rule on that island. They knew that if I changed my mind, I could turn the council on them with a smile and a few words. My power was too dangerous. *I* was too dangerous. Because I could overthrow them."

"But you were his son. You told him you didn't want the throne."

He shrugged one shoulder. "Such things don't matter when power is involved."

We fell into silence for a long moment. This was one of those times when I felt like a child. I kept assuming other people held the same values I did. A quiet, peaceful life. Family. Close friends. Laughter.

If I was honest with myself, it was one of the reasons I'd wanted to have my cousin watched. I'd hoped he was a good man. A man who would join us and be part of what little family we had left. No wonder Demos was frustrated with me. He'd been raised to understand just how the world truly worked.

"What are you thinking?"

Rythos had made his own family. Lorian and the others would die before they willingly betrayed him. I could make my own family too.

"It's not important. Thank you. For doing this. For helping me visit the hybrid kingdom."

He sighed. "It's not just for you, Pris. Part of it is for my own conscience."

"What do you mean?"

"My people could have helped during the fae wars. Hell, we could have helped when your kingdom was invaded. There were ships close enough that they could have gotten there in time."

My mouth went dry. "Why didn't they?"

"While my father rules, such decisions are made by consensus. The council votes."

I clenched my hand around the railing. Rythos dropped his gaze, and when our eyes met once more, his expression was tight. "One vote, Pris. Your people lost by one vote."

Leaning over the side of the ship, I heaved.

Lorian was there in an instant, holding my hair off my face.

"Ugh, leave me alone," I croaked out.

He brought a waterskin to my lips. "Never."

I managed a few sips, and he stroked my back. "It won't be long, wildcat."

I still had no idea what they meant when they said that, but I lifted my head, finding Rythos watching me, his dark eyes glinting with repressed rage.

"They won't get to stay out of things this time, Prisca. Regner will learn my people were involved. And when you eventually go to my father and demand our fleet—which I know you're already planning to do—" he grinned at me, and I didn't have the energy to pretend I hadn't been daydreaming about what that fleet could do for us "—he'll know he can no longer pretend impartiality."

Lorian's arm tightened around me, and I shifted my gaze to the other side of the deck.

"Found this one hiding below deck." Galon was holding Fendrel by the back of his neck.

Rythos's curses turned the air blue.

PRISCA

Three days later, we were still traveling. Although this time, my stomach was just fine.

When Lorian and Rythos had said it "wouldn't

be long," they hadn't been referring to the trip itself—although that was much faster than expected as well. No, they'd been referring to the point when we were far enough away from the island that Rythos touched the ship's helm, said a word that echoed through my brain, and the ship began to sink beneath the waves.

The blood had drained from my face in such a rush, I'd swayed on my feet. Asinia had launched herself toward us, Telean following at a much more sedate pace.

"What's happening?" Asinia had demanded.

We were going to die. That was what was happening.

The ship seemed to vibrate with power. And a dome-like ward slid up from the railing surrounding the deck, encasing it in a protective bubble.

I'd automatically sucked in a breath, only releasing it when Lorian poked a finger into my ribs.

"Is there…"

"Enough air for the trip? Yes."

"You could have told me…"

"That not only would you be on a ship, but you'd be under the water?" He'd quirked one eyebrow, and despite the situation, I'd smiled.

I would have been enveloped in dread from the moment I learned about our planned transportation until the moment it happened. Still, I'd given him my best hard stare. "We're going to talk about your high-handed ways."

He'd sent me a wicked grin.

If I thought too much about what it meant to travel beneath the waves—and what would happen if that strange ward somehow popped—I grew light-headed. But when I pushed those thoughts out of my mind…

It was…peaceful.

"Are you ready, wildcat?"

I glanced over my shoulder as Lorian stalked toward me. Would I always be endlessly fascinated by the sight of him doing simple things like walking?

My heart twisted. One day, these memories would be all I had of him. And I wanted them solidified in my mind for the rest of my life.

"Ready?" I asked.

"We'll be emerging soon."

Even knowing we would return on this ship, some part of me mourned that the trip was ending. The ship's strange ward cast colors I'd never seen before into the waters surrounding us, the cool glow illuminating the underwater world. I never could have imagined just how much there was to see beneath the waves.

Vibrant, diverse marine life swam past us. Sleek fish with shimmering scales of gold and silver, majestic manta rays gliding effortlessly through the water, schools of tiny iridescent fish, no larger than one of my fingers.

But over the past three days, I'd occasionally glimpsed creatures of a more strange, magical nature. I'd never seen enough to understand what I'd caught sight of—they only seemed to appear in the corner of my eye— but I'd known they were there. Watching us.

With nothing else to do, we'd spent our time eating— Rythos had somehow ensured this ship was fully stocked with food. Of course Lorian and Galon had insisted we train for hours each morning, and when we were finally exhausted, we'd played King's Web.

The biggest surprise? No longer did Asinia struggle to hide her thoughts. Now, she'd even beaten Marth.

My aunt was also good at the game. In her case, her expertise had come from years in the queen's employ.

Fendrel was absolutely terrible at deception, but his sly, self-deprecating humor meant that he fit right in with the rest of us.

When we'd gotten tired of King's Web, we'd told ludicrous stories and tasteless jokes. Rythos had been more than a little annoyed to learn Fendrel had snuck back on to the ship, but they'd spent hours drinking and reminiscing together. Fendrel had a limitless knowledge of drinking songs and other bawdy tunes—one of which had made Asinia laugh until wine dripped from her nose.

The ship began to rise. My heart pounded. I'd gotten used to the steady direction we'd been traveling and the occasional right turns to correct our course around the southern coast of the fae lands.

"Our bodies aren't designed to stay beneath the water for long," Lorian murmured in my ear. "The magic of this ship counteracts the pressure of the surrounding water."

Asinia appeared on the dock, shooting me a wide-eyed look. I nodded back at her. Of all the incredible sights we'd both seen since we left our village, this had to be the most awe-inspiring.

The ship continued to shoot up from beneath the

waves, water pouring from the surrounding dome. The rolling of the ship would have told me we were now above the waves if the dome hadn't disappeared a moment later.

Fresh air swept across the ship, and I tilted my face up. A gull shrieked, the ship creaked, and everything seemed suddenly too loud. The sunlight cast a dazzling glint on the water, and the salty breeze ruffled my hair. Above us, Aquilus circled, swooping down to land on Lorian's shoulder. He plucked the message from his hawk and handed it to me. "From Demos."

I scanned it, decoding it as I read. They hadn't yet located the hourglass. But… "Vicer convinced Tibris and Demos to help with a group of hybrids in Eprotha near the Gromalian border. They're going to travel with them across the border to make sure they get there safely."

I knew Demos well enough to know he would have preferred to keep looking for the hourglass, while Tibris would have insisted they escort the hybrids personally.

I was sure that argument had lasted for hours.

"Pris," Asinia said, and her voice cracked.

I swung my gaze to where she was pointing.

To our left, shreds of heavy fog clung to the waves, yet as we drew closer, fleeting glimpses of…something began to present themselves. My hands turned slick with sweat. This land, any hybrids who'd hidden during the attack and managed to stay alive…they were what we were fighting for.

The mist thinned, and I could make out the faintest suggestions of some kind of towering structure. Perhaps walls. Part of a castle? Or the once-fortified boundary of a city?

But we weren't traveling toward the kingdom. No, we were turning back toward the east.

Telean stepped up next to us, wrapping an arm around my waist. She peered into the distance, her expression tight with grief. "We can't go any closer," she said. "Already, we risk much by traveling this far into the Sleeping Sea."

We anchored offshore on the western coast of Eprotha, boarding a smaller boat to take us to the peninsula. The beginning of the Asric Pass was just a few thousand foot-spans away.

Demos had said if I was judged worthy, I would be taken across the sea. I had no idea who or what would be judging me, but it was clear we weren't welcome in the hybrid kingdom until such a thing happened.

Lorian murmured something to Rythos, who nodded. "Regner will be having this area watched," Lorian told me. He glanced at Telean, Asinia, and me. "Galon and Cavis will do a sweep of the forest nearby while Rythos and I check the beach. No wandering off alone."

I nodded. Hopefully, we would all be back on the ship soon and crossing the Sleeping Sea toward the hybrid kingdom—as long as I was found worthy. My stomach churned at the possibility that we'd instead be turned away, but I forced that thought out of my mind, refusing to consider it until it happened. If we could find allies here, if there were still people with magic who were willing to fight…

Perhaps we would have a chance against Regner's armies.

Lorian jumped over the side of the boat, landing gracefully next to Rythos, who was already standing on the rocky shore. If I attempted to do such a thing, I'd break a leg.

My gaze drifted toward the horizon, where the sea met the sky in a seamless embrace. Something caught my eye. A dark shape broke the surface, its movement disrupting the tranquility of the water. I squinted, and my heart skipped a beat as realization washed over me.

This was one of the monsters the hybrids had whispered about.

The creature surged upward, its sinuous body undulating with mesmerizing grace as it arched through the air. Scales, shimmering like a thousand suns, adorned its massive form, reflecting the sunlight in a kaleidoscope of iridescent hues. The monster's serpentine neck stretched high above the waves, its regal, triangular head crowned with an array of twisting, pointed horns.

It opened Its mouth, displaying teeth the size of my fingers, and my lungs seized. Those teeth had been designed to snag its prey and hold it beneath the water.

The creature unfurled its vast wings, the membrane between the bones glistening with droplets of sea spray. The wings, resembling those of a bat but on a colossal scale, cast enormous shadows upon the water. The monster flexed its muscular tail, the fins at the end propelling it through the water with astonishing speed and power.

I got the sense it was…preening.

The creature's eyes, pools of molten gold, bored into mine with an intelligence that made my stomach churn. A shiver ran down my spine at the keen curiosity behind that gaze.

The sea dragon was studying me just as intently as I was studying it.

"Gods," Asinia whispered next to me. "What exactly are you supposed to do now, Pris?"

The monster dove back into the depths, its mighty wings folding against its body. I swallowed. "I have no idea."

Telean stepped up next to me. "Now, we wait."

"Wait for what?"

"To see if anyone comes."

An arrow went whistling past my head. I dropped low, and Telean raised her hand, forming a shield. Several more arrows thunked into the shield, and we both ducked even lower until her shield disappeared, her power spent. My vision narrowed, blood pounded in my ears, and I bared my teeth. Iron guards. They'd waited for us as if we were their prey.

"I'm sorry," Telean said. "My power…"

I pulled the threads of my magic toward me and stood. I hadn't had a clear look, so I'd stopped time for everyone. But…there. At the edge of the forest. They were using the trees as cover so they could pick us off. We needed to lure them out.

Time resumed, but I knew where our attackers were now. I strained, until time stopped just for them.

"They're in the forest, using the trees for cover!" I screamed. In the distance, Galon and Cavis began roaring curses.

"Stay there," Lorian snarled from the beach below us, and then he was gone, sprinting toward the copse of trees with Rythos.

The threads began to slip. No. It was too early. If I dropped them now…

I held on with all my might.

"Pris!" Asinia was crawling along the dock toward me. I just shook my head, clenching my eyes closed as I focused on holding time still on land.

"Quiet, girl. Don't distract her. Take a crossbow and prepare yourself," Telean ordered.

Blood dripped from my nose.

"Release it, or you will lose consciousness," Telean warned at my side.

"Lorian…"

"Is merrily slaughtering our enemies with the others."

I released my hold and gasped, my head spinning. Telean handed me a cloth, and I pressed it to my face, using the side of the boat to haul myself to my feet.

Sun glinted off something to our left. More iron guards were creeping toward Lorian, Rythos, and the others. From behind.

Launching into motion, I swung myself over the edge of the boat, hitting knee-high water and splashing toward the shore. Telean's shield appeared once more, covering me. Asinia fired a bolt toward the enemy.

"Holy gods, I hit him," she crowed. "I guess Demos knows what he's talking about after all."

"Less bragging, more shooting!" I yelled back. She got to work, and the air filled with arrows. I dropped to the rocky shore and crouched. Galon was standing close to the edge of the forest, several iron guards advancing on him. My heart thundered, but he was already raising his hand, water from the sea lifting in a long, narrow spout that flew toward him. He used it as a shield, sprinting to the left, then dumped it over one of the iron guards' heads, using the distraction to stab him in the throat.

Cavis had launched to the right, preventing the iron guard from backing us toward the sea. The air suddenly smelled like a thunderstorm, the sharp, distinct scent of lightning making it clear Lorian was using his own power. But I couldn't see him. My breaths turned into panicked pants, and I scanned the shore.

Movement caught my eye. Near the edge of the forest, Fendrel hit the ground. I dashed toward him, zigzagging to avoid the arrows. A sob ripped through my chest.

An arrow was jutting out from his throat.

I dropped to my knees, my hands fluttering near his neck. But there was nothing to be done, Fendrel's eyes blank as he stared up at the sky.

I reached for my power, wrath burning through me. I would make them *pay*.

Shouts came from behind me, but I could hear the

clash of metal on metal in the forest ahead. Climbing to my feet, I pulled my sword and headed toward the sound.

The ground disappeared from beneath my feet. The last thing I heard was Lorian roaring my name.

19

PRISCA

I was standing in some kind of… tunnel.

The walls were smooth rock that glistened with veins of precious stones. Logically, I knew those walls weren't actually closing in on me.

But my body didn't seem to know that.

Lorian would be losing his mind. I'd heard the fury and fear in his voice when he'd roared my name. What if…what if the distraction had been enough for one of the iron guards to kill him?

My power had been helping us against the countless iron guards lying in wait. Now, my friends were all alone, fighting for their lives.

I panted, icy sweat dripping down my back. Daring a glance over my shoulder, I sucked in a breath. Nothing but a wall of solid rock. Above my head, there should have been a hole. I'd fallen down—I was sure of it. But it had disappeared.

Stretching in front of me, the

tunnel was dimly lit with the occasional orb of light. I had no other way to go except forward.

Something nudged my back. I whirled, swinging my sword.

There was nothing there.

Another nudge, this time poking at my shoulder. It was an invisible nudge. A magical nudge.

Someone was playing with me.

"Put me back," I hissed. "My friends need me."

Nudge.

Nudge, nudge, nudge.

I clenched my teeth and stalked down the tunnel. I'd find whoever had brought me here, and I'd make them eat this sword.

The tunnel seemed to go on forever, and yet I lost all sense of time. When I turned, the wall was still at my back, yet I'd been walking for long enough that my mouth was dry.

This was a strange, magical place. And yet, it was almost familiar. I quickened my steps, and something glinted in the distance.

A wooden ladder. Something unwound in my gut. I wouldn't be stuck down here forever. I could get out. My claustrophobia was unfortunate at the best of times, but I could practically hear Lorian in my ear, ordering me to stay exactly where I was and not to leave the tunnel.

My hand was clasping the wood of the ladder a moment later. Perhaps if my earliest memory hadn't involved being kidnapped and shoved into a dark satchel,

I would've been able to sit in this tunnel and wait for someone to rescue me.

Then again, that didn't sound much like the woman I was becoming.

Sheathing my sword, I hauled myself up the ladder toward the light above my head. I was climbing out of another hole in the ground. My vision speckled as my eyes adjusted to the light, and a long moment stretched where anyone standing above me could have killed me as I was blinded by the sun. Rolling over the edge, I breathed in the sweet, fresh air and then launched myself to my feet, surveying the area.

I was standing in some kind of clearing. Alone.

Someone or something had brought me here. But why?

A guttural growl sounded, shattering the quiet. I froze.

A massive, furred creature slunk from the shadows, black eyes fixed upon me. Those eyes were elongated and narrow…faintly feline. Unkempt, mottled fur covered its muscular body, ensuring it blended seamlessly with the surrounding foliage. A thick mane ran along its spine, adding to its overall bulk, while two curved horns jutted from its head—the ends so sharp they glinted as the creature stepped into the dappled sunlight.

My entire body went numb. The creature could likely sense fear, because it bared its wickedly sharp teeth in a snarl, inching closer with each thud of my heart. It padded forward, crouching, coiled, waiting to spring.

Distantly, I attempted to figure out what it was. It moved with the feline grace of a cat, and yet it looked more like some kind of huge, wild hound. It stepped closer, and its tail came into view. Long, bushy, and *white*, the tail was a tuft of fur that didn't seem to match its body in any way.

I reached for the thread of my power. Whatever it was, I'd freeze it and run for my life. The creature opened its mouth and hissed at me.

I yanked at my power, pulling so much I was dizzy with the influx of magic. But the creature merely yowled, as if my attempt was annoying it.

It was…immune to my power.

And I was going to die.

LORIAN

I roared, digging at the dirt where Prisca had disappeared. I'd been too far from her. I never should have left her side.

"Where did she go?" Asinia demanded.

I could barely speak, rage clamping tight around my throat. I would find her. I would find her, and whoever had taken her would die screaming for mercy.

Cavis took a step closer to me, still panting from

killing the remaining iron guards. "She disappeared. It was the strangest thing. I saw it too. The ground opened up, she fell, and then the hole sealed over like nothing had happened."

Telean was sitting on a log at the edge of the forest, her face in the shade. And she didn't look nearly concerned enough to suit me. I slowly got to my feet. Stalking over to her, I waited until she slowly lifted her gaze.

"Nelayra will be fine," she told me. "Our people want to meet her alone."

I didn't give a fuck what their people wanted. "How could they take her from this kingdom?"

She gave me a faint smile. "This was just one of the ways we were able to get so many across to this side when we were under attack."

"And you weren't planning to warn us?" I hissed. If I'd known, I would have made sure I was standing right next to Prisca during the battle. She wouldn't be alone and in danger now.

Telean frowned at me. "It didn't occur to me that she would be taken in such a manner. But this is a good thing. It means important people are interested in her."

If I told Telean exactly what I thought of *that*, my wildcat would likely castrate me when she returned.

And she *would* return. Or I would find a way to get to that fucking kingdom. Sea serpents be damned.

"It may feel as if you will die without her clamped to your side," Telean said softly, "but that is not the case, Prince. And this is something that you both should learn sooner rather than later."

I bared my teeth, and she was wise enough to drop her gaze. Pivoting, I stalked back toward the hole. And this time, I examined it with my power. There was no ward hiding the magic that had taken Prisca. It was as if she truly had disappeared.

If they harmed her in any way…if they made her afraid…I would—

"Lorian," Galon said softly.

I slowly turned, finding him watching me. "We will find her," he said. "If she doesn't return to us, we will cross the Sleeping Sea and hunt those who took her. For now…" He glanced at Rythos, and I followed his gaze.

Rythos was sitting at Fendrel's side, his head bowed. I reached deep for control. Rythos was one of my brothers. And I could practically hear Prisca snarling at me to pay attention.

Getting to my feet, I crossed the rocky shore and sat next to him in silence, until he lifted his head, his eyes wet.

"He wanted off that island, and all I did was get him killed," he said.

"He hid on the ship. He knew you wouldn't allow him to come for this very reason. He's never seen true battle."

Rythos just shook his head. "And now, he never will."

"It's not your fault."

"My father was right," he muttered. "All I am to

them is poison."

Rythos's father had never deserved him. But sometimes a man had to learn such lessons for himself.

Marth finished searching the bodies and approached, crouching next to Fendrel's body.

"Fendrel would be disappointed to find you wallowing in guilt."

Rythos shook his head, blocking all of us out.

I turned my face toward the hybrid kingdom. Where the fuck was she?

The Queen

My heartbeat thundered against my rib cage as I walked toward the throne room, Pelysian's message tucked into my bodice. His mother had agreed to try my suggestion.

But that voice in my head taunted me with the knowledge that Sabium was somehow always one step ahead of me.

According to Pelysian's mother, her kind of power was unpredictable. Risky. Often experimental.

I strolled into the throne room, finding Sabium staring at his general. He ignored me, and I slipped past, taking a seat on my throne.

I studied him, my blood rushing in my ears. Sabium was becoming increasingly paranoid and had installed even more spies at court. Thankfully, he was currently distracted by Tymedes, who wore the resigned expression of one who knew these words might be his last.

"The heir has reached the western coastline, Your Majesty."

Sabium's face turned purple.

"I *ordered* you to ensure that didn't happen," he hissed.

"I had an entire legion hidden in the Asric Pass, Your Majesty."

"Then what happened?"

"They didn't travel through the pass, Your Majesty."

"Then how *did* they travel?"

"By some kind of strange, fae ship we believe. It traveled much quicker than anticipated. Our people were lying in wait close to the shoreline."

"And?" Sabium's voice was very quiet. The general's face was almost bloodless now.

"And we killed one of the fae."

"One of them?"

"Yes."

"And the others?"

"They slaughtered our men."

"All of them?"

"All except one. He ran for his pigeon so he could send a message to us. The…the Bloodthirsty Prince was there. And the others."

"And the girl?"

"She disappeared."

Not for the first time, I wished I'd had my own spies infiltrate the legion Tymedes had sent. But I'd heard many theories about the strange workings of the hybrid kingdom. If the heir had disappeared, it was likely she'd made it to that kingdom.

Sabium sat back on his throne, his brow furrowed. For one moment, I saw the man I'd thought I might one day fall in love with. The one who had always seemed to be thinking deeply.

Then, I'd assumed those thoughts would mean great things for this kingdom.

But I had been a stupid girl.

"It's time to create repercussions for anyone who attempts to help the girl. She will learn that it's not just her life in the balance. She cares so much about innocent lives?" He smiled. "Send the iron guards to her village."

My mind whirled. If the hybrid heir was broken by Sabium's actions, she would never last long enough to do what I needed her to do.

"There will be consequences to this," I murmured.

Sabium spared me a glance. "Your point?"

I swallowed, choosing my words carefully. "There are those in that village who have remained loyal to you. If you choose not to spare them, others may question their own loyalty."

He smiled. "It won't be *my* people who attack that village. It will be the hybrid heir and her little friends."

Sabium got to his feet, ignoring the advisers who immediately bowed. He strolled toward the door. I didn't release the breath I was holding until he was gone.

Then I slowly got to my feet.

"Another headache, Your Majesty?"

I went still, my gaze finding Tymedes. I searched his face, looking for some hint that he knew my plans.

Nothing but polite interest.

I didn't trust it.

"Yes," I said.

"Would you like me to contact the healer?"

"I suggest you focus your attention on ensuring your men stay alive," I said coldly. "I have more than enough servants to attend me."

"Of course, Your Majesty."

I felt his eyes on me as I walked toward the door, careful to keep my pace unhurried. When I finally reached my chambers, I was shaking.

Half an hour spent listening to my ladies gossip over tea, although they certainly weren't putting any effort into being interesting. When I finally dismissed them, they practically bolted from the room.

And I stared at myself in the mirror.

This wasn't the only mirror that was not truly a mirror in this castle. Compared to Sabium's hidden mirror, this was a simple enchantment. But I'd ensured it had traveled with me when I'd married him, leaving its twin with Pelysian.

I had never used it myself, some part of me terrified

that I would get stuck at that point between places.

But I agreed with Pelysian. It was far too dangerous for his mother to use her power in this castle. Her magic was dark, with a heavy scent of death.

Lifting my gown with one hand, I straightened my shoulders. Before I could talk myself out of it, I stepped into the mirror.

For one terrifying moment, I was blind and deaf, surrounded by nothing but an unusual, cool magic.

Strong hands grabbed me, and a strange sound hiccupped from me. It was almost a whimper, and I scanned my surroundings. Pelysian had pulled me through, and his mother sat at a scarred wooden table, her gaze on me. I only recognized her because Pelysian had once brought her to court for a ball. She was a small woman, fine-boned, with deep-set lines creasing her face.

I wanted to kill her for witnessing my terror. Pelysian's mother smiled as if she knew.

"Your Majesty," she said mockingly. "My son tells me you have a need for me."

I was the queen of this kingdom, and yet this woman somehow managed to make me feel as if *she* was the one with all of the power.

"Yes," I said.

"What you want will not be easy. Tell me, if I can find this person for you, will you use that knowledge for evil?"

"No."

The glint in her eye said she didn't believe me.

"What will you use it for?"

"Why do you presume to ask me such questions?"

Pelysian stiffened. "Your Majesty—"

"Let me ask you a *different* question, then," the hag murmured, slowly getting to her feet. "Do you serve the king?"

"No."

She folded her hands on the table and waited. Grinding my teeth, I took the risk. Pelysian had never betrayed me. I had to believe he wouldn't allow his mother to either. "I wish to help the hybrid heir."

"So you can put your false son on the throne."

I slowly turned my head, pinning Pelysian with a stare. "I didn't say anything," he said softly. "My mother has the knowing."

I wasn't sure I believed in the knowing. But whether the gods truly whispered in her ear or whether she had somehow found other magical means to spy on me was irrelevant. I at least knew she had the ability to locate those I needed.

"Yes. I wish for my son to rule."

She waved a gnarled hand, and I stepped forward, taking a seat at her table. A glance at her son, and he sat next to me.

"There are some things you need to know," Pelysian said. "My mother can tie her awareness to the person you choose. It will last for as long as both of them live."

Anticipation sparked along my skin. "Yes, this is what I want."

"Don't agree so freely, Your Majesty," the hag said. "This kind of power is forbidden by all but those who worship the dark gods. And the dark gods demand sacrifice."

I kept my face blank, even as my stomach spiraled. "What kind of sacrifice?"

"Something so precious, most in your position would never pay it."

"Cease dancing around the point."

"Very well. If you choose this sacrifice, you will save many lives. One day, you will be remembered for it."

"I care nothing for those lives. Tell me of my son."

"The future is murky, but I can tell you that by opening up communication with the one you seek, you will almost certainly prevent his sacrifice."

My heart pounded. "Sabium won't kill him?"

"You will buy him time, Your Majesty. What he does with that time—what you do with it—is not my concern."

Time. That was what I needed most. Sabium had four hundred years of scheming, and he had used his own time well. "And if I choose not to sacrifice?"

"Your son will be slaughtered for the power Sabium has been channeling into him for years."

My lungs seized, and a metallic taste flooded my mouth. "When?"

Her gaze turned distant. "I cannot see the exact time, but it is before the next full moon."

I did this, or my son was dead. If I could buy him this time she spoke of, I would use it to save his life. I was sure of it.

"I'll do it."

"You haven't heard the sacrifice required."

"I don't need to."

Pelysian shifted in his chair. "Please, Your Majesty. Listen."

I folded my hands in my lap with an impatient huff.

"Tell me, then."

"If the current thread of fate continues to unravel undisturbed, you will one day grow heavy with child."

The room seemed to tilt around me. Pelysian held out his hand as if he would steady me but instantly dropped it.

My breath stilled in my chest. "You think to taunt me?"

"I tell you only what I know, Your Majesty." Her voice was quiet now, almost pitying. "If nothing changes from this moment, you have a child."

My lips were numb. "How?"

"I cannot see this."

"The father?"

"I cannot see this either. You must choose. But know this. If you sacrifice this opportunity, it will never be gifted again. Your womb will never ripen. You will never feel a child stir within you. You will never hold your daughter."

My heart stumbled, grief stealing the air from my lungs.

"Mother," Pelysian said.

"Quiet," she snapped. "In order for a sacrifice to happen, it has to *mean* something."

A daughter.

Of my own. A baby that would come from me. Would be mine alone. I would keep her safe.

But if I chose that future, my son would die.

Tiny feet thumping down the hall. The mischievous chortle that urged all who heard it to smile. Green eyes, locked on mine.

"Mama!"

"I'll do it," I croaked. "I'll make the sacrifice."

I opened my eyes. The pity on the hag's face made me want to crawl beneath the table to weep. Gone was my urge to kill any who saw me this vulnerable. Now, I could barely feel anything at all.

The hag raised her knife, gesturing for me to place my hand on the table.

"Picture the one you seek. Picture only this person, or the magic won't strike true."

I had given everything for this. So I brought that face into my mind and pushed everything else aside.

"The name?"

According to Pelysian, the best chance of success was for me to choose one person to attempt to locate. The person I knew best.

And that person wasn't the hybrid heir.

I took a deep breath. "Madinia."

PRISCA

The creature hissed at me. "I don't want to hurt you," I murmured.

Was that...amusement flashing through its eyes? How much did it understand?

I tried again. "I know this is your territory. I don't want to intrude. Please don't eat me."

The creature took a step closer, and I pulled at my power once more. It snapped its teeth at me.

I knew nothing about the unusual creatures found in fae and hybrid lands. Any such creatures that might have been found in the human kingdoms had likely been slaughtered centuries ago. How exactly did I convince it not to eat me?

I was fast. How fast was this creature? I didn't know where I was, but if I could lose it, I could hide up a tree or something.

"It takes humility, bravery, and true strength to be able to bow before such creatures. If you ever see one, do not run."

I shook my head as the creature stared at me, still seemingly waiting for me to do something.

It was a bedtime story. My adoptive father had told Tibris and me many such stories over the years. Was I truly going to do this?

I hope you weren't creating those stories out of nowhere, Papa.

I reached for my dagger. The creature let out another yowl and bared long, sharp teeth. When I dropped the dagger onto the ground in front of us, it angled its head but went silent.

My hand shook. If this creature didn't kill me, and Lorian ever learned of me disarming myself this way...

My knees barely supported my weight, my skin turning clammy. My heart pounded in my ears.

Was I so desperate to feel close to Papa that I was about to die for it? Was I so eager to clutch at any kind of meaning in his words that I would risk everything?

I studied the creature in front of me. It stared back. Waiting.

My limbs turned numb as I slowly reached for my sword. It showed me its teeth again.

"I'm not going to hurt you unless you hurt me," I told it.

Its eyes were on my sword.

I pulled it free.

Dropping it onto the ground between us might have been the most difficult thing I'd done in my life.

Bowing my head, I waited for it to rip out my throat.

I could feel it padding closer, a flash of fur out the corner of my eye. I braced for the burst of agony.

The creature's breath was hot on my face. This was it. A *stupid* way to die. My family and friends would never forgive me. Lorian would... Lorian...

A rough tongue licked my cheek.

Lifting my head, I met those black eyes. "You're not going to kill me?"

It turned and wandered to the edge of the clearing, sniffing at something I couldn't see.

"So you tamed the Drakoryx," a voice said.

I whirled. An old man stood at the edge of the clearing, a wooden staff in his hand.

"The Drakoryx?"

He nodded, but his gaze swept over my muddy leather breeches, ripped shirt, and up the curls that had come free from my braid. He didn't look impressed.

But I was becoming less and less interested in whether the powerful men I was coming into contact with found me *acceptable*.

I studied his own clothes—neat and clean—his beard—trimmed and shot through with silver—and finally, his eyes—glimmering with interest. It was gone in an instant.

"There is a reason the elders insisted you meet the Drakoryx first," he said, glancing at the creature behind me. "He has judged you worthy."

"And if he didn't?"

The old man gave me a sharp smile. "Then I wouldn't have needed to make this journey."

Cute.

"Follow me," the old man said, turning back toward the forest.

I stayed put. He glanced over his shoulder and frowned at me.

"You just told me you risked my life without my knowledge or consent. Why would I follow you?"

His eyebrows shot up, as if he hadn't considered I might be a little annoyed by my brush with death. "Because the Drakoryx would only approve of someone it considered fit to rule this kingdom," he said, and his tone made it clear he didn't agree with the creature. "Which means you can now meet those who have risked their lives for your people while you grew up safe in your village."

Clearly, he wanted me to lose my temper. If there was one thing I'd learned so far, it was to never give my enemies what they wanted. So I gave him a cool smile, sheathed both of my weapons, and followed him into the forest.

The Drakoryx followed too.

The old man seemed bemused by this. But he was smart enough not to argue.

"My name is Rivenlor. I have been tasked with bringing you to the elders."

"And who are the elders?"

"They are the ones who have ruled in your stead."

In my stead. And what exactly did that mean?

"Will you follow me?"

"I'm still deciding."

He bowed his head. "I understand you are... unhappy."

That was putting it mildly. But I was here. In the hybrid kingdom. So I tucked away the worst of my rage. "Fine."

Turning, he led me deeper into the forest. But I kept one hand on the hilt of my dagger, just in case he decided to try anything.

After a few minutes, Rivenlor stopped in front of a rock about eight foot-spans high and several times wider than my body. He waved his hand in front of it, and the front of the rock simply disappeared, revealing a passage. "After you."

I tightened my hand around the hilt of my dagger. "I don't think so."

He shook his head as if I was being overly dramatic. I waited him out. Finally, he huffed out a breath and stepped inside the rock. I glanced at the Drakoryx, but it had already lain down in a patch of sun, closing its eyes. No longer did it seem like a vicious monster. No, it now reminded me of Herica's cat napping in the late afternoon.

The inside of the passage was about as dimly lit as I would have expected, those same light orbs hovering in the air at regular intervals along the spiral staircase.

Why did so many of these trips involve dark, confined spaces? If the gods truly were interested in our lives, I had no doubt one of them was playing with me.

The stairs went on and on, until we had to be deep within the earth. My heart raced, slamming against my ribs, and the hand I'd placed against the side of the wall trembled.

"Almost there," Rivenlor grunted.

Finally, *finally*, we reached the end of the staircase. A huge stone wall blocked our way, and Rivenlor held up one hand, pressing it to the center of the wall.

A door handle appeared, and he turned it, swinging the wall open and stepping into the room.

Four people were waiting for us. They watched me silently, all of them seated around a scarred circular wooden table. Rivenlor waved his hand at me to sit, doing the same on the opposite side of the table.

I sat, surveying the elders who watched me so closely. Two women and three men. All of them wore extravagant jewels—earrings and necklaces for the women, large rings for the men. Their clothes appeared to be made of the finest materials, reminding me of the courtiers in Regner's castle.

A dull fury burned in my belly. These people had managed to hoard wealth while so many of the hybrids were living in poverty and starving?

"How dare they put on such a display when our people are fleeing for their lives?" a woman intoned.

I went still, meeting her eyes. Could she...?

"Yes." Her smile was slow and smug. "I can read your mind."

Rivenlor cleared his throat. "This is Ysara," he said. "The man to her left is Tymriel. To his left is Gavros. Next to him is Sylphina."

Ysara was still watching me in the same unnerving way. Her eyes were so dark they seemed to glow against skin that was so pale I wouldn't have been surprised if I were told she had never stepped outside.

Tymriel was a small man, his shoulders hunched,

his face lined with wrinkles. But his eyes sparkled at me from across the table. Gavros was broad-shouldered and bearded, with the kind of bulk that told me he was used to swinging a sword.

Sylphina was thin and willowy, with light brown skin, her glossy black hair braided like mine, only her braid was sleek and tidy.

"Why have you brought me here?" I asked.

"The better question is, why did you come?" Gavros asked.

I explained about the fae king and his request for allies. They listened silently. When I was done, no one spoke.

I'd seen Lorian use the same tactic, and I refused to break the silence. Finally, Sylphina tilted her head. "You've told us what the fae king wants and the benefits of allying with him. But you haven't told us why *you* have come."

This was awkward. "He told me to" didn't seem like a good enough answer, even if it was the truth.

"And do you always do as men tell you?" Ysara asked, clearly still reading my mind.

I bared my teeth in a humorless smile. "Delve a little deeper and see for yourself."

She stared at me, clearly unimpressed. I took a deep breath. "We have close to eleven thousand hybrids in the fae lands. More of them are arriving every day. We're trying to save as many of them as we can, but Regner is on a murderous rampage. The fae king will ally with me if I can find others who will join us. Will you help us?"

"You don't want to rule," Ysara said. "You chose to look to your cousin instead. Even now, you wonder if when all this is over, *we* will continue to rule in your stead."

How could I be polite with someone who could read my mind?

"It's not that I don't want to rule," I said carefully. "It's that I know I'm not the best person for the position. I was raised in a small village. I only recently learned that I have any claim to the throne. I will do everything I can to help our people. I will lay down my life for them. But I have seen what happens when someone who is unfit to rule sits on a throne."

Rivenlor raised one eyebrow. "You compare yourself to the mad king?"

"He not only believed he was the best choice at the time of his rule, he believes he is the best choice to rule *forever*. Power corrupts."

"And you believe yourself corruptible?" He glanced at Ysara as if I'd proven his point.

I smiled at his attempt to bait me. "Everyone is corruptible at their core."

"It's not just that you are afraid of being a tyrant," Ysara said, her tone biting. "You don't believe you would be a fit queen."

"No," I said. The certainty of it ate away at me every day I had to pretend to be someone who wanted to rule. "I don't." Being forced to admit the truth was a relief.

"And instead of choosing to *learn* how to rule, you're giving it up before you truly try."

"Ruling a kingdom is not something you *try*," I snapped. "Would you prefer I bumbled my way on to the throne and put everyone at risk?"

"They're already at risk," Tymriel intoned. Everyone went silent. "Such cowardice would shame your mother if she could hear it."

Getting to my feet, I strode toward the door. I'd find my way back to Lorian and the others myself.

The door slammed closed, and I whirled. "You want a puppet on the throne? Pick someone else," I hissed.

Ysara smiled, and it was terrible. "The woman who stole you has damaged you irreparably," she said. "But never mind that. We can fix you."

Agony engulfed me. I dropped to my knees and screamed.

20

PRISCA

Someone was speaking in a low, melodious tone. I was…floating. A chill slid over me. Where was I?

"You're safe, Nelayra."

"Who…" My voice was hoarse, my throat sore. As if I'd been screaming.

Because I'd been burning alive. At least that's what it had felt like.

"Sometimes pain is necessary for growth," the voice said.

Could she…

"Read your mind? Yes. Just breathe. It will come to you."

Ysara. She'd done something to me.

"Yes. It's time for you to *see*."

Oh, I planned to see. I would see my dagger slam into her throat at the first opportunity.

A long pause. "Your thoughts are rather…murderous."

Was she laughing at me?

"Just a little. That wrath is a *good* thing. Your rage must be nurtured until you become exactly who you should be."

Oh, my rage was being nurtured. But she wasn't going to like the result.

"Enough, Nelayra. Look down."

Perhaps if I did what she wanted, she would let me out of this nightmare. I tilted my head, and a gasp left my throat.

The kingdom stretched across a diverse landscape. Past the coastline, rolling hills, shimmering lakes, and dense forests spread toward the northeast, where rugged mountains took watch, their snowcapped peaks jutting above a low layer of clouds.

Rivers and streams wound from those mountains, fed by the melting snow, meandering through the valleys and nourishing the land. In the south, a carpet of verdant plains unfurled, dotted with crops and wild flowers. To the west, ancient trees stood tall and proud, the woodlands teeming with life.

Ysara moved us past the plains of wild flowers, until we hovered over expansive wetlands overrun by strange creatures that popped their heads out of the water.

She lowered us, sweeping us north, until I could see villages dotting the landscape, turning to towns and cities closer to the center of the kingdom. When we were near the eastern coast, she dropped us closer to the buildings.

"The hybrid kingdom was known as Lyrinore," Ysara murmured. "And this was the capital city."

I blinked, and we were hovering above cobbled streets. It was dusk in the city, and thousands of tiny silver creatures flitted to and fro, peeking out of baskets of flowers and slipping inside baskets of fruit.

Intricate mosaics adorned the city walls, showcasing fierce battles, breathtaking scenery, and faces I didn't know.

"The city was named Celestara."

We lowered farther, and I could see the hybrids. They looked human, except there were no blue marks on their temples. They gathered in teahouses, sitting at tables outside, faces tipped up to the sun. In the marketplace, vendors and merchants set up their stalls, displaying handcrafted goods, exotic spices, fresh produce. Children ran in packs, laughing and playing, while somewhere, a bell rang, announcing the hour.

Ysara swept us above the city, until I had to close my eyes, dizzy. When I opened them once more, I was gazing down at the castle. Sculpted from ivory stone, it was almost as if it had been designed from pieces of the clouds. Vines and flowers draped over its walls, while the grand entrance was guarded by a pair of intricately carved statues that looked suspiciously like the Drakoryx.

The towering silver gates were opened to reveal the courtyard. Carriages arrived, carrying nobles and visitors—the ladies in gauzy, glittering gowns, the man in cloaks of ermine and velvet. The massive silver gates slid open, allowing another carriage entrance, and I peered closer.

A blink, and I was inside the castle. Vaulted ceilings adorned with frescoes rose high above the polished marble floors. At the heart of the castle, a magnificent throne room sprawled—currently empty. Rows of tall, stately columns ran the length of the room, their surfaces covered in ornate carvings of mythical creatures. The high ceiling was painted with a lifelike mural of ancient gods among a night sky, while tapestries hanging along one wall depicted the history of the kingdom. The floor was a vast expanse of polished marble, speckled with silver and pearl, which glowed gently beneath the golden light orbs hovering throughout the grand space. At the end of the room, two thrones sat, side by side. Crafted from some strange pearl-like material, the back of each throne formed wings, flaring outward.

My heart stuttered in my chest, but we were already moving again. My mouth went dry, and I instantly knew we were in the royal quarters.

Because that was my mother standing next to the window, my father behind her.

All I could see were their backs. But I knew instinctively it was them. My mother had my blond curls. And my father nuzzled one of them aside, leaning down to lay a kiss on her cheek.

We began moving again, and I choked out a sob.

"No, please!"

"There is more to see, Nelayra. You cannot linger here."

My heart cracked as my parents disappeared.

Ysara lifted me over the city. Higher and higher, we went, until I could see the Sleeping Sea. Could see the glistening, iridescent ward surrounding our kingdom.

The ward disappeared. Ships appeared in the distance—previously hidden by magic.

Ysara took us back to the marketplace, where a bell began ringing again and again and again.

The expressions on the hybrids' faces changed to blind terror.

Children were swept up by the nearest adult, and the hybrids ran for cover, ducking beneath tables, wagons, anything they could find. The humans were attacking.

I spotted a hybrid with fire magic like Madinia's. He bought the children time, sending his power arcing through the air toward the human attackers. Next to him, several hybrid women used their own elemental powers.

But Regner had ensured his people brought weapons filled with fae iron. Those weapons flew through the air, spewing tiny bolts of iron when they landed. The iron buried deep into hybrid bodies, killing the unlucky and severing others from their power. Even knowing this had happened long ago, my heart thundered, my instincts urging me to join the fight.

"Where are the defenses?"

"The wards were gone. Without them, the serpents didn't know to attack. Until directed."

Ysara showed me a woman climbing a hill overlooking the shoreline. She was tall, graceful, her face lined with age. But those eyes...

"Is she—"

"Your grandmother. The current hybrid queen."

She was at the top of the hill now. From there, she

could see her people fleeing. Could see them dying. Her face twisted in fierce grief, and she threw back her head with a scream.

The sea serpents were sinking enemy ships now, tails slamming into wooden hulls, as if they could hear my grandmother scream her rage and were responding accordingly.

"Look closely," Ysara ordered.

"The hourglass," I murmured. "On a chain around her neck." It called to me like a lover, as if some part of me had been missing until I saw it.

A strange wind began to swirl around my grandmother.

"What is she doing?"

"The humans came from what is now known as the Cursed City in Eprotha. It is named such because your grandmother gave her life to see it so. As she gasped out her last dying breath, the hybrid queen cursed the city from which those ships had come. As long as her people had no home, neither would they. Nothing would grow on the lands around their city. Sickness would ravage the city, and death would haunt it, until those who had lived there fled deeper into human lands. If she could have cursed the entire human kingdom, I believe she would have."

Was that *amusement* in Ysara's voice?

She pulled me higher, until we were above the ships, close to the Eprothan kingdom. And I watched as they began to sink.

"Regner sent more forces. But the curse had already

taken hold. Any ships carrying humans with hate in their hearts would sink. Your grandmother's curse protected what was left of our kingdom for hundreds of years."

I was related to that woman. Pride mingled with an odd kind of anxiety in my chest. Ysara showed me one last glimpse of her, slumping to her knees on that hill. Eprothan guards were sprinting toward her, and she cast out what was left of her power.

She...*aged* them.

I gaped as the guards' hair turned gray and then white. They became hunched and elderly, stumbling instead of sprinting.

But her power was drained. With a final scream, the hybrid queen collapsed to the ground. And one of Regner's guards took his sword and sliced it through her neck.

Even knowing this had already occurred, I let out a helpless scream. The guard spat on my grandmother's body, snatched the hourglass, and moved back down the hill.

Ysara pulled us back toward Eprotha. Someone had already used their power to create the tunnel, and families were pouring from it, running toward the pass. The hybrid army bought them time, laying down their lives so their people could get to safety.

Many of the hybrids traveled with only the clothes on their backs. A few of them wore nothing but thin slippers on their feet.

"And so our people fled through the pass," Ysara said. "Many of them froze. Hundreds of them were children."

She showed me the Asric Pass next. The hybrids traveled in groups, and the trail was littered with...

Bodies. The ground was frozen, and there was no time to bury them. Bile flooded my throat as Ysara showed me a tiny girl, no more than four summers, lying with a doll in her arms. Her mother lay beside her, clearly unable to continue without her daughter.

"Stop," I croaked out. "Please."

"No." Ysara's voice was pitiless, and she showed me more and more. The bodies, the hybrids who arrived in villages, begging for help. Some of those villagers took them in. Too many of them turned them away. More and more died every day. Those who lived were shadows of themselves. My blood burned for retribution.

Ysara showed me those who made it to the fae lands, only to pound on that impenetrable ward, right as Regner's guards caught up to them.

Even knowing Conreth and Lorian weren't responsible...

Fury burned through my insides.

"Nourish the spark of your rage, Nelayra."

"Why?"

"When you have to, you will change the worlds. If I have to torture you to convince you that you're the only one who can do it..." I *felt* her shrug. "Well, what must be done must be done."

Another person attempting to use me for their own goals.

"End this. Now."

"Or?"

"Or I'll make you *pay*."

"That's better."

I woke up on the ground. Every muscle in my body burned as if I truly had been set aflame. My gaze met Ysara's. And then I scanned the rest of them. I was drained, my body numb, my limbs strangely light.

None of them were wearing jewels or finery No, they wore clothes similar to me. Another one of their manipulations. Who knew why?

"It pleased us that you were someone who judged us for turning to such things," Ysara said.

Rivenlor nodded. "You may have been someone who saw such wealth and longed for it." Something about his tone made me wonder if he was disappointed that I *hadn't*.

All I longed for was to get the fuck out of here.

"So that's a no on the allying?" I guessed, getting to my feet.

Tymriel gestured at my sword. "The blade of your sword was repeatedly heated and then hammered into shape. Not only did it give it the desired form, but it strengthened the sword by aligning the internal structure of the metal."

I stared at him, exhausted. "And?"

"Just as your blade had to endure the intense heat and the force of the hammer to become a strong, reliable weapon, so must you. Except you must choose to be forged in fire so you will become the queen we need."

I tried again. I couldn't just leave empty-handed. I needed *something*. "I want to know the state of your armed forces. How many people are left? Is there any kind of army on this continent?"

They just watched me.

"I need to know what we are working with. Surely there's some kind of general or leader I can talk to."

Nothing.

That strange, frustrated fury bubbled within me once more. "I'm trying to save this kingdom," I snarled.

More silence.

Fine. "Play your power games," I hissed. "I'll save our people without you."

Tymriel *smiled*. "You have seen more horror than anyone of so few winters should have to. But you are still hiding. Become the queen we know you can be, and we will do whatever we can to help you."

Ysara watched me, this time with sympathy in her eyes. "And enjoy your time with your fae prince. But know this—you cannot keep him."

PRISCA

Thankfully, I didn't have to drag myself up the spiral staircase. Tymriel waved a hand, and the wall slid open, revealing the forest. I scampered out before they could change their minds. Likely, the staircase had just been another way to unnerve me.

I wanted to scream at them, but I bit back the curses on my tongue. Ysara could probably hear me anyway.

The forest was far too quiet and peaceful after everything I'd just seen. I sucked the fresh, earthy air into my lungs.

The Drakoryx opened one eye, its head still on its paws.

I eyed it back. "Thank you for not eating me."

It slowly got to its feet. Perhaps I'd spoken too soon.

No, it was wandering toward me, that strange fluffy white tail flicking through the air. "Any chance you know how I can get back to my friends?"

It turned and stepped off the main path. I hesitated, and it looked over its shoulder, as if waiting for me.

"Fine."

The ladder was where I'd left it, and I blew out a breath. My trip here had been an epic failure, but at least I could get back to the others. Fendrel's face flashed through my mind, and I froze.

All for nothing. One of our people was dead, and it was for nothing.

The elders had taken one look at me and found me wanting.

The Drakoryx nudged my hand with its nose.

"Fine. Goodbye." I hauled myself down the ladder, took a few steps, and whirled as the Drakoryx landed next to me.

It was probably escorting me through the tunnel so I

didn't get any ideas about returning and begging for help.

This time, the walk was much shorter. Also unsurprising.

Another ladder was at the end of the tunnel, but I saw no hole for me to climb through to the others. My gut clenched. I would find a way to let Lorian know I was here. Maybe his power could break through the stone.

I climbed the ladder and pushed against the ceiling.

My hand went straight through. Something grabbed it, and I yelped.

And then I was hauled into Lorian's arms, and he was carrying me away from the ladder, pressing kisses to my face.

"I take it you missed me." I attempted a lighthearted grin, but he nuzzled my cheeks, and I realized he was kissing my tears away.

He went still.

My head whirled as he thrust me behind him.

"What. Is. That?"

"A Drakoryx. I think you're supposed to throw down your weapons and bow to him."

Outraged silence.

Lorian slowly turned his head to look at me, and the expression on his face made it clear he would be doing no such thing. I sighed, glancing past him at the Drakoryx.

It was paying no attention to the sharp metallic scent that had filled the air or the sparks now rising from Lorian's skin. If anything, it was ignoring him.

"It's immune to my power," I said. "I'm pretty sure

it's not supposed to be here."

The Drakoryx pinned its ears to its head and showed me its teeth, obviously taking offense to the idea that it was *supposed* to be anywhere.

Lorian took a step toward it, letting out a growl of his own.

"Protection."

I froze. So did Lorian.

"Did you hear that?'

"Yes," he said. "The creature wants protection."

The Drakoryx let out a yowling sound that made the hair on the back of my neck stand up.

I choked out a laugh. "I don't think that's it. I think it's offering us protection."

"Not us," Lorian said. "You." The lightning in his eyes disappeared, and he nodded at the Drakoryx. "Welcome to the group."

I stared at him.

He just shrugged. "Anything that wants to protect you can stick around. Especially when you're going to disappear at any moment."

"I didn't do it on purpose," I grumbled.

Voices sounded from farther down the coast, and I peered around Lorian's body. Asinia was running toward me, her face pale.

"*There* you are. You scared all of us."

"Is everyone…"

"Alive?" Her eyes filled. "Everyone except Fendrel. Rythos is still sitting with the body. It's been hours."

"Hours?"

Asinia waved a hand at the sun currently about to set in the sky. It had been midmorning when we'd arrived. While it had felt like I'd only been gone for an hour or two, it had clearly been a lot longer than that. No wonder Lorian was hovering.

"Uh, Pris…what is that?"

"That's a Drakoryx. He followed me from the hybrid kingdom. From…Lyrinore." Grief clutched my throat, and Asinia nudged me.

"Are you—"

"I'm not ready to talk about it. The Drakoryx will have to return. We can't take him with us."

"No."

We both fell silent, staring at the beast. "Did it just…"

"Talk in our heads? Yes. From the voice—and the arrogance—I think it's a male."

The Drakoryx met my eyes, but I was all out of fear. Now that I was back, I was attempting to process everything I'd seen and heard so far.

Asinia crouched and angled her head. "Yup. He's a boy monster. Do you have a name?" she asked him.

"Vynthar."

I couldn't deal with this. "You want to come with us? Fine. But no eating anyone."

He gave me a patient look, as if the very idea was ridiculous and he hadn't been threatening to kill me just hours ago.

Turning, I shook my head and headed back toward

our ship. Lorian stayed behind, murmuring something to the Drakoryx. Asinia fell into step with me.

"Pris."

"I don't want to talk about it."

"Pris." Her voice cracked. "It's *me*."

My throat burned, and I sucked in a breath that felt like shards of glass shredding my lungs. "I met the elders. They showed me the day Lyrinore was attacked. My grandmother is the reason the Cursed City is what it is, and the reason Regner's ships sank whenever he attempted to return to Lyrinore. She gave her life to protect the hybrids."

Asinia winced. "Wow."

"She killed the enemy, but also thousands of innocent people in that city. The elders won't help, Asinia. Not until I'm *the queen they know I can be*. They wouldn't tell me anything about who we have over there, if we have weapons, anyone who can fight. All of this was for nothing. Rythos lost his friend for nothing."

Asinia's face turned cold. "Not nothing. If the elders live in Lyrinore, others do too. So if they won't help, we'll find a way to go around them and find help from elsewhere. Fuck their declarations."

I attempted a smile, and she wrapped her arms around me. "No one gets to choose if you're worthy of that crown except you."

"Thanks, Asinia."

"Rythos…"

"I know. I'll find him now." My chest ached. He'd

finally reconnected with Fendrel, and he'd died in vain. Because of me.

Rythos was sitting where Fendrel had died, clutching one of his friend's hands in both of his. I stepped up next to him, my chest tight. I hadn't known Fendrel well, but I'd liked what I'd seen.

Rythos turned and pressed his head against my thigh. My throat tightened until I could barely breathe. I'd half expected him to be unable to look at me.

I stroked his hair. "I'm sorry."

"Thank you."

Guilt engulfed me as I stared down at the man who'd been so eager to come with us. Who'd just wanted to spend time with his friend.

"I know you're not thinking this is your fault," Rythos said.

I could barely talk around the lump in my throat, so I just let out a noncommittal sound. He raised his head. "This was Regner. *Regner*. And we're going to make him pay for it."

"Yes. Yes, we are."

"I need to take him home," Rythos said.

"I know."

"You'll take him with Galon and Marth," Lorian said.

Rythos nodded, glancing up at Lorian. They shared a look I couldn't read.

I took a step backward, my pulse stuttering. "I need a minute."

Lorian nodded, his green eyes flickering with concern. Turning, I strode down toward the waves lapping at the shore.

My heart ached as if I were bleeding out.

I'd thought if I could just get to our kingdom, it would all be all right. In reality, things were worse than ever.

The crown was meant for someone stronger. Someone more deserving. Someone who understood diplomacy and strategy. The kind of queen my grandmother had been. The kind of queen my mother would have been.

My cousin was a murderer and his parents the reason our people had lost everything.

The elders were busy playing their power games.

Demos didn't have time magic.

My kingdom needed a leader.

No, I wasn't the perfect choice. I was about as far from it as you could get. But my people needed someone who would stand with them. Someone who would fight with them. Someone who cared for them.

I finally understood. And it had nothing to do with anything the elders had said. Nothing to do with the words my aunt had continually murmured in my ear.

A crown wasn't just a title or a symbol. It was a promise. A promise that I would do whatever was necessary to protect my people.

Asinia's words echoed in my head. *"No one gets to choose if you're worthy of that crown except you."*

I stared across the sea toward my kingdom, and I made a vow.

I may not be a worthy ruler yet. But I would become one.

Not for the elders.

Certainly not for myself.

For my grandmother, who had loved her people with a fierce, all-consuming love that had turned to helpless rage.

For my parents, who had led their people through the Asric Pass, only to watch as their safe haven was destroyed once more.

And for the hybrids themselves, who had been hiding and suffering and dying under Regner's rule.

No, I wasn't perfect. There were many people who could likely rule far better than I could. I would stumble and fall. But each time, I would rise. I would grow stronger. I would become the queen my people deserved.

And no one would fight harder for them than I would.

Taking a deep breath, I allowed the weight of my decision to settle on my shoulders. It was heavy. But when I looked back at who I'd already become since I'd left my village, I felt...pride.

I thought back to that village girl, who wanted nothing more than a small life. Peace, quiet, predictability. For the first time, I wasn't ashamed of those wants. I didn't blame her for them. I was still attempting to unravel the ways Vuena had twisted my mind. The way Papa had attempted to erase her work.

But that village girl wouldn't win us a war. So, I took

those dreams of an uninterrupted life.

And I said goodbye.

When I turned, Lorian was standing just foot-spans behind me, watching me with dark eyes.

"The elders won't help me. They say I'm not enough." I'd managed to slap a bandage over that wound, and my tone was factual, voice clear.

Lorian's nostrils flared. "That doesn't make sense."

My heart strained. He'd always seen the best in me. Always seen the potential. I hoped he still would by the time this war was over.

"Wildcat." He stepped closer and grabbed my shoulders. "What exactly did they say?"

"I'm not yet ready to be queen, and they won't help. Oh, and I can't keep you. As if we didn't already know that."

Lorian bared his teeth in a feral smile. "I'll ignore that last part for now. *Think*, Prisca. Why would they turn you away?"

I shook my head. "Ysara and Tymriel seemed the most likely to support me—although not until I'm the *queen they know I can be*. Ysara showed me the hybrid kingdom and the day we lost everything, and she seemed invested in my becoming stronger. Sylphina, Rivenlor, and Gavros…they were focused on how I was raised in that village and know nothing about ruling. I may be the only one with time magic, but…"

The realization slammed into me. I *wasn't* the only one with time magic.

"There you go," Lorian said grimly.

It sank in. "My cousin. Zathrian. He got to them first."

Lorian nodded. "The elders are playing both sides. I have no doubt they would like you to prove you can be the queen they would hope for you to be. But by now, they probably know Zathrian. He was young enough when his parents dropped the wards that even you thought he could be innocent."

"He played them," I marveled. "He got here first. It's why he killed our spy. He wanted to make sure we wouldn't send anyone else—at least right now—so we wouldn't know what he was up to."

I turned to pace. I had no doubt Ysara would prefer me as queen, but only if I could prove to be a better choice than Zathrian. I was relatively sure Tymriel was on my side too. Zathrian had three of the elders, and I had two.

Rage swept through me. "What has he done all these years? Our people have been dying since the day Regner arrived. And he's known about it since he'd seen twelve winters."

"I don't know, wildcat, but we need to find out exactly what he has been up to."

The elders had made me feel like I wasn't enough. And I'd let them. I hadn't seen it, because some part of me had been relieved that we were all in agreement about my deficiencies.

I'd let them make me feel small. When in reality, they'd been playing me against my cousin. I glanced at

Lorian. "You saw what they were doing so easily."

"I've been dealing with these kinds of situations for a very long time."

My jaw ached from clenching my teeth. I could use this to make myself feel insecure and unworthy, or I could use it as fuel.

They wanted me to grow stronger? On that, we were in perfect agreement.

My eyes met Lorian's. "I need to go to Gromalia."

Understanding flickered across his face, and he stepped closer. "You're going to attempt to convince Eryndan to ally with you."

"Yes."

"We will need to cross the border by land. The Arslan won't allow humans to see their ships, and Rythos would never break that law."

I nodded. "Any word from Demos and the others?"

"No. I'll send some messages once we're in Gromalia."

"Thank you."

"What are you thinking?"

"I'm doing it, Lorian." My voice cracked, and then I was in his arms.

"You're taking your crown."

"I am. And if, at the end of it all, when my people are safe, they want someone else…I'll step aside."

Gladly. I'd step aside gladly. But in the meantime, I'd do whatever it took to bring them home.

He pulled me closer, his expression unreadable. I

peered up at him. "I thought you'd be pleased."

He'd always been the one to see things in me I couldn't see myself. The one who'd insisted I live up to my potential.

"Pleased is the wrong word. I'm *proud*, Prisca. I know you can do it. But this war will change you. You'll lose people you love. You'll lose parts of yourself. I could never want that for you, even as I know you will save your people."

I took a deep breath. "I'm afraid," I admitted.

His huge hand cupped my cheek. "I know. It's how you act despite your fear that counts."

His mouth brushed mine, and my eyes stung.

"Enjoy your time with your fae prince. But know this—you cannot keep him."

21

LORIAN

Prisca was quiet for most of the trip back to Quorith. Rythos spent the majority of his time in his cabin, while Galon bullied him to ensure he ate. Marth was stalking up and down the deck like a caged animal—uncomfortable with not being on land as usual—and Cavis stood statue-still, staring into the distance the way he did when he was mentally with his family.

Asinia had found a brush and a comb somewhere, and the Drakoryx had allowed her to tease the knots out of its matted fur. Prisca had given them an incredulous look and shaken her head, stalking away.

Telean had paled when she first saw the Drakoryx, her gaze jumping to Prisca. I'd asked her to explain the significance, and she'd informed me that Drakoryx were the ultimate test for anyone wanting to claim the hybrid throne.

The creatures had a unique ability to see the true heart of a person. Before ascending to the throne, all potential rulers were given a waterskin and a knife and led into Drakoryx territory. If they made it out alive, they were considered worthy to rule.

"What does it mean that one of them *followed* her?"

"I don't know. Perhaps it means she is worthy but it wants to watch over her to ensure she remains so. It is something I've never encountered before."

The Drakoryx had opened one eye, clearly listening, and I'd given it a slow smile. "If you attempt to 'change your mind' and harm her in any way, I will make your death a horror you cannot imagine."

The Drakoryx lifted one side of its lip, halfheartedly displaying a few teeth, and closed its eyes.

Prisca stood near the helm of the ship, her gaze on the underwater creatures drifting past us. She was quiet, and I attempted to give her the space she needed.

I'd never doubted for one moment that she would take her crown. Even as I'd known what had been done to make her fear such a thing, I'd known she would conquer all of it and put her people first.

Finally, we docked at the edge of fae territory, Rythos using his ward to ensure we remained unseen.

Cavis and I would travel with Prisca, Telean, and Asinia to Gromalia.

The Drakoryx had decided to continue following us. Prisca seemed entirely bemused by the creature, who seemed just as interested in watching everything she did.

My instincts told me it was safe, but I was closely

monitoring it all the same. I'd also warned it not to draw attention to us, and it had responded by curling its lip and flashing sharp white teeth at me. I'd done the same, and we'd understood each other.

We crossed into Gromalia in the dead of night, Cavis and I in our human forms, all of us cloaked and heavily armed. In the first town, we procured fresh horses, and by the time we broke through the forest near the city gates, I was more than ready to sleep in a bed once more.

Telean asked for a brief break. Prisca gave her a concerned look, and her aunt waved a hand at her. "I need to stretch."

Prisca glanced at me, still looking concerned for her aunt. "Where are we staying?"

"The Golden Goblet."

Her lower lip stuck out. "Isn't that where we stopped on our way out of the city?"

"Yes."

She sucked her lip into her mouth, and I stared, entranced.

"What's wrong with that inn?"

She shook her head. "It's fine." She stalked away to mount her horse.

"I can help you out here," Asinia said from behind me.

I turned and eyed her. "And why would you do that?" Her loyalty was to Prisca. As it should be.

"Because giving you this hint might help you take your foot out of your mouth. And Prisca has far too many important things to worry about to be brooding over you."

"And what do you want in return?"

She gave me a sharp smile. "A favor of my choosing at an unspecified time in the future. You fae have been teaching us the value of such things."

I glanced at Prisca, who was scowling into the forest.

"Fine," I grumbled. "Do you want a blood vow?"

Asinia slowly shook her head. "If I didn't think your word could be trusted, I'd be urging Prisca to leave you at the first opportunity."

I stiffened. "Getting between us would be a mistake."

She rolled her eyes at me. "I'm the sister of her heart. You're just a fae prince with murderous urges and a leash connecting you to your brother."

Sparks flicked from my skin. Asinia was watching me closely, no trace of fear on her face.

"You're pushing me. Why?"

Asinia gave me a wide smile. "You and I haven't spent nearly enough time together. I don't know enough about you to know whether you're the best or worst thing to ever happen to her. So I'm collecting evidence."

I pinned her with a hard stare. "Evidence?"

"We don't have time to go into all of that." She gave a wave of her hand. "Do we have a deal?"

"I said we did."

"Good. Think back to the inn. And the fae woman who was all over you."

Not much surprised me, but that was enough for my mouth to fall open. I'd accused Prisca of being jealous that day, but it had obviously impacted her more than I'd known if she didn't want to risk running into the woman again.

Lust roared through me without warning. Asinia turned and wandered away. "You're welcome," she threw over her shoulder.

Prisca didn't take her gaze off the forest when I mounted and steered my horse over to her.

"I chose that inn because it's run by those loyal to the fae. But we can find somewhere else if you don't want to stay there."

Prisca's eyes were very gold as she glanced at me. "You're being exceptionally reasonable."

"I know what it is to be eaten alive by the thought of you with another man. I'll always spare you from that."

Her cheeks heated. "I'm not usually the jealous type."

"I like it," I said. "In fact, I'm so fucking hard right now, all I want to do is pull you from that horse and take you behind the nearest tree."

Her breath hitched.

"Ahem." Cavis cleared his throat. "The horses have all been watered."

Prisca knelt in front of the Drakoryx and explained that it couldn't come inside the city with us.

"It's too dangerous," she said. "You could get hurt."

The Drakoryx yowled. After a long, tense standoff where they stared at each other, it turned and melted away into the forest.

"Do you think we need to worry about him eating people?" Prisca asked.

I shrugged. "It sounds like he only eats bad people."

The Golden Goblet was quiet by the time we arrived—most people having already eaten lunch. Cavis and Asinia chatted quietly while Telean excused herself, announcing that she needed a nap.

"You need to eat," I told Prisca.

Prisca gave me a look. But her stomach chose that moment to let out a rumble. She glowered down at it as if it had betrayed her.

"I want to take a walk," Asinia said.

Prisca frowned. "Are you sure? I can come with you."

"No." Asinia smiled. "I'm fine, I promise. I just want to stretch my legs, think a little."

Prisca nodded, and I glanced at Cavis. "I'll take watch," he told me.

It was my turn. "Thank you." I glanced back at Prisca. "Looks like it's just you and me, wildcat. Take a seat."

I kept one eye on her while I paid the innkeeper for our stay, sliding the key to our room into my pocket. Prisca didn't have the best luck in either taverns or inns, and I was taking no chances. The barmaid nodded at me, and I sat, watching as Prisca frowned down at the table.

"What are you thinking?"

"How reliant is the Gromalian king on Regner?"

"In terms of trade, both of them are equally reliant on

each other when it comes to food. However, Regner has access to iron deposits, which he trades with Eryndan—not just for construction, but so he can create fae iron."

Prisca glowered at that. "And just where are these iron deposits?"

The barmaid plunked two plates of food in front of us, along with water and ale.

Prisca surveyed her heaping plate, and my lips twitched. "What is it?"

"Mostly wondering how all this food is going to fit in my stomach. But Galon was right. Look at this." Prisca rolled up her sleeve and flexed her arm proudly. Her arm was sleek and toned, her biceps clearly gaining in definition. But it was the pride on her face that made me lean forward and kiss the tip of her nose.

"You're definitely…filling out," I said, dropping my gaze to her breasts.

She burst out laughing. "I'll tell Galon you approve of his training and food plan."

I scowled. "Don't tell Galon anything about your breasts."

She shook her head at me, taking a bite. "Are you going to tell me why we stopped here the first time?"

"My spies have been searching for the amulets. I received some news that seemed positive, but Regner has created several guarded residences in various locations to throw us off."

She nodded, eating some more. I watched her. It probably wasn't normal that I wished I had access to every single one of her thoughts. But at least I knew her well enough to guess where her mind had gone.

"What are you going to do about your cousin, wildcat?"

Prisca sighed. "I've been thinking about it. For now, we need to focus on finding allies. But...it's pretty likely he will become a threat." Her lips curved. "You've got that look in your eyes."

"What look?"

"The look that screams 'murder.' His parents are the reason our kingdom was invaded. But...even after what he did to that man, some part of me wondered if he could be redeemed somehow. Now that I know he went to the elders, I won't trust him. But I still wish..." She shook her head. "It's stupid."

I sighed. "It's not stupid. You value family. You wish he could be a part of that family."

She was quiet. "You were raised with everyone thinking you were a monster."

"I *am* a monster."

She glowered at me. I shrugged.

"You know the difference between right and wrong. Even with all your power, and the loneliness, you never let it make you...evil. How did you..."

"Stay sane?" I asked, and her mouth curved.

Darkness seemed to roll over the room, and I was suddenly little more than a boy, with barely ten winters behind me, struggling to lift a sword.

"I'm sorry, Lorian. I shouldn't have asked."

"No," I said. "I'm beginning to learn that pain left untended doesn't fade—it festers. One day, I'd like to talk about it. With you."

Her breath caught, and I drew back in time to see her looking at me like I'd created all the stars in the sky, just for her.

Had I given this woman so little of myself that the mere mention of a potential conversation at some point in the future was enough to put that light in her eyes?

"We can talk about it now," I offered hoarsely, my throat closing at the thought of ripping that wound open.

"No," she said. "No, Lorian. I get it. You were so young, and Regner took everything from you. Even your reputation."

I raised one eyebrow. "Don't be mistaken, wildcat. I've spent years earning that reputation. I *am* the Bloodthirsty Prince."

"I know." She nodded. "But you're not bloodthirsty when it comes to my people—or your own."

"No."

That look was in her eyes again, and all I wanted to do was roll her beneath me. "Are you finished?"

She blinked. "Finished?"

"With your food, wildcat."

She glanced down at her mostly empty plate and nodded.

"In that case…" Launching myself to my feet, I grabbed her wrist, pulling her toward the stairs. Her delighted laugh rang out behind me. It was the best sound

I'd ever heard.

She tripped up the stairs, and I pulled her into my arms, making my way up to the room I preferred on the third floor. Within moments, I was slamming the door behind us, locking it with a flick of my wrist, and placing Prisca on the floor in front of me.

My hand was suddenly buried in her hair, my mouth covering hers, swallowing her surprised yelp. She pushed my shirt up, and I chuckled, enjoying how desperate she was for me. *Only* for me. If any other man ever saw her like this, I would kill him.

I leaned back enough to rip my shirt off, before pulling her tunic over her head, her breasts spilling free from the undergarment I unwrapped. She whimpered as I slid my hands up to her full breasts, cupping them, gently brushing her nipples before squeezing.

She went languid against me, swaying on her feet.

Made for me.

I pushed her back until her legs hit the bed, following her down so I could strip her leggings from her. She lay spread beneath me, naked and ready, her eyes heated, her cheeks flushed, her body eager for mine.

Placing my hand around her neck, I gently squeezed, enjoying her sharp intake of breath, the way her eyes flared. I let my hand trail down her body until I cupped her pussy, smiling at the feel of her, so wet for me.

She groaned, arching her back as I pushed one finger inside her, using the heel of my hand to drive against her clit. Her body jerked, and I added a second finger, lowering my head to tongue her.

The sweet taste of her drove me wild, filling my senses with *her*.

Within moments, she was rocking desperately into my fingers, inconsolable with need. I sucked on her clit, thrusting my fingers deeper, and she let out a long moan, clamping down around my fingers.

Pulling them out, I licked them, watching as her eyes opened to half-mast, more gold than brown.

"Delicious," I told her, and her cheeks flushed brighter.

Stripping off my pants, I caught her hand as she attempted to grasp my cock. I slid into her instead, a groan of pleasure leaving my throat. Pushing her thighs wider so I could get deeper, I began to thrust.

Prisca wrapped her legs around my hips, and I leaned down, taking her mouth. She was making those tiny gasps now, her thighs shaking in the way she did when she was close.

Pulling back, I slammed forward, watching her carefully. My wildcat was still getting used to my size. But she lifted her hips, tightening her legs around me, urging me on.

My mouth found her nipple, and I bit down gently. It was enough to make her stiffen.

"Lorian…"

Fuck, I loved it when she said my name in that needy tone.

"Something you want, Prisca?"

She glared up at me and I laughed, but the sound was choked. I trailed kisses up her neck, pounding into her. She let out a tiny whimper, her pussy clamping down around me as she shuddered in my arms. I sucked in a breath, thrust deep, and followed her over.

PRISCA

I hadn't thought about what we would wear to meet the Gromalian king.

Thankfully, Lorian and Telean had. This explained where they'd disappeared to yesterday afternoon while both Asinia and I had napped.

The dress fit perfectly. Intricate embroidery adorned the bodice, tendrils of silver thread weaving across it. The flowing sleeves draped elegantly from my shoulders, while the skirt was somehow both conservative and daring. Voluminous layers of fabric parted, the high slit revealing a hint of thigh with my every step.

But some kind of unusual material had been inserted into the bodice, making it stiff and uncomfortable. I was frowning and wrestling with the dress when Lorian walked in.

"You look beautiful. What's wrong?"

"There's something stiff in here."

"It's a fae material that repels iron. I had it sewn into the dress."

I stopped pulling on the bodice and glanced up. "You think someone will try to stab me in the Gromalian castle?"

He looked vaguely offended. "Of course not. Or you wouldn't be going."

I folded my arms. "Try that again."

He gave me a smile he likely thought was charming. In reality, it was wicked and just a little smug.

"I don't want any surprises. This way, if anyone tries to stab you in the back, before either I can get to you or you can use your power, you'll be safe."

I opened my mouth, and he raised one eyebrow. "I had it sewn into Asinia's and Telean's gowns as well. Asinia isn't happy. She says it's too uncomfortable and she'll only wear it if you do."

And he'd outmaneuvered me yet again. I squinted at him. "Where's *your* armor?"

His mouth twitched, and I sighed. He *was* armor. No one would dare attack me with him by my side.

"Fine."

He leaned close. "You look very regal."

"Is that right?"

"Yes. I want to lift up that dress and—"

"The carriage is here," Asinia called.

Lorian sighed. I stepped back and took a look at him.

Unsurprisingly, he wore black. He'd once told me it was because it hid bloodstains. His doublet was cut from a rich material that seemed to drink in the light, the silver detailing similar to mine. Beneath the doublet, he wore a black silken shirt, which was tucked into his breeches. My gaze got stuck on his muscular thighs before tapering down to his polished black leather boots.

My mouth watered.

Lorian's eyes darkened. "That look on your face is going to get you fucked."

"No, it's not," Asinia called, slamming her hand on the door. "We need to *go*."

He cut his gaze to the door, but his mouth twitched. "We're coming."

"No, you're not." Asinia was laughing now.

"Go away," I called.

Cavis's low voice sounded. Asinia replied. And then *he* started laughing.

Lorian shook his head. "Are you ready?"

"No. But I will be."

He gave me that dark, approving look that made my toes curl. "I know you will."

Lorian had sent a messenger to Eryndan, asking for an audience. And the king had sent one of his carriages to the inn. Several people were gathered outside, eyes wide as they watched the uniformed driver open the door for us. Lorian swept his gaze over them, and most of them turned away, finding something else to look at.

The driver held out his hand, and I allowed him to help me into the carriage, holding out my own hand to Telean, who sat beside me. Asinia sat in front of us next to Lorian, who watched me thoughtfully.

"Cavis?" I murmured.

"He'll sit up with the driver."

"Has anyone seen the Drakoryx?"

"No," Lorian said. "But if he came into the city, he would be hunted. He's smart enough to stay away."

We were quiet as the carriage left the inn. This was it. I pictured all of the hybrids in those cages in Sabium's dungeon and let myself imagine the daily burnings in the city. The screams. It hurt. But it cleared my mind.

Telean reached out and squeezed my hand.

I met her eyes. "I wish my mother were here."

She knew I wasn't talking about Vuena. Her expression softened.

"You can do this, Nelayra."

The name hung in the air. At first, I'd loathed it. It was a reminder of who I might have been if Vuena had chosen slightly differently. If she'd warned my parents of the attack, or even found a way to get me to Demos as a child. And yet I couldn't regret growing up in that village. Couldn't imagine never knowing Tibris.

Prisca was who I'd made myself. Even if it had been Vuena who'd named me. Nelayra...one day, perhaps I would be worthy of that name too.

The carriage bumped over the cobblestones, and Lorian's hard thigh pressed against mine, a silent support.

"We need allies," Telean said. "Just remember, when it came to her kingdom, there was nothing your mother *wouldn't* do."

I replayed her words over and over. My mother had been forced to flee her kingdom when they were invaded without warning. But Telean had told me a few stories about her, grief tightening her face. My mother had never forgotten her people. She was the one who'd ensured Crawyth would be safe for them. And she should have still been alive, still fighting for our kingdom.

Instead, she'd died crazed with grief as she searched for me in an empty house.

So I had to take her place. Had to be the ruler she would have been.

I kept my head high as we drove through the castle gates and into the courtyard.

The courtyard was filled with statues—each more detailed than the last. They depicted various people seemingly caught in motion, as if they had been merely living their lives before they were turned to stone. I shuddered.

We filed out of the carriage, and I surveyed the castle, conscious I was being watched. Like Regner's, it had been built with dark stone bricks, only in place of towers, the Gromalian castle spread out wider, with countless wings jutting from the main building. At least thirty Gromalian guards were waiting for us. All wore thick armor and carried longswords, as if expecting to be attacked at any moment. Was this due to our sudden visit? Or was Eryndan simply the paranoid type?

One of the guards stepped forward, forgoing a bow for a shallow nod.

I just smiled coldly, allowing him to see I'd noted the disrespect.

"His Majesty Eryndan Marovier awaits your presence." The guard shifted, his gaze flicking to Lorian. I glanced at the fae prince. But he was simply standing next to us, a mild expression on his face.

"By all means," Lorian said when I didn't speak. "Escort us to him."

The guard nodded. And just like that, *I* was one of *Lorian's* companions.

I chewed on that. To get a reputation like Lorian's— to strike fear in the hearts of men who'd never met me—I would need to spend years doling out the kind of brutality Lorian had.

So I would take advantage of the fact that my potential allies—and my enemies—were wary of the Bloodthirsty Prince.

Perhaps I was just as bad as Conreth after all. The thought made my stomach twist.

The guard swallowed. "Please follow me."

We fell into step behind him, walking into the dimly lit entrance. A strategic move by Eryndan, as it took several seconds for my eyes to adjust to the change in light. Anyone who managed to get past his guards would need those same seconds.

At least, anyone human. Who knew what Lorian and Cavis needed?

The guard led us into the throne room, where the Gromalian king sat, waiting. He was a large man, but his build was the kind of hard fat that said he trained with his men each day. His beard was trim, interspersed with gray, and his bushy brows lowered as he watched us approach.

Next to him, his son sat on a throne of his own. His hair was red, brighter than Madinia's, and fell past his shoulders. But his green eyes gleamed with curiosity as they met mine.

I bowed—just low enough to show respect, but not low enough to imply Eryndan ruled me. Telean had made me practice that bow over and over last night.

"Your Majesty," I said. "Thank you for seeing us."

He raised one brow, the picture of languid indifference, but I caught the way his hand tightened on the arm of his throne. "You managed to get the pirate queen on your side. And then you swaggered through my kingdom without even a visit."

"A simple bargain."

He shook his head. "Nothing with that woman is simple. Your second mistake."

I raised a brow. "And what was my first?"

"Working with the fae next to you."

"Lorian and I both had separate tasks to achieve in Sabium's castle," I said carefully.

"Yes, I know all about how you freed the hybrids."

He said *hybrids* like it was a dirty word, and I stared him down.

"Tell me," Prince Rekja said, his gaze on Lorian. "Did you enjoy pretending to be me?"

Lorian sent him a feral grin.

This wasn't going well. I cleared my throat. "We came here to talk about the threat Sabium presents to all of us," I said.

Rekja's eyes met mine. They were surprisingly clear, and they glittered with good humor. He wasn't what I expected.

Eryndan snorted, and I returned my attention to the king. *He*, on the other hand, was exactly what I'd expected.

"Sabium presents no threat to me and mine," Eryndan said. "And neither do you."

"My people are hidden across this continent," I said. "They're powerful, and they're *angry*. If you don't think that makes them a threat, you're about to see just how Sabium underestimated them."

"Underestimated them? The man holds three fae amulets, along with the hourglass. The symbol of your kingdom. And you want to wage war against him?"

"I *will* wage war," I said. I glanced at Lorian.

He pulled his amulet out from beneath his shirt, sending the king a wicked, deranged grin. Power darted along every inch of his body, crackling, sparking.

"Sabium holds *two* fae amulets." Lorian flashed his teeth at Eryndan. "Temporarily."

The Gromalian king's hands tightened around the arms of his throne. And he speared his guard with a furious scowl. "You allowed the Bloodthirsty Prince in here with his full power?"

The guard had turned ashen. "I'm sorry, Your

Majesty. I didn't know."

"Get out."

The guard fled. Meanwhile, Lorian was still sparking. I squinted at him, and he packed his power away.

It was time to put all our cards on the table. Eryndan wasn't going to help us otherwise. There was nothing in it for him.

"Sabium's real name is Regner," I said. "He has been alive all this time."

"Don't be *ridiculous*."

Lorian's smile could never be mistaken for amusement. "Careful," he said, his voice low, his eyes flat. He focused on Eryndan with a predatory stare, and everyone froze.

The guards barely breathed. A furious flush climbed up Eryndan's cheeks. Next to me, Telean sighed. So far, all we'd done was antagonize and frighten the king in his own castle. Unless I could communicate exactly how dangerous Sabium was, Eryndan's ego would prevent him from listening to us now.

"I would like to hear this theory," Rekja said quietly. Eryndan snarled, but I was already talking.

"It's not a theory." I told them everything I knew. Well, I told them most of it.

When I was finished, both the prince and the king sat in silence.

"You still haven't told me how this is relevant to me," Eryndan finally said.

"You can't be serious," I breathed. "Do you think

he's aiming to conquer every inch of this continent *except* for Gromalia?"

"I think you would say anything to get what you need for your war."

I took a steadying breath and reached deep for a spark of patience. "It doesn't have to be like this," I said. "People on this continent don't have to suffer and bleed just because one man has decided he wants to play at being a god. We can make a better future."

"You're a child playing at being a queen."

Behind me, Asinia sucked in a breath. My hands shook with fury, and I buried them in the folds of my dress.

I needed to be diplomatic. Tactful.

"In that case, don't come to me once Sabium has learned not to fuck with the hybrids or the fae. When he decides to turn his attention to easier targets."

So much for diplomacy.

Next to me, Lorian shook with silent laughter. He'd likely been waiting for me to reach this point. My temper was almost as bad as his.

"And you'd allow that, would you? You, who just spoke to me of *hope* and a better future. What of the humans who live in my kingdom?"

I shook my head. "Clearly, you can't be reasoned with." I thought about what Conreth had said. "My loyalty is to my own people."

He sneered at me. "Instead of attempting to ally with us, you stand next to the Bloodthirsty Prince. And I know you've been in the fae lands with their king. You've certainly cozied up to the fae since you've left Eprotha, *Your Majesty.*"

Those two words oozed sarcasm. We weren't going to get what we needed here. I turned to go.

"Wait," Rekja said, and I glanced over my shoulder. "Join us for dinner. If this is the one and only time we will meet before war breaks out, we should use that time wisely. Don't you agree, Father?"

Eryndan gave him a look. "You are your mother's son."

Rekja smiled back at him, but when Eryndan glanced away, I caught the wounded expression on his face.

"Fine," Eryndan said. "We will discuss this civilly over a meal. And when you travel back to the fae lands, you can tell the fae king that I listened to your explanation."

22

PRISCA

One of Eryndan's guards showed us to a set of rooms. We filed in, and I swept my gaze over the main chamber. It was huge, with rich tapestries decorating the walls, a grand hearth, and a large window overlooking the courtyard. Several doors led to private rooms for sleeping and bathing, and I caught a glimpse of a wide four-poster bed through one of the doorways.

My throat was so tight I could barely speak. "I'm sorry," I murmured to Telean as we stepped inside. There were no words for how badly I'd blown our chances.

"Do not apologize. It's not over," Telean said. She hobbled toward a bedroom to the right.

Asinia shot me a questioning look. I just shrugged. She jerked her head at Cavis, and they disappeared into another room.

Lorian was prowling around the room, his skin sparking once more.

I kept my voice low, conscious of

spies. Lorian would hear me with those fae senses of his. "The Gromalian king is too cozy with Regner. We need to do something about it."

"Both kingdoms are mostly home to humans. And even if he attempts to deny it, Eryndan knows there's something unnatural about Regner. He also knows it wouldn't take much for Regner to decide that if Eryndan won't give him his armies, he'll simply take Gromalia and enjoy those armies himself."

"Then why won't he ally with us?"

"I don't know. He has always loathed the fae. As far as I'm aware, we haven't given him any reason for such a deep hatred."

I stalked to the window, looking down at the courtyard below us and the strange statues placed throughout it. "Is there anyone from Eprotha in the area? Anyone important?"

"An ambassador from Eprotha is due to arrive tonight after dinner. I'd planned for us to leave before he was announced."

I glanced over my shoulder at him, the beginning of a plan coming together. "You said Demos and Tibris were in Eprotha. Near the Gromalian border."

Lorian nodded.

The thought of actively putting my brothers in danger made me want to lose my stomach. And yet both of them would scowl at me if they could hear my thoughts.

"Demos is recognizable."

"Yes. There are flyers with both of your faces across

the kingdom, along with any hybrids who escaped. Including Asinia. And you." A spark left his skin and darted into the air. The fae were powerful, territorial, and snarly at the best of times. And Lorian was their prince. Being here, in Eryndan's castle, was clearly making it difficult for him to keep his control.

"Should I be worried?"

He met my gaze. "About this?" He raised his hand, and another spark flew into the air. "No. I would tell you if I was concerned."

I nodded, letting it go. I trusted him.

"If Demos and the others were seen crossing into Gromalia, would Regner's men chase them down?"

"Likely. Historically, the Eprothans have simply told the Gromalian guards at the border that they're searching for escaped hybrids, and they've been allowed entry."

"You and Marth wore Gromalian uniforms when you were in Eprotha."

He slowly nodded, and I could see him figuring out what I needed. "We have plenty of contacts to get various attire. That is likely the easiest part of whatever you're planning."

I crossed the room to the desk and found some parchment, scrawling my note in code. "I need you to get this message to Tibris." Lorian took it, and our hands brushed. That strange awareness burned between us, and the gleam in his eyes told me he felt it too.

"Aquilus will get it to him within a few hours."

"Hmm?"

His smile was smug. He knew what he did to me.

"My hawk will get the message to Tibris."

My cheeks flushed, and I forced myself to focus. "What do we know about Rekja and Eryndan?"

"Rekja is an only child. His mother died when he was young, and Eryndan oversaw every minute of his education. I vaguely remember Conreth mentioning that Rekja is in love with one of his father's guards. The guard is well-known, and she has spent years moving up the ranks. Eryndan would not be pleased if he learned of this. In fact, her life would be in danger."

Would I weaponize Rekja's forbidden love if it helped my people?

Without a second thought.

I rubbed at my temple. A headache had begun drilling through my head. If the plan I was putting together was going to work, we needed to stay for a few days.

And I knew just how I was going to get invited.

Lorian moved closer, raising his hand to my head. "I'll call for a healer."

"I'm fine."

He smoothed my hair back from my face, clearly unhappy. I gave in to the impulse and leaned my head against his chest. His heart thumped, steady and strong, and I wished we could stay just like this for hours.

"Do you know exactly what time the ambassador is due to arrive?" I mumbled.

He stroked my hair. "I can find out."

I nodded against his chest, breathing in his scent. His other hand found my waist, holding me against him.

"I wish we could have one day," I said, lifting my head. "Just one day to spend together."

Lorian leaned down, pressing a kiss to my forehead. "We'll have it. We'll have days and days just like this."

I met his eyes. His gaze was so serious. For just this moment, I couldn't think about all the reasons those days would never happen. Instead, I gave in to the urge to daydream with him. Taking his hand, I pressed a kiss to the center of his palm. "You promise?"

"I promise."

A door opened. "Nelayra?"

Lorian turned me so we could both see Telean, standing in the doorway. A pillow crease lined one of her cheeks, but she didn't look any more rested. The travel had been hard on all of us, but especially her.

"It's time to dress for dinner."

I nodded, reluctantly pulling away from Lorian and following Telean into the room.

She'd unpacked, and her bed was a mountain of lace, silk, velvet, with glimpses of tiny pearled buttons and thin gloves, all of it in colors that would suit my skin tone.

"How did you have time to find all of these?

"I took your original measurements from the castle and added onto them slightly to account for the regular meals you've now been eating." My lips twitched and she shrugged. "I began designing the gowns when we were still on the ship."

Something about the thought of Telean working so hard even after leaving the castle made my eyes burn.

"Thank you."

She shrugged one curved shoulder. "Thank the prince. He insisted on paying for them."

"He did?"

"You gave most of our money to the others. Demos left me more than enough should we run into problems, but your fae insisted he be the one to provide you with what you needed."

That sounded like Lorian.

"Do I have time to wash?"

Telean nodded. "Make it quick."

At some point, a maid knocked on the main door and offered to help me get ready for dinner. Telean sent Asinia out to tell her I didn't need help, and I took a quick bath, piling my hair onto my head so it wouldn't get wet.

The gown Telean had designed for dinner was a deep green. The bodice cut in at the waist, drawing attention to the curve of my hips, while intricate embroidery swept up from the bottom of the skirt to the bodice, resembling gold vines that twisted around my torso.

Like the first gown I'd worn, the skirt was also fashioned from layers of fine, diaphanous fabric, only there was no split, and the material seemed to whisper with each step I took. And just like the first gown, the bodice was stiff with Lorian's armor.

Telean handed me an emerald necklace.

"Also from your prince."

My heart tripped at the gleam of diamonds and gems, and I fastened it around my neck.

"And this."

I swallowed at the sight of the matching diadem. Fashioned out of glimmering white gold, the band was shaped like intertwining vines, designed to rest upon my brow. The centerpiece was a large emerald that perfectly matched Lorian's eyes. Along the band, meticulously placed diamonds glimmered, decorating the vine—staggered in size.

It was delicate, unique, and perfect. Telean gestured for me to lower my head. Carefully placing the diadem, she stepped back, admiring her work. "He convinced me you would need to work up to a crown."

"He was right."

Asinia stepped into the room and met my eyes in the mirror. "You look beautiful."

I attempted a smile, and her eyes sharpened. Telean stepped into my line of sight.

"Take that heart of yours and turn it to stone," she ordered me. "Tonight, you are not a woman who *feels* anything for the Bloodthirsty Prince. He is a tool you have chosen to wield, and you are a monarch who will do whatever it takes for your people."

Telean waited until I'd nodded. Then she pressed a kiss to my forehead and walked out the door, closing it gently behind her.

Asinia blew out a breath. "Your aunt can be a little scary."

"I know."

Asinia frowned. "What's wrong, Pris?"

I filled her in about my plan for Demos and Tibris.

"You're worried."

"Of course."

She patted the bed next to her, and I sat down, careful not to wrinkle my dress.

"I won't bother telling you they can look after themselves. But I will tell you they wouldn't want you to worry about them."

"I know. But I can't help it. Are you sure you don't want to come to this dinner?"

She immediately shook her head. "I'm going to eat with your aunt and Cavis, and then I'm going to beat Cavis at King's Web. We'd be a distraction at dinner, and you've got this." She studied my face, seeming to come to some decision. "I know you're trying not to think about what will happen with you and Lorian, but...I wanted to let you know I like him."

"You do?"

"I do. He's short-tempered and brutal, but I've never seen a man look at a woman the way he looks at you. As if you're his entire reason for breathing."

I took a deep, shuddering breath. "The elders said I couldn't keep him."

"Why are you still thinking about anything they said?"

I got up to pace. "I'm scared, Asinia. I'm scared to want him this much."

"A little fear is good for you, Pris. Just don't let that fear steal your happiness."

Telean opened the door. "It's time."

LORIAN

It wasn't my job to debate the political ramifications of murder.

Usually, I left those kinds of musings to my brother.

However, if the Gromalian king didn't stop sneering at Prisca—in between the glances he stole at her breasts—I would gut him. Perhaps then, his son would be more open to an alliance.

Currently, the king was using this time to taunt Prisca. It would be so, so easy to remove his head from his body. And yet, it would simply create more complications. *This* was why my brother didn't send me for these kinds of political maneuverings. And why I was the weapon he pointed at our enemies instead.

Something dark settled in my gut at the thought.

"We have an alliance with the Eprothan king," Eryndan was saying, and I lifted my head, watching as he took a hefty bite of creamed potato. "An uneasy alliance, but an agreement not to wage war on the other."

Prisca stared at him, condemnation gleaming in her eyes. "Tell me, Your Majesty, do the *gods* take your people's power in this kingdom?"

Eryndan's expression turned sly. "No, I didn't make

any such agreements with the gods." His lips twitched, and Prisca's hand tightened around her knife. "However," Eryndan continued, "while there have been some... distasteful aspects of Sabium's great lie, there is no denying the positive outcomes."

The table went silent. Even Rekja placed his fork back on his plate.

"The positive outcomes?" Prisca breathed, and I had to fight the urge to reach for her hand beneath the table. I wanted to pull her into my arms. Right after I speared Eryndan with enough lightning to make him dance as he died.

"Sometimes, great power is found in the most surprising places. Why should that power be wasted in tiny villages by small-minded peasants when it could be used for the greater good?"

The blood had drained from Prisca's cheeks. Anyone who looked at her right now would assume she was exactly what she appeared to be. Weak.

And yet I recognized the wrath in her eyes. Eryndan didn't realize it yet, but he wasn't long for this world. Someday, no matter how long it took, Prisca would see him dead.

I hoped I'd get to see it.

"And how many hybrids did you send back to Regner?" Her voice was lifeless now.

"Countless," he hissed. "What could your people do for me, except die in new and unusual ways and keep Regner occupied?"

Her eyes glittered with a restrained wrath. "Was that why the Gromalians didn't step in when Sabium attacked my kingdom?"

"You'd have to ask my grandfather, who sadly passed not long after that little skirmish." He wagged his finger at her, obviously enjoying himself now. "If I were you, *Hybrid Heir*, I wouldn't go counting your thrones before you're sitting on them."

I'd promised Prisca I would leash my temper. So far, this conversation was going the way we'd anticipated. But I looked forward to the day Eryndan took his last breath.

Prisca gave Eryndan a cool smile that made me want to kiss her. "You'll forgive me if I don't take advice from a man who is waiting to drop to one knee for Regner."

The smile fell from Eryndan's face. Across the table, Rekja sent me a warning look.

"Why don't you ask yourself where the fae were?" Eryndan suggested. "Those with such similar life-spans and power to your hybrids? Those who once shared a kingdom with you?"

Prisca's eyes met mine, and I held her gaze, keeping my voice carefully neutral as we'd agreed. "Not helping our hybrid cousins remains my people's greatest shame."

The messenger I'd bribed slipped into the room, whispering in my ear. I didn't so much as glance Prisca's way. She knew what this meant.

"If you know what is good for you, you will disappear." Eryndan smiled at Prisca. "Run, and hope that time magic of yours keeps you safe for at least a few years. If you're lucky, you'll be able to pop out a few heirs of your own, and perhaps one day, they'll have more success swaying allies to your side."

Fury flashed across Prisca's face. But her eyes flooded with tears. Even knowing her reaction was planned, I wanted to slit Eryndan's throat.

"I need some air," Prisca mumbled, getting to her feet.

She glanced around the table, eyes skating over my form and landing on Rekja.

He stood, offering his arm. "Allow me to escort you to the gardens."

She gave him a shaky smile and wrapped her hand around his arm. Sparks jumped off my skin, and I wrestled my power, shoving it down deep. I could feel Eryndan's amusement as he watched me watching them. Good.

"I noticed some unique statues in the courtyard," Prisca said softly to Rekja as they walked past me. "Would you show them to me?"

"Of course."

I repressed my every instinct, tamping down the rage that burned through my body. Ignoring Eryndan's low laugh, I allowed them to leave together.

PRISCA

Rekja was polite and charming. He led me through the courtyard, staying quiet while I collected myself. Eventually, he seemed unable to handle the silence—and my quiet sniffles—because he launched into a story about the time he'd embarrassed the king at a dinner. Eryndan had ordered him to clean every statue in the courtyard, and Rekja had worked with one of his best friends to create a spell to do the work for them.

Only, that spell had blown the head off his father's favorite statue—a war hero from Gromalia's earliest days.

I chuckled, genuinely amused. Rekja was…kinder than I'd expected. I'd only known him for a few hours, but he seemed mildly embarrassed by his father. And yet, if he had any conflicting thoughts about Regner, he was keeping them to himself.

I didn't *want* to complicate his life. Didn't want to make him an enemy.

"When it came to her kingdom, there was nothing your mother wouldn't *do."*

Rekja had been raised by his father. The man who was sending the hybrids back to Regner to burn. I might like him as a person, but I had no proof he wouldn't do the exact same if he ever took that throne from his father.

Unless I began to make life exceedingly difficult for him.

"Nelayra?"

Taking a deep breath, I smiled up at the prince. He'd stepped closer, and I raised my hand, allowing my fingers to trail through the ends of his red hair.

Surprise flashed across his face, and he caught my hand in his. "Are you attempting to encourage your lover to kill me?"

I shook my head, taking a tiny step closer. And that was when Rekja turned his head to our left.

The Eprothan ambassador stood on the other side of the courtyard, his eyes flinty. Hopefully, he was mentally noting just how close the prince and I stood.

Rekja tightened his hold on my hand as he glanced at the ambassador. "You're much better at scheming than I gave you credit for."

I smiled sunnily at him. "Why is it that men are considered to be cunning planners, while women are usually called conniving schemers, do you think?"

Despite the dull fury in Rekja's eyes, his mouth twitched. "Your fae prince will have his hands full with you."

It was my turn to go still, and he shook his head at me. "You'll need to control that weakness before my father uses it to control you."

I tipped my head back and let my laugh ring out across the courtyard. In the corner of my eye, I caught the ambassador's mouth twist as he raised a hand, gesturing for a messenger. With any hope, the rumors I'd started would also reach the ambassador's ears tonight.

The rumors of an impending engagement between the Gromalian prince and the hybrid heir.

Rekja gave a long-suffering sigh. "Are you finished?"

"For now." I allowed him to lead me back toward the castle.

"My father has never been one to think clearly when his back is against the wall."

"I figured."

"I don't think you're hearing what I'm saying." Rekja stopped and leaned close, lowering his voice. "Pushing him won't get you what you're looking for."

"Neither will meekly turning and leaving his kingdom with my tail between my legs. I want him to learn just how easily I can tie our fates together. If my people go down, he goes down with them."

His gaze darted over my face. "You grew up in a tiny village. I know that much about you."

My throat closed at the reminder of my home, and I nodded.

"So how did you become like this so quickly?"

I let out a hollow laugh. It was evident *like this* was not a compliment.

"It's simple, really. I saw what Regner had done to the hybrids. I learned that no one came to our aid when we were invaded. Not the Gromalians. Not the fae. Not the *gods*. And I realized no one was going to save us except ourselves."

I would become every bit as ruthless as these old kings and twice as conniving.

I leveled Rekja with a hard stare. "I need you to invite us to stay for a couple of days."

His red brows shot up. "And why would I do that?"

"Because you know we're speaking the truth when we tell you that Regner will come for this kingdom."

"I may believe you, but my loyalties still lie with my father. I'm sorry. I wish it could be different."

I'd expected this answer, even as I'd hoped he'd take the easy option. "Reconsider. Please."

"I can't."

I hadn't wanted to use this, but I would if I had to. "Then invite me to stay because I know about your relationship with your father's guard."

Rekja's expression turned cold. My skin prickled. I wasn't sure what power he had, but I wasn't about to find out.

Pulling the threads of my power toward me, I slid behind him, then released the hold I had on time. He jumped, pivoting to face me.

"Relax, Rekja. I have no intention of telling your father anything about your life. And if we ever end up across the battlefield from each other, I will order that your guard is spared."

Rekja snarled, and I stepped into one of the many alcoves along this corridor. He followed me. I knew that expression. He wasn't used to power like mine, and he responded to fear with rage.

"We could have been allies," he said softly.

"We will be," I said.

Rekja slowly shook his head. "You have two days. But I strongly suggest you stay away from me, Nelayra." He turned and stalked away. I buried my hands in my gown until they stopped shaking. It was becoming increasingly rare that I had a moment alone, and I stood in the silence, taking deep breaths.

It shouldn't matter, that I'd threatened the life of Rekja's lover. I would do much, much worse before this was over.

And yet…

And yet.

Footsteps sounded on the stone, and I stepped out of the alcove, smiling at the servant who hurried past me. By the time I made it back to my room, I was firmly in control of my emotions.

At least I was until my eyes met Lorian's.

I closed the door behind me. "We're staying. But he's not going to work with us unless we make sure he has nowhere else to turn. You said his mother died when he was young?"

Lorian leaned back and watched me, his gaze steady.

"Yes. There was some mystery surrounding her death."

"What kind of mystery?"

"I can't say I kept track."

Telean stepped through the door. Her shoulders seemed more hunched than usual, as if the weight of the world were pressing down.

"I have been speaking to the servants about the

queen," she said. "One of them is distantly related to a woman I knew in Crawyth. I will attempt to find out whatever I can."

"Thank you." I glanced at Lorian. "Are we ready?"

He gave me a slow, feral smile. "We're ready."

23

PRISCA

In the early hours of the next morning, while most of the castle was asleep, Cavis took Telean and Asinia back to the inn, along with all our luggage.

I stood by the window and watched their carriage leave while Lorian ran his fingers through my hair. I arched my neck, chasing his fingers as if I were the wildcat he'd named me.

"Are you ready?" he murmured.

I smiled up at him, pleased to finally be leaving this place. "Oh, I'm ready. Are you?"

"I'm always ready to play with you, wildcat," he purred. "Especially when you're putting arrogant human bastards in their place."

My smile widened. A knock sounded on the door. Lorian's eyes glittered with suppressed amusement.

"Come in," he said.

A messenger stepped into the room. "The king asks that you join him for breakfast."

I was relatively sure he hadn't put his request in such polite terms. "That sounds lovely," I said.

We followed the messenger down the hall, where one of Eryndan's guards opened a door.

Eryndan and Rekja sat at a table laden with plates. The old king's face was purple, and when he looked up, his eyes glittered with fury.

Perfect.

I sauntered toward the table, smiling at Lorian as he nudged a servant out of the way and pulled my chair out himself. The silence stretched as we both sat.

"You," Eryndan hissed, his gaze on me.

Lorian went still in that fae way of his. I nudged him with my foot beneath the table.

Rekja pinched the bridge of his nose. "What is it, Father?"

"The Eprothans crossed into Gromalia to hunt one of the hybrid groups," he said between his teeth. "Only to be attacked by a group of *border guards* wearing *our colors*."

I feigned a wince. "Clearly, your men no longer agree with your choices, Eryndan."

His face darkened further. Hopefully, he'd drop dead right here, and we could begin negotiations with his son.

Eryndan ignored me, turning to his son. "The Eprothan ambassador is under the impression you are betrothed to the hybrid heir. Do you have any inkling of why he would believe this?"

Rekja's eyes met mine. I didn't breathe.

After a long, tense moment, he shrugged. "I have no idea, Father. Likely court gossip that got out of hand."

"Sabium believes we are *allied* with the hybrids," Eryndan snarled.

I smiled, pushed back my chair, and stood, glancing at Lorian. His expression was blank, but amusement gleamed in his eyes when he looked at me. Amusement and lust.

"You're not going anywhere until you fix this," Eryndan said.

The amusement drained from Lorian's eyes. "Consider your words carefully," he said, slowly getting to his feet. He held out his arm for me. I took it.

I met Rekja's gaze. His expression was unreadable.

"You believe you have won?" Eryndan laughed. "A simple letter to Sabium, and our alliance will be steadier than ever."

I gave him a slow smile and didn't say a word. We both knew the Eprothan king. While Regner would perhaps believe Eryndan the first time, I would do everything I could to break their alliance. I would make it seem as if the Gromalians were working with everyone *but* the Eprothans.

Regner already didn't trust the Gromalians. I'd learned that soon after I'd arrived at the castle when I was one of the queen's ladies.

The Gromalians had attempted to stay carefully neutral when Regner first went to war with the fae.

"King Sabium may need Gromalia to help us shore

up our borders, but he'll make them pay for siding with the fae last time." Alcandre's voice had dripped with disdain for the Gromalians.

Now, Regner would believe they were ruining his plans once more. Not just by staying out of his war, but by actively siding with his enemies. A small part of me hoped Regner came for Eryndan. I hoped he felt one drop of the helplessness the hybrids had felt for all these years.

"Did you hear me?" Eryndan hissed.

"Write your letter," I said. "Perhaps you should keep your parchment close by for the next letter you'll need to write. And the one after that."

"And what is that supposed to mean?"

I angled my head. "I'm going to use small words so you can understand me. We will do whatever it takes to ruin your alliance with Regner. We will make him think you have betrayed him over and over again, until eventually, so much evidence piles up that he declares war. I suggest you consider whether you want to face that war alone."

I nodded at Rekja and squeezed Lorian's arm. He began leading me away from the table.

"You will *fix this*," Eryndan snarled.

His guards spilled through the door, into the room, instantly surrounding us.

Rekja heaved a sigh.

One of the guards drew his sword.

A single spark drifted up from Lorian's hand.

Flames exploded in a circle around us, burning blue at the center.

I choked on my next breath. Lorian couldn't just summon fire. He could summon *fae fire*.

The fire that was impossible to put out without damask weed mixed with the water. The fire that could burn through this castle and everyone in it.

The blood drained from the guards' faces, and it was evident they knew exactly what they were looking at.

"Lorian," I murmured.

He didn't reply, his gaze remote as he watched the guards.

Lorian had spent the majority of his life with only a small amount of his power. And now that it had been returned, that power was bubbling up inside him, likely urging him to kill the humans who would attempt to stop him from leaving.

So I turned to Eryndan instead. "If I were you, I would call off your guards."

He stared at Lorian in horror. Rekja's expression was tight as he glanced between Lorian and his father.

"Lorian."

His eyes met mine. There was no green left in them—just darkness.

"Go, Prisca," he murmured.

"Lorian," I tried again.

"I won't kill them. Go."

I needed to attempt to fix the situation. We'd decided not to kill Eryndan for a reason. So I began walking toward the door. Lorian's fire moved with me. It wasn't encircling him. It was encircling *me*.

I was the one he was attempting to protect. His power had leaked out because I was in danger.

My heart pounded. I'd deal with this later.

Glancing over my shoulder, I caught Lorian leaning close to Eryndan. He murmured something I couldn't hear. Something that made the old king turn gray. Then he was stalking back toward me.

He stepped through the fae fire. "I know you wanted to swagger out under your own steam," he said tightly. "I apologize."

It was rare that Lorian apologized for anything. I swallowed my surprise and shrugged. "Eryndan knows not to mess with us. That was what we wanted to achieve."

His flames disappeared, and I blew out a relieved breath. Unsurprisingly, the guards didn't attempt to stop us as we walked down the wide staircase and into the courtyard.

Lorian narrowed his eyes at me, clearly wondering if I was being sarcastic. I sighed. "We both got out of there alive. We messed with his little alliance and taught him that the hybrids are a threat. He already thought we were tied together. And in that case, you're more powerful than me." I surveyed him. His face was blank, but he still had a strange, glazed look in his eyes. I'd never seen him wield fae fire before. I had a feeling this was…new. "Is everything…"

"I'm fine."

He wasn't fine. Lorian was nothing if not controlled.

When he used his power, and when he killed, it was because he *chose* to. We'd discussed how we would leave Eryndan's castle, and a ring of fae fire hadn't exactly been part of the plan.

I wasn't sure what had just happened, but all I could do was give Lorian some time to come to terms with it.

And then we would talk.

PRISCA

When Telean had left the castle that morning, she'd insisted on returning to the seamstress. I'd reminded her that we didn't have any further royal engagements, and she'd just patted my hand. I had no doubt she would work with Lorian to ensure the elaborate gowns she favored would find their way to me the next time I needed them.

Even knowing she could look after herself, I wondered if I should go looking for her when we made it back to the inn.

"She'll be fine, wildcat," Lorian said. "I suggest you focus on whatever you're planning next."

I raised an eyebrow. "I'm not sure I understand your meaning."

He pinched my ass, and I laughed. The laugh died as Asinia burst from the inn. Her face was ashen, her eyes lifeless.

A strange metallic taste flooded my mouth, and my limbs turned to water.

"What—"

"It's bad, Prisca," she said.

I tore up the stairs, toward the rooms we'd continued to rent while visiting the castle.

Strong hands caught me, and Tibris pulled me close. "Pris."

He was alive. I squeezed him tighter. "Demos?"

"He's fine. Prisca…"

I pushed out of his arms and opened the door.

Thol's eyes met mine.

For a long moment, I wondered if I was seeing things.

Then Lorian burst into the room, stepping close to me, Cavis moving next to him.

Thol's expression turned blank. "Tell your Bloodthirsty Prince I'm not here to challenge him," he said bitterly.

Across the room, Demos pushed off the wall, threat dripping from his every movement. I cut him a warning glare and scanned his body. Healthy. Safe. My chest cracked open, but my heart still pounded. This room was far too small.

Thol was filthy, covered in healing scabs and a few new scars.

"What happened?" I got out.

His eyes were bitter as they met mine. "*You* happened."

Lorian prowled toward Thol, murder written across his face, and I shoved my hand out, slamming it against his chest.

"Stop it," Asinia snapped. We all looked at her, and she met my eyes.

"Regner learned you'd visited your kingdom," she said, her voice tight. "In retaliation, he sent his iron guards to our village."

"No." My denial was instant, but grief twisted Asinia's expression. Demos stepped toward her as if he couldn't help himself.

"Everyone is dead," Thol said, voice empty. "Everyone except me."

His words punched into me, like a fist to the gut. My vision spiraled, and numbness swept over my face.

His eyes were still on mine. My throat locked up, and I fought to get the word out. "Chista?"

Thol's face crumpled. His sister was dead. Asinia crossed the room to him, wrapping an arm around him to lead him to the bed. "Sit," she said.

He sat. Now that he'd said the words, it was as if he had nothing else left. He looked drained.

"They came in the middle of the night," he said quietly. "I'd gone hunting and was on my way back. I heard the screams and ran."

I could picture him desperately sprinting through the forest to get to our village. There were two kinds of people—those who heard screaming and ran in the opposite direction, and those who ran toward it to help.

Thol had always been someone who helped.

"I tripped on a fucking rock," Thol said, his eyes hollow. "I hit my head. I can't have been out for long, but when I woke up, there weren't so many screams."

It had been night in the forest, and he'd been running as fast as he could. A dangerous task for anyone. But Thol would blame himself for tripping for the rest of his life.

Something broke in my chest. And the pain made it impossible to speak.

This was my fault. I should have known. This was what Regner did. He'd proven throughout his history that he had no problem targeting innocent people to make his enemies suffer.

I should have—

Thol ran a hand over his face. "Chista…Chista tried to run. I found her body near the bakery. The guard she was in love with had attempted to protect her. They'd both been cut down."

The horror of it choked me, until all I could see in my mind was our village, the people dead. Our friends…

They weren't my friends anymore. Likely hadn't been since the moment they heard I was *corrupt*. But none of that mattered.

"Kreilor was still alive when I got there. He'd tried to buy the others time to run, and the guards had tortured him."

I closed my eyes, attempting to block out the vision that appeared in my mind, but it was no use.

"Kreilor said they let a few of them go at first. And

then hunted them through the forest for sport. My father was the first to die. Apparently it was his fault that the corrupt had been allowed to flourish in our village."

Every word he said was like a hammer inside my mind. My head spun, and the ringing in my ears was so loud I could barely hear his next words.

I opened my eyes to find Thol staring steadily at me. "They said this was because of you."

Lorian let out a low warning growl next to me. But he couldn't protect me from this.

"They had someone who wielded lightning, and they laughed as they tortured Kreilor, because now the whole kingdom will think you did it as revenge for not helping you." The rancor had disappeared from Thol's gaze, and there was nothing left but agony.

Lightning. So the Bloodthirsty Prince would be blamed once again. And so would I.

Demos and Tibris were both silent, likely considering the implications of that—and what it would mean when Vicer attempted to convince the hybrids they could find safety with us.

"You're a hybrid," Thol said. "A rebel. That's why Sabium did this, isn't it?"

"Sabium did this because he's a tyrant and a liar, and he knows Prisca is a threat to him," Tibris said.

"How?" Thol's voice cracked incredulously. "How is she a threat?"

Of course he wouldn't know. I opened my mouth, closed it. Opened it again. Lorian took my hand. "She's the heir to the hybrid kingdom," he said.

Thol replied, but I couldn't hear it. All I could hear was the blood pounding in my ears. All I could see were the faces of the people I'd once seen every day.

Herica. Natan. The families. The *children*.

I'd heard over and over again how Regner involved innocent people in his plans. How he decimated villages whenever necessary.

Ever since I'd left the castle, I'd barely given our village a second thought. I could have protected them. Instead, I'd been safe in the fae kingdom, training for a war I would never be prepared for, while Regner was already making his moves.

I mumbled something to Thol, pulled my hand from Lorian's, and walked toward the door. It was as if I were floating above myself, watching my body move without me. Lorian spoke, but all I could hear were the screams of those villagers as they died.

I stood in the hall, staring at nothing. Lorian caught my hand and pulled me into another room, sitting me on the edge of the bed.

He crouched in front of me.

"What can I do for you?" His words sounded as if they were echoing from the end of a long tunnel.

I shook my head. No one could do anything. I was the *cause* of all this.

Lorian pulled off my slippers and loosened the back of my dress, his fingers exceedingly gentle. Guiding me down to the bed, he curled up behind me and held me close.

"Shh," he said, and I realized I was making a strange whimpering sound. "I've got you, wildcat."

LORIAN

I didn't know what to do for her.

It had been two days. She wouldn't eat. Neither would Thol. Asinia ate only because Demos somehow convinced her to take a few bites. Cavis kept watch, in case anyone had followed Thol from the village and tracked him as he met up with Prisca's brothers.

The innkeeper had ensured all other guests stayed downstairs or on the second floor, allowing us to have the third floor to ourselves.

I slipped out of our room, intending to find some food to bring back for Prisca. She was in such a deep sleep, something that might have been panic chewed at my rib cage.

A scuffle sounded on the wooden floor. My gaze met Asinia's. Her face was still drained of color, her eyes glazed.

"I'll stay with her," she said.

I nodded, stepping aside as she cracked open the door.

Tibris and Demos sat downstairs at a table in the tavern, speaking in hushed voices. They nodded at me when I sat next to them.

"We got Prisca's note, and everything went to plan," Demos said quietly.

Prisca had translated the code, letting me know what her message had said.

Charge at the Eprothans and create as much confusion as possible. Leave one alive so he can run home and tell the king about how the Gromalians turned on them. All he will remember is that the group wore Gromalian colors and attacked without negotiating.

"We'd found a few hybrids who were traveling with us, and one of them can wield sound."

I nodded. Being able to deafen an enemy was an incredibly valuable power to have.

Regner would receive word of the fight just as his ambassador informed him that she'd been seen getting close enough to the Gromalian prince that it was clear he was enamored with her. Not to mention the rumors flying that an engagement was soon to be announced.

Prisca was clever. Cunning. She'd proven that much—not just in Eprotha, but with the way she'd hit out at the alliance between Eprotha and Gromalia. But she was also tenderhearted and prone to blaming herself for things she couldn't have known were coming. The village was a good example.

I had enough experience that *I* was the one who should have anticipated Regner's actions. But this was insane, even for him.

Telean appeared. She'd merely nodded when Demos

had told her about the village—presumably numb to the horror Regner wielded after so many years. She sat next to us, nodding to indicate we should continue our conversation.

"We were crossing over the border when Thol found us," Demos said.

That was enough to prick my attention. "And just how did he find you?"

Tibris picked up a piece of bread and tore it in two. "He's a tracker. That's what his power does. Like all of us humans, he's not working anywhere near his full potential, but it was obviously enough for him to find us."

"Can he find objects or just people?"

"Just people," Demos said. "Believe me, I've asked."

"And how did he know to find you?"

"He said he focused on Prisca. His power brought him to us because we were the closest and we could get him directly to the person he sought."

I didn't like it. "And why did he want to find Prisca?"

"So he could kill her," Demos said.

Every muscle in my body locked up, and I was glancing at the stairs before he'd finished speaking.

"He's not here," Demos said. "He went to get some air."

"He wasn't himself," Tibris said carefully. "He said at first he blamed Prisca for all of it and wanted her dead too. But once he stole a horse, the journey took long enough that he realized that wouldn't help anything. By the time he found us, it was because he needed answers.

And because he had nowhere else to go."

I watched Prisca's brothers. They were young. Tibris, in particular, had been sheltered in his village for years before he finally left. Demos, on the other hand, had lived a difficult life. The kind of life that had shaped him into someone who understood the choices people made when they were at their worst.

Telean waved a hand at a barmaid, who nodded at her. "It would be foolish to allow him to be alone with her right now," she murmured. "From what you told me of Nelayra's reaction yesterday, I find it difficult to believe she would defend herself appropriately if he were to attack."

Fury burned through my gut at the thought.

"You don't give her enough credit," Demos said, his eyes hard.

Telean shook her head at him. I pondered her for a long moment.

Occasionally, Prisca's aunt saw her as little more than a tool to wield against their enemies. I recognized it, because my brother had used me the same way since I'd reached nine winters. The difference was that I was a born killer. Prisca was a born protector. And if Telean thought I would allow her to break Prisca and mold her into a weapon, she would soon learn differently.

Telean glanced at me, her eyebrows lifting at whatever she saw on my face. I watched her until she looked away.

Everything in me urged me to return upstairs. To shake Prisca from this depression. To dote on her. To do *anything* to see her smile.

There was no use denying it anymore. The dreams that both of us had shared, the killing calm that had overtaken me when I'd learned of Conreth's duplicity, the deep *knowing* that had settled in my chest when I looked at Prisca.

She was my mate.

And I couldn't tell her.

Prisca didn't choose to be born the hybrid heir. She didn't choose to go to war. She'd had so few choices in her life so far, I refused to take any further choices from her.

Oh, she knew mates didn't *have* to stay together. But I wouldn't place the weight of more expectation on her shoulders.

And…some part of me, a part I'd never acknowledged before…it needed her to *choose* me. Of her own free will. Not because the fates had decided we would be best for each other, or because we'd been thrown together by those same fates. But because she looked at me and saw me as a man who was more than just the Bloodthirsty Prince. Because she saw a man who was worth tying herself to for the rest of her life.

I wasn't blind to my people's flaws. We were a capricious race, obsessive and prone to violence. But our mating—rare as it was—was a gift. The other half of our soul waiting for us to love. To cherish.

I wanted that. With her. And if there was one thing I had, it was patience. I could wait.

At least, for a little while.

24

The Queen

Sabium's rage was evident in the twitching of his fingers as he pressed them to his thigh over and over again.

"The Gromalians attacked? You're sure?"

Patriarch Greve nodded. He had been given Farrow's lands, and in return, Sabium had insisted he take a greater role in the rebellion.

"One survivor," he said. "Just like last time." He jerked his head, and one of the iron guards was brought forward, shoved on his knees before Sabium's throne. The guard had been beaten, both of his eyes black, several of his teeth missing. He favored one arm, cradling it with the other. Clearly, he'd been denied a healer.

"Speak," Sabium said.

The guard's lip trembled. "They were wearing Gromalian colors, Your Majesty. They told our men they would no longer be allowed to waltz into their kingdom as we pleased. And then they killed everyone but me."

Sabium narrowed his eyes. And I saw the moment he realized his tactics had failed. He'd assumed the hybrid heir was nothing but a nuisance. One who would go away—at least for the short term. One who might rally her people, but those numbers were so low, they wouldn't stand a chance against him. And so she'd bleed out on a muddy battlefield somewhere, forgotten to history.

Instead, Nelayra had made the first move. I had no doubt she was behind this "attack." Finally, she was acting as I'd hoped.

Sabium drummed his fingers with increasing vigor.

"You said the ambassador saw her with the Gromalian prince." He addressed Greve, who took out a handkerchief and patted at his sweaty forehead, clearly wary of the king's current mood.

"Yes, Your Majesty. They were…clearly close. Speculation was rife that the two will be married. Speculation the ambassador said he would have ignored had he not seen just how close they were with his own eyes."

Sabium stared at Greve as if he was considering having *his* eyes plucked from his head.

Greve went very still.

"And Eryndan?"

"He sent this message, Your Majesty."

Sabium took it, swept his gaze over it, and sneered. "He wants me to accept platitudes and promises of loyalty? No. Send a message back. Instruct him that I know of a corrupt stronghold within his city walls. If he truly wants to remain allies, he will take the appropriate steps."

My mind raced. If I were Eryndan, I would be attempting to play both sides for the time being. With this coercion, Sabium was forcing him to take a stand. And if the hybrid heir learned of Eryndan's attack on her people, any alliance they might have had would be dead.

The inkling of an idea came to me. If I was caught, I was dead. But it might just buy me some time.

Thanks to Pelysian, I knew where Madinia was now. And the flame-spitting viper wouldn't trust me without a show of faith.

This would be the perfect opportunity.

PRISCA

I woke to find Asinia's gaze on me. I rolled onto my back. "Were you watching me sleep?"

"It was difficult not to. You've been sleeping for two days. Someone needed to check if you were still breathing."

My mind was still muddled with sleep, so it took me a moment to remember.

The pain blindsided me, and I gasped out a breath.

Asinia reached for my hand. "I know."

We lay in silence for a long time. At some point, I

stumbled to the bathing room. When I shambled back toward the bed, Asinia eyed me.

"Lorian is downstairs getting something to eat."

I just nodded, taking in her limp hair and pale face. She watched me back. "I know you're blaming yourself," she said.

I didn't bother trying to deny it.

She sat up, bringing her knees to her chest. "You're probably thinking none of this would have happened if you hadn't lost your temper with Kreilor and used your power that day."

It was the truth. Asinia shook her head at me. "You were running. And you would have made it on to a ship. I know you would have. Especially after Tibris found you. But instead, you walked into that castle because I was there."

My stomach clenched. "Asinia—"

"No, listen."

I clamped my mouth shut.

Asinia's mouth twisted. "I can just as easily blame myself. I should have run the moment I knew you were gone. But I was too slow. And you risked everything to save *me*. You would never have saved all those hybrids if I hadn't been down in that dungeon. And that's what made Regner so furious."

I sighed. "It always would have come to this. At some point, I would have learned who I was."

"And Regner would have burned our village and killed all those people as retaliation. Always. It's his tried and true method whenever he decides to lash out. Both of us could blame ourselves. Truthfully, Chista should carry some blame too if we're playing that game, but I won't speak badly of the dead."

I winced, but I understood where Asinia was going with this. Still, the pain burrowed deep, until my head spun with it.

"All of them, Asinia."

Her eyes filled. "I know. But if we blame ourselves, if we allow it to cripple us, he wins. You're allowed to feel like shit. You're allowed to sleep for a couple of days and shut out the world. But then you have to get up and keep moving. Because we're all counting on you."

I took a deep breath. Part of me wanted to crawl back into bed, but the rest of me knew she was right. I had to keep moving. And I could do it, because of her. Because of Lorian, my brothers, Cavis, and the others. "Thank you. For being here."

Her smile was fragile, broken. "Where else would I be?"

Lorian

Demos made a small sound, and I turned as Prisca appeared at the bottom of the stairs. Something inside my chest unlocked. I glanced at her brothers. From the twin looks of relief on their faces, they felt the same.

Telean took a bite of stew. Clearly, she'd expected nothing less.

Asinia trailed after Prisca. She looked drained but resolute.

I took Prisca's hand and pulled her into the seat next to me as Asinia took the seat across from her.

Prisca met my eyes. "Cavis?"

I kept hold of her hand, needing to touch her. "He's on watch."

She nodded. I signaled for more stew.

"Thol?" Asinia asked.

"Taking a walk."

Two more bowls of stew and a plate of fresh bread were placed on the table in front of them. Both women began to eat, and something settled within me as a little color returned to Prisca's cheeks.

A man dressed in Gromalian green approached us. I slid to my feet, stepping between the messenger and the table. The messenger gulped, his hand trembling as he gave me the parchment. Taking the message, I handed it to Prisca.

Demos dropped a couple of coins in the messenger's hand. No one spoke until he'd scampered out of the inn.

Prisca scanned the message, and I wanted to slaughter Eryndan for the desolation on her face.

"The Gromalian king has given us a choice. He'll break his alliance with Regner and join with us if...if we handle his *uprising* in the west." Her eyes were dull, her voice drained. She handed me the note, and I scanned it.

Rebels had taken a large swath of land in western Gromalia, along the Gromalian and Eprothan borders. I'd told Prisca about them when we were traveling to the fae lands.

According to the message, they had become even more of a threat recently.

They'd created their own army and laid traps around the territory they'd claimed as their own. Eryndan's men kept attempting to take the territory back, and each time, more of them died.

Prisca's gaze met mine, and those amber eyes held so much misery, it took everything in me not to stalk out of the inn and slaughter the Gromalian king myself. That beast inside me didn't care about the political ramifications. Didn't even care about war, or the lives that would be lost. No, it only cared about her.

It hurt, shoving that beast back down where it belonged. Especially when Prisca's eyes glittered. "Those rebels are people who want a better life," she whispered. "People just like—"

"No," Telean said, her voice harder than I'd ever heard it. "Our kingdom was invaded for no reason other than Regner wanted what we had. Our people were entirely innocent, slaughtered merely because we had a power he believed he deserved. And they've been in hiding ever since, forced to watch as their children were killed too. Don't forget who you're fighting for, Nelayra."

Prisca's mouth tightened, but she nodded. "Perhaps… perhaps, the rebels can be convinced to disband if we tell them about the threat coming their way."

I shook my head. "They consider that territory to be their own now. They would no more abandon it than you would hand over the hybrid kingdom." I held up the letter. "This gives us free passage through Gromalia, which is the fastest way to get to the rebels' territory. But if you prefer, we can skirt the rebels and travel directly back to the hybrid camp where you can determine what you want to do about the Gromalian rebels."

"We can't." Demos had been exceptionally quiet, but he glanced at Tibris, and something silent passed between them.

Asinia went still, and understanding flashed across Prisca's face. Something told me this was why they had been meeting so often in the hybrid camp.

I leaned back in my chair. "How about you tell me what you've been hiding from me all this time, hmm?"

There was only one reason why Demos and Tibris wouldn't want us to go directly to the rebels in an attempt to gain the Gromalian king's support. They were going after the hourglass. Prisca had been careful not to mention it to me, but I'd known when she read my message that she would figure out a way to find it. Pride shot through me, and it took everything in me not to haul her onto my lap and slam my mouth down on hers.

Pride was tempered by something darker. Prisca knew if she told me the location, and I told my brother, Conreth could beat us there.

Oh, he wouldn't actively fight Prisca for it. But he

could send a small team to sneak in and steal it from under her. I knew exactly who he'd pick for such a mission. Galon and I had trained some of them ourselves.

"You can trust me, wildcat."

I had said the words quietly, but Telean still let out a snort.

"Your loyalty is to your brother, Lorian," Prisca said softly. "It's not a bad thing. I understand it. But it means I can't tell you everything."

Her words shouldn't have wounded me. She was right. But I had to force my expression to turn blank.

"You are very helpful with your sword and your lightning." Telean addressed me. "But this relationship between the two of you cannot last. You know it, we know it."

Something ancient and feral opened one eye inside me. Something that wanted to lay waste to anyone and anything that would take my wildcat from my side.

Prisca's breath hitched, as if her aunt's words had burrowed deep into her chest and hit a lung. I wanted to wrap my arm around her, but I wasn't even sure if she would welcome it at this moment.

"I'll make a blood vow," I conceded. "Swearing that I will not tell Conreth of this until it is safe."

"Until *I* say it's safe," Prisca clarified, and I smiled.

"Agreed."

"You will make the vow with Demos," Telean told me.

Prisca stiffened. She slowly turned her head and

pinned her aunt with a dangerous look. "Are you suggesting my judgment has been compromised? That I would risk our kingdom and all the lives at stake?"

The table was silent. Telean stared back at her niece. And whatever she saw in Prisca's cold expression must have pleased her, because she smiled.

"No," she said softly. "I'm not suggesting that at all." Her gaze flicked to me. "Make your vow, Prince."

There was one person I would tolerate taking orders from, and even Conreth was careful with his phrasing. I gave Telean a long look, and she dropped her gaze.

A few minutes later, two white lines sliced across Prisca's palm—one from me and one from the pirate queen.

Thol walked in as I was finishing the vow. The man looked as if he was a ghost, barely of this world. "What is happening?" he asked.

"We need to tell Prisca some important information," Tibris said. It was clear he liked the other man. If Prisca had somehow managed to stay in that village and had married Thol, Tibris would have treated him as a brother without question. I barely suppressed a snarl.

That was the future Prisca had wanted. The future she might still long for now, even with the knowledge that her village was nothing but ash.

"You can talk in front of me," Thol said. "I won't tell anyone."

"Of course," Prisca said softly. "Just as soon as you make the blood vow."

I had to turn in my seat to stare at her, wondering if I'd somehow misheard her words. A strange kind of elation flickered in my gut.

Thol's mouth dropped open.

Tibris shifted in his seat. "Prisca."

She glanced at her brother. "If the man who has saved my life over and over again needs to take a vow, then the one who was planning to kill me should make the same vow, don't you think?"

Thol had the decency to flush. Tibris sucked in a breath, and Prisca's eyes met his once more. "Did you think I wouldn't figure it out?"

"No," Tibris said softly. "Thol was insane with grief."

"And now he's lost in rage, which is perfectly understandable." She turned her attention back to Thol. "You don't have to remain here for this conversation."

"No," Thol said, his teeth clenched. "I'll vow."

Next to her, Asinia was staring at her best friend as if she'd never seen her before. Her eyes met mine, and I gave her a warning look. She dropped her gaze before Prisca could see that expression on her face.

Thol made his vow. Prisca now carried three marks on her palm. Jealousy shot through me at the fact that Thol had marked her body in any way, even if it was just a blood vow.

Only a few people were sitting at the tables surrounding us at this time of the day, but I created a silence ward anyway.

Prisca raised a brow. "I thought only Conreth could do that."

I shook my head. "Now that I have my full power back, I can do it too." I wasn't ready to talk about the fae fire. *That* power had come from somewhere else within me. Somewhere I'd never felt magic before. It was as if it had been lifted directly from my soul.

Demos pushed his plate away. "It took us a while to put it together, but we're certain now."

"How?" Prisca asked, twisting her hands in her lap.

"We followed one of Regner's guards. He'd been in the area. Tibris heard him boasting to someone that the hybrids would never be able to challenge Sabium. Not with their precious hourglass still under the human king's control."

Of course.

"Some of the hybrids who took a certain route would have traveled right above it on the way to the fae lands."

The twisting increased. "Where?" Prisca demanded.

Demos's eyes were dark with grief. "Close to Crawyth," he said, his voice hoarse. "The forest runs across the Gromalian and Eprothan borders, although most of it is on the Eprothan side. According to the information we found, water has been moving beneath the forest—through the soil and rock layers—creating voids and passages for thousands of years. Those passages are now a large labyrinth of caves. And somewhere in those caves is the hourglass that was given to our ancestors."

Prisca closed her eyes. "So close."

Yes. The hourglass had been so close to her parents. To her mother, who could have used the hourglass to save her people. I had no doubt Regner had enjoyed that knowledge.

Everyone was silent as Prisca attempted to come to terms with the information. Finally, she opened her eyes. "The note said it's possible the hourglass could be moved soon. What do you know about that?"

"He's still planning to move it. But he's well aware that moving it will be the most dangerous time. He knows we have spies watching him."

"If we were to wait until he moved it, he'd use it as bait and trap us," Asinia said.

Demos nodded. "We need to go for it. Quickly."

"The caves could stretch out for thousands of foot-spans," Prisca said. "How will we narrow down where the hourglass is?"

Demos's smile was a grim twist of his lips. "I have someone near Crawyth. He lives in the area and has mapped parts of the caves throughout the years. I'll request a copy of those maps, and we'll refine the area to search from there."

It was a good plan. At least, it was now that Cavis and I would be traveling with them.

The conversation wrapped up relatively quickly after that. Tibris took watch and Cavis stumbled in, ruffling Prisca's hair. "Good to see you." He sat at the table, gulped down some stew, and meandered upstairs for some sleep.

"I want to go with you," Thol said.

I tamped down my instant denial. He might only be able to track people, but that power would be extremely helpful after we found the hourglass. Besides, as much as I would prefer for him to be far from my wildcat, this would at least allow me to keep an eye on him.

Prisca gazed at him. "We can leave you with enough coin to start a new life somewhere, Thol," she said gently.

He gave her a venomous look that almost got him killed. I let out a low growl, and Thol cleared his expression. "I have nowhere to go. No one left. If finding this hourglass will allow you to fight Regner, I want to go too. If this is my life now, then I'll spend it making him pay for what he has done."

Prisca nodded. "Very well."

Demos didn't look convinced, but Thol got to his feet, turned, and walked away.

PRISCA

"Talk to me, wildcat," Lorian urged from behind me. I kept my gaze on the street below us, where people went about their normal days, buying food for dinner from the market, complaining about their husbands, managing their children.

"Tibris is waiting for me. I need to go speak with him soon."

"Speak with him?"

"He knows what needs to happen next, and he's waiting for me to ask." I blew out a breath and turned, meeting his eyes. "Tibris is a healer. All the time he spent traveling from home to home, healing wounds and sicknesses...it allowed him to understand people. He knows how to talk to them in ways that they respond the best to. He became the only person some of them *could* talk to, and they would call him back not just to treat their external wounds, but to help them with their internal wounds as well."

He frowned. "You're thinking of sending him to the rebels."

I nodded. The thought made me want to heave, but Tibris was smart, trained, and a healer. If we attempted to send a group, they would likely be attacked. By sending a healer, we were telling the rebels we trusted them not to hurt one of our own, and that we didn't want to hurt them either.

"It still takes me by surprise sometimes," Lorian murmured.

"What does?"

"How natural you are at this."

My mouth fell open, and his eyes darkened as they dropped to my lips. But he raised his gaze once more. "Not only are you a natural-born leader, but the trauma of your past has shaped you into exactly who you need to be."

"How?"

"You had to pay excruciatingly close attention to anyone and everyone. You had to know who could potentially be trusted, and you had to understand the strengths and weaknesses of those around you. Because if you were suddenly discovered, even those who might try to save you could become a liability. The terror you lived with has given you an incredible ability to evaluate people and determine where they are best used."

"I don't want to use the people around me," I whispered. "Tibris is my brother." I refused to ever be Conreth. *My* brother was more than a tool I could use when the time came.

The corner of Lorian's mouth turned up. Maybe he'd followed my thoughts.

"Your brother *wants* to be useful. All of them do. They deserve to fight for your people as well, Prisca."

He was right. I knew he was right. But if something happened to Tibris...

I squashed that thought. "I know. It's why I'm going to send him, alone, into rebel territory."

He crossed the room and pulled me into his arms. "I'm sorry."

"For what?"

"For all of it. For the choices you have to make. For the weight on your shoulders. If I'd found a way to kill Regner before this, you might have had that quiet life you dreamed of." His eyes blazed at the thought, but I knew him well enough to know he'd give me that quiet life if he could.

I no longer wanted it.

The thought of him having killed Regner before I was discovered… It was horrifying.

Because it would mean I never would have met him.

My gut twisted. So many people had died. My brother had been in a cage for two years. And the thought of it not happening, of never knowing… "Lorian…"

"What is it, Prisca?" His voice was gentle. As if he knew.

"I never would have met you," I got out. "If you'd killed Regner."

"Oh, wildcat. Don't you know by now? I would have found you. No matter what happens, I will *always* find you."

My heart skipped a beat and then raced. He smiled at me, and my knees turned weak. The certainty in his voice…

I believed him. He would have found me. Somehow.

"Enjoy your time with your fae prince. But know this—you cannot keep him."

Lorian's mouth found mine, and I let him push Ysara's voice from my mind, basking in the feel of him. His scent. His lips, skilled and firm against my own. He slid his hand to my back and pulled me close, and I thrilled at the feel of him hard and ready.

I managed to pull myself out of his arms. His eyes were so dark, the green had almost completely disappeared.

"I need to find Tibris. And then…" I glanced down

at myself. "A bath."

He gave me a wicked smile. "It just so happens I also need to bathe."

Lorian's hawk flew in the open window. I ducked as it swooped overhead, but it went to Lorian's shoulder, and he read the message. His mouth twitched, and he looked up at me.

"It's an update from Hevdrin. About the fae and the hybrids."

"No change?"

He shook his head.

Chewing on my lower lip, I crossed to the window. "Do you think it was a mistake?"

"No, but I think they need a common enemy."

"They *have* a common enemy."

"Yes, but right now, Regner is a theoretical kind of enemy."

I took a deep breath. "We need to send some of them out. If Vicer manages to get the hybrid camp leader to cooperate, the entire camp will need to move down to the fae lands. It will draw a lot of attention. The fae and hybrids are probably tired of training. They're bored, and they want to be doing something." We needed a distraction. Something that would make them *have* to cooperate... "We hold a competition," I said.

"A competition?"

"Yes. Something that requires them to work together in teams of hybrid and fae. The best teams get to go and escort the hybrid camp down."

"You believe Vicer can convince them to move down to the fae lands?"

"I think once we tell him what happened to my village, he'll start playing dirty."

"I'll let Hevdrin know." Lorian glanced toward the door, his expression tightening. "How well can you trust Thol?"

Surprise flashed through me. "What do you mean?"

"He says the village was attacked, but we have no proof of such a thing. If I were Regner and I wanted to slip someone in here and ensure they learned everything they could…"

Bile climbed up my throat at the thought of Thol lying. At the way Asinia and I had fallen apart. "He took a blood vow."

"Only for the hourglass. There are plenty of other things he could tell Regner. All I'm saying is it's incredibly convenient that the only person who survived was the man who had the ability to track you."

My stomach clenched. I hated that Lorian had a point.

"We'll be careful about what we say in front of him. And I'll speak to Demos. We'll all keep a close eye on him. But I can't just leave him here, Lorian. If he really is on our side, I'm responsible for everything that happened to him. If he's not lying, his sister is *dead*." My voice cracked. I couldn't blame him for wanting to kill me, even if he said he no longer wanted me dead. If it had been Tibris who had died with the rest of our village…

Lorian's big hands caught my hips, and he pulled me into him, until my back was against his chest. He pressed a kiss to my cheek. "We'll watch him. It will be all right. Your brother said he's a tracker. But he can't track objects."

I blew out a breath. "That's right. If…if this works, and we find the hourglass, maybe he would help us find Jamic." We needed to find him, and none of Demos's spies had learned anything about his location so far. Thol could save us weeks. Maybe months.

"If he's being honest, the distraction would likely be good for him."

I nodded, and Lorian leaned down, nuzzling my neck. My toes curled. "I need to go talk to Tibris."

He pressed a row of kisses up to my jaw, finding my mouth. I leaned into him, and his hand slipped up, settling just below my breast. Our kiss was slow, achingly tender, his tongue teasing mine. When I finally pulled away, my heart was pounding.

"You're far too distracting."

He gave me a smug smile and lifted my hand, pressing a kiss to my palm. "I'll be waiting."

Somehow, I found the willpower to walk out of the room instead of jumping into his arms. I found Cavis wandering the hall, looking confused. "What's wrong?"

He jolted, staring at me as if he'd never seen me before. "Strange dreams."

This was taking a toll on all of us, and Cavis had been filling in the gaps. He was the one who was constantly taking watch. "You want me to go get you something?"

"No thank you. Who are you looking for?"

"Tibris."

He smiled. "I'll show you."

It was a good thing I didn't fear heights, because my brother was sitting on the roof. All things considered, it made the perfect spot to keep watch, with the ability to see in all directions.

"Go get some sleep," I told Cavis, who yawned, blinked blearily, and nodded.

Tibris patted the spot next to him. "Would you like to begin a long, impassioned speech about how useful I am here, but how I'd be much more helpful winning over the Gromalian rebels? And how I can say no at any point and you won't hold it against me and it's just an idea, but you thought about it and you really believe I'm the best person for the job?"

I glowered at him. "You can be a real bastard sometimes, you know that?" I'd been working on that speech in the back of my mind since I'd read the Gromalian king's message.

My brother grinned at me. "I've got this, Prisca. If you didn't suggest it, I would have. And I would have insisted." His smile turned grim. "We're running out of options."

We were. I'd failed in the hybrid kingdom, no help would be coming from Conreth unless I found allies, Rythos had lost his friend, our entire village was dead, and Eryndan wouldn't ally with us anytime soon.

The war had barely begun. And we were already losing.

25
LORIAN

Prisca's lower lip trembled as she hugged her brother goodbye the next morning. She valiantly managed to hold it together after making him swear over and over again that he would be careful. When she suggested a blood vow to hold him to such a promise, he'd rolled his eyes, extricated himself from her arms, and given Demos a look that told him to step in.

Unsurprisingly, Asinia was the one to jolt Prisca from her anxiety. "Are you serious? Tibris is a healer and will probably be welcomed with open arms. We're going into a labyrinth of *caves*—as quickly as we can before Conreth's men beat us there." She sneered at me as if the order had come from my mouth. "Not to mention, Regner probably has his people lying in wait at every entrance. You want to worry about someone? Worry about us."

Prisca laughed. Cavis grinned at Asinia, while Telean shook her head. After some negotiation, she'd agreed to stay behind, admitting that the trip would be too much for her. I was satisfied with that. One less person to keep alive in those caves.

Tibris made a quick escape, and the stable hands brought out our horses. After our stay in Thobirea, they were well-rested and ready, and soon we were all back on the road.

Cavis pulled up next to me, his gaze distant. "It's not too late to change your mind," I reminded him. "Galon and the others know where to meet us, so you can get back to Sybella and Piperia."

He sighed, longing flickering over his face. "I can't explain it," he said. "But I feel as if something is prodding me to go with you."

I nodded. I'd learned early in life to pay attention to such instincts.

As soon as we reached the forest, I caught a glimpse of the Drakoryx through the trees. Our eyes met, and I pointed him out to Prisca, who let out a relieved breath. "He's all right."

Asinia gave her a wide-eyed look. "He'll be just fine. It's everyone else you need to be worried about."

The Drakoryx disappeared once more, but every now and then, I caught sight of his fur.

Something caught my eye, and I glanced up. Aquilus was flying above our heads, the hawk circling down until she landed on my shoulder. Giving her a stroke, I took the message tied to her foot and scanned it.

Prisca immediately reined in her horse. "What is it?" she asked.

"One of my spies believes he has located one of the amulets."

Her eyes widened. "You need to go."

I gave her the look that comment deserved.

She sighed. "Lorian."

"I'm getting tired of it, Prisca. Tired of you taking any chance to push me away."

She waved at the others to keep riding. "That's not what this is. We both have duties to our people. Demos and I will get the hourglass with Asinia. You and Cavis go get the amulet. We'll meet—"

A dull fury took up residence in my gut at the thought of her going into those caves without me. "Listen to me very carefully. I will never leave you to do something that dangerous without me. Never."

She glanced away. "You're making choices that you can't take back, Lorian. What will happen when your brother learns you knew where the amulet was, and instead of finding it, you came with me?"

An odd kind of tenderness sparked through my chest. "Stop trying to protect me."

"I will. Just as soon as you do the same."

My mouth twitched, and she rolled her eyes at me.

"I'll make you a deal," she said.

Few things intrigued me like bargaining with this woman. "What kind of deal?"

"I'll allow you to come with me to find the hourglass, but the moment it's in my hands, you go after the amulet."

"Why would I make such a deal?"

"Because you respect me and you know if I wanted, I could leave you at any time."

"Perhaps I would simply follow you."

"Lorian."

She looked so serious. I hated that this world seemed designed to push us apart. But I had to trust that with the hourglass in her hands, she could keep herself safe while I went after the amulet.

I sighed. The reality was, while Conreth had given me three weeks, he hadn't needed to add an "or else" to that threat. Because while he may not be able to punish me, he *could* punish Galon and the others. He could force them to take the most dangerous missions, could ensure Cavis was continually away from his family. He could separate us for years if he felt like it. He'd done it before when I'd displeased him, and that time, Marth had almost died.

Fury burned in gut. I knew what Rythos and the others would say if they learned just how Conreth had leashed me over the years. But if not for each of them standing beside me, I would have become utterly irredeemable by now.

My gaze found Prisca's. This war would separate us again and again. As much as it felt almost impossible, I had to trust that she would stay alive. She was clever and cunning, and she had people around her who would help keep her safe.

"Lorian?"

"I'm thinking."

Her mouth twitched.

I knew that stubborn expression. This was a threshold she would not cross.

Choices.

I had to do this. Not just for Prisca, but for my brothers. For my people. For the war. This was our chance to deal Regner a blow he wouldn't soon recover from—especially after the loss of the hourglass.

"Fine, wildcat. As soon as you have that hourglass in your hands, I will go after the amulet."

It wasn't triumph in her eyes. No, she looked as if she was already mourning. As if she already missed me. No one had ever looked at me like that before.

I caught her hand and pressed a kiss to her palm. "As soon as I have that amulet, I will come for you. I promise."

She took a deep breath. "I'm holding you to that promise."

"I told you, wildcat. I'll always find you."

PRISCA

The caves swallowed us whole, a beast of stone and shadow with dark pockets even our light orbs couldn't counter. The stony path beneath our boots twined and coiled as we trudged along it, continually tripping those of us without natural fae grace.

Demos cursed as he stumbled.

"Watch your step," Asinia muttered, and whatever he snarled back was too low for me to hear.

We'd found a group of Regner's guards at the entrance we'd planned to use. After several moments of hissed deliberation, we'd decided to use my power instead of slaughtering them.

There was no point letting Regner know we were here just yet—although it was only a matter of time before he learned of our presence.

The Drakoryx had refused to step one paw into the caves. Since he'd had no problem trotting down the tunnel near the hybrid kingdom, his refusal was disconcerting, to say the least.

"If there was ever a time that we needed him, it's now," Demos had growled.

I had to admit, I would've appreciated having Vynthar with us. The caves were…eerie.

Even the air seemed ancient, holding on to the whispers of those who'd attempted to navigate the caves before us. More than once, we'd found a collection of bones hidden in some corner—someone who'd gotten lost, broken an ankle, starved to death.

Something glinted on the wall in front of me, and I squinted.

A hand wrapped around the back of my cloak and

pulled me backward. I let out an embarrassing squeak.

"What—"

"Trap," Thol ground out. Lorian held a knife to his throat, which Thol was ignoring.

I gave Lorian a warning look, and he waited until Thol released my cloak before sliding the knife back into its sheath. Thol just pointed at something low on the ground.

"What is it?" I breathed.

"A trap," he said again, directing his light orb closer. Lorian crouched and examined it.

"He's right."

The intricate whirl of silver glowing on the cave wall in front of us made sense now. Unwary travelers would find their attention drawn by the sparkle, not noticing the trap at their feet until it was too late.

"How does it work?"

"It's an incredibly thin rope, bound with magic," Demos said, stepping up behind us. "You step into it, and it pulls on something nasty. Likely, something magical and nasty."

"Everyone step over it. Carefully," Lorian warned. "We'll leave it as a little gift for anyone following us. If we have to run out this way…"

"Be careful," Cavis advised.

One by one, they stepped over the thin rope, a sigh of relief echoing in the cavernous space. Finally, it was my turn, Lorian close behind me. I had a feeling he wanted to lift me over the rope, and I slid him a narrow-eyed stare as he crowded me.

Sucking in a breath, I lifted one foot, half expecting to trip and doom us all. Moments later, we were all on the other side of the rope, and I let out the breath I was holding.

The labyrinth wound deeper, its twisting paths and blind corners filled with more traps. Claustrophobia coiled around my chest and squeezed, until I was covered in an ice-cold sweat.

Lorian caught my hand, leaning close. "Take a deep breath. Again. Look at me."

The others waited, and my cheeks blazed. No one said a word, but I *hated* this weakness. Lorian's green gaze drilled into mine. I peered up at him, slowing my breath, blocking out everything but his face. He cupped my cheek. "Better?"

I nodded. He pressed a kiss to my forehead, and we kept moving. The fear came in waves, but I refused to give in to it.

Every few minutes, we encountered something new—more thin ropes at ankle height, magical glyphs that seemed saturated in dark power—Lorian and Cavis handled them together, both of them panting by the time the glyphs were nullified.

Just as we were about to step into the next passage, Lorian went still. He held up a hand, and we all froze. At his signal, the rest of us melted into the closest cave and waited. We'd agreed to this part, but I still ached to help as they lay in wait for Regner's men. Obviously, at least some of them had survived the traps.

The screams were blood-curdling. When Regner's men were dead, Lorian and Cavis ordered us to wait, hiding the bodies in another cave. Hopefully, when the next group was sent in after us, this first group wouldn't be found.

We spent the night huddled in one of the smaller caverns, two of us taking watch at any time—each guarding one of the entrances. When we woke, we trudged on, until I began to lose all sense of time.

On what was likely the third day, we crossed paths with our own trail. Demos stared down at it, horrified.

"How?" he got out.

My heart sank. This place would make us all insane if we let it.

Lorian took the map, and they put their heads together, muttering quietly.

"Prisca. Can I talk to you?" Thol murmured while the others took the opportunity to eat.

"Of course."

Lorian glanced at us, and I knew he was conscious of every move Thol made.

We stepped to the outer wall of the cavern, lowering our voices. "I want to apologize," Thol said, shoving a hand through his curls.

"Thol…"

"No, listen. I should never have blamed you. I lived a life where I ignored the worst around me, because I knew I would benefit from the best of it."

"You're a good man, Thol. I always admired the way

you looked after the people who were struggling. You hunted for them, you helped them when you could—"

"To soothe my conscience. I recognized you in that castle, you know. I told myself I didn't. You looked so different—you even carried yourself differently. But I'd memorized your face by the time I was sixteen winters."

My chest clenched. "Why didn't you say anything?"

"Because in my heart, I was a coward. I knew why you were there. The moment they took Asinia, you would have done whatever it took to free her. I couldn't tell my father or the king you were there, but I couldn't help you either. I would have lived my life like that. Sitting on the fence. Never making a decision. Too cowardly to make a choice against one side or the other. If I'd joined you that day, I could have gotten Chista out."

Heat seared the backs of my eyes. "She wouldn't have left, Thol."

"I would have dragged her out of that village kicking and screaming." His voice cracked, and he ran a hand over his face. "That was my job as her brother. And she'd still be alive."

"You can't think like that. You couldn't have known what would happen."

"My father knew about your people. I learned they weren't really *corrupt* after the ball. He'd overheard one of the king's patriarchs talking. I knew you were victims, and I would have done nothing."

My heart thundered in my ears. "Do you want me to hate you?" I managed to get out. "Is that it?"

He shoved a hand through his hair. "I don't know what I want. Maybe it's for you to stop looking at me with pity and understanding in your eyes when I was planning your murder not all that long ago."

I flinched. Lorian was instantly there. "Enough," he rumbled.

Thol didn't argue. He just slung his pack over his shoulders and followed Cavis into the next cave.

I watched him go. I'd thought I loved him once. I hadn't even known what love was. I'd thought if I could just pretend to be normal, if I could just find a way to hide who I was, we could have a safe, happy life together.

"Wildcat?"

I swallowed around the lump in my throat. "I'm all right." I glanced at Demos. "Do we know where we're going now?"

He nodded.

"Then let's keep moving."

LORIAN

On the evening of the third day navigating the caves, a pounding headache took up residence at the base of my skull. I glanced at Cavis, who nodded back at me. He felt it too.

The hybrids began to slow their pace. "What's happening?" Demos muttered. "Feels like I'm back in that dungeon."

"Fae iron," I said. "Regner has had it melded into the walls. Perhaps hidden beneath our feet."

Prisca sent Cavis and me a concerned look. "Do you both feel all right?"

I pressed a kiss to her forehead. "We're grumpy and tired. Our power will be weakened—perhaps significantly if the search takes much longer. Since hybrids are half-human, it will take longer to impact you, but you'll begin feeling symptoms, and when you reach for your power, it won't work as well. Eventually, it may temporarily drain until you don't have anything left. I'll get you out of here before that happens."

"No, you won't," Prisca said. "I remember how awful it felt when that arrow went through my arm. I was completely incapacitated. This is nowhere near that bad."

The only one unaffected was Thol. Fae iron didn't affect humans. Prisca noticed where my gaze was stuck and elbowed me in the ribs.

We spent the next few hours focusing on the constant traps and finding ways to ensure we didn't get lost. We were now so deep within the caves, the map was useless.

We'd assumed Regner's iron guards would follow us into the caves. And each time one of them caught up to us, Cavis and I took care of the threat—only two or three of the guards at a time.

A boot scuffed against the dirt floor. Not one of ours.

I bared my teeth, moving farther into the cavern as six men appeared, encircling us and sealing off the exits. The cavern was the perfect spot for an ambush. These men were more intelligent than any who'd attacked so far, and they'd managed to mask their scents from Cavis and me.

Not the iron guard. While they looked strong and fast, this was just a warning. A way to tire us, pick off the weakest among us, and to drive cracks through our morale.

"Finally," Demos muttered. "Some exercise."

Asinia sent him an incredulous look. Cavis snorted, and I positioned myself next to Prisca. "Try to conserve your power," I ordered our people.

One of the men sneered. His eyes met mine, and his face slowly drained of color. His sword was too long for him—a bad choice in a confined space such as this.

A long-haired man charged. Demos launched forward to meet the sword aimed at his head. He moved like the fae, incredibly fast. The others attacked as one, and I slammed the pommel of my sword into the next guard's temple. The guard crumpled, and I kicked him in the face for good measure.

I risked a glance at the others. Prisca whirled, slashing out with her knife as another guard swung at Asinia. Dropping, Prisca sliced his hamstrings. Pride rumbled in my chest. I'd taught her that move.

My distraction almost cost me. I swung my head back, the next sword singing within an inch of my throat. My back hit someone, and I palmed my dagger with my other hand, only to find Thol backing toward me, dodging a giant of a man.

"Faster," I snapped at him. There was no fucking room to move in this cavern. If I wasn't careful, I'd slice into one of our people.

Regner's guard laughed. "Worry about yourself." A bearded human gave up on his attempts to slice through me. He gestured with his other hand.

"Duck," I roared. Ice slashed over my head, sharp enough to take a man's head off.

I launched myself to my feet and reached for Asinia, who'd dropped to her knees next to me. My hand found her tunic, and I hauled her to her feet.

Panic stabbed into my chest. Where was my wildcat?

I caught one glimpse of her, fighting back-to-back with Demos, and then the ice-wielder made that same gesture. Powerful, but he clearly had issues channeling it if he relied on his hand movements.

With a roar, I barreled toward him before he could finish summoning his power. My knife slid into his throat like it was butter, and by the time I got to my feet, Cavis was removing the final man's head from his shoulders.

The head bounced on the dirt floor. Asinia leaned over and threw up.

PRISCA

I'd only used a hint of my power during the attack—mostly because it was all I could summon. And I was still as tired as if I'd been using it all day. My nose dripped blood, and Lorian reached into his pack, pulled out a shirt, and ripped off a piece, handing it to me. He wrapped his arm around me, pulling me just outside the cave. His huge hand stroked my cheek, his gaze searching mine. "Are you all right?"

"I'm fine."

I'd barely been able to concentrate during that attack—with all of us surrounded. And I'd watched as he'd roared at Thol, keeping him safe. Lorian considered Thol a threat, and yet he'd saved him anyway.

Sliding my hand up, I urged him to lean down to meet me. His mouth found mine, and I sighed against his lips.

"We should get back," I murmured against his mouth.

In the cavern, Demos and Cavis searched the bodies. Asinia apologized profusely for vomiting, while Thol stared at the bloody remains on the ground.

"We have their food and weapons." Demos lifted his head. "Is everyone ready to continue?"

"It's going to get worse from here," Lorian said. "These attacks are designed to tire us. Regner may weaken us physically, but he can't weaken our resolve.

Stay together and think smart."

"You should save what little power you have until after Prisca has the hourglass," Demos said.

It was a good idea. "We don't know what else will be waiting for us on the way out," I said, and Lorian nodded. But I could see the frustration in his eyes. None of us had expected the fae iron in these caves.

The next attack came a few hours later. I received a long, shallow cut down my forearm. Lorian took it *very* personally. By the time he'd finished with Regner's guard, his face had been unrecognizable.

We all needed to rest. Demos nodded at us to stay put, and he and Lorian split up, searching for the best cavern for us to get a few hours of sleep. On the other side of the cave, Thol murmured quietly to Cavis.

"Your prince seems wound tightly," Asinia whispered, handing me a bandage from Demos's satchel. I sighed, and Asinia turned, giving me *the look*. "What did you do?"

"Made him promise that as soon as I have the hourglass, he'll go find the second amulet."

"What?"

"One of his spies has located it. The fae need it. And the hybrids need the fae to be as powerful as possible since they could end up being our only allies. Not to mention, Lorian needs to protect his people. It's how he was built. No matter what his brother did to him, he can't turn his back on him."

Asinia shook her head at me. "So you threatened to

leave him unless he agreed to go after the amulet?"

"Not exactly."

She folded her arms. "I love you, Pris, but if he'd manipulated you that way, you would have vowed revenge. You've taken his choice away. He wouldn't do that to you."

I stared at her. Clearly, Lorian had been working his charms on my best friend. "He would do it in a *second* if he thought he was protecting me. If he could, he would haul me over his shoulder and dump me somewhere well guarded until this war is over. Since he can't, he's doing everything he can to make sure I'm as strong and well trained as possible. But make no mistake, Lorian would do the exact same thing."

"Then I suppose you're perfect for each other." Asinia turned away.

I caught her hand. "Sin."

"I'm sorry, Pris. I just don't want you to become someone you're not. This war is going to change all of us. Answer one question honestly, and I'll leave it alone."

I nodded. "Anything."

"Did some part of you decide to send him away because you think it will be easier that way? Because you've fallen in love with him, and you don't think you can be together? Because you're trying to protect your heart from any further damage?"

Tears stung my eyes. She hauled me into her arms. "I thought so."

"It was the right choice," I whispered.

"Maybe. For both kingdoms. But not for you, Pris."

Asinia was right. I wanted to protect Lorian. But I also wanted to protect myself. My memory painted Lorian's expression into my mind. The resolved, determined look he'd given me right before he promised to leave.

He knew. He knew, and he'd promised anyway. Because Lorian was nothing if not patient.

I pulled away and took a deep breath. "When I'm with him…I'm a better person. I'm stronger. Braver. Smarter. He makes me face the demons I want to hide from. And he teaches me how to kill those demons myself."

The thought of not having him around…it made me want to roar my frustration.

"Maybe that's what love is. Finding someone who brings out the best in you."

"That's the problem," I murmured, careful to keep my voice low. "Since he met me, Lorian has committed treason, defied his brother, and prioritized our hourglass over the amulet. He brings out the best in me, and I bring out the worst in him."

"Maybe you should let him be the one who decides that," Asinia said.

Lorian appeared, his gaze sweeping over me, as if I might have somehow become injured in the few minutes he'd been gone. Our eyes met. Had he heard the last part of our conversation?

Demos stepped back into the cave behind Lorian. "We found somewhere for us to sleep tonight." His voice had an undertone of suppressed excitement, and I raised one eyebrow. Asinia got to her feet, holding out her hand, and I let her haul me up.

Cavis handed Lorian his waterskin, and Lorian gave me a look of dark promise. "You're going to like this, wildcat."

We picked up our packs and followed Demos out of the cave. He rolled his shoulders, and Asinia elbowed me with a smirk. It wasn't often that Demos seemed this pleased by something. Especially recently.

He led us away from the main series of caverns and to the right, through several caves that got progressively larger. Slowly, the air became noticeably warmer, the heat gently massaging the goose bumps from my skin. We rounded a bend, and my heart thrummed against my ribs as a soft amber glow broke through the shadows.

A natural pool, with steam rising from the surface. Large enough to comfortably hold ten or more people, it carried the faint scent of damp earth and minerals. The tinkling sound of a small waterfall danced through the air, and I craned my head. The water dripped down the side of the cave wall and into the pool, continually recirculating the water.

"There are several of them," Demos said, nodding to another cave entrance. "I found at least five more, all of them in this area."

Cavis stepped closer, dropped his hand into the water, and smiled. All of us could use a bath.

"We'll take turns," Lorian said. "Demos and Thol first. Then we'll switch."

We filed out. All of us except Asinia. I gave Lorian wide eyes, and he smiled, throwing his arm around my neck and steering me into the smaller cave several caverns away. With only one opening to guard, it would mean only one of us had to be on watch at any one time.

Asinia joined us a little later, a dark scowl on her face, her clothes soaked and dripping. I gaped at her.

She squeezed out her tunic. "Your brother pulled me in. He thinks he's amusing."

"Uh-huh. You must have stayed in the water with him for a while."

She squinted at me. My mouth twitched. "Sorry. I mean, 'How dare he?'"

Rolling her eyes, she grabbed new clothes, stalking away to dress. Demos returned not long after, his expression blank, eyes smug.

Cavis had wandered away to find a pool of his own, while Thol had already returned and was busy eating dried meat by the handful. I glanced at Lorian. He was already moving, reaching for my hand and tugging me out of the cave after him.

The pool Lorian led me to was several caves away, and he laid our weapons on the stone within reach. We undressed silently, slipping into the warm water, Lorian's light orbs floating in the air surrounding us. His eyes were half wild, and he stroked one finger along my cheek. He touched me like I was precious, breakable. Like he couldn't believe I was real.

My breath hitched, and I moved into his arms,

straddling him, our faces so close they were almost touching.

"You don't bring out the worst in me," he said.

Ah. So he had heard that.

He pressed his forehead to mine. "Something in me died the night I lost my parents. And then I met you. You brought me back to life, Prisca."

My eyes filled, a tear escaping to trail down my cheek. Lorian pressed his lips to it.

I wouldn't let him throw away his future for me. No one had ever protected him before. Oh, Conreth had sheltered him for a few years, but the moment he'd seen Lorian's potential, he'd sent him away to be trained. Then Conreth had ordered tokens to be delivered to Lorian— the same way Hestia used to drop treats at her cat's feet when she was attempting to train her.

Lorian deserved more.

"What are you thinking, Prisca?"

I'd promised myself we would make the most of every moment we had together. So I leaned down, gently pressing my mouth to his.

Lorian slid his hands to my hips, guiding me down until he was nestled against me. Our kiss deepened, tongues twining together, until I was writhing, grinding against his cock. His big hands held me in place, limiting my movement.

"Gently. Slowly," he murmured against my lips. "I want to savor you, wildcat."

He moved my hair aside, running his mouth down

my neck. I shivered, my hands sliding to his hair, holding his head to me. He leaned me backward, kissing his way down to my nipples, stroking, caressing. I moaned for him, and he tightened his hands around me.

One of those hands slipped down to my clit, one finger slowly stroking me, until I wanted to scream my impatience.

I knew what he was doing. We'd always fallen into each other's arms so easily, even when we couldn't agree on anything else. Now, he was forcing us both to pay attention to each tender moment. Moments that would end soon.

My breath hitched, and he lifted his head. He continued to move his hand, rubbing and playing, and he watched my every reaction, his green eyes alight with lust. Lust, and something else. Something I couldn't place.

I closed my eyes, and he nipped my lower lip. "Look at me," he growled.

"You're so demanding." The words were breathless, and my thighs trembled, my head falling back as a groan left my throat. He slid his hand into my hair, holding my head up, and I opened my eyes to half-mast.

"I'll take everything from you, wildcat. You're mine."

I ignored the way his words made my stomach flutter, leveling him with what I hoped was a stern frown. From the way his lips twitched, I wasn't successful.

"Mine," he said again. I narrowed my eyes, but he was already tightening his hand in my hair, holding me steady as he plundered my mouth. He kissed me like it was the last time we'd ever be together, and I kissed him back, basking in the feel of him.

His tongue slid into my mouth, and I licked it with mine. He growled, further tightening his hand in my hair, and I panted against him, desperate to feel him inside me. He was still stroking me, achingly gently, and I let out a needy moan, attempting to grind into his hand.

"Lorian."

He loosened his grip, guiding me onto him. My breath caught as he pressed against my entrance, pushing inside, his thick cock stretching me. When I attempted to slide all the way down, he tightened his hands again. "Slowly."

I wrapped my arms around his neck, holding him close. He lifted me, then lowered me once more, guiding me until I was fully seated, stretched around him. He let out a low growl, his chest rumbling, and I contracted around him.

Water splashed around us as he effortlessly lifted me again, guiding me up and down. I rocked, stomach clenched, thighs trembling, muscles locking up. My head fell back as he sucked and bit at my throat.

Lorian guided me backward, the new angle making me gasp as he thrust into me. I ran my hands over his chest, his shoulders, his face, as if I could lock the feel of him into my mind. As if I could memorize the hard planes of his body. As if this moment could last forever.

I was clamping around him, and he circled my throat

with his hand. My gaze jumped to his. Lorian's eyes were so dark they were almost black in the dim light, and the way he watched me…

I cried out, pleasure crashing through every muscle and nerve in my body. He kept moving, guiding me onto him, stretching out my release as I shuddered in his arms. I wrapped my arms around him again, holding him close as he buried his head in my neck and emptied himself inside me with a husky groan.

We stayed like that for a long time, then rinsed, still kissing and touching and stroking. Finally, we dressed, making our way back to the cave.

I wasn't particularly hungry, but I ate a little dried fruit and sipped at some water, curling up next to Lorian.

But I couldn't sleep.

Across the cave, Asinia tossed and turned restlessly, while Demos sat up and drank some water. Eventually, it was my turn to take watch, and I sat by the cave entrance until Demos joined me.

"Can't sleep?" I whispered.

"I don't think any of us can. Well, except Cavis."

I cracked a smile. His soft snores cut through the silence of the cave.

"You feel it too?" I'd thought it was just my claustrophobia getting the best of me once more.

He nodded. "Something is wrong. My instincts are screaming at me. But I can't understand what it could be."

I glanced behind us. Asinia was sitting up, brushing her hair and pulling it into a braid. Lorian leaned against the cave wall, watching me.

"So, no one is sleeping?" I asked.

"Not anymore," Cavis muttered, and Thol snorted.

"In that case, let's keep moving," Lorian said.

We packed up, falling into the same rhythm as we continued our search. I might not have been able to sleep, but I felt better after bathing and eating. Still, panic pricked at me. How much longer would we be down here? Would we ever find the hourglass?

I was so immersed in my thoughts, I jolted when Demos grabbed my shoulder, hauling me toward him.

A cracking sound echoed through the cavern, like the grinding of ancient bones. The rocky ground beneath us shifted. I dropped into a crouch, slamming one hand against the cavern wall.

A glint of metal caught my eye. Silhouettes peeled themselves from the shadows, all of them moving with an almost unnatural grace. My skin turned clammy, and I gulped frantically for air.

The iron guards.

They wore sleek, blackened iron armor, designed for maximum mobility and protection. Their helmets would make it even more difficult to kill them, although there was a slice of flesh unguarded between their armor and helmets.

I backed up, hitting Asinia. Thol was to my left, Lorian on my right. Cavis and Demos must be on the other side. We'd formed a rough circle, but in this limited space, it would only make things more difficult. I counted them. Five. More than enough of the elite fighters to prove challenging with so many of us in such a small area. And with the fae iron eating away at our strength and power.

"Give us the heir," one of them demanded. "And we will allow you to live."

It was a lie. I knew it was a lie. Even if I went with them, they'd never let the others go.

His armor was subtly different, adorned with silver trim on the edges.

Telean had told me what that meant. He was a captain, answering only to the Iron Commander.

"Leave," Cavis said. "Or die."

The captain ignored that, his gaze flicking between Asinia and me. He focused on me, likely recognizing my description.

"We slaughtered everyone in your village, Hybrid *Heir*. The only thing you're the heir to is death."

If suffering had a sound, it was the choked noise that left Thol's throat.

This was it. I had to summon my power. It had to work for me. The iron guards were fresh, with access to stolen magic. We'd been down here for days, slowly weakening.

Reaching for my power, I glanced at Lorian. He nodded. I could buy them a few seconds. It would have to be enough.

Please. Please don't fail me. Please just give us some time.

My power was nothing but the smallest ember inside

me. Barely burning. Demos stepped forward, breaking the circle. He cut me a single look and said something pithy to one of the iron guards. Buying me a few moments.

Next to me, Thol shuddered with repressed rage.

I reached deeper. The cave disappeared around me. Pain exploded inside my head. I took the few threads I could find and *yanked*.

"Go," I choked out. My vision cleared. The guards froze. Our people jumped into motion. The world dissolved into a gray cloud of agony, cocooning me until it felt as if my head would burst right here.

I fell to my knees.

The threads of my power disappeared. I raised my head in time to see three of the iron guard falling. Lorian, Demos, and Asinia had each taken one, while Thol was still running toward the captain. The man who'd taunted me about our village. Thol was enraged. Not thinking clearly.

"Lorian," I choked out.

His eyes were wild as his gaze found mine. He swung that gaze to Thol and ducked, shoving the other man, protecting him from the iron guard and the knife swinging toward his chest.

It found Lorian's shoulder instead.

I screamed.

Lorian ripped the knife free and threw it at the other guard. Demos and Cavis pinned the guard between them, their swords clanging as they drove him toward the back of the cavern.

"You're weak," the captain hissed at Thol. "The gods will punish you for associating with the corrupt."

Thol swung his sword. I'd once thought he was a great swordsman. Now, after just weeks of training with the fae, I could see his lack of form. Could see the way each of his movements foreshadowed his thrust.

The captain swung.

I reached for my power, pulling deep. Time slowed.

But it didn't stop.

Lorian launched himself toward Thol, his own sword swinging toward the captain.

The threads were nowhere to be found. I dug deeper. "Please…"

Lorian couldn't have heard me. But I caught the slight tilt of his head as if he had. He flew across the cave, leaving himself wide open.

The captain's sword thrust into Thol's chest.

Lorian shoved his own sword into the captain's throat.

Time sped up once more.

Thol sank to the ground. I launched myself across the cave and dropped to my knees next to him. Demos and Cavis must have killed the final guard because they were suddenly there, holding their hands against Thol's wound.

It was useless. Blood spilled out over their hands. Behind me, Asinia choked on a sob. Lorian dropped next to us.

"Healer!" I screamed. Oh gods, we needed…

We needed Tibris. And I'd sent him away.

We were here with no healer because I'd sent him away.

I met Thol's eyes. "You're going to be fine. You're fine. Just keep breathing."

He attempted a smile.

His eyes turned blank.

He was gone.

26

PRISCA

The kind, handsome man who'd looked after the poorest and weakest in our village was dead.

And it was my fault.

I'd known Thol wasn't thinking clearly. He'd just lost everyone he'd loved. He'd learned that everything he'd been told was a lie. And I'd allowed him to come with us.

If I'd practiced more with my power.

If I'd made the decision to be queen earlier.

If I'd brought Tibris with us.

If I'd fought next to him and watched his back…

If I'd done *any* of those things, Thol would still be alive. He'd still be furious and bitter and grief-stricken. But he'd be alive.

The cold seeped into my bones, chilling me. I wrapped my arms around myself, but it seemed unlikely that I would ever be warm again. My gaze was locked on to Thol's body—

some part of me still waiting for him to sit up and tell us he was all right. His eyes were still open, glazed with death. Asinia leaned over and closed them, her shoulders shaking with suppressed sobs.

He would have had a better death if he'd died in that village with his friends and family. Instead, he'd traveled through cold and hunger, only to end up here. Dead in a dark cave, far from home.

How many more would die before we faced Regner? How many would die when we met on the battlefield?

My throat ached, my eyes burned, but I couldn't cry. It was as if the simple release from tears was barred to me. Something was shattering in my chest, and I sucked in a deep breath.

Distantly, I could hear the others murmuring in low voices.

What good was I? How could I save the hybrids when I couldn't even save a man I'd grown up with?

Faces flashed in front of my eyes. Herica. Vuena. Asinia's mother. Thol. Chista. The villagers who'd done nothing except have the bad luck to know me.

Wila.

Her eyes, burning with wrath. *"Promise me, Prisca. Promise me you'll free them. And one day, you'll come back and burn this fucking place to the ground."*

An agonizing knot twisted in my stomach. She'd deserved better. So had Thol. All of the hybrids, those innocent villages, *all* of us deserved better.

Something stirred in the depths of my mind. A

whisper of truth.

It didn't have to be this way.

Regner had made it this way.

He was the one who had done this. He was responsible for all of it. I would carry this guilt and grief with me for the rest of my life. But Regner was the one who'd killed and burned and tortured for centuries now.

He wanted to break us. If I let him, he would win.

I crawled closer to Thol. Asinia moved aside, and I leaned down, murmuring into his ear. "I swear to you, I will make him pay."

Making it to my knees took everything in me. But we had work to do. My friends, my family, they were waiting. One foot, and then two. My head spun dizzily, and I was weaker than I'd ever been.

But I was on my feet.

I surveyed the others.

Demos's gaze met mine. Pride gleamed in his eyes. He reached down and helped Asinia up. She kept her gaze on Thol, while Lorian was watching me with intent focus.

"Cavis?" I asked, my voice hoarse.

"Taking watch," Lorian said.

All of us were covered in blood. Demos began riffling through the iron guards' belongings for more bandages, water, food. Asinia watched him for a long moment and then did the same.

Blood covered Lorian's shirt, and I stepped close to him, pushing it aside. The wound on his shoulder wasn't closing the way it usually would, the fae iron around us suppressing his healing.

Rummaging through one of our packs, I found our healing supplies and bandaged him, my hands shaking.

"I'm sorry, wildcat," he murmured.

I lifted my head. "What for?"

"For not saving him. I know you loved him."

I stared at him. Gods, I didn't want him to feel guilty for what had just happened. I'd seen how hard he'd tried to save Thol. "You think I...loved him?"

"Not the way you will love me," he said, and my heart skipped a beat. Lorian arched his brow in that arrogant way I secretly adored. "But you still loved him. And I failed you."

"You didn't fail me, Lorian. And yes, I loved Thol. Once, I thought it was romantic love, and I was mistaken. I admired him greatly, and I wish he'd lived. But he didn't die through anything you did."

Lorian went still. "I know you're not blaming yourself."

I returned my attention to cleaning and bandaging his wound. "I'll carry a piece of it with me. But I know who is truly responsible."

His hands caught mine. "You bought us precious seconds at the start. You're covered in blood." He swiped one finger along my lip and showed it to me. "You're so pale, I want to roar at you. You had nothing left to give, Prisca."

My lower lip trembled. I knew I'd see that moment in my nightmares. Forever. Time crawling while Thol leaped to his death, blinded by rage.

"He was foolish," Demos announced from where he was now leaning against the cave wall, cleaning his sword. "He wasn't trained, and if he'd just waited, he would have watched as Lorian cut down the man responsible for killing his sister. Instead, he died for no reason."

Asinia sucked in a ragged breath. "You're a heartless bastard."

Demos cut her a hard look. "Take this as a lesson. You will *train*, Asinia. Until your hands are callused and you move without thinking. Because you came close to dying yourself today. Don't think I didn't see it." His gaze swept the room, and I could see the leader he'd been before Regner had imprisoned him. "There is no room for emotion in a fight." His amber eyes met mine. "If you allow your emotions to overtake your logic, you are dead. Thol didn't have to die today. And that's all the more tragic. But Lorian didn't kill him. Prisca didn't kill him. He threw his life away."

Demos stalked out of the cave. Asinia no longer looked like she was drowning in grief. Her face was coldly enraged. But she picked herself up off the ground and launched herself out the cave entrance after my brother.

Find a weak spot and poke at it. Perhaps it was a family trait. I would have to ask Telean.

Panic had begun burning in my chest. I hadn't realized just what it would feel like to be completely powerless. All of us were impatient, exhausted, worn down. Thol was *dead*. I had to find the hourglass. This couldn't all be for nothing.

"We're going to find it, wildcat."

Lorian was watching me. I attempted a smile. "How do you know?"

"Because I'm not leaving this place until you have it."

He radiated calm certainty, and his expression made it clear he would accept no other outcome.

"Thank you, Lorian. For everything."

"You never have to thank me, Prisca."

"At some point, when all of this is done, we need to talk."

"We will." He leaned down and brushed my hair back from my face. "I once told you that until you faced up to the reality of your life, you would continue to be a victim to it. And my reality is this—I'm in love with you."

I let out a strangled sound and his eyes crinkled at the corners, but his expression remained serious.

"You can't be."

"Yes, wildcat. I can."

My breath hitched, and my mouth opened. He covered my mouth with one of his fingers. "Don't say it back."

I raised one eyebrow, and a hint of vulnerability flickered through his eyes. "When you say it…when you *feel* it, and you will," he said, as arrogant as ever, "I want you to be sure. I need that from you."

He was fae. And if there was one thing Lorian had, it was patience.

Lorian had never had anyone choose him before—not because of his reputation or his position as fae prince or what he could do for them, but because of who he was.

And yet we *couldn't* choose each other. As much as I'd begun to fantasize about a future with him, he belonged with his brother. His people. And I belonged with mine.

I'd been silent for too long. Lorian gave me a smile that dripped with promise. "We need to continue moving," he said.

I glanced at Thol's body, and my chest seized. Lorian stroked my hair. "We'll come back for him. I promise."

I nodded. I knew we couldn't take him with us. As soon as we left this place, I would find a peaceful spot to bury him. Somewhere near the water.

Demos was waiting for us outside the cave. "Asinia?" I asked.

"With Cavis."

"You might have to work on your rallying speeches," I teased him.

Demos just looked at me. "Tibris would have said the right thing. He always knows what to say at such times."

I reached out and squeezed his shoulder. "Tibris knew Thol well. He'll be devastated when he learns what happened. But he has habit of only seeing the best in people. You're able to see their strengths and weaknesses. It's a good thing, Demos. Just…be gentle with Asinia."

His mouth firmed. "The last thing that woman needs is coddling."

I rolled my eyes. "I don't want to hear about it when

she gets her revenge."

Lorian stepped up behind me, and Demos glanced at him.

"The hourglass has to be close," Demos said. "Regner had his iron guards waiting there for a reason. If his plan had worked, we would all be dead."

But Regner would also assume we would have at least one fae with us.

We were missing something. It itched at me. But I couldn't understand what it could be.

Cavis and Asinia joined us. Her expression was carefully blank, whatever she was feeling locked away.

"I feel it too," Cavis said. "Something doesn't make sense."

Asinia and Demos were carefully avoiding looking at each other, but they stepped into our agreed formation, ready to continue walking.

"Our only choice is to keep moving," Lorian said.

We continued our progress, all of us silent. There was an empty spot where Thol should have been walking, and I spent the time imagining all the various ways I would kill Regner one day.

I was so lost in blood lust, it took me a moment to realize we'd stopped moving. Lorian reached out his hand and prevented me from slamming into Demos's back.

The path had split. We had two choices—continue straight or turn to the right. The path to the right was so narrow, just looking at it made my breath short. It appeared to be a dead end. But Lorian was studying it.

He pulled his dagger, stepping down the path. "Wait here," he ordered, disappearing into the gloom. My heartbeats quickened as I lost sight of him.

Just moments later, he returned, expression triumphant.

"This way."

I'd been able to manage my claustrophobia up until that point, but within a few steps down the narrow passage, it was as if the walls were moving, edging closer and closer, about to squeeze my body like a grape.

I shuddered, counting my steps in an attempt to slow my breathing. The air was musty, damp, and my skin broke out in goose bumps.

We slowly made our way down the narrow passage, until I was standing directly behind Lorian. And then I saw it. It wasn't a dead end at all. One side was a recessed continuation of the passage, bending sharply away from the viewpoint of anyone who approached.

"It's a natural illusion," Asinia said, peering over my shoulder.

Lorian's light orb slid farther from us, lighting our way. It was so narrow, we would need to shuffle sideways.

Even Lorian looked unhappy at this. But he slid into the cramped crevice, and his eyes met mine, his gaze steady, unrelenting. "You can do this."

I swallowed, my mouth bone-dry. "I know."

He began to inch his way down the passage. I followed, Asinia behind me, with Demos and Cavis guarding our backs.

"I'm glad I didn't have a second helping of dinner last night," Cavis called in a clear attempt to distract me.

"If I didn't already want to kill Regner, this would do it," Asinia muttered. She was too close. I was surrounded on all sides by rock and people and—

My throat constricted, my fingertips tingled, and my stomach spiraled until I could only focus on my feet, shuffling one at a time, over and over again.

Just when I was sure I would freeze, unable to move any farther, the passage spat us out into a cave so small, there was barely enough room for all of us to stand and face the next cavern entrance.

Lorian swept his gaze over me. "Behind me," Lorian ordered, and I didn't bother arguing, my head still spinning. He stepped through the entrance, and we filed in after him.

And there it was.

Barely bigger than my hand, the hourglass sat on a stone pedestal, a chain draping from a tiny hoop on the top. Its polished gold surface seemed to glow in the dim light of the cave. Twin reservoirs held the sand—not ordinary grains, but some kind of glittering manifestation of moments past and yet to come. I'd only seen the hourglass in Ysara's vision, yet some part of me recognized it deep in my soul.

My breath caught, and I took a step closer. Lorian caught my arm.

"It's protected by a ward."

Now that he'd pointed it out, I could see hints of the

ward, flickering around the pedestal.

"Can you break it?" Demos asked.

Lorian's gaze stayed on the ward. I knew that look.

"Give him some time," I said.

I took off my pack and rolled my shoulders, already dreading the trip back through that fucking passage.

Lorian cut his forearm and flicked his blade toward the hourglass. The ward was suddenly visible, marbled with black and red.

Lorian glanced at me. "Regner has tied it to his blood. But I have a theory." He nodded at my own blade.

I pulled my blade free and sliced my blade down my forearm, hissing at the sting. I flicked my own blade at the ward, the scent of my blood sliding up my nostrils.

Drops of blood hit the ward. It glowed a silver so bright I had to glance away.

Lorian smiled. "Regner didn't account for the power from the hourglass itself. The hourglass has molded the ward. It won't just accept his blood. It will also accept the blood of the hybrid heir."

An arm came around my throat. Terror exploded through my stomach, and I clawed at the arm, head spinning. A trap. We hadn't killed all the iron guards.

Lorian sucked in an audible breath. It was as if he'd been gut punched. "Cavis…"

The arm tightened. "Lorian, I don't know what's happening."

My heart hammered against my ribs, and my mind went momentarily blank.

Demos was yelling something. Asinia had begun begging Cavis to let me go. The blood had drained from Lorian's face.

I managed to crane my head, peering up at Cavis. My breath dried up, denial slowly giving way to realization.

One side of his face was covered with a spider web. The mark glowed black and gold beneath his skin.

The king's web.

No. Not Cavis. Fury clawed at my throat. Regner couldn't have him.

"Release her," Lorian bit out. "We can fix this. *I'll* fix this. We'll undo what Regner has done."

Lorian's gaze found mine, and for the first time since I'd met him, his eyes held true terror. He flicked a glance to the knife at my side, and I swallowed.

Could I stab Cavis?

Lorian's eyes burned into mine. Demanding compliance.

My hand drifted down. Cavis caught it, tightening his other hand around my throat.

"I'm sorry," he said. His voice cracked, and for a moment, he sounded like a small child.

Demos was slipping to the right, attempting to get behind us. Cavis snarled, tightening his hold further, and Demos froze.

"You'll snap her neck," Asinia said, her voice low and soothing. "Ease up, Cavis."

He did. Likely because Regner wanted me alive.

My gaze met Asinia's. This would ruin Tibris and

Demos. She had to be there for them. Her dark eyes filled as she stared back at me. She shook her head, her mouth trembling.

But I knew she would support my brothers.

I reached for my power, but it was gone. Snuffed out by fae iron. Blood dripped from my nose at the attempt.

"Kill me, Lorian," Cavis snarled. "Hurry. I can't hold off for much longer."

I closed my eyes, and all I could see was Cavis, traveling with us, fighting with us, laughing with us. The unconditional love he had for Lorian, Marth, Rythos, and Galon and their years of brotherhood. His quiet humor, his steady presence. The way he'd looked at Sybella, as if he couldn't quite believe she was his. And his daughter, so tiny clasped in his arms.

"We don't need to kill you, Cavis." I opened my eyes. "We just need to fix you."

He let out a hollow laugh and took a step back, pulling me with him. His entire body was trembling as he fought whatever orders had awoken him.

"Tell Sybella I'm sorry. And Piperia..."

I craned my head and found Cavis's eyes on Lorian's.

Lorian looked like he'd just been stabbed in his chest. "I've got her, brother," he choked out. "Piperia will have a beautiful life. She will know you were a man of courage and honor."

My eyes met Demos's, and I glanced at the hourglass.

His blood was mine. If I couldn't take it, he had to. Before Regner moved it.

Demos nodded, his expression tight with suppressed rage. His eyes darted, and as he attempted to find some kind of way out of this.

Cavis was shuddering now. Something warm hit my forehead. Blood. Dripping from his eyes. Because he was fighting as hard as he could.

Lorian's dagger was in his hand. He looked at me.

No. I refused. I wouldn't let Cavis die for me. We'd undo whatever Regner had done to him.

Lorian's gaze turned hard. And then Cavis dragged me to the left, giving Lorian a clear shot at him. It was a movement that only took a single moment.

Lorian's dagger was already flying. Straight toward Cavis's head.

My scream was ripped from my lungs.

Cavis's arm tightened around me. The ground was crumbling beneath our feet, and I stumbled. Lorian's dagger lodged in the wall. I had one moment to meet his eyes.

He let out a roar that seemed to shake the walls around us, launching himself at me, teeth bared.

Cavis pulled me to him. And then we were falling through the air.

THE END.

Thank you so much for reading *A Kingdom This Cursed and Empty*. I hope you enjoyed reading it as much as I've enjoyed writing it. The next book is *A Crown This Cold and Heavy*. Turn over for a sneak preview...

If you'd like to keep up with my latest updates, including new releases, bonus scenes, sales, and more, sign up for my newsletter at staciastark.com.

ACKNOWLEDGMENTS:

First and most importantly, thank you to Alex, who kept me going throughout all of the book 2 shenanigans. Thank you for the long plot chats, for talking me off the author ledge, and for giving me a reality check when I was unable to see the forest for the trees.

To each and every person who made this book possible: Dawn, Fay, Lo, Elli, Deb, Angela, @samaiya.art for the gorgeous character art, Bianca from Moonpress for my cover (and anyone else I've forgotten during deadline hell), thank you from the bottom of my exhausted heart.

To my readers: Thank you for coming along on this journey with me. There will never be enough words for me to express how much I appreciate you.

Stacia x

PRISCA

Click.
Click.
Click.

The sound scratched at my senses. My eyelids were so heavy, it took everything in me to open them even to slits.

Sunlight stabbed into my eyes, and I instantly slammed them closed. But I'd gotten a glimpse.

A carriage.

I was in a carriage. Moving. I tensed my hands. Tied. My mind whirled. What was I doing—

Lorian.

Demos.

Asinia.

Oh gods. *Cavis.*

The web on his face. The web that meant he was one of the human king's spiders. Those who were often planted in foreign courts as children.

Lorian's words drifted into my mind.

"Cavis was from Jadynmire. One of Galon's men found him wandering

alone and barefoot in the forest. He was the only survivor."

He'd only reached six winters. And Regner had already gotten to him, twisted his mind, used his filthy magic to plant a seed in Cavis that he could use at any time.

Fury blazed through me. And this time, I managed to keep my eyes open.

They met bright-blue eyes. Eyes that laughed at me.

I knew those eyes.

The man smiled at me, and I went still in the way of prey. His smile widened.

"I'm not exactly sure how you've woken so soon," he said. "But it's rather impressive."

I kept my expression blank. Dark hair, wide shoulders, and those amused blue eyes. I'd met him at an inn soon after Lorian and I had docked in Gromalia. I'd been consumed with bitter jealousy as Lorian spoke to a beautiful fae woman, and this man had approached me.

"You're far too beautiful to be frowning into the flames."

How long had he been following us? Who was he? And how quickly could I slit his throat and jump from this carriage?

His mouth twitched. "You're sitting there, half drugged, clamped in fae iron, yet you're actively planning my murder, aren't you?"

Ignoring him, I turned my attention to the other man in the carriage. The one I hadn't yet been able to look at.

Cavis stared straight ahead, as if he wasn't present.

Blood slipped from his nose in a steady drip. Dread coiled in my stomach, my throat clamped shut, and the world spun around me. Cavis had done everything he could to let Lorian kill him before he took me. Now…he looked like he was gone.

"What did you do to him?"

The man tutted. "That's from fighting the compulsion, I'm afraid. Regner will be *very* interested to see this."

My breath shuddered from my lungs. It might not look like it, but Cavis was still fighting. Looking at him was agonizing, and the man who'd put me in this carriage was obviously enjoying my pain. I turned my gaze back to him.

"What exactly do you want from me?"

"Perhaps I'm interested to see who the hybrid heir is when she's not clamped to the side of that fae bastard."

I gave him a pitying look. "If you think he'd beat you in a fight, just say that. This is unnecessary."

His smile was cold. "Let me guess. You think he's coming for you."

I knew he was.

He angled his head. "Do you truly believe we didn't have something special waiting for the Bloodthirsty Prince, your brother, and anyone else stupid enough to travel with you? They're not going to rescue you. By now, they're all dead. So I suggest you begin learning how to cooperate if you want to save yourself some pain."

My stomach clenched, and I clamped down on the urge to heave. It was a lie. They weren't dead. I would know, deep in my bones, if they were. I would feel it. He was trying to get under my skin.

"Don't believe me?" He shook his head. "You will."

His fist flew toward my temple, and the world turned black.

LORIAN

The creature smashed through the labyrinth walls, tossing stone and fae iron aside as if they were nothing.

Four colossal legs, gnarled and twisted—the bark-like skin resembling ancient tree trunks. Those legs ended in wickedly curved talons that gleamed in the light orbs.

Asinia ducked, narrowly missing a rock to the side of her head. A rock the creature had kicked at her.

That told me it had some level of intelligence.

"Watch for the traps!" Demos roared as we sprinted toward the entrance.

"It's almost on us," Asinia panted. She tripped, and Demos caught her arm, pulling her faster.

I brought up the rear, guarding their backs. The creature's fetid breath dampened the air, and I cursed. "We need to make a stand."

Demos darted around another rock. "We need to get closer to the entrance first."

He didn't say the words we were all thinking. With the way the creature's vicious horns were slamming into the roof of the caves, they could crumble at any moment.

We'd spent two days down here, moving as quickly as we could. Regner had arranged for the creature to find us at the worst possible time—when we were running out of food, water, and patience.

I risked a glance over my shoulder, aiming my power in a thin bolt toward its feet. I had so little left, I was almost completely drained. Useless.

The creature roared, falling back. But not before I caught another glimpse of it.

It looked like something out of my worst nightmares.

My worst nightmares *before* I'd met Prisca. Now, the slobbering beast behind us was nothing compared to the knowledge that she was gone.

That she had been *taken*.

Right in front of me.

Demos wore her hourglass around his neck. And he was moving faster, while my own steps slowed.

The hourglass was countering the fae iron. Because it recognized his blood.

"Use your power," I snarled.

"I am. My power is telling us to fucking run."

I didn't even have the energy to curse. Asinia launched herself over one of the traps, and I followed, sending another bolt over my shoulder.

The creature snarled.

Prisca had already lost too many people. Of the three

of us, I had the best odds of survival. "I'm going to distract it." I lunged over one of the traps. "Get out of here."

"Not happening," Demos snarled back, ducking beneath the low ceiling of the next cavern. "Prisca needs you. You're our best chance to get her back."

I didn't bother arguing. He was as stubborn as his sister, and it would just waste time. Silver flashed on one of the walls, catching my attention. I recognized these caverns. We'd hidden a few dead bodies around here somewhere. "Where are the guards we killed?"

Behind us, the creature roared. Asinia let out a choked sound that might've been a laugh. "Something tells me the monster set off one of the traps. Hopefully that distracts it for a while."

"The bodies are three caverns to our left," Demos said. "I think."

"I have an idea."

MADÎNIA

"Do you need anything else?"

I smiled at the innkeeper's wife. "No thank you. I'm going to rest."

"Well, be sure to lock your door."

I kept the smile on my face, nodding as I closed the

door. I'd need to find new accommodations soon. This woman was far too nosy.

Her insistence on making sure meals were delivered to my rooms had made it much too difficult to eavesdrop on drunk patrons. I ground my teeth. Eavesdropping was my best chance at finding the smallest seed of information about Jamic's whereabouts. If we could find Regner's false son, we could prevent the human king from reinforcing his barrier.

I needed *something*. A direction. A whisper about guards gathering somewhere remote. A sighting of one of Regner's generals in a place he shouldn't be.

Instead, drunk travelers had spoken of strange creatures being bred near various mountains, of wards in unlikely places, of armies gathered in the ashes of several northern villages.

So I traveled through Eprotha in the guise of a rich widow, listening for anything we could use.

I traveled alone. I ate alone. I slept alone.

And it was glorious.

There was no one to look at me with censure in their eyes. No one to demand *obedience*. No one to stare at me as if *I* were the great betrayer.

Father's ashen face flashed through my mind.

"How? Gods, how? How did I miss such a thing?"

And then, to learn he knew I wasn't corrupt. Knew my magic wasn't a rejection of the gods but was instead from my mother's bloodline…

Prisca had made my father admit to being weak. And

a hypocrite. At the time, I'd wanted to slap her. Now, I recognized it for the gift it was.

Because I didn't have either the time or the inclination to mourn a weak hypocrite.

Striding to the window, I threw it open, gazing down into the bustling street. I'd made it to a fishing village north of Thobirea. An area of the kingdom I'd never been to before. I wanted to be out, roaming the city like a stray cat, soaking up everything I could. Unfortunately, I had to be careful not to draw attention from the guards. The priestesses. Even with the wash of blue on my temple declaring me *legal*.

A knock sounded on my door. The innkeeper's wife. Again. My skin burned at her intrusiveness, but I pasted on a smile and crossed the room.

The boy who blinked at me was unfamiliar. He was also dressed in Regner's colors. I went still, summoning my fire until my hand heated—the warmth a comfort.

"Are you Madinia Farrow?"

My hand heated further, and he swallowed as if he knew just how close to the edge I leaned.

One second to kill the messenger, another three to drag his body inside. My bag was packed, and I'd already climbed from the window my first night here to ensure I'd never be trapped.

"Message from Her Majesty," he said, slowly holding it out.

My heart stopped and then restarted again, pounding double time. How exactly had that bitch found me? I wasn't even due to cross into Eprotha until three days from now.

I'd found a woman who'd helped me dye my hair the moment I'd left the fae lands, and it was now a dark brown. I kept to myself and had sent no messages except to let Prisca know where I was.

The safest approach would be my first plan. And yet, my hand rose as if on its own, plucked the message from his hand, and left a coin.

My curiosity would always be my downfall.

"Go," I said.

He went.

Turning, I moved back to the window, watching as he left the boarding house, glancing over his shoulder. No one followed him.

I opened the message.

Madinia,

A clever woman would notice Gromalian forces gathering in the eastern sector of Thobirea.

You always were far too clever for your own good.

No signature, but that wasn't surprising. Besides, I'd recognize Regner's queen's handwriting anywhere.

The question? Was she leading us into a trap?

I'd seen Kaliera commit a number of atrocities over the years. This could be her attempt to regain trust with Regner. He would enjoy sentencing me. And he'd certainly enjoy watching Prisca burn.

My mind provided me with an image of my father's head hitting the ground. Directly before the rest of his body. I fisted my hand, crumpling the letter.

Before we'd left the camp, Lorian had given us all fae-bred pigeons to ensure we could communicate.

But…Prisca needed to find the hourglass. Tibris wasn't an option either. He'd left to negotiate with Gromalian rebels, and the last I'd heard, Demos had gone with Prisca. Besides, Demos was an inflexible bastard.

Vicer would be deep in Eprotha by now, attempting to convince the hybrids to travel south to the fae lands. But…he might have people on the ground. If he didn't, he could probably put a team together.

Scrawling a quick note of my own, I took my pigeon out of her cage. I didn't understand how the birds knew which of us to travel to, but Lorian had simply told us to clearly state the name of the person we wanted to contact.

"Take this to Vicer," I said.